The Sisterhood

Emily Barr

W F HOWES LTD

This large print edition published in 2008 by
W F Howes Ltd
Unit 4, Rearsby Business Park, Gaddesby Lane,
Rearsby, Leicester LE7 4YH

1 3 5 7 9 10 8 6 4 2

First published in the United Kingdom in 2008
by Headline Review

A CIP catalogue record for this book is available
from the British Library

ISBN 978 1 40742 488 0

Typeset by Palimpsest Book Production Limited,
Grangemouth, Stirlingshire
Printed and bound in Great Britain
by MPG Books Ltd, Bodmin, Cornwall

FSC
Mixed Sources
Product group from well-managed
forests and other controlled sources

Cert no. SGS-COC-2953
www.fsc.org
© 1996 Forest Stewardship Council

For James, Gabe, Seb and Lottie

Thanks to Harriet Evans, Emily Furniss and everyone else at Headline; Jonny Geller, Doug Kean, Carole Jackson and everybody at Curtis Brown. Thanks to Lisa McLean, Helen Stewart, Samantha Hand, Sylvie Bod, Bridget Guzek, Maria Gentile, Adam Barr, and Tansy Evans. And much love, as always, to James, Gabe, Seb and Lottie.

PROLOGUE

HELEN

Next summer

When I get out of the airport, I look around in wonder. I am on the other side of the world. I have never been so far from home. I could not get any further than this, unless I went into space.

The air is clear, and I take deep breaths. I am grateful to be off the plane, away from the hordes of strangers and the stale air. Nothing here looks particularly weird, but it feels odd. I am disconnected, disorientated. Two days ago I was in Spain. The day before that I was in France. It is confusing to be so far from everything that I know.

I look around for a taxi. I take the piece of paper out of my pocket, although I memorised her address long ago.

'I need somewhere to stay in Ponsonby,' I tell the driver.

He looks at me, and at my big rucksack. 'A hotel?' he asks. 'A backpackers? There's a backpackers in Ponsonby. Nice place, I've heard.'

I consider it for a moment. The days when I was

too scared to stay in backpackers' accommodation are long gone, I decide.

'That would be perfect,' I tell him. I get in, and settle back. I am smiling, showing Auckland that I want to belong. I am a European backpacker, and I happily stay in hostels.

I will find her. This time it will all be different.

I breathe deeply in the cab. I have done everything I can to forget all the things that happened last year. I toss back my dark hair and pull at the hem of my dress, pulling it almost to my knees. Last year is the past. It is what brought me here. It is all a part of my story.

As the flat, green landscape passes by, I realise how much I have grown up. I was nobody, when this started. I was nothing. I used to hang around at home, in France, talking to my little brother. I used to lie back, in the sun, and wait. I waited and waited for something to happen.

'You have to make things happen,' Tom said to me, once. We were lying by the pool. I was trying to make him get me a drink. We had done nothing at all for days. 'They don't just happen by themselves.'

'How am I supposed to do that?' I asked him.

He shrugged and stretched out his arms and legs, like a starfish.

I knew he was right. In the end, I did make things happen.

I had an adventure, and it is still going on. Here I am, one year and ten months later, in New

Zealand. I would never have imagined that the trail would lead me here.

Finally, I have the confidence to do my own thing. I know what I want, and I am going to stay in Ponsonby until I've got it. I am going to find her, and this time it's going to work out perfectly. This is just the beginning.

CHAPTER 1

ELIZABETH GREENE

London, 31 October

It was Halloween, and a few people were dressed in stupid costumes. Everyone ignored them. I stood on the Northern Line, gripping a red pole and swaying in the familiar rush-hour crush, and I decided that I was going to start to make an effort. When Steve and I got together, we were starry-eyed 27-year-olds. Now we were close to forty, with nothing but a mortgaged flat to show for it.

It was natural, I decided, that we had fallen into a rut. I pictured a huge tractor ploughing a muddy field. There we were, Steve and me, tiny little figures struggling in an enormous earthen rut. He tried to give me a leg up, but I toppled back into the mud. He climbed on to my shoulders, but we overbalanced. My hair was covered in damp earth. We were stuck. This was what I thought, at least, on Halloween. My whole life was a rut. I was doing the job I had trained for, as a stopgap, sixteen years earlier, when people with English degrees who didn't want to go into the media did a PGCE as something to fall back on. I was bored with teaching, but I didn't know what else to do.

Someone lurched into me. 'Sorry,' I told him, without thinking.

A lot of other people I knew had babies. Maybe that was good, I thought. Perhaps it gave a relationship a new focus. Perhaps a baby gave a couple something to look at, other than each other. It certainly gave them something to talk about, endlessly. I didn't want a baby, though, and neither did Steve. What I wanted was a holiday. I was trying to work out whether I could arrange something as a surprise for Steve, whether he could take several weeks off work, and how far away we could get without flying. I was thinking of Italy, or Russia, or a great train trip like the Trans-Siberian. In the year since we'd both decided to stop air travel, we had been no further afield than Brighton. Although we'd often talked about taking off on the Eurostar and having romantic holidays centring on European stations with big clocks and well-dressed people, Steve seemed to be in the process of downgrading this summer's excursion to a weekend at Glastonbury.

I sighed as the doors opened and twenty-two more people forced themselves into the scrum. My shoulders were up against everyone else's, as usual. I blew the hair off my face and tried not to feel claustrophobic. I hated feeling that I had failed myself. The dreams I'd had, when I was young, had never included being jammed on to the Northern and Victoria Lines twice a day. They hadn't involved trying to ram D.H. Lawrence down the throats of unresponsive fifteen-year-olds, when everyone in the room – myself included – would rather be drinking, smoking and shagging. I was fed up with my life, and I was worried about my relationship, too. Last week, I'd put a lot of time and effort into seducing Steve. To my horror, it had been difficult. I'd had to force him into it, and before that we hadn't had sex for months. Tonight, I was going to try again.

Steve was the great love of my life. From the moment we met, we belonged together. He was a part of me. Over the years, we had been best friends, lovers, soulmates. We had always been equals. Now, suddenly, things felt wrong. We were distant, slightly wary of each other. I wondered whether we would split up. It was unthinkable. I wished we were married, because that would have made it harder for us to part. Neither of us had ever wanted marriage. We had been to so many of our friends' weddings that there had long ago ceased to be any attraction in having our own: we would have been forced either to re-enact a ceremony we had already been to many times over, or to be self-consciously different just for the hell of it. On top of that, I had been married before, for two sad years in my early twenties. I married my university boyfriend, feeling enormously grown up. My father paid for a registry office and a party in the upstairs room of a pub in the Lanes

7

in Brighton. Within six months I could hardly bear to look at my husband. I had never fancied being a double divorcee. That was another reason why I had not married Steve.

The train pulled into my station and as I came out of the Tube, I decided, with a sudden fierce conviction, that I had to do everything I could to bring us close again. I would start that night, by putting on an ironic Halloween party for the two of us. We would get drunk, laugh, be silly, and remember why we were together. When I was drunk enough, I would steer the conversation to my insecurity, and to holidays and the fact that life was no longer as much fun as it ought to be. Actually, I was rubbish at playing games. I would have a drink and tell Steve exactly how I felt. Then it would be up to him.

It was a clean, crisp day, even in London. The air I breathed was impregnated with exhaust fumes, but I was used to that. Whenever I left the city, my lungs protested, scalded by fresh air. The sun had disappeared behind a tower block, low in the sky, but above me everything was blue and cloudless. My breath fogged in front of me, and the nip of incipient night was making my nose red and my fingertips numb. I threw fifty pence at the homeless boy on the pavement, aware of the pathetic nature of my token gesture, and wondering how he was going to get through the winter with a skimpy sleeping bag and a 50p coin. Then I forgot about him, and went to Waitrose.

There was always something soothing about Waitrose. That was a sad state of affairs, but it was true. It was its own world, where everything was clean and orderly. Instantly, I felt I could make things right.

If I could put on a good enough Halloween spread, then everything was going to work out the way I wanted it to. I dashed around, feeling harassed and trying to order my mind. In my anxiety, I filled a small trolley with a big pumpkin, several bags of crisps, two Pizza Express pizzas, two bottles of expensive champagne and a box of Belgian chocolates. Then, almost hysterical, I added an orange plastic tablecloth with witches on it, two novelty black pointed hats, and a pair of plastic champagne glasses with spiders on them. Not long ago, Steve would have loved something this kitsch. Drunken, ironic evenings were the sort of thing we used to do together, winding each other up to fever pitch, laughing and staying up all night. I contemplated face paints, but decided that I should stop short of making myself look mad. I would redo my make-up instead. I would put on some sexy underwear.

Years ago, on my thirtieth birthday, we had a party, just Steve and me. We had just bought our flat. He cooked dinner, and we drank and laughed and ate, and sat on our sofa with the curtains open and the lights off, and talked until it got light. I adored Steve. I had loved him passionately from the day I met him, and I was not letting him go.

I was excited when I got back to the flat. We lived on the top two floors of a large terraced house in Kentish Town. We had been there for years and years, since we were twenty-nine, and had watched our friends gradually having families and moving out to the suburbs and beyond, generally just before the second baby arrived. These days the only people I knew locally were shopkeepers, the barman at the local café, and a few neighbours.

The big black front door slammed shut behind me. I checked the post on the sideboard, though there was nothing for us. I unlocked our front door, which was a cheap plywood effort in the hall, and took the stairs two at a time.

'Hiya!' I shouted, always hating the sound of my voice in a potentially empty space. 'I'm back,' I added, my voice tailing off. I listened. There were footsteps upstairs.

'Lizzy!' he called. A herd of elephants gallumphed down to meet me. Steve leapt down the last five steps, landing with a crash in front of me. He smiled a broad smile, but he looked unsettled.

Steve had changed after work, and was wearing a baggy shirt, unbuttoned almost to the waist. He had lost weight recently, which made me conscious of the fact that I hadn't. He was trying, at the moment, to compensate for his receding hairline by growing what remained, so it touched the back of his collar. To my surprise, he looked distinguished like that. It suited his face.

He ran a hand through his hair.

'You're back!' he exclaimed, frowning and smiling at the same time. 'Are you early?'

I shook my head. 'Maybe a bit,' I said. 'Left school at four for once.' I held up my hands, a laden carrier bag in each. 'Went to Waitrose. Got stuff for tonight.' I listened to myself. I could tell that I was nervous, because I was missing off personal pronouns. The atmosphere was odder than usual.

Steve nodded. 'OK. Cool. I'm just sorting some stuff upstairs. Be down in a minute.'

'Sure.'

Steve was often home before me, even though he supposedly worked until half past five. I had never quite worked out how he did it, though when I thought about it, I knew that I usually stayed later than four, and he often bunked off early. I worked further from home than he did. My school was in Pimlico. I travelled eight stops on two Tube lines, while he rode a bike for ten minutes. It did add up, in a way.

I looked around the kitchen. There were two cups, washed up, on the draining board. Otherwise it was spotless. Our kitchen was filled with cheap wooden units that we painted blue and yellow after we visited Monet's house on holiday, years ago. I remembered feeling proud and grown up, standing up a ladder with a paintbrush in my hand. These days it was tatty, but it was home, and I would not have swapped it because our history, in our happy days, was in this kitchen.

I put the radio on, determined to work myself up into a party mood. Radio Four was eager to tell me about a reporter for one of the British papers who had been kidnapped in Iraq. I felt fairly sure that the details weren't going to crank up my adrenaline levels and make me irresistible, and so I twiddled the dial. Eventually, I found an easy listening station that allowed me to attempt to harmonise with Sinatra in 'Something Stupid'. I chilled the champagne in the freezer, and poured myself a gin and tonic. I hollowed out the pumpkin as best I could, and put the pathetic scrapings I took from its middle into the fridge, where I supposed they would sit in a bowl for a week or so before we threw them away.

By the time Steve reappeared, the oven was pre-heated, ready for the pizzas, and the table was set with the tasteless tablecloth and five candles. I was pleased with the overall effect. I had even remembered to close the sitting-room door at the front of the house, with lights off and curtains drawn, to discourage trick or treaters.

I was singing along, enjoying myself, when Steve came back downstairs, and I stopped with the words 'I love you' in my throat, suddenly shy.

He looked around.

'Heeeeeyyyy,' he said. He was trying hard to be appreciative.

'Do you like it?' I pretended his reaction was incidental, as if the whole point of the evening was not to get him back.

He smiled warmly, and put an arm around my shoulders.

'Of course I like it. What can I do?'

I cuddled into him, appreciating the rare physical contact.

'Did you switch everything off upstairs? So we look like we're out?'

'Scared of your students coming to terrorise you?'

'They live too far away. Thank Christ. Scared of the local five-year-olds, though.'

'Scared of drunk teenagers armed with flour and eggs.'

'Fireworks and handguns, more like.'

'Well, it's all switched off upstairs, yes.'

We put the pizzas in the oven, and I opened the first bottle of champagne. The plastic flutes made a dull clunk against each other.

'Cheers,' said Steve, and he sat down at the table. The atmosphere between us was suddenly stranger than it should have been. I looked at him, the beautiful man who had adored me for years, who had made me laugh and cry with happiness. My first husband had never been anything. Steve was everything to me. I made myself speak. I couldn't try to manipulate the conversation like a 'Venus' woman. I had to come straight out with it.

'OK,' I said, levelly. 'Steve. Honey. I think we need to talk about a few things.'

Steve stared at the table.

'Talk about a few things?' He snorted gently.

'Yes. I've been wondering if you'd picked up on anything.'

I looked at him, surprised. 'Picked up on what?'

'You tell me.'

'No. You tell me.'

'You started it.'

'I don't think I've "picked up on anything".' I tried to fit my concerns into a framework of picking up. It didn't work.

'So what did you want to say?' he asked, fiddling with his plastic champagne glass, a glass which suddenly looked stupid.

'I'm going to the loo,' I announced suddenly, scared. 'Then we both have to talk.'

'Deal.'

I looked at him. He smiled and winked. It was a shadow of the way we used to be, a trace of the old days. I felt a mounting fear, because I sensed that the foundations of my life were shifting.

I lurched upstairs, already slightly drunk. More than that, though, I was starting to panic. I knew Steve inside out, and I knew that he had something big to tell me. It was going to be something disastrous. I wondered whether he was ill. He had lost a lot of weight. We hadn't talked about it.

I stared into the bathroom mirror, which had a little mosaic around it. I was hiding from what might be coming. I saw that the fear, and the alcohol, had made my cheeks pink, my eyes wide. I drew my fingers through my curly hair and tried to be positive.

14

I looked good. I was slightly heavier than I would have liked, but my features were strong and even. I looked a bit stupid in my work clothes, so I thought I would go and change. This was something I should face in what Steve called my 'glad rags'.

Then I stopped myself. I wasn't going to hide upstairs, in the bathroom. I wasn't going to put on a dress. This was not a job interview. This was Steve and me. I told him everything. We were partners. He was probably in financial trouble. We would work through it together.

Someone moved in our bedroom. I wondered how Steve had got up there without my hearing him. I didn't even need to go to the loo. As I opened the bathroom door, I heard footsteps jumping down the stairs, taking all of them in three or four jumps. Steve was standing at the bottom, but there was someone else there too.

Within seconds, I was in the kitchen. Steve grabbed me around the waist, and held me back. Our visitor was going down the other stairs, now, in a panicky blur. The plywood door downstairs slammed shut. I kneed Steve in the balls and jumped down, taking the stairs in fours and fives.

I had only seen Steve's face for a second, but it was all there. I knew.

He chased me down the stairs, trying to catch me as I tumbled over and grabbed the banister. I had to find her, had to know who she was. As I opened our flimsy front door, I saw a slight figure

15

silhouetted in the frame of the main door. That door slammed with a noise that shook the building. I ran to it, yanked it open, and stared at the person on the steps.

I was expecting a young woman. In the few seconds since I'd realised what was happening – since I had started to 'pick up on it' – I had formed a picture of a 22-year-old girl with peachy skin. Many things had instantly fallen into place. Steve wasn't interested in sex with me. He came home from work early, presumably not alone. He often changed the sheets on our bed, which he never used to do. He was too polite to me, like a stranger, and he had wanted to talk. When I was about to tell him how much I loved him, how much I wanted to be with him for ever, he was working up to telling me that he'd met someone else, and that the woman in question was hiding in our bedroom.

But this was not a peachy young woman. It was just a boy. He was a teenager, handsome in a young, callow way. He was wearing a pair of jeans and Steve's grey jumper. As he turned and looked at me, I saw that I had missed everything. I was a stupid woman who had no idea about things that went on under her nose. I knew nothing, nothing at all. Steve and I had been leading separate lives, and I had thought it was all about commitment.

I grabbed the boy's arm. He looked at my hand, and then at my face. His face was young, younger

16

than I would have thought possible. He looked like the more knowing children in my GCSE classes. His skin was slightly pitted and his eyes were wild, as if he were high.

As I stared, he looked back at me. He began to smile. Then he chuckled, and within a few seconds, he was laughing loudly, in my face.

Steve's face was flushed, his expression unreadable. As I watched, he covered his mouth with his hand. I had no idea whether he was laughing too, or whether he was mortified.

'Um,' he said. 'I imagine this clarifies things.' I could not make a reply. 'I guess I'd better go,' he added. 'I'm sorry that it's been . . . I'm sorry, Liz. It's just . . .'

I didn't want him to leave. All the same, I stood on the pavement, outside our house, in the cold of an autumn evening that was turning to night, and watched my boyfriend of ten years leaving me with a boy who was probably illegal.

The boy looked back over his shoulder, and smiled contemptuously. He put a hand possessively on Steve's bum, and Steve didn't stop him. Not even for my sake.

Across the road, three children dressed as vampires were going from house to house.

CHAPTER 2

HELEN

Bordeaux, 31 October

Mother and Papa were away for the weekend, so I made a visit to their house. Apart from the compulsory Sunday lunches, I made a point of visiting only when they were out. I thought we got on better that way. On Sundays, I visited the dining room, the kitchen and the downstairs loo. When they weren't there, I poked in every corner, checked every cupboard.

I had lived in that house for eighteen years, so it was horribly familiar. The smell of it hit me straightaway. The floor cleaner that Madame Allemand used for the tiles every Saturday morning. The leftover cooking smells, with top notes of garlic and breadiness. The haze of red wine. I was fifteen again. I was twelve. I was four. It made me sick.

I was thankful that I didn't have to live there any more. Because of the business they were in, the parents had a lot of outbuildings. Some of them had been derelict for years, and, a few years ago, the parents did them up, as cheaply as they

18

could. Some became holiday cottages, and others were now workers' accommodation for harvest time. The smallest one was my home. I moved in the day after I finished my bac. It was an ineffectual gesture on my part, one that was intended to show that I would like to move out even though I couldn't work up the motivation to do it properly. All the same, it was good to be out of here.

I hated the ugly furniture which everyone pretended was beautiful because it was old. The house was stuffed with oversized varnished cupboards and bulky chests. The rooms were dark. The tiled floors were so cold that you needed to wear slippers all year round. I nosed around the place, noticing a few things that had changed since I'd last been in. The sitting-room furniture had been moved about a bit. There were some different, but equally boring, pictures on the walls. There were never any photos of Tom or me. Mother said putting photos of your children up around the house was crass. Everything had to be done properly. It was all correct and joyless. My parents were snobs. They were horrible.

I wandered around for a while, taking it all in. I took some biscuits from the cupboard and a bowl of posh ice cream from the freezer. Tom joined me. We poured drinks. We both hate red wine, but we managed to knock back our own approximation of a vodka martini, complete with olives. Then I set to work. Tom trailed after me, giggling to himself. He always got drunk quickly.

I glanced back at him. His cheeks were red and his eyes were wide.

Thankfully, Tom had no idea how good-looking he was. When I was his age, teenage boys stared sullenly at the floor, their skin already scarred by acne. They slouched and avoided eye contact. They were horrible. Tom had creamy skin, and he smiled and charmed everybody. Even as his big sister, I could see that he was amazing. I would never have told him that.

I felt bad, going into the parents' room. It lasted a few seconds, and then I felt better. Luckily, the room was so sterile that I could avoid thinking about them having sex. The bed was covered by a white counterpane with small flowers printed on it, and this was pulled so tight that I couldn't imagine anyone sitting on it, let alone anything else.

I was looking for excitement, but I had no idea what it might be. Perhaps I thought Papa would have some porn, though the idea was laughable. He was far too uptight. If he did have porn, it would have to be extreme and disturbing. Maybe I thought Mother would secretly have a drawer full of sexy underwear and nurses' uniforms, though that was, if anything, even less likely. Still, I set to work, hunting through drawers of carefully folded jumpers and swishing past rows of immaculately ironed skirts and shirts. Tom just sat on the floor and laughed. He always did that. I was never silly; all my silliness seemed to have gone to Tom.

After fifteen minutes' careful searching, I struck gold. At the back of Mother's wardrobe was a neat little cardboard box, sealed on all sides with thick brown tape. I debated opening it. It would probably be something dull, and then I was going to be stuck trying to close it again. I didn't know where to find the right tape, so I was bound to botch it. Still, I couldn't imagine what it was, so I decided to prise it open anyway, as carefully as I could, and deal with the consequences later. I peeled the tape back, and hoped that whatever was inside was going to be worth it.

I wouldn't get into trouble. Nobody ever talked about anything in our family. We were not really a family at all. Mother would notice that someone had been into her special box, and she would know it had been me. It would not occur to her that Tom, the golden boy, could have done such a thing, and she would be right. He wouldn't. She would be colder to me than ever, but she would never, ever mention it. I ripped away the rest of the tape, threw it on the wooden floor, and reached inside the box.

It seemed I had found her Achilles heel. Most parents kept photographs of their children in albums, or in frames. My mother preferred to seal hers in a box and hide it in the back of her wardrobe. Nonetheless, here was the evidence: she did think we were worth recording after all. I held the picture by the edges, amazed that she had kept this photograph of me, toddling around the

21

garden, clutching a teddy I still owned and looking grumpy. My white-blonde hair was cut in an uncompromising fringe, and I was wearing a strange little smock. There were six pictures of me, up to the age of about five. There were pictures of Tom, too, as a tiny baby. In a couple of them, he was propped on my lap while I clutched him protectively. I slipped one of those shots into the back pocket of my jeans.

Then there was a photo with Mother in it. She was sitting up in a hospital bed, with a tiny baby in her arms. Obviously, she wasn't smiling. She wasn't looking at the camera, either. She was just staring away into a corner, looking grim.

It took me a few seconds to realise that the baby was neither me nor Tom. Mother was incredibly young. In this picture, she looked about the same age that I was now, and the colours were strange and faded. She had funny hair that was long and straight and parted in the middle: hippy hair. I could do mine like that, if I wanted to, which I didn't. And there was a man standing behind her, but when I looked closely at him (it was a crap photo; he was in the shade) he was definitely not my papa. I looked again at the woman. That was her, all right. Mother had had a baby, with somebody else.

'Hey,' I said to my brother. 'Hey, Tom. Look at this.'

The other stuff in the box filled in a few gaps. There were a few more pictures of the baby, mostly with Mother looking at it in a bored and disappointed manner. The poor child was togged up in lacy knitted jackets and ribboned bootees. There was a newspaper cutting with a birth announcement, circled by an ancient red pen, marking the following arrival: 'GREENE: To William and Mary, a girl, Elizabeth Rosemary.' The birth date was 21 October 1969. The baby was born at the Royal Sussex Hospital in Brighton.

Mother's name was Mary but I had never heard the name Greene in my life. I had also never heard her mention anyone called Elizabeth.

Tom sat on the floor and examined everything I passed to him. He leaned forward, intent on his task, and his fringe flopped forwards over his face.

'This is weird,' he noted. 'Do you think the baby died?'

I shook my head. I hated the idea that a baby could die.

'No,' I said.

'Why not? If it didn't, that would mean we'd have a sister. We'd know if we had a sister.' He looked at me, big-eyed. 'Wouldn't we?'

'Yes, because Mother is such an open person, she could never keep a secret. Particularly not from us.'

'But she couldn't hide a child.'

'She could have had it adopted. That's what people used to do, if they didn't want it or whatever. And if it had died, there'd be a death notice with this birth one. Maybe.'

'Have you checked?'

'No.' I tipped out everything that remained in the box. Five envelopes were held together by a rubber band. I took off the band and threw a couple of envelopes over to Tom. They were all addressed to Miss Elizabeth Greene, c/o Mr William Greene, with an address in Brighton, Angleterre. They didn't have stamps on.

I opened one. I didn't care now that she was going to know that we knew. In fact, I was glad.

The letter was typical of her.

> Dear Elizabeth,
>
> Happy birthday to you. I hope this finds you well.
>
> I am sorry not to be there with you. I am, however, sure that your father is looking after you properly. Please find enclosed a birthday present of five pounds. I hope your father buys you something nice with it.
>
> I do think about you and miss you. I hope we will meet again one day. In the meantime, I wish you a very happy second birthday.
>
> With best wishes,
> Mother. x

That was my mother all over: warm, affectionate and supportive. She had not had the baby adopted, and it hadn't died. She had just left it with its dad, for ever. We read the letters, put everything back as authentically as we could, and rushed over to my cottage to get on to the internet.

Since I had left school my life had been deadly boring. I was stuck in the countryside in the middle of *N'importe-où*, France, with no job, parents whom I hated and who hated me, and a little brother who was at school most of the time. Nobody took any notice of me. They all thought I was meek and dull. Nobody, apart from Tom, knew what I was like inside. I had been longing for something like this to happen. I had been desperate for excitement, and now it had arrived. I had known that something would happen, eventually.

It was time to get to work. It appeared that we had a sister. It would be rude of us not to try to find her.

CHAPTER 3

LIZ

November

My hands shook all the time. I was used to that, now. I was used to the feeling that I was always one step away from vomiting with misery. I was used to arranging my features into the rictus grin of someone who was 'coping really well', and I was used to people taking my assertion that I was fine at face value, because it was easier for them if they could say, 'Liz is doing brilliantly.'

I marched into the bar and sat down on a sofa next to a low table. This was my neighbourhood bar, somewhere that Steve and I used to come to at least once a week. It was a rare thing in London: a genuinely local café with such a loyal clientele that when Costa opened a branch opposite, a few years ago, everyone boycotted them and Costa closed six months later. I was comfortable in here. This was the sort of place where anybody, even a lone woman, could sit without feeling conspicuous. It was a café by day, a bar by night, and was run and staffed exclusively by a man called Matt.

Matt was a shocking gossip, and nurtured a community feeling by telling his regulars all about each other's private lives. I dreaded to think what mileage he was getting out of Steve and me.

He smiled and waved.

'What can I get you, Lizzy?' he called across the room. 'Double arsenic and tonic?'

'Fuck off,' I said, and cheered up a little in spite of myself. 'Large glass of white. And a bowl of deadly nightshade on the side.'

'Coming right up!'

I sank back into the sofa. It was all right here. It was better than being at home. The lighting was low, and the sofa was soft, with thick cushions. There was a small candle in a glass holder on the little table. The floors were boarded with thickly varnished wood. That old Air album was playing discreetly in the background. This room was as close as it could get to being someone's living room, but with a bar at one end and a handsome man serving drinks.

I tried to breathe properly, tried not to be sick. That feeling had not let up over the past two weeks. It was as if I was living a dream. I was reeling from it: Steve, and a boy. I woke up in the mornings thinking about them. At night, I lay awake trying to forget them. Despite my best efforts, I pictured them together. I did it all the time. I imagined them naked, in bed, somewhere in London. I had no idea where Steve was, nor whether he was in some monogamous relationship with his young lover, or

27

whether he was out pulling men all the time. I imagined them in our bed, fucking furiously. I couldn't get them out of my head. I hoped, irrationally, that Steve had turned the picture of my mother away while he was screwing.

My doctor had prescribed me pills to help me sleep. I took them all the time. They kept me spaced out, but they didn't stop me imagining.

When Steve had come for his things, a few days after Halloween, I had managed to string a sentence together, through the fug.

'Why did you bring him here?' I had asked dully. 'Why not go to his place? He didn't look as if he had a girlfriend.'

Steve had looked at the floor. He'd shuffled his feet and cleared his throat.

'Erm,' he had said, in the end. 'That'll be because Miles lives with his, er, family.'

'Parents, you mean.'

'I do mean, yes.'

I hadn't had anything to say to that. I hoped Steve had taken my silence to be cutting and judgemental, rather than woolly and confused.

I took off my coat and draped it on the arm of the sofa. Drops of rain began to splatter on the huge window. London in November could be grim. Christmas was going to arrive suddenly, and after that the cold grey time would stretch out until spring. I felt a spasm of terror. That cold grey time was mine. I could spend it how I wanted. People kept telling me that there were things I could do.

28

'At least there aren't children involved,' they said. 'What a blessing. You should go travelling. You could go to Asia or Africa.' But I don't fly, I told them, on principle. 'So go overland!' they said. 'Join an expedition.' And so on. And I knew I could. I could leave my job, sell up, go travelling, learn something new. Instead, I would probably carry on working at a job I was rarely much good at. I would drink. I would wait to feel better, and I would, perhaps, one day try to cut down on my Valium. I was craving company, because living on my own was turning out not to be much fun. I had grown up doing things on my own, and here I was again.

The last time I felt this bleak was during my brief marriage. At least when I finally managed to leave Adrian, I'd felt better. In fact I had been overwhelmed by a surge of unadulterated joy that lasted for more than a year. I wondered whether Steve was feeling that way now. I pictured him, high on life or something else, laughing about how fat and nagging I was, telling Miles that I'd put him off women for life.

I took a magazine out of my red handbag. This bag was a present to myself, last week, which probably fell into the category of the pathetic post-break-up behaviour that I was keen to avoid. Yet what was I supposed to have done? The bag was perfect, capacious enough for my work stuff, the right colour for my coat, and it was cheap. Not buying it would have been perverse, and so I bent the rules.

I stared at the magazine and sipped my drink.

Steve hadn't come back, that night. I'd half expected him to reappear, at least to offer some sort of explanation. I could not believe that the man I had hitched myself to for ten long years – the man I adored, the man I still adored after all this – would saunter off down the street with a teenage boy without a backward glance. Yet he had. He called me during my lunch hour the next day, to arrange, stiffly, to come over after work and 'pick up a few of my bits and bobs'. A week later, he was back for the rest.

He had wasted no time in coming out to the world. Most of our friends had announced that they'd suspected it all along.

'We did wonder, didn't we?' said a woman called Camilla, previously one of 'our' best friends, and now somebody I would ignore if I passed her on the street. She looked to her partner for confirmation. 'When a man starts wearing pink shirts, that's when you worry. And he liked Kylie. And he cooked that fabulous salmon en croute.' Her partner, Giles, didn't manage to answer because the baby was being sick into his chest hair, but he nodded. I hated them. I particularly hated them because I knew we made a hilarious anecdote. I pictured Camilla sharing the details of my heart-break with the women she called 'my mummy friends', a group of them marvelling at my stupidity, and insisting that I 'must have known really'. I was cutting people off, left, right and

30

centre. I was handing all the joint friends to Steve, on a plate. They all wanted gay friends, anyway. They didn't want me. The women thought I would try to seduce their husbands, and the men wondered whether I was HIV positive. I assumed that Camilla and her ilk were lying. I was sure no one else had guessed either. She just wanted to sound perceptive. I didn't care. I reminded myself of that, and wondered whether to calm my rage with another pill. 'I *don't care*,' I whispered, finished my wine, and signalled to Matt to bring me another.

I was sick, constantly sick. The worst thing, and the thing that I had, so far, admitted to no one, was the visceral feeling that had hit me, with awful timing, on 1 November. Once I realised that Steve really had gone, I discovered that, after all, I wanted a baby. I told myself that I wanted one because it was no longer an option. I had no idea if that was true. All I knew was that, suddenly, I was stopping mothers on the street and smiling maniacally into pushchairs until the occupant smiled back. I was noticing the softness of small children's cheeks, and the gentle wisps of their hair. I was becoming the sort of person I'd always despised, and it scared me.

I was never going to reproduce. I was under no illusions about that. I had turned, suddenly, into a cliché: a superannuated 'career woman', single and broody. I had read all the newspaper articles about us and I knew that we didn't get happy endings.

We turned psychotic in our pursuit of sperm and when it didn't come our way, we either spent a million pounds having donor IVF, or we ran up enormous debts on credit cards in an attempt to compensate for the love we were missing, and ended up bankrupt with nowhere to go to but AA meetings.

It was his fucking cowardice that was eating me up. This was the twenty-first century: being gay was all right. It was not shameful. It was cool. If Steve had suddenly started having feelings for young men at work, then he should have taken the trouble to dump me first. He had an answer for everything, of course.

'I was confused,' he said. 'I wasn't sure what was going on. I didn't want to hurt you. It was the first time it happened.' Under questioning, it transpired that Halloween wasn't the first time, but allegedly it was no more than the sixth or so. In the end, though, Steve didn't really care. He was pleased that events had forced the issue. He had a different life now.

I sipped my wine and screwed up my face, yet again, at the vision I could not dispel. I was obsessed with the idea of Steve and Miles having penetrative sex. Although Steve hadn't been interested in my body for quite some time, I had managed to force him into some token sex the week before Halloween. I had been on the pill for years, so of course we didn't use condoms.

When I thought about this, I wanted to throw

things and scream and shout and curl up into a foetal position and cry for my mummy. This was unfortunate, as I didn't have a mummy, and my father, even with my stepmother in tow, just did not quite cut it. Part of me, too, looked back on the seduction with a glimmer of hopeless hope. I wondered whether I could have got pregnant. The chances were low: not only was I on the pill, but I'd had a period since. There was no chance at all, in fact.

It was taking steely self-control, and it was taking pills, but I was getting through so far. I was, I felt, presenting the outside world with an unusually dignified façade. I had always been strong, because I had never had much choice about it. Therefore, and thanks in part to the pills, I had managed not to have a dramatic haircut. Nor had I joined a gym, telephoned a sperm bank, left blank or abusive messages on Steve's voicemail, or sat around with my girlfriends listing his bad points (not least because my girlfriends were probably sitting around with him, ticking off my faults on their fingers). I had neither gorged myself on chocolate nor starved myself down two dress sizes to show him what he was missing (that would have been a perverse strategy, under the circum-stances). I had not cruised online personal adverts, nor picked up random strangers for a shag. I had not ambushed him outside his office at lunchtime.

And tonight, I had not been able to stay at home on my own, because if I had, I would have felt myself teetering on the brink of various of the above courses of action, and to do any of them would make me stupid, a fool. So, here I was: a single woman, in a London bar, having a civilised glass of wine by herself. Here I was, relieved of the pathological liar who had been holding me back for all these years. I imagined myself in various locations around the world where I wouldn't be able to sit here like this, on my own, with a drink. In much of the world, I would be a grandmother by now. In many places, I would still be married to Adrian. All things considered, I was privileged to be doing this. I took a deep breath and tried to feel good.

The wine was reacting with the pills. My head spun gently. I leaned back on the sofa and sighed. I had never felt so alone in my life. This felt a bit like rock bottom.

When the woman smiled from across the room, I smiled back, dizzy and unfocused. I told myself that there was a connection between us. We were two single women. Thanks to the discreet lighting, and thanks, perhaps, to the state I was in, I could not make out her features, but I could see that she was pretty, with long dark hair. I had always made myself blonder than I naturally was, but, looking at this woman's glossy hair hanging darkly down her back, I thought that perhaps I should try life as a brunette. I might seem intriguing that way. I shook my head. That would be classic 'dumped' behaviour.

Suddenly, she was above me.

'Hi,' she said. She seemed more confident than me. She swam as I attempted to focus on her. I made an effort and moved my mouth in what I hoped was the shape of the word 'hello'. Someone had come to talk to me. That was good.

I pointed to the other cushion on my sofa. 'Ungh?' I managed to say.

'Thanks.'

She sat down, crossed her legs, and finished her drink in one gulp. I made an effort to pull myself together. I was certain that if I closed my eyes, I would pass out, so I opened them wide.

'Drink?' she asked.

I nodded, and tried hard to sound rational.

'Something to wake me up a bit,' I said carefully. She looked at me, laughed, and disappeared.

She came back with a foul liquid that I hadn't tasted for years.

'Fernet branca,' said my new friend. This woke me up enough to start talking, at least.

'. . . and now I'm thirty-seven,' I slurred, close to the end of my story, 'and it's all looking a bit . . . what's the word? . . . Stark. I am thirty-seven. Single. I'll never have a child. Or a partner. And my fucking boyfriend's fucking gay! But I still love him! How stupid?'

She narrowed her eyes at me. She was beautifully dressed, and her voice was low. When I spoke, I found myself trying to make my own voice husky too. She looked young, but she seemed wise.

'Forget about him. Loser. Do you *want* a child?' she demanded.

'I don't *not* want one. Not any more.'

'Because most women, if they'd wanted a child, and if they'd been with someone for – how long were you with this "Steve" tosser?' She made quote marks with her fingers when she said his name, distancing herself from him as if he were a nasty infectious disease.

'Ten years.'

'Since you were twenty-seven. So, if you'd actually wanted a baby, you'd have pushed the issue with him about five years ago, wouldn't you? He'd have given it all this "but I'm not ready" crap, you'd have been able to ditch him and meet someone else. Or maybe he would have said, actually I might be swinging the other way, sorry.' She twiddled her hair around her finger. 'Anyway, you're thirty-seven. Not fifty-seven. It's hardly impossible.'

'Mmm. Tricky, though. A man my age who wants a family looks for a woman who's about twenty-eight. A nice little breeder.'

I bought Rosa another vodka and tonic, and knocked back two more fernet brancas, pleased with the effect they were having. I realised that I should be asking Rosa about herself, and I tried, but she waved my questions away and said that I was more interesting than she was, which I doubted was true. Still, I returned, gratefully, to the subject of myself.

36

It was good to talk about it. I talked and talked, glad that she was a stranger, pleased that I would never see her again. I could tell her anything, and I did.

'I don't even miss him all that much,' I confided. 'But sometimes I miss him so much that I want to find out where he's living and go and throw rocks through his window. But most of the time I can manage without him. Which is just as well.'

She took out a red lipstick and used the window as a mirror. A passer-by stopped and stared at her. Rosa stuck her tongue out.

'Of course you can,' she said. 'You can do more than manage. It's his loss, not yours.'

Two or three drinks later, I tried to leave. I had work in the morning and was already dreading it. If I turned up with an obvious hangover on a Tuesday, everyone would mutter about me. Being hungover on a Friday or even a Monday was cool: my colleagues and the kids would have been pleased to see I was officially 'not moping'. Being the worse for wear on a Tuesday would reek of solitary drinking and desperation.

Rosa smiled and pushed me back down on to the cushions. For the first time, I noticed that although her nails were beautifully manicured, her hands were big and knobbly.

'I'm drunk enough now,' she said, raising her immaculately plucked eyebrows, 'to tell you my little secret.' She gave me a piercing look. 'Unless you've worked it out already. If you have, you're good at covering up. Normally the eyes go straight from the hands to the Adam's apple, and then they try to glimpse my legs. At which point, shiftiness kicks in.' She smiled a wobbly smile. 'Normally, once people work it out, they stop looking me in the eye but at the same time they can't let me go until they've made me confirm it, so they ask all sorts of leading questions about my early life.' She shuddered, waving the inept people away with her large hands. I was proud that I was so wasted I wouldn't have recognised my own father, had he walked into the room. There was no way I was noticing Adam's apples, not tonight. Thanks to this, I had clearly passed the test.

'Well,' I said, hoping that I was jumping to the right conclusion, peering at her neck, 'I can guess what it is *now*, but I didn't before. I really didn't. You should give yourself more credit.' I looked at her hands, and her legs. 'I would never have known. Honestly. You look just wonderful. You have amazing legs.'

She leaned over and kissed my cheek, her hand resting on my thigh. Her perfume was subtle and musky. 'You're very kind.'

'So.' I knew I had to follow up with an intelligent question, but I couldn't think of anything to say. 'Um,' I muttered. 'What stage are you at? May one ask?'

She smiled broadly. 'Gearing up! Hence, out here trawling around for drinking partners. Dutch courage. I've been Rosa for two years. That makes it very nearly D-day.'

I interrupted. 'Who did you used to be?'

She winced, shaking her head at my tactless question.

'Ross,' she whispered. 'We don't talk about him. But the day of reckoning is at hand. It all starts for me next week. Hormone treatment, and then surgery. Then I'm truly Rosa, for ever.' She looked nervous. 'What do you think of that? That for the past couple of hours you've been sharing your secrets with . . . well, with someone like me?'

I laughed. 'Great!' I told her. 'I think it's cool. I do! It's brilliant. I mean, you're only young. Aren't you?' This wasn't what I'd planned to say, but it was what came out.

'I'm thirty-two.'

'Jesus. Much younger than me.'

'But I'll never have babies either.'

'Adopt one? From China or something? Maybe I'll do that . . .' I tailed off, pleased with this new train of thought.

She snorted. 'Yeah, right.'

I thought of something else.

'Tell me to shut up. But do you still have, you know, a willy?'

She paused. 'Not for long.'

I looked at her face. 'You must have been a gorgeous man.' She frowned, and shook her head. She pushed the idea away with both hands.

'I mean it,' I told her. 'If Ross was here I'd be trying to tempt him back to my flat. I would.'

'You can tempt Rosa. I'd like to see where you live.'

I looked around. The bar was about to shut, and we were the last people left. Matt caught my eye. His fringe was always hanging over half his face. I wished he would get it cut.

'Sorry, Liz,' he called over. 'Chucking out time. You too, mate. Lizzy, can you stand up OK?'

Rosa flicked a finger at him, and leaned over to me.

'So, am I invited chez Liz?'

I grinned and swayed. 'Of course you are.'

She stood up and pulled me to my feet.

The very last thing I had been planning when I went out for my solo drink was to bring someone back, so our flat – my flat – was not geared up for company. Steve was a neat-freak, and without him there, I had let it descend into chaos.

In fact, through my blurred vision, I saw that it was a temple to miserable self-indulgence. The sink was full of dirty cups and glasses. The paint on the blue and yellow cupboards was peeling. As if for the first time, I saw the heap of washing, the ironing board with half-ironed blouse draped over it, the exercise books piled precariously on the table. Every corner seemed to be a repository for something. I hoped Rosa would notice that, beneath the mess, there was a homely flat with

40

colourful walls, and polished floors, and mirrors with mosaics around the edge.

I could see that the decor was too studenty. The sitting-room walls were pillar-box red. I thought that, now I was on my own, and now that I was so old, I should probably update it and paint a few walls beige, like they did on television.

I tried to say something to this effect, but my legs started to wobble, and I quickly sat down instead. After a while, I noticed that Rosa was clearing up. She picked up all my clean washing from the other end of the sofa, and moved it on to the stairs. Then she sat next to me.

'Can I have a drink?' she asked. 'Shall I get one myself? What would you like?'

'Oh,' I said, and tried to think. 'Coffee? Tea? Water?'

'Gin?' countered my new friend. 'Or a *digestif* of some sort?'

'Um.' I hauled myself up, pulling on the arm of the sofa. Together, we went to the kitchen, and I knelt, unsteadily, and looked through some kitchen cupboards. 'There's port here,' I said, as bottles dissolved before my eyes. 'And other things. Not quite sure what. Um. Tequila. Something from Brazil. Something from duty free.'

Rosa smiled and nodded. 'Tequila. What else? Can we line up a few in shot glasses? I haven't done that for months.' She looked around uncertainly. 'Do you have such things?'

41

'*Course*,' I slurred. 'I'm a woman of the world.' I checked, clumsily, at the backs of a few cupboards, and managed to locate them. 'Look at this. Steve's *not* a selfish pig. Thank you, Steve. You fucked a teenager but at least you left the shot glasses.'

I moved some old newspapers from the kitchen table to the floor, and put six small glasses on it. I let Rosa do the pouring. While she did it, I thought about how stupid I was being. Even through the haze of Valium, wine and fernet branca, I could see that tequila was a terrible idea. There was no way I was going to work in the morning. I didn't think I would go to work ever again.

Rosa took the shots back to the sitting room, and I followed. I sat close to her, back on the sofa.

'I love you,' I told her, sleepily.

'Oh, shut up! And drink!'

We clinked glasses and gulped back our drinks. I shifted closer to Rosa. A small alert part of me was looking on, disgusted. I hated myself and I hated my life. I was sensible. I never got talking to strangers in bars. I certainly never invited them home with me. And I never did this, either.

I stroked her arm. 'Rosa?' I asked.

'Oh fuck it. Why not?' Tequila and my nagging had made her suddenly aggressive. She sounded male, all of a sudden. 'You want to know if it still works? Let's find out. You want a curiosity fuck? So have one. It's the last chance for me, I suppose. My ceremonial good riddance.'

She turned to me. I gazed at her. There was no trace remaining of Ross's facial hair. She had already told me that she had had everything but the most delicate of eyebrows removed by electrolysis. But her bone structure was masculine.

I was propelled by alcohol and pills and self-disgust. I hated myself. I hated what I was doing. I was worthless. It didn't matter what I did, because it just proved how horrible I was.

Sick with everything, I moved in and forced myself to kiss her. I pulled away in disgust, and so did she. I swallowed and overcame my horror. I was going to do this. I was. I thought of Steve and Miles, and I pushed myself to carry on. I had to take control, because Rosa was not enjoying this any more than I was. I pushed my mouth on to hers. Everything about it was wrong. Her mouth was soft, like mine. The intimacy when our tongues touched made my whole body shudder. She tasted different from Steve. I recoiled, but I carried on. I was propelled by a grim and determined self-hatred.

With an effort, I stood up and pulled Rosa in the direction of the stairs. As I did it, I knew how much I was going to regret this in the morning, and I took satisfaction from that, and redoubled my efforts.

It took a lot of hard work to get Rosa to a point where she was ready for sex. I pressed onwards, not letting myself stop for a second, working with hands and fingers and mouth. I felt like a prostitute, going through the motions without feeling anything. But no one was going to pay me. I was just doing this out of perversity. Then I started to feel a little thrill, in spite of myself.

Twenty minutes later, we were lying on the bed. The bedside lamp was on, illuminating the debauched scene. I looked at the photograph of my mother, which had always stood on my bedside table. She was holding me, a few minutes after my birth. Her face was pale, and there were bags under her eyes. It was the only image I had of her. All the photos stopped when I was a few months old.

Rosa prodded my naked body. I couldn't even be bothered to be ashamed of it. There were parts of my stomach and thighs that I kept meaning to lose, but that meant nothing.

'*This* is everything I've ever wanted,' she said, pulling my left nipple hard between her finger and thumb. I winced. 'See, I don't care if it hurts, because you've got everything I should have had. You've seen me.' She was dressed by now, ashamed of her hairless male body. She had only half undressed to start with. 'You've seen the mess I am. That was Ross's last outing. He's not proud of himself and he's going to leave now. He's not coming back.'

'Good,' I told her. I didn't want to be her friend any more. I couldn't bear the sight of her.

'So I'm going.' She shook her head. 'Because I

know what's about to happen. I'm going to sober up, and I'm going to hate myself with a vengeance that might seem disproportionate. I'm already disgusted. So I'll say au revoir while I can still speak to you, and we won't swap numbers.'

'Me too,' I told her. 'Don't slam the door when you go.'

She picked up all her things and left without saying anything else. I heard the door slam. It was half past three. I left a message on Derek's voice-mail, trying, and definitely failing, to sound sober as I excused myself from work the next day. Then I took two Nurofen with a pint of water, followed them with two sleeping pills, and passed out.

CHAPTER 4

HELEN

Bordeaux

Papa was waiting for me in the car, his face looking old and strange in the half-light of the underground car park.

'*Bonjour*,' he said to me, more formally than a parent ought to speak to their child. He folded his copy of *Le Figaro*, and pulled his seat forward.

'Hello, Papa,' I said, tightly, and I put my bags of shopping in the back, and slid into the passenger seat. The car smelt of stale wine and old people. I tried to think of something to say.

I never had anything to say to Papa. He would only speak to me in French. I spoke English back, because Mother had always insisted that we speak English at home. I had been to English school, and I read books in English and in French, but I had never been to England. In fact, I had never left France. That was how twisted my life was. I once went to Paris on a school trip, and I'd been to the mountains, but that was it. Mother didn't like anyone going anywhere. She liked us all to stay put. 'This is our haven,' she said firmly.

'This is where we belong.' I used to wonder why she didn't want to go away. Now I thought it might be because she was scared. If I had an ex-husband and an abandoned baby, I might want to hide as well.

Papa never spoke Engish. I often thought how funny his life would look, to a normal person. He was surrounded by people who spoke to him in a foreign language, which he understood, and who understood him when he spoke back in French. Most people would not consider that to be a satisfying family life. There were too many barriers there for it to be normal.

On the surface, Papa and I understood each other. But I always felt that we were speaking different languages on another level as well. I wanted him to be proud of me. I had never told him that, but if he and Mother had been proud of me, I would have been able to do anything. I knew that it would never occur to him. I was his daughter, but that appeared to mean that I was another item to be managed in his busy life.

'Did you buy anything nice?' he asked as he started up the car and reversed far too quickly. He always parked in a state-of-the-art underground car park that Tom called the Bat Cave, because it had curving walls at the entrance and rows of colour-coded lights showing you where to park.

'A few clothes. Some shoes.' While I couldn't see Papa's expression, I imagined that it denoted boredom. I always bought clothes and shoes. Most of the time I never even wore them once. I had no idea why I bothered, but my parents seemed to expect me to spend their money on clothes and shoes, and so, as part of my quest for their approval, I did it.

'Good,' he said, in his deadpan manner. His hair was all white now, and wild like Einstein's.

He set off, at some speed, for the exit. It would take us twenty-five minutes to get home. I didn't care if we sat in silence. On the other hand, there were things I needed to know.

'How old was Mother when you met her?' I said, after a while. I was looking out at the grand façades of Bordeaux's riverfront buildings. I liked the architecture here. For a while, I had wanted to study architecture. If I went to university, that was what I would have done. But I couldn't imagine that it was going to happen.

The autumn was still freakishly warm. People wandered around in shirt sleeves, even though it was November.

'How old was your mother?' he checked, in French.

'Yes.'

'I never ask a lady her age.'

I rolled my eyes, without letting him see. 'She must have been about thirty.'

'Perhaps.'

'But she didn't have me until she was thirty-eight, did she?'

48

'If you say so.'

I bit back a retort. 'And then she had Tom.'

He looked at me.

'Yes,' he said. 'Then she had Tom.'

'Why did it take her so long to have babies? When you'd met years before?'

My father tutted and stared straight ahead. He performed a couple of aggressive overtaking manoeuvres, his hand on the horn.

'Hélène,' he said, chastising me. 'Some things are private. Some things are in the past. Some things are both.'

I didn't dare ask again.

'Sorry,' I said, meekly.

He knew about Elizabeth Greene. He knew that Mother had been married before, that she had loved William Greene enough to wear his ring and have his child. That was obvious.

I wondered what had happened in her first marriage, to send Mother away to France. I was itching to find out. Tom and I were doing our best but, so far, it was proving hard to track down the right Elizabeth Greene.

CHAPTER 5

LIZ

29 November

Four weeks later, the grace period ended. As soon as I realised that my period was fifteen days late, I knew that I had, somewhere in my brain, known all along. It had taken me two weeks to face the possibility.

At the same time, I didn't believe it. I didn't believe it for an instant. I felt that this was another of life's sick jokes, and that if I ignored it, something else would happen instead. Perhaps it would turn out to be the menopause. I kept the positive pregnancy test around the flat for a while, but it seemed like a curiosity, a random item that meant nothing very much. I had seen that blue line once before, when I was twenty-one. It felt disastrous then, whereas now I felt nothing. Back in my youth, it had barely occurred to me that I could have had a baby. A blue line meant an abortion, which happened as quickly and quietly as possible. I didn't even mention it to my father; it was my stepmother, Sue, who drove me to the hospital, waited for me, and took me home again. I never regretted it. I did, however, go on to marry the father, out of some strange feeling that the fact that we had conceived meant that we were made for each other. That stupid romantic notion was soon brutally dismissed.

This time, the line, which glowed like neon, had many potential meanings. It could mean that my body had overcome the obstacles, and got itself pregnant when I threw myself at Steve, the week before I found out what was going on. I knew this was unlikely, but I looked it up on the internet, and found that there were a lot of people out there who had had a period but still been pregnant. There was a chance that this was his baby. It could mean that Rosa was still fertile, a notion that had barely occurred to me. It could mean another abortion. Or it might mean that, after the fuck-ups and disasters of the past two months, after all the rejection and the self-destruction, the pills and the alcohol and the mind-spinning weirdness, finally something positive was happening. I had no idea what to do.

I changed my mind many times a day. I stopped drinking and stopped my pills, just in case. I had no idea what I was going to do.

I was fairly sure, however, that I wouldn't marry the father this time.

The idea that Rosa might have impregnated me made me sick to the core. I shuddered at the risks we had taken: when I rifled through my hazy, desperate, drunken memories of that night, I saw no condom. I didn't think it had even occurred

51

to me, because she was a woman, and because I was so fixated on taking the worst possible course of action for me and for her.

The night Steve left, I had thrown my contraceptive pills in the bin, and had quickly filled their place on the shelves with temazepam.

I suddenly, chillingly, hoped that Rosa hadn't given me anything else. To risk AIDS twice in one month certainly felt like carelessness. To get pregnant by someone who had now, presumably, been voluntarily castrated also seemed perverse.

I couldn't tell her. I didn't dare. I knew I could never contact her again. Neither of us would ever be able to look each other in the eye. If I tried to tell her about this, she would probably go ballistic. She would cry and she would hate me even more than she already did. I could not confide in anyone else until I knew what I was going to do, because to talk to anyone about this would make it real, and I thought that I preferred to keep it half imaginary for the moment. I was horrified by the idea of telling anyone about what I had done with Rosa. I felt terrible about it, and the idea that it seemed to have had the most serious of consequences was unbearable.

On my own, I tried to see the future. If I did nothing, I could be a mother in seven and a half months. If I stepped in to prevent that happening, I would probably never have the chance again. I looked on this dilemma with a strange sort of detachment.

I would have the baby. I would not. I hoped for a miscarriage. I worried about abnormalities. I stopped drinking. I started again, but found I couldn't swallow even a mouthful of my favourite white wine. I started being sick in the mornings. Symptom piled upon symptom. I went to bed at eight o'clock every night, and slept for twelve hours, even without tranquillisers. I lived my life, as far as I could, as normal. I did my very best to ignore it all.

I stumbled along, teaching my classes on autopilot, using a fraction of the mental energy I usually used. During classes, I mastered the lazy teacher's manoeuvre of nodding and saying, 'That's a very good question. Anyone?' It occasionally made my life easier, though more often I was greeted with blank looks and shrugs. I marked homework without really looking at what I was doing, sitting in the corner of the staffroom nibbling a ginger biscuit, and waiting for this particular crisis to go away. I invented a mystery virus to throw colleagues off the scent, and when they looked at me knowingly, sympathetically, I realised that they thought I was still bogged down being devastated about Steve. That, I decided, was as good an excuse for wan, stressed sickness as anything. I agreed with them. 'It's only just hit me,' I said, sadly. 'Ten years of my life, down the pan.' In fact, I wasn't feeling anything any more. I didn't care about Steve, and I didn't care about anyone.

After a week, on impulse, I went to the doctor. I sat in the waiting room for forty minutes, staring at an old copy of *Marie Claire*, and avoiding looking at a selection of posters about not drinking, smoking or injecting heroin while pregnant. I gazed, instead, at a government warning on osteoporosis. By the time I went in, I was starting to shake.

My GP was a lovely woman, my own age but responsible. I had tried four different doctors before I found her, and I trusted her. I knew she thought I was coming for more tranquillisers. As I walked into the room, I saw her face arranging itself into a sympathetic 'you shouldn't get dependent' expression.

I found myself unexpectedly holding back tears.

'I'm pregnant,' I told her curtly, blinking. 'And, as you know, single.'

Dr Grey gave nothing away.

'Oh!' she said, with a sage nod. 'Right. How do you feel about that?'

I sniffed and rubbed my forehead. 'If you'd said "congratulations",' I told her, 'that would have been a sign. If you'd picked up the phone and booked me in to see a termination counsellor, that would have been a sign, too. Where did you learn to be so non-committal?'

'It's my job.' Dr Grey smiled sympathetically. I knew she had three children. She had a photo of them on her desk, looking wholesome in their school uniforms. Each of them had a different variation on their mother's dark red hair, brown eyes, and freckles. She was, I always thought, my opposite; how I could have been, in a different universe. She had been to medical school when I was drinking and slacking my way through an English degree. She had known from a young age what she wanted to be when she grew up, and as soon as she graduated, she was a doctor. I still had no idea what I really wanted to be.

Dr Grey fixed me with her dark eyes. She had, no doubt, planned her own conceptions.

'So,' she said. 'I repeat. How do you feel about it?'

I sighed. 'I don't. I've been going out of my way not to think about it for quite some time. But it seems that my legs have walked me here and I suppose I have to face it. Sometimes I think, oh, a lovely baby to dress in cute little outfits – it'll be like a lovely doll, or a kitten. Other times . . .' I tailed off, then made myself continue. 'I was in the bookshop the other day,' I said, fiddling with a paperweight on her desk. The paperweight was a gift from some pharmaceuticals company, emblazoned with the name of a drug I had never heard of. 'And I found myself sitting on the floor reading baby books. Looking at diagrams. But you can't buy pregnancy books if you're not even sure if you can go through with it. A month ago I thought I didn't have a maternal bone in my body. A week after that, I felt desperate for a baby. I don't know if I can do it on my own. I'm getting old, and this is probably my last chance.' I passed the paperweight from hand to hand, staring at it. 'I do Google searches for all the things that can go wrong,' I told it. In my peripheral vision, Dr Grey was shaking her head, about to say something. 'I know,' I told her. 'This morning I learned about Edwards Syndrome. It's that phrase they use, "incompatible with life". It sounds innocuous at first, and then you realise what they're saying. How can I not want the baby and be scared of Edwards Syndrome at the same time?'

'Very easily. You're confused.'

'Yes.'

'So the first thing you do is you stop Googling. Are you still taking the tempazepam?' I shook my head. 'Well done. When was your last period?'

I didn't ask her whether there was a chance that I could have conceived before my last period, because I didn't want to hear her answer. I told her, and she gave me a due date in the middle of August. A part of me was thrilled. I had never expected that I would utter, or want to utter, the words 'my due date'. As Dr Grey said the words, 'August the seventh,' my abortion receded over the horizon. I strongly believed in abortion on principle, but right now, it was not looking like an option.

Suddenly, I was staring at the prospect of single motherhood. I cast around wildly for a support network. My father would help. He had brought me up on his own, and he was a shambling mess. If he could do it, then so could I. He met Sue when I was twelve, and she was slightly more clued up than he was. She would, in fact, be a far greater help than he could possibly be. I had friends with children, though they had all become more distant as their worlds and mine diverged over the past ten years. At the moment, of course, most of them were clinging to Steve, hoping to make him an Elton John-style godfather to their babies. But some of them would, surely, let me back into the fold, if I had a child.

I knew the internet was full of baby websites, because a couple of my colleagues monopolised the computer room whenever they got the chance, posting messages about night feeds and hilarious comments their toddlers had come out with. I might be able to get on the internet and find some new friends. This was London: there were other women out there in my situation, more or less, and I ought to be able to find some of them.

Dr Grey was looking at me sympathetically. 'Come back in a week,' she said. 'I don't think you're ready for me to refer you anywhere. You're only seven weeks. You've got time to make your decision.'

I looked at her.

'Do you know something weird?' I asked her, feeling dizzy and terrified.

'What's that?'

'There's only one thing in the world that I want less than to have a baby, right now, on my own.'

'And that is?'

'Not to have it.'

As I left the surgery, I placed my hands experimentally, protectively over my abdomen. It would be a challenge, I told myself. And I was not going to run away from a challenge. I made an effort to pull myself together. I was mortified at the way I'd behaved on the night I met Rosa. That pathetic, self-loathing creature was not me. Life was giving me a chance to prove that I was better than that.

For a second, as I stamped through the cold drizzle, towards the Tube, I was exhilarated. I was on my own. This might be Steve's, and it might be Rosa's. I hoped it was Steve's, but either way, nobody but me had any claim on this implausible embryo. The course of my life had changed. I was going to be a mother. I barely had a concept of what that meant.

A baby would love me. It would be mine, for ever. I tried to tell myself that the fact that I had no mother myself did not necessarily mean that I was incapable of being one. I was not my own mother. History would not repeat itself. I would be there for this baby. I was there for it already. I was its entire world. I encircled it. I enclosed it. Everything was filtered for it, by me. It wasn't a baby yet. It was just a cluster of miraculous cells.

I hadn't decided to have it. I could shrug it off, forget this had ever happened, and carry on with my life in peace.

★　　★　　★

I found a site that I liked the look of. It was called Babytalk, and it didn't contain any patronising articles by health professionals, or any government advice. It was made up of apparently endless discussion forums. I looked down their names. Pregnancy, Baby, Toddlers, Over-threes, Teens and tweens, Relationships, Gossip, Stress, and many more. I clicked on Pregnancy, amazed to find myself doing such a thing. A bubble popped up telling me I had to register, so I filled in a form and registered as LizGreene. I had never seen the appeal of the kooky username: Liz Greene was who I was. Then I typed a message on the pregnancy forum.

'Hi,' I wrote. 'May I join you? My name is Liz. I'm 37 and I seem to be headed for single motherhood in August. Are there any other single mothers out there? This pregnancy was not planned and I'm overwhelmed and still trying to come to terms with it. Hoping to hear from somebody – anybody. Thanks, Liz.'

I went to bed, feeling strangely tranquil. In the morning, to my amazement, I had five replies. Four were friendly and welcoming. One was from someone called 'Fluffball' who was also expecting a baby on her own. Three said I should talk to Fluffball. The fifth took me to task for 'your extreme insensitivity in parading your good fortune when there are so many of us on here who've been TTC2L and would give anything to be in your shoes'. I had no idea what TTC2L might mean, but I thought I got her drift.

I paused for my morning vomit, then sipped at weak lemon and ginger tea and got to work, determined to reply to everyone before I had to go to school.

CHAPTER 6

HELEN

Bordeaux, 30 November

I put my head in my hands. I had been sitting at the computer for weeks, and I had got nowhere. There were millions of Elizabeth Greenes in the world, and none of them fitted. The ages were wrong, the ethnicity was wrong. Every time I thought I might have found her, it turned out to be an eight-year-old, or someone on a family tree an American child had assembled for a school project. The same Elizabeth Greenes came up again and again. There was an American astrologer, an actress who had made one horror film, a classics lecturer and a metal-smithing instructor. None of them could have been her. I had checked and checked. I had even emailed two of them, just in case.

My computer was set up on a rickety table downstairs. It was raining outside, though the sun was trying to poke through. I had to find her. I knew that this woman would be my ticket out of here. I didn't want to get a boring job like everyone else. I needed a challenge, and Elizabeth

Greene was going to be it. The more I thought about it, the more I knew that she would solve everything. I was absolutely convinced that everything was going to be all right. It was my destiny. This was the adventure I had been waiting for, all my life.

The trouble was, I was beginning to despair. I couldn't fall at the first hurdle, but so far, I had no idea where to find her.

Tom ruffled the back of my hair.

'How long have you been there?' I demanded, whipping round. He was wearing a white sweatshirt and black jeans. Tom loved black and white.

'Just got here.'

'How come I haven't seen you for days?'

He dropped his bag and shrugged. 'School. Football. Mates. You know. Life.' He pulled up a chair. 'Found her?'

I shook my head. 'You're younger than me,' I said, pulling my hair back into a ponytail. 'You're good at the internet. You do it.'

'Still putting her name into Google?'

I nodded. 'I think Mother did it on purpose. Gave her a name with hundreds of variations. I've done Elizabeth, Beth, Betty, Lizzie-with-an-"ie", Lizzy-with-a-y, Liz . . . And I've trawled through pages and pages of Google for all of them.'

Tom motioned with his head for me to move aside. I stood up and let him take my place. He started typing.

'What are you doing?' I asked him.

'We'll try some other ways,' he said, without looking up. 'First of all, name a few cities.'

'God knows. Brighton, where the letters were addressed? London? Some other cities in England? Erm, Edinburgh? Manchester? New York?'

He looked at me shrewdly. 'You wish.'

'What do you mean?'

'You're going to go and get her.'

'No I'm not.' I knew I didn't sound convincing.

'I'm psychic, I know these things. You're going to bring her to Mother. A little present.'

I looked away. 'You're mad.'

'Well, we'll find her. Don't worry.'

He stared at the screen, a little frown of concentration on his forehead. I twirled a strand of hair around my finger and stood on one foot, feeling anxious. He typed, then sat back and waited.

'Trouble is, there are millions of E. Greenes in all those places, and she might not even be one of them. She's probably married by now and changed her name. Let's try narrowing down Google a bit.'

'How? Type "my mother abandoned me" next to her name?'

We stared at each other, both frustrated.

'Try us,' I said. 'See if we exist online. If we don't, she might not, either. Then we could try to find her the old-fashioned way.'

Tom snorted. 'Which is?'

I sucked my lip and tried to think of an answer. 'Hire a private detective!' I said triumphantly.

63

'Follow the paper trail! Start with the address on the envelopes and take it from there.'

'Are we going to put you in a beret and send you slinking around England smoking a cigarette and stumbling on clues?' He rolled his eyes. 'Do private detectives even exist? Aren't they just a construct serving the various branches of the fiction industry?' He pointed at the screen. 'Hey, here you are! Helen Labenne – you're on the school site.'

'Jesus. What for?' I wanted to tell him off for talking like a professor when he was fifteen years old, but this was too interesting, so I let it drop.

'Ummm. Hang on, just clicking it. Here we go. Bordeaux International School. Why in God's name did they put you on there? You are in a long list, I must say.' He smiled. 'A long list of students who passed the International Bac last year. So, in fact, everyone.'

'Cheers. What about you?'

He tapped some more. 'As far as the World Wide Web's concerned, I don't exist. Not as Tom, and not as Thomas, not even anyone else with my name. Anyway, let's get back to our big sister. She's nearly forty. The internet *must* have heard of her by now.'

Ten fruitless minutes later, the phone rang. I picked it up reluctantly, because I knew who it was going to be.

'Helen,' said Mother. 'It's nearly lunchtime.'

'OK,' I mumbled. 'Be there in a bit.'

Sunday lunch was a ritual of my parents', and while I was living at home, I had to go along with it. Tom was adept at excusing himself but, somehow, I never, ever managed to get out of it. I supposed they saw him all the time because he lived with them, in term time. I kept myself as far away as I could, but I was utterly dependent on their money. Their insistence that I sit down with them and submit to a cringingly formal meal once a week was their way of reminding me that they owned me.

I did not want to be owned. I was aching with frustration. I was holed up here, on this stupid over-sized estate, and the whole world had forgotten about me. I knew I should leave, but because I didn't have to, I hadn't dared. The moment we found Elizabeth, I would be out of there.

I knew the parents were glad when I left the big house, even though they never said it. They exchanged glances when they thought I wasn't looking, whenever I was in the same room as them, and they thought I didn't notice. Tom had spotted them doing it too, so I knew it wasn't my imagination. We looked at each other and rolled our eyes when they spoke, in retaliation.

I liked things tidy, and when I took it over, the little house was in a state. Before I moved in, I vacuumed all the floors and washed the linen. I polished every wooden surface and dusted away a citadel of spider webs. I mopped the downstairs tiles. I bought a few curtains for the bare windows.

None of this got rid of the musty smell. The downstairs floor was paved with cheap orange tiles, some of which I had covered with rugs. The upstairs floors were wooden, and they creaked, even when there was no one there. Sometimes I had a feeling that there was a ghost, but then I laughed at myself, because I knew that there were no such things, that credulous people invented them to make life more interesting.

I had a little kitchen, kitted out as cheaply as possible by my unstintingly generous parents (I even had to boil water in a tinny little pan on the gas ring, in true French fashion, because they didn't stretch to a kettle). The tiny sitting room had a foldaway table at one end, which presently bore my laptop and broadband connection. Upstairs, I had two poky bedrooms and a crappy little bathroom.

Tom had to live with Mum and Dad because he was still at school. He was gratifyingly jealous of my freedom. In the holidays, he came to live in my spare room. It was a tiny room, but a light, bright one. He had white sheets on the bed, and he made the place come alive. When he was there, I was the boss. I liked being bossy to Tom. It was the only area of my life over which I had control.

Now I left him on the computer, and dragged my feet along the gravel path that separated my old shed from the big house. The vines were half hidden in thick, low cloud. It was hard to see exactly where the sky began. There was no sign of the sun. The cold instantly made my jumper and jeans irrelevant. I might as well have been naked. The parents had become so exasperated by my turning up frozen last winter that, for my birthday, they bought me an expensive coat. When I wore it, I felt like a spy. It was beige, or rather 'camel', and it was an incredible disguise for me. It reached halfway down my calves, and its belted waist and wide, luxurious sleeves made me into someone else entirely. I adored it. Unfortunately, my relationship with my parents could not have accommodated my raising my hands in joy and exclaiming, 'I love it!' This meant, perversely, that I only wore it if I knew they weren't going to see me. I couldn't bear to let them think that they had got something right.

Mother was waiting at the top of the nine steps that led up to the front door. I looked at the front of the house as I approached. It was bleak and enormous. The outside was grey and weather-beaten, and although it could look all right in the summer, when the flowers were out in front, in the winter it was austere and grim. There were rooms and rooms in there that were never used, which were dotted with ugly pieces of dark brown furniture covered in dust sheets. The parts they did use had barely changed since my earliest childhood, and I knew, although I never went back there, that my bedroom was fully intact, and probably always would be, with its pink bedlinen and posters of musicians I'd never really known but had put up in an attempt to become like the other girls at school, to fit in. This was in spite of the fact that I'd barely ever brought a friend home. I knew the atmosphere in our house was weird, and I'd instinctively kept home and school apart. Tom did the same. He had millions of friends but, even though we lived in a chateau, they never came to visit.

'Helen!' Mother widened her eyes in exasperation. 'Where is your *coat*, Helen? Come on in.' She tutted at me, and, as I reached the top of the steps, she reached for my hand. 'You're freezing,' she scolded. I shrugged, avoiding her face. I knew she didn't really care. She tried to act like a mother around me, and I had always known she was faking it. Now that I knew that she had abandoned a baby before me, I could understand why she was like this. She was one of those women who was never meant to be a mother. I wondered why she'd had two more children after running out on Elizabeth (Lizzie, Betty, Beth). Having failed so spectacularly the first time, she should have steered well clear.

I stepped into the hall and stared into her face, trying to divine whether she wished she had aborted me. Abortion was legal when she was pregnant with me. It had even been legal when she got pregnant with Elizabeth. She shouldn't have kept having unwanted babies when she could have flushed us all away.

She was looking at me, a strange expression on her face. Mother was fifty-eight but she didn't look old yet. She was tall, with long fair hair, like me, though she wore her hair in a severe chignon and I left mine loose. She should have been pretty, even at her age, but she was tense and her face was lined with pent-up worry and anger. I could never have asked her how she was feeling. I did wonder, though.

We stared into each other's face, unspeaking. I wondered whether she was looking at me like she was because she knew that I knew her secret. Abruptly, she turned her back, and I followed her into the dining room, which was formal and oppressive, with portraits of people we didn't know on the walls. Her heels clipped across the parquet floor. My trainers squeaked.

'Hélène!' My father was sixty-five, and he was the one who looked old, because he was.

'*Oui, Papa,*' I said, and let him hold my shoulders and kiss each of my cheeks. He handed me an aperitif, a glass of sweet wine, and stood and looked at me. They both did. I turned away. Self-conscious, I took a deep gulp of wine, and felt it go immediately to my head. They always made me drink in the middle of the day. It made me so drowsy that I had to go home and sleep all afternoon.

'What have you been doing this week, Helen?' asked Mother, crisply.

As if you didn't know, I answered silently. As if you didn't stand at the window watching my comings and goings.

'Not much,' I told her, meekly. 'And you?'

'You know what we've been doing. All the usual things that we do. But what about you? You don't seem to have been out and about. Do you have a plan?' She touched my arm. 'Have you thought any more about university?'

I smiled, and shook my head. This was what I wanted to say: 'You can't wait to get rid of me, can you? You can't even have me in the house for five minutes without asking when I'm moving out.' I tried to let my eyebrows say it for me.

Papa frowned. 'Think about getting some work, Hélène,' he said, in French. 'If you had a job in Bordeaux, I could drive you in, in the mornings, and I could pick you up afterwards. It wouldn't be a problem. You can go to university next year, in Bordeaux. You had good results. You need to meet people.' He looked at my face. 'We want you to be happy,' he added. I watched him looking at Mother, saw the expression that passed between them, and I hated them both.

Mother pitched in. 'Sylvie's daughter, you know, Ophélie? She's started working at one of those clothes shops in town. She said she could look out for something for you if you'd like her to.'

I shrugged, incensed. 'If she likes,' I hissed. Then I took a deep breath, exhaled slowly, and breathed in again. 'Actually,' I said, 'I might go somewhere further afield. I might go abroad. We've never been abroad, and I want to see what it's like.'

Mother pursed her lips. Papa took a step towards me. I stepped back.

'Where, abroad?' he asked. He looked alarmed.

'Perhaps to England. I do speak the language, after all.'

Mother shook her head. 'You don't want to go there,' she said, flatly.

'Or America.'

'No.'

'Why not?'

'Because you've never been anywhere on your own. You wouldn't last five minutes.' She looked at me, and her expression softened slightly. 'I'm glad you're curious, all the same. I had itchy feet at your age. There's nothing like it.'

I narrowed my eyes at her. 'Did you actually travel?'

Mother smiled to herself. 'Further than you could possibly imagine. Until I met your father.' Again, they looked at each other. Again, I felt excluded and unwanted.

'You can't have gone very far then,' I pointed out, 'because France is next door to England.'

'I came the long way round,' said Mother.

I put my empty glass down on the table. I was giddy with alcohol. Although I hated confrontations, Elizabeth Greene was more important than anything in the world, so I was going to break our unspoken rules.

'Do we have family in England?' I asked loudly. 'Is there anyone I can go to see? Cousins or anything?'

Before I'd even finished speaking, she was shaking her head. She looked cross.

'No, Helen. There's no one.'

'What about your parents? My grandparents. What happened to them?'

'Oh, they didn't approve of my lifestyle. You know that. Travelling was bad enough – nice girls didn't do it in those days. Marrying a Frenchman was worse.' She and my father shared the smug despicable smile of the long-married. 'We never kept in touch. I've told you that before. They disowned me and I never felt the need to go crawling back. Good riddance, say I.'

'Can't I go and find them? Build some bridges? They'd like to meet their granddaughter. It's one thing for them not to want to talk to you, but it's not fair for them not even to know that I exist.'

She took a deep breath, and used her no-arguing-back voice.

'No, Helen,' she said, 'you absolutely cannot. Sit down. I'll serve up.'

I hated my mother's cooking. Everything was meaty, and there were too many vegetables. Today she had cooked pork, with cabbage and peas and roast potatoes. I watched, half disgusted, as she and Papa poured a thick red wine gravy over everything. The French didn't do gravy, but my parents certainly did.

I set to work, knowing I had to force down at least half of what was on my plate. Our cutlery scraped, and we cast around for things to talk about. I barely said a word. The parents made forced conversation about the garden and the weather. If Tom had been there, it would have been all right.

I stared at the grandfather clock that stood against the opposite wall, and jigged my leg, excitedly, under the table. As soon as I found my sister, my whole life would come into focus. I tried to imagine Mother's reaction when I came back with her lost baby. It would be the best present she had ever had. Tom was right about my plan. I was going to surprise everyone. I would find my sister, and make friends with her, and bring her back. No one would imagine I could pull off something like that, but I knew that I could do it.

I pictured Mother's face. Finally, the tension was going to fall away. She would be open. She would be joyful. She and Elizabeth would be reconciled, and I would have a sister, a soulmate. Everything was going to change. My parents were going to love me.

They carried on talking, in their bored, formal way, about the vineyard, and about last year's wines, and about the neighbours. I let it all drift past. The parents were on reasonable terms with everyone in the village. I hardly knew anybody, because I never knew what to say to anyone, and they all thought I was snobbish and cold. Nobody invited me anywhere. I had gone to International School because Mother wanted English to be my first language. Tom and I both wished we had gone to the local school. That way we would have known everyone, and we would have felt properly French. As things stood, I was neither French nor English. There was nowhere that I belonged, apart from here, in this weird, messed-up family, in this big, wasteful chateau.

I swallowed. Nobody spoke for a few minutes. I could hear Papa chewing his meat. The sound turned my stomach. Mother looked at me, and looked away again. She drained the red wine from her glass.

'Helen,' she said, in her formal little voice. 'Could you possibly manage to pass me the peas?'

I sighed. 'Yes, of course,' I said. As I passed them, I forced myself to speak again. 'How far away would you let me go?' I demanded, avoiding eye contact. 'Could I go to Paris?'

They looked at each other, in shared, suppressed amusement.

'Do you *want* to go to Paris?' asked Mother, carefully.

I looked at her, and then at Papa.

'I don't know,' I told them. 'I haven't decided yet.'

By the time I returned home, waving away the parents' predictable suggestion that I stay in the big house with them all afternoon, the cloud had closed in. The fog was so thick that I couldn't see my own cottage. I stumbled because of the wine.

The gravel path was the whole world. I looked back. It was good to see the chateau swallowed up. The day was still and damp, and I stood for a moment to savour the cold.

Tom was standing at the door of the cottage. As soon as I was close enough for him to hear, he shouted.

'I think I've found her!' he yelled.

I ran. 'How? Where?' The door banged shut behind me, and I raced to the computer, the end of my nose cold, my fingers frozen.

'Look,' he said, pointing. There was a site up on screen. 'Babytalk,' it said at the top. 'Pregnancy Forum' was written underneath.

'A baby website?' I asked. 'Pregnancy?'

'She registered last night. Look.' Tom double clicked on a message, and it filled the screen. We read it together.

'Hi,' it read. 'May I join you? My name is Liz. I'm 37 and I seem to be headed for single mother-hood in August. Are there any other single mothers out there? This pregnancy was not planned and I'm overwhelmed and still trying to come to terms with it. Hoping to hear from somebody – anybody. Thanks, Liz.'

'She hasn't been doing this for long,' said Tom, with a smile. 'Look at her username. LizGreene. It took me about five seconds to find her.'

'We don't know it's her,' I objected.

'That's why you've just registered. You have a new identity, H. From now on, you're Frenchmaid.

75

Look, I've written you a profile. So you're on here because you're broody, even though you're young. OK? Start asking questions. We'll soon suss her out.'

I sat down. Nervously, I clicked on the 'reply' button under her message.

'Here goes,' I said to Tom, and I started typing.

'Hello Liz!' read my message, by the time I posted it. 'I'm not in your situation but I want to lend you some support. I'm sure you will be fine though it probably seems difficult at the moment. Can your own mother help you out? Any time you want a shoulder to cry on, I'm around. Love, Frenchmaid.'

'What do you think?' I asked Tom. He nodded, and I clicked the 'submit' button.

In the evening, she responded.

'Thanks for your message,' she wrote. 'Your support means a lot. Unfortunately I don't have a mother – my dad brought me up on his own. He and my stepmother don't know about the pregnancy yet but you're right, I'm sure they'll do what they can. I'm in London and they're in Sussex, which actually isn't too far away. Thanks again. I guess I'll cope when the news sinks in. Liz x.'

We looked at each other.

'She hasn't got a mother,' I said. Tom was right behind me. I turned round and looked up at him. 'Her father lives in Sussex,' I added.

'Then I would say,' he told me, 'that she is our best bet.'

I nodded, thrilled. 'I'd say she's our only bet.'

My life had a purpose. I had a mission.

CHAPTER 7

LIZ

1 January

I hoped the café was open on New Year's Day. Matt used to have a sign up that promised, 'We never close,' but after a few weeks, he crossed out the word 'never' and changed it to 'rarely'.

I put my hands in my pockets, pulled my scarf tightly around my face, and stomped up the street. It was eerie, the silence. Curtains were drawn; in some cases, sarongs were nailed to window frames. Some windows didn't have curtains, but there was a gaping darkness behind them. Everybody except me had stayed up long after midnight. Everyone else was groggily sleeping it off.

I could hear cars in the distance, but other than that, I seemed to have Kentish Town to myself. There were light grey clouds overhead, and the cold was making my nose shine and my fingertips tingle. I felt as if I were out at five in the morning, and checked my watch. It was almost eleven o'clock. A car passed, the first I had seen.

I was nauseous, and still no one had guessed

my secret. I had shut myself off from all my old friends, had pushed them firmly towards Steve, because I couldn't bear to confide in anybody. I didn't want anyone to know about my night with Rosa. I didn't want to talk about my pregnancy, to deal with the questions that would arise, so I had busily ignored everyone. At work, though, I felt it must be written on my face. No one had noticed that I spent most of the morning holding a handkerchief over my nose, trying to screen the smells that made my stomach heave. Nobody had commented on the fact that I stroked my stomach ceaselessly, and they were probably all relieved that I'd stopped moaning about the fact that I would never have children.

My New Year's Eve had been mainly miserable, leavened with a tiny glug of excitement. I had a bath, watched some television, and went to bed at ten, as usual. I was woken at ten seconds to midnight by a roared countdown from the pub up the road, swiftly followed by Big Ben in surround sound from radios in the area, and then fireworks which sounded as if they were in the neighbours' garden. At that point, sleep eluded me entirely and I tossed and turned, got up, agonised and felt sorry for myself until four in the morning. I went on the forum, briefly, and exchanged odd messages with Frenchmaid, who was the only other one sad enough to be online in the early hours of New Year's Day.

'Happy New Year,' she'd written. 'The year when

your baby's going to be born! It's going to be a brilliant year for you, I can tell.'

'Thanks,' I wrote back, pleased with the illusion of company. 'You too. What are your resolutions?'

'Leave home,' she replied. 'Go abroad, probably. I've got plans for an adventure.'

'Well, come to London then,' I told her. 'And whatever you do, try not to give in to your broodiness. You've got your whole life ahead of you, you lucky, lucky person.'

She was enthusiastic and friendly, and I hoped she had no idea how pained I was by the contrast between her life – a twenty-year-old girl who seemed to have the world at her feet – and mine.

My life was all bad, except that it wasn't. Frenchmaid was right: this was the year in which I was going to become a single mother. Somehow, that prospect was at the same time the most terrifying thing that had ever happened to me and wildly exciting. There were going to be two of us, against the world. I knew it would be difficult. I dreaded almost everything about my immediate future. Yet I could not stop a few moments of elation. I was going to have a baby. I would be a mother. Two months ago, that had seemed utterly impossible, and now it was happening.

Christmas had been horrible, as I spent two days with Dad and Sue pretending to drink, and the rest of the holidays wallowing by myself. Next Christmas would be different, because if all went

80

well, I would have a four-month-old baby. That was beyond my capabilities to imagine.

Lying in bed, listening to the parties going on around me, I wondered whether it was really going to be harder doing it on my own than it would have been with Steve. I concluded that I would have ended up on my own pretty swiftly anyway. It didn't really matter.

What mattered was that I had a network, that my baby had other people than me in its life. I was trying to persuade myself that Rosa really was the father, although until I had a dating scan, I was going to cling to the shred of hope that it might be Steve's.

Lying in bed last night, listening to other people having fun, I'd made a resolution. Although my instincts were still yelling at me to leave Rosa out of my life and my baby's life, I was going to try to overcome my fear and contact her. That was the mature thing to do. However bizarre the circumstances, Rosa had fathered my baby, and she had a right to know about it. I was trying to convince myself to stop being afraid of her, and ashamed of what I'd done that night. I was going to do my best to track her down and share the news. I would not be scared of her reaction. I would just tell her. Then I would walk away and leave her alone until she wanted to talk to me, if she ever did.

I vaguely remembered that Matt had addressed her as 'mate', and that she had given him the finger. This made me think that he'd known her for a while. He was the only lead I had. As soon as I'd had a scan, I was going to tell the father. If it was Rosa, she would hate me. I hoped she might come around to the idea, in time. If it was Steve, he would assume I had done it on purpose, that I was trying to trap him. Either way, I was going to piss somebody off.

I was nearly at the café when I gradually became half aware that someone was walking towards me. Without looking up, I moved to the edge of the pavement, to let them pass. They didn't. They stopped in front of me and put their hands on my shoulders. I looked up. When I saw who it was, I shrugged his hands away.

'Steve,' I said, and turned away. At least my bizarre conception had stopped me obsessing over him. I tried to think of something to say. I didn't look at his face. 'Hello,' I said, and tried to keep walking.

'Hi, Lizzy,' he said, and finally I looked at him. Unfortunately, it still gave me a pang. I had loved him for years and years. Nothing changed that. He had a handsome face that was getting craggy as he got older. It suited him. So did his hair, which was now professorially long and messy. The black was sprinkled with more grey than I remembered.

'Hello,' I said again. 'What brings you here?'

He smiled. 'New Year's resolution,' he said. 'Can I come back for a coffee?'

'I was on my way to Matt's.'

'Join you?'

It felt odd, to be walking with him again. We reached the top of the road, and turned right. Every shop on the little row was closed. The scummy newsagent, the grotty, expensive food shop. These were the retail outlets of our life together. As far as these shut and barred façades were concerned, Steve and Liz were walking together to the café, as usual. Nothing had changed, in their view.

We didn't say anything as we walked. I was suddenly tired, exhausted to the point where I had no idea whether I would be able to reach our destination without stopping for a quick nap in someone's doorway. I wished I had stayed in bed. I could have listened to Steve ringing the bell, and I could have ignored him. I wouldn't have done, though. I would have answered it.

I wanted to tell him. I couldn't tell him.

The café's windows were half misted over, and I could see a couple of figures inside. When we stepped in, it was unfeasibly warm. Frank Sinatra was playing on the stereo. Matt looked at us, and did a small double take.

'Happy New Year,' he said, uncertainly.

'Happy New Year to you, too, Matthew,' Steve replied, too jovially. We took a table in the furthest corner. It was not the table where I had sat with Rosa.

Coffee made me sick, so I ordered mint tea. Steve raised his eyebrows.

83

'Given up the hard stuff?' he asked, clearing his throat.

'Just for today.'

'Good night last night?'

'Fabulous.' I looked at him, and saw that he believed me. 'Are you having a croissant?'

'Sure.'

Steve shouted our order over to Matt, who pushed his blond fringe aside and got to work. We sat in silence for a while. To my annoyance, I cracked first.

'Were you coming to see me?'

Steve sighed and looked down.

'I want to apologise,' he said quickly, fiddling with the sugar. 'I'm sorry about everything I've put you through. It's shitty.'

I thought of the tiny embryo and tried to rise above this.

'It's OK,' I said as casually as I could. My voice betrayed me with a wobble. 'It's in the past.'

He looked up and frowned. 'Not very far in the past.'

'What is this?' I demanded. 'New year, new, caring Steve? Suddenly realised that sauntering off down the fucking street with a teenager's hand on your arse wasn't your finest moment? Come back to say a pathetic sorry so you can start to feel good about yourself again?'

He nodded slowly, acknowledging my point with a grimace. 'Something like that.'

I tutted and rolled my eyes, because I knew that

he hated it. He sighed and ran both hands through his greying hair.

'It's Miles,' he said, eventually. 'He's spent the holidays at home. With his parents. And it's rather struck me, since we've been apart, that he's seventeen. And I'm thirty-eight. I've been infatuated, I'll be the first to admit that. I'd never known anything like it, when I met Miles. Sorry. I feel like a fool. I mean, bringing him to the flat and everything. It wasn't the greatest behaviour on my part.'

I swallowed. 'Seventeen-year-olds are young and stupid and they think they own the world. I see too many of them at work.'

'Good thing I'm not in your line of work.'

'You'd be in prison.'

'What do they call it – the nonce's wing?'

'So you and Miles?' I was numb. I was trying not to care. I was pretending to myself that Steve and I had no history, that he was just someone I'd met in the street, or a friend of a friend. I wanted to yell at him, 'I might be having your baby!' but I didn't. It did not seem appropriate.

'I might call it a day.' He looked at me quickly. 'But I'm still gay.'

'I see.'

'So, that's it really. Sorry that I've been such a bastard.'

I considered letting rip at him, but I lacked the energy. 'It's all right,' I said. I chewed my croissant. Over the past few weeks, I had discovered that it was possible to be nauseous and starving at the same time, and I ate quickly before the sick feeling caught up with me.

We sat in silence. Steve tried to start a couple of conversations.

'How's your dad?' he asked.

'Fine.'

'And Sue?'

'She's all right.'

'How about Kathy? She must hate me.' Kathy was my best friend at work.

'Pretty much.' In the end I turned on him. 'Steve,' I said, wearily. 'I appreciate your coming over and trying to be nice. But if you're thinking we can "still be friends" or anything like that, please fuck off. You go and live your life. I'll live mine.' I opened my mouth to tell him I was pregnant. I closed it again. I needed him away from me.

'That's it?'

'That's it.'

He looked at me for a while, then stood up and went to pay at the counter. From the corner of my eye, I was aware of him pausing, wondering whether or not to kiss me. I didn't look round, and he went.

As soon as he'd gone, I went to the counter and sat on a tall stool.

'Jeez,' said Matt, flicking a croissant crumb from his black T-shirt. Matt was tall and burly, and he had very annoying hair. He always wore black. 'What was going on there?'

I shrugged. 'Steve was trying to feel better about himself. Now he can walk away feeling all fluffy, telling himself that he's done the right thing. He wanted to be friends. Tempting as that was, I turned him down.'

'It never works, does it, the "can we still be friends" thing?'

'Particularly not under our circumstances.'

Matt leaned forwards on his elbows. 'Do you think it's better or worse, though, being left for a man? On the one hand, it's like it's nothing personal – it's the whole of womankind that's not doing it for him. On the other hand, he's left you for a boy, and that's just not normal, is it?'

I sighed. 'Thanks, Matt. Thanks for the analysis.'

'Just thinking aloud. You know it's quiet here today. And apart from you and Steve, no one's given me any interesting gossip for weeks.'

'You should start doing food. Proper food, I mean. Not the croissanty stuff. Then everyone would come for their hangover breakfasts.'

He nodded, slowly, several times. 'I'm thinking about it. Big expense. I'd need to get a proper kitchen, and a few people to work it, and that would take more space. And money. But I know where you're coming from, and you're right.'

I remembered why, originally, I had been on my way here. 'Hey, Matt?'

'Mmm?'

'Remember about six weeks ago? I was in here and I got talking to a woman? Rosa?'

87

He stepped back, looked at me, and laughed loudly. '"Got talking to" her?' he bellowed. Two people drinking milky coffees at a nearby table looked round. 'Got wildly drunk with her, more like. Yes, I do remember. I remember listening to you moaning to her about how you'd never have a baby.'

I winced. 'Does she come in often?'

He shrugged. 'Mmm. From time to time. Used to come in when he was a bloke. Gave me a shock the first time he rocked up in a dress.'

'I'm sure you got over it. Does she live round here?'

'Over by the station, I think. Why? Do you want to renew the friendship?'

I ignored the unmistakable sarcasm.

'I want to talk to her about something.' I swallowed. 'It's important. Does she have a boyfriend? Or a girlfriend?'

He blew his hair off his face. 'Either. Both. Plenty, I'd say. Sometimes she's on her own, and other times she's on a date. Gets them off the internet, I reckon. They have special sites, you know.'

I looked at him. 'I guess she's had the operation by now.'

He held up his hands. 'Too much information, thank you.'

'Look, if you see her, um, can you just say that I was asking after her?' I handed him a piece of paper. 'Give her my number?'

He looked at me, sizing me up. 'Is this a sneaky way of giving me your number? Is it Rosa you want to call you, or is it me?'

I laughed. 'You flatter yourself.'

A couple came through the door, and Matt turned to them with a professional smile. They ignored him, white with hangovers.

'Seriously,' he said, out of the corner of his mouth. 'I'd give her a wide berth. She's nice, but she's trouble.'

CHAPTER 8

HELEN

10 January

I had to gasp for breath when I saw what I had supposedly written. It was horrible. A stream of abuse had snaked its way down wires and across national borders from my little laptop to the computer, wherever it was, that belonged to the most important woman in the world. I stared at it, in my sent messages folder, unable to take it in. Words jumped off the screen. They were random, splenetic abuse. *Promiscuous bitch*, I had apparently written. *What makes you think you can have a baby? Going to be a crap mother just like yours. You make us all sick. You deserve all the misery.*

Liz had received this, from me. Tears streamed down my cheeks. Every moment of my life was consumed by my relationship with Liz. I imagined her, tall and slender like Mother and me. I pictured myself meeting her for the first time. I thought, all the time, about the scene, the wonderful scene, that would take place when I brought her back here, the way she would light up the chateau.

'Tom!' I yelled. 'Tom, you get your fucking arse down here *right now!*'

Of course, he did not. He was hiding, upstairs.

'Tom!' I shouted again. I waited. 'I've just read it.' I stopped shouting, and spoke normally. 'You've ruined everything,' I said quietly.

'I haven't.' He appeared by my shoulder. He had not been upstairs after all. He giggled, wildly. 'You must admit, it's a good test,' he chuckled. 'If she decided you're mad and never wants to speak to you again, that means she wouldn't have been up to the task, anyway. If she can't take this, then she certainly can't take Mother.'

I held my head in my hands, watching my future curl up and die. Everything looked hopeless now. 'Tom,' I said, wretched. 'She doesn't know about Mother. Liz and I are friends now. I've worked on this non-stop for weeks and weeks. Every time she posts a message, I reply to it. I've been so careful to say the right thing all the time. She trusts me, or she did. We only graduated to personal emails a couple of weeks ago.' I checked the time of the message. It had been sent four minutes ago. Liz had probably read it by now. 'What have you *said*?' I wailed. 'Vicious personal abuse? She isn't going to want to be friends with someone who calls her a slut.' I turned round and lunged at him. 'You stupid bastard.'

He stopped laughing, grabbed my arms, and we tussled until we ended up on the floor. He pulled my hair. I pulled his, harder. We sat up and stared at each other.

'Sorry,' he said. 'I wasn't thinking.'

I turned to look at him. Tom had strange turns, occasionally. He said they were like out-of-body experiences. He could see what he was doing, but he couldn't stop himself. He would send reams of abuse to someone, or trash the house, or smash up something important just because he thought it was looking at him strangely. It was odd that he was the one who did these things. Normally, I was the one who didn't cope with life.

This time he had trashed the most important thing we had.

'Right,' I told him, shooing him away. 'Let me see if there's anything at all I can do to salvage this.'

I got to work, quickly composing an apologetic email to Liz. 'I'm blaming you,' I said, half looking over my shoulder, as I frantically explained to Liz that my eccentric younger brother had written a load of nonsense to her from my computer. I implied that he was nine or so, rather than fifteen. It seemed more plausible that way. Then I realised it would have taken an alarmingly precocious nine-year-old to compose the filthy tirade that had just flown Liz's way, so I rewrote it. I hoped she was going to believe me. I dropped in a couple of hints about his mental state.

'I am so sorry,' I finished up. 'I've now got my mail password-protected. Believe me, it won't happen again. Hope the morning sickness truly has gone for good. Speak to you soon, H x.'

'Right,' I told Tom. 'Now we just have to hope. Time for the walk.'

We took a walk together every afternoon. We had done for years. From the moment I learned to toddle along on my own, Mother had pushed me out into the garden at three o'clock and insisted that I get some exercise and stay out for an hour. I hated it when I was four – I knew she just wanted me out of sight so she could forget about me – but when Tom started coming too, it got a lot better. I remembered our first walk together. Tom was only three. I looked round, and he was coming up behind me, wearing a thick black duffle coat.

'Hello,' I said to him, and waited for him to catch up.

He looked at me with big, trusting eyes. 'Where are we going?' he asked, in his careful, babyish voice.

'To the woods,' I told him, and took his hand. I was pleased to be able to look after him.

The habit was ingrained now. We went out every afternoon, even though Mother couldn't make us do anything we didn't want to do. Now, it would never occur to her to be concerned about our physical well-being.

We always walked around the vineyard. People seemed to think it was glamorous to have parents who owned a vineyard. It was not. It was just loads of fields full of vines, which, for half the year, looked like sticks linked together with wire. For the other half, they demanded constant attention. The parents always tried to rope us in, but we generally managed to avoid manual labour, to leave it to the workers. My horror was not of the work (there was something appealing in the idea of physical labour), but of the social interaction. The workers scared me. They were confident and loud and they laughed and shouted at each other. I preferred to stalk past, ignoring them, pretending to be aloof.

This was a miserable January day, but nothing prevented the walk. We put on thick coats and woolly hats. I wore my camel coat, because I was sure that Mother and Papa wouldn't see me. As soon as I put it on, I felt I could do anything. I knew, though, that it looked funny with my bobble hat. When I went to London, I was going to have to pay attention to details like that.

Tom's coat was just his old black parka, but he still managed to look like someone from one of those cool British bands. I would have looked like a spanner if I'd put it on.

We did the walk that went away from the main house, because we didn't particularly want to risk bumping into our progenitors. The path followed the edge of the first field, and then sloped off downhill, towards the woods. It was a freezing day. I was sure that winter was worse where we lived than it was in places with people and shops. Some places were alive whatever the weather. Out here in the sticks, everything was all right in summer when the place was full of tourists on their wine tours and each village had a wild summer fête which involved vast amounts of merriment. It went dead in winter.

Today, the trees were black and bare. The sky was grey and full of clouds. The vines were sticks poking out of brown earth. Everybody seemed to hibernate. I had no idea know what they did. Presumably, they stayed indoors until the leaf buds and the daffodils appeared. When you walked past someone's house, you smelt meat cooking, which proved they were in there. Probably, they were in there looking out at me from far enough back in the room for me not to be able to see them, as long as the lights were off. Almost certainly they were muttering about the stuck-up English girl who never spoke to anyone, and her charming brother who was so funny and friendly and helpful when his sister wasn't around.

'I can't wait to go to London,' I told Tom.

'Mmmm,' he agreed. 'Me neither.' He looked around at the nothingness that surrounded us. An animal ran through the dead undergrowth, some-where nearby.

'London!' he said. 'Big red buses and big black taxis.'

'Nelson's column,' I countered. 'With lions around it.'

'Lots of people. No one watching us. Nobody

at all interested in anything we do, because there are too many other people for anyone to bother to gossip about us.'

'Radical Islamic fundamentalists. Big Ben. The Queen.'

Tom and I occasionally watched *Newsround* on the BBC. That was largely where our view of London came from.

'You know you're not coming though,' I told him, offhand. 'Just me.'

He frowned. 'Of course I'm coming. This is our project. Joint. Because she's our sister. Joint. And I was the one that found her.'

I shook my head. I wanted Tom to come with me, but I knew it was something I needed to do on my own.

'No way,' I told him. 'You've got school. I'm doing this one myself. *Particularly* after that email you just sent.' I tried to catch his eye, but he looked away, up into a tree with clumps of mistletoe at the top. 'You've probably ruined it all, you know,' I added. 'I probably won't be able to go, anyway.' It was true. I felt sick to my stomach.

We had reached the middle of the woods. Tom marched in ahead of me. I could see from his face that he was marshalling his arguments. The dead leaves had long since rotted away, and the ground was absolutely bare. We skirted the rotting stump of a tree. It had been there for ever. A bird flew through the branches above us, and then everything was silent. I pushed some ivy aside. When Tom turned round his nose was red.

'You need me to come because she's mine as well,' he said, a tremor in his voice. 'And you can't go from here, from this . . .' He showed me what he meant by waving his arm at the dead wood, the mistletoe high in the trees, the looming black sky. 'From this, to London! On your own! You've never been anywhere like London. You've never done anything without me. You've left school but you haven't even had a job. You just bum around here, and now you think you can go to London. It's not going to work. You need someone with you, Hels. I'm sorry about that mail, but I'll make it all right. I promise. You need me.'

I shook my head. 'I don't.' I said it with conviction, because suddenly I knew that it was time for me to get away from here. 'You'd be surprised what I can do, on my own.'

Mother stepped out in front of us, when we were nearly home.

'Are you all right?' she asked. She looked at my coat and smiled. 'Nice to see you wearing that thing for once.'

I was annoyed. 'Yeah. Fine. thanks.'

'Why wouldn't we be?' added Tom.

Mother stared into my face. 'You're sure?' she said. 'You're acting a bit strangely, Helen. Are you plotting something?'

'Why would we be plotting something?' demanded Tom, rudely.

'Well, are you?' she asked again. 'Tell me.'

'What makes you think that?' I asked.

'Oh. Something about the look on your face. You're excited about something. Come in. Come on. Come in and have a cup of tea and a biscuit.'

I was almost tempted. Tom pulled my sleeve.

'No thanks,' we said together, and we turned and went home.

When we got back to the cottage, hot from the walking but cold on the outside, two emails sat in my inbox. Each subject line contained five words that made me grin with relief and grab my brother and hug him in delight and forgiveness. Liz had a Hotmail account, and Hotmail accounts were always filling up or being deleted or timing out. The gods had smiled on us today, and uttered the beautiful words that restored my faith in the world. 'Undeliverable mail,' it said, 'returned to sender.'

CHAPTER 9

LIZ

26 January

I was sitting in the midwife's waiting room, concentrating hard on my nausea, when I saw a woman I recognised. She had a small bump, which I looked at uneasily, and long black hair. She was frowning, puffing, and looking at her watch.

I decided to risk it. Pushing aside a curtain of nausea and fatigue, I cleared my throat.

'Um, hello,' I said, sounding stupid.

She looked at me, quizzically.

'Hello?' she said.

'I think we're neighbours.'

The woman frowned at me. Then her face cleared. 'You live over the road! Your boyfriend's gay.' She had a slight accent. I thought she was Spanish.

I had to take a deep breath before replying to this.

'How do you know that?' I asked, trying to sound nonchalant. 'I thought Londoners weren't meant to know anything about their neighbours.'

'Oh, sorry. The guy in the café told me. Sorry, I didn't mean to upset you.'

'That's all right. The gay boyfriend upset me more than you. Though I'll also be having a stern word with Matt. I knew he'd been gossiping about me with his clientèle, but all the same . . .'

'Jesus, he is a terrible gossip. You shouldn't tell him anything.'

'Yeah, you're right.'

The waiting room smelt of disinfectant, with an undertone of bodily functions. I had taken an appointment before school, on the basis that the midwife could not possibly be running late at 8 a.m. It was now 8.31, and although I had a late start today, I was still due to be teaching year seven at 9.45.

'What time's your appointment?' I asked the woman.

She tutted. 'Quarter past eight. How about you?'

'Eight o'clock.'

'Oh, no way. No fucking way. I asked for an appointment before work because I actually have to go to work. This happened last time, as well.'

'Me too.'

She smiled tightly at me. 'I'm Anna.'

'Hi, Anna. I'm Liz.'

'Hi, Liz. So you're having a baby?'

'Yes.' I gripped my handbag tightly as I said it. This was the first time I had told anyone, apart from the doctor, face to face. Anna looked at me, the question in her eyes, and I gave in.

'It's not Steve's,' I said, firmly.

'Steve is the gay one?'

'Yes. It's not his. I'm having this baby on my own.'

She whistled. 'Wow. Well, good luck to you.'

'So, you have a partner?'

'A husband, yes. Jeremy. He's English.'

The midwife's door opened and a heavily pregnant woman emerged. I avoided looking at her bump, and stood up.

'See you again sometime,' I said to Anna. 'And please, could you not tell Matt at the café that you saw me here? I can't bear to have him telling the neighbourhood. I'm not telling anyone until I've had a scan.'

She smiled, a sudden, brilliant smile. 'My lips are sealed. Come over and drink some tea,' she said. 'Number forty-five. I mean it, whenever you like. Or send me an email at work.' She took out a card, and quickly put it into my hand.

The midwife was flustered. Her hair was in a bun, which had half fallen down. This was the first time I had seen her, and I would have preferred Dr Grey.

'Sit down, Elizabeth,' she said. She was filling in the previous woman's notes as she spoke to me. I tried to read them upside down but her writing was too messy. 'So you're, what, twelve weeks or so along, you think? Shall we get you a scan appointment? How are you feeling? Any nausea?'

She picked up the phone and chatted incessantly while waiting for someone at the other end to answer. I looked around the room, aware, once again, that my life was taking an unexpected turn. After six weeks of guarding my precious, incredible secret, I was about to make it official. I was to be transformed into a Pregnant Lady. It was unsettling. Soon, if everything went well, I would have to start telling people. I thought that I preferred the lonely panic, after all. Matt was going to gossip. Dad and Sue would worry about me. Kathy would be horrified. Our friendship had been founded on the fact that neither of us wanted children. Together we had long been exasperated by friends who stopped being interested in the environment or politics or anything from the wider world, and focused exclusively on their wombs, their offspring.

Eventually, the midwife booked me a hospital appointment for 6 February, for a scan. That in itself was a surreal prospect. She took my blood pressure, asked a few questions, noting my single status without comment, surprise, or supplementary question.

'Why don't you hop up on here,' she said, as I was getting ready to leave. She patted the couch.

I climbed up gracelessly, and uncovered my abdomen. 'Look at that,' I said, pinching my flab. 'Lucky I have an excuse.'

'Oh, you're fine,' she said, absently. 'You should see some of the ladies who come through that door. The worst is when they take offence when I talk about their weight. Hello? Gestational diabetes? Now, I'm going to use this doppler to try to find the heartbeat, but we often can't find it this early, so don't worry for a moment if I don't get it. I'm only trying because you seem sensible, and because you said there was a chance you might be a bit further on.'

It took her a few attempts to locate it. Then, time stopped. The room was taken over by a swooshy galloping noise. It raced along, unfeasibly fast. I forgot to breathe.

'There you go,' the midwife said, with a small smile. 'Nothing wrong with that. Right. The scan's on the sixth, remember. I'll see you again in a month.'

The world looked different. It was tinged with wonder.

Inside me, two hearts were beating. I held tightly to that knowledge. Nothing else mattered Even though I was heinously late, I stopped at the receptionist's desk on my way out.

'Excuse me,' I said, as quietly as I could. I looked around the general waiting room. Here was a mass of ailing humanity.

'Yes?' said the woman, slightly tetchily, I thought. She had a phone to her ear and was sorting through a pile of papers.

I cleared my throat. 'Um, do you know a woman called Rosa? I'm not sure whether she's a patient here. I'm trying to get in touch with her.' I lowered my voice. 'She's a transsexual. Her name used to be Ross.'

The woman was wearing bright pink lipstick. She looked up at me and pouted. 'I don't, but even if I did, we're strictly not allowed to divulge information about our patients. *Particularly* not sensitive information.'

'I didn't want you to divulge information, exactly . . .' She had turned back to her paperwork. Then she began to speak animatedly into the telephone.

'Hello, Mrs Bennett,' she said in a sing-song voice. 'It's the surgery here . . .'

I turned and headed out. As far as I could tell, Rosa had vanished.

Although I was wrapped up against the cold, it still shocked me when I stepped out of the warmth of the surgery. The sky was heavy with clouds, and my breath puffed out around me. I pulled my scarf tightly around the lower part of my face, pushed my hands into my pockets, and looked down as I strode as quickly as possible towards the Tube, making sure I was avoiding the frozen dog shit. The baby's heartbeat pumped through my head. It stayed there all day.

I got through the day on automatic pilot, as usual. At four o'clock, I collapsed, relieved, on to my special staffroom chair, and patted my stomach, hoping no one was looking. I made an effort to think nice thoughts towards the baby.

The staffroom was large, crowded and untidy.

The posters on the walls dated back several years, though many of the older ones had been papered over with Stop the War Coalition offerings. There was always a mixture of fluster and laziness in here. I liked it. I had always tried to ignore the politics and use it as a recharging station, a place to ingest caffeine and sugar.

My special chair, though, was horrible. I leaned back on a metal support, and wiggled myself into a semi-comfortable position, my legs awkwardly tucked underneath me, my bulk slightly too large to be comfortable in any position on this scrappy reject of a seat. Sometimes I dashed off at four, but, at the moment, the end of school marked the arrival of my appetite. I was starving. I clutched my tea, which I'd made in someone else's mug, and ate a ginger biscuit. The cup I was using bore the KitKat logo, and that was enough to make me realise that I needed more sustenance. I took a muesli bar from the bottom of my handbag and demolished it, then looked around to find out what was next. Not for the first time, I cursed the fact that the junk food vending machine had been removed over the summer holidays, and replaced by one that dispensed fruit.

Kathy appeared next to me. She looked businesslike in a crisp suit and sensible shoes. Kathy was a slim and lovely black woman, and she took no nonsense. The sixth form called her Condi. I'd never known whether she minded.

'Hey,' she said. 'Not rushing away?'

'Nope,' I said, through my third ginger biscuit. 'Home is a bit boring to go back to these days.'

She smiled. 'Drink?'

My heart sank. 'Can't. Sorry.' Kathy had been my best friend for years, at work, and we often went straight to the pub after school. For six weeks I had been finding excuses, because Kathy was the one person who would notice that I was avoiding alcohol, and ask me why. It was time to come clean.

'Actually, yes,' I said. 'Why not? I've got something to tell you.'

It was a standard London pub, aimed largely at tourists, with low lights, a dartboard, and many beers on tap. Three of our year tens sat at a corner table, thinking we hadn't noticed them, their pint glasses half empty. I bought two packets of crisps, a glass of wine for Kathy, and a lemonade. Then I sat down, and steeled myself.

Kathy had no interest in children, and we had always consoled each other when friends and colleagues made pregnancy announcements. 'Congratulations,' we would say, looking at each other and rolling our eyes. 'Another one bites the dust,' we would tut, later, in the pub. Over the years, we had bemoaned the loss of dozens of friends, as they went over to the other side, the side where the babies were.

But I had heard the heartbeat. I was twelve weeks pregnant, and my baby, whoever's it was, was alive.

I was going for a scan, and that in itself was enough to take me to the other side, the weird world I had never wanted to be a part of.

'Cheers,' she said, clinking glasses. 'So, what's new? Is it Steve? Has he changed orientation again?'

I forced a smile. 'That's not going to happen. He calls from time to time. He's desperate to be able to think of himself as a good guy. But no, he never mentions coming back. I think he's screwing round the gay bars, which will probably take him a few years.' I shuddered. I was nowhere near getting over the fact that I had never known him.

'But you want to tell me something.'

I nodded. 'Can you keep it confidential, for the moment?'

'You're leaving school, aren't you? Good on you. Are you going travelling?'

'I'm having a baby.'

I watched her reaction carefully. Her eyes widened. Her jaw dropped slightly. She stared at me, seeking confirmation. I nodded.

'I'm twelve weeks pregnant. I heard the heartbeat today and it was . . .' I tailed off. Kathy wasn't going to be interested in the heartbeat. 'That's why I was late for work. The pregnancy was a huge surprise. As you can imagine.' I steeled myself to say the next bit. 'And it isn't Steve's,' I told her, although I was far from sure. The strong heartbeat was making me think that it might be.

She was still gaping at me. 'It isn't Steve's?' she managed to echo. 'Are you sure?'

'Uh-huh.'

'So whose is it?'

'Just a one-night stand I had with someone I met when I was drunk. I've been trying to track them down. I'm certain they won't want to know. But I feel I have to try. It seems only polite.'

'Jesus fucking Christ, Liz.'

'I know.'

'You're actually having it? I mean, you're well within the time limits . . .'

'I know. I thought about it. I know I never wanted a baby, I know we've both said that for years. But now I've got one. I've been living with this for weeks, and I've made my decision. I heard its heart. It was amazing.'

'Are you going to cope?'

'I don't think I have the choice.'

'You're one hundred per cent certain you want to go through with it? Because if you don't, I'll be there, you know?'

I nodded. Kathy was saying what I would have said in her position. 'I know. And I appreciate that. But this is probably my only chance, and it's the strangest thing, but now I do want to be a mother.'

'Fucking hell.'

'Yes.' I drew a deep breath. I hoped that, at some point, somebody might congratulate me. If I'd still been with Steve, Kathy would have been pleased for me, or, at least, she would not have been able to be as rude as this. 'You're the first person I've told,' I said. 'Apart from a woman who lives over the road who I met in the midwife's waiting room this morning. I'm going to see Dad and Sue on Friday. But for now, it's just you.'

Kathy finished her drink. 'So you're going to be deserting me and Sandrine?' she said, looking away. Sandrine taught French, and was the third member of our clique. She wore tight miniskirts, and our school boasted a surprising number of teenage boys who were interested in French as a result. 'You're going to hang out with all the mothers, now. You're going to be coming in with baby snot on your shoulder,' she continued, 'and wearing the same clothes you've worn all week, and you'll never have time to get your highlights done. You're going to talk about "nap time" and "poos on the potty", and you're going to tell Sandrine and me that we could never understand. We're all going to have to cover your lessons when your baby's got chickenpox. Aren't we?'

I felt myself sagging. 'I hope not,' I said. Then I started to feel angry. 'And thanks for the support, Kathy. Thanks very much. It's great that that's how you feel.' I looked at her. She looked back, defiant. 'You're the very first person I've come to. I guess this is what it's going to be like.'

She was calm. 'It doesn't have to be like this. You could still get rid of it. From where I sit, it looks as though you're in the process of ruining your life. I'd quite like to encourage you to think again. Because it really isn't too late.' She laughed. 'Jesus. This is like the little chats we all end up having with year tens from time to time. And another thing, which you know very well. What about the environment? Is bringing another person into the world really a good idea? You're going to be chucking out bags full of disposable nappies before you know it. You're going to be getting cheap flights, after all, because it'll be easier than lugging a baby on the train. You know as well as I do that the planet is vastly overpopulated, and anyone who worries about the falling birth rate in western Europe is just saying they want more nice white babies and fewer pesky brown ones.'

I stood up. 'Cheers.' As I left, I called back over my shoulder: 'You know I'm as pro-choice as you are, Kathy. But that doesn't mean I think everyone should abort every pregnancy. This is my baby, and don't you dare tell me to get rid of it. It's my *baby*.'

I was halfway out of the door before I remembered that the year tens were right there, giggling into their lager.

I cried while I made my rudimentary dinner. Extreme emotional distress would not overcome my fixation with food. I cooked some pasta, and added anything I could find in the fridge: carrots, some tomatoes, and a bit of hard cheese. I was desperately alone. As soon as the pasta was in a bowl, I took it to the computer, and logged on, as quickly as I could, to Babytalk. Here, I knew I had sympathetic listeners. Nobody on the forum would dare to speak to me like Kathy had done.

I signed in, and scanned through the days' messages on the pregnancy board. I saw a couple of messages from my fellow single mother-to-be, Fluffball, who signed herself 'Jem'. I liked Jem. Her very existence was a comfort to me. Her boyfriend had walked out a few weeks into her pregnancy, and her baby was due a month before mine. She had got through, so far, by herself, and this showed me that there was a way. I always replied to her messages and she always replied to mine. I was steeling myself to suggest swapping email addresses and becoming real friends, even though she lived in Bolton. I'd hoped she would suggest it, but she hadn't yet. She was one of the more popular forumites, so I supposed she had more than enough friends.

There was no sign of Frenchmaid on the forum, but there was an email from her in my inbox. Frenchmaid's name, I had discovered, was Helen Labenne, and in contrast to Fluffball, she was eager to exchange emails. She was almost spookily kind and supportive. I could not understand why someone so young would choose to spend her time on a website that was mainly populated by hormonal women in their thirties. 'I've always been fascinated by the idea of having a baby,' was her explanation, and I was vaguely worried that,

111

some day soon, she was going to post what was known as a 'blue line post'.

I skimmed her email: it seemed she was coming to London, as I'd suggested, and I supposed I would meet her, which would be nice. All the same, Helen was only twenty. I craved a real friend. I wanted to meet someone who understood just how terrifying a prospect this baby actually was. I wanted someone who would see what Kathy's reaction had done to me.

Today, Jem was worried about her mother coming to stay when her baby was born, and taking over everything.

'How can I set the boundaries?' she wrote. 'I don't want her to think I don't appreciate her help. But she said to my dad the other day, "Jemima doesn't know one end of a baby from the other," and I'm worried she's going to march in and want to control everything. Is it selfish of me to want enough of her help to stop me going mad, but not too much? And how do I go about discussing it with her?'

I smiled and opened a banana. 'Hi, Fluffball,' I typed. 'That's one dilemma I don't *think* I'm going to have . . .'

Before I could even start to libel Kathy, my phone rang. I took a big bite of banana, and then answered it.

'Hello?' I demanded, speaking with my mouth full, wedging the phone between shoulder and ear, and continuing to type. I typed the words 'My dad'.

112

'Hello,' said my dad. 'It's your father.'

I sighed, and pushed the keyboard away. 'Hi, Dad. I was just talking about you. Sort of. How are you?'

'Oh, we're all right. You know. How about you?'

'Mmm. Not too bad. Considering.' I finished the banana, and cast around for chocolate. Then I realised that my dad was treating me to one of his silences.

'So,' I said, filling the gap. 'I'm coming down this weekend if that's still OK.'

'Of course,' he said. 'Of course. We're all looking forward to seeing you. All of us.'

'All?'

'Mmm. Oh, yes. Roberto and Julie are here for a while.'

I put on a fake 'delighted' voice. 'Great! It'll be fun to catch up with them!' I rolled my eyes at myself. *It'll be fun*, indeed. Nobody over the age of five used such a phrase unless they were lying. I had no desire to make my announcement so publicly.

My stepbrother Roberto and I had always antagonised each other. Although he had been nice to me since Steve's departure, gruffly confiding that Steve had always seemed a bit of a wanker to him, the paranoid part of me felt he must be glad at my misfortunes. Julie had been with him for a few years, but I barely had an impression of her at all. Her appearance was bland, and I could hardly recall what her face was like. She was a bit pasty, with

113

hair of no particular colour. I wondered whether she would react to my news at all. Certainly, no one in Haywards Heath would manage a polite 'congratulations'.

'Right,' said Dad. 'Yes. Good.'

He was impossible. I adored my father, not least because I had to. He had brought me up on his own and done a good, if baffled, job. If I didn't love him, I had no one. Dad and I had been thrown together when I was a baby, he having to look after me, me dependent on him for everything. As I grew up, he nurtured me in his eccentric way. My typical packed lunch at primary school contained two mustard sandwiches, a trio of cold potatoes, and orange squash in a jam jar. In the school holidays, I would do whatever I fancied, while he watched the cricket. He took me to dinner parties where I would read in the corner until midnight, then curl up and sleep while he and his bizarre friends continued drinking. Once I found a box of my mother's clothes in the attic, and delighted myself by dressing up in outlandish, too-big sixties outfits. I'd wear a purple smock to school, with green socks and a wide straw hat, and it would never have occurred to my father that anything was amiss. My hair was long and tangled, my reading matter anything I happened to pluck from a shelf (for a long time I had a copy of *The Joy of Sex* under my bed) and the fields around the house were my domain. Despite everything, and despite what everyone thought, I grew

114

up happy, even though I was always aware that someone was missing.

When I was twelve, he met Sue.

'How's Sue?' I said now.

'Oh, yes. Fine. You know.'

'Good. And Roberto and Julie? They're OK?'

'Yes, yes, they're doing well.' He paused. 'At something of a hiatus.' He stopped.

There always came a point in a conversation like this when I wanted to yell: '*You* rang *me*!' I usually restrained myself. Today I just gave an exasperated sigh.

'How long are they staying for?'

'Hmm? Well, for the moment. Just until they find something else. I think that's the plan, anyway.'

'Right.'

Sue had arrived in a long purple dress, smelling of incense and smiling at me with the determinedly kind manner of someone who was going to do whatever it took to become my friend. A tubby boy stood behind her, holding her skirts and scowling, first at my father, and then at me. My stepbrother was five years my junior and possessed of a glamorous Italian father he visited in the holidays. For the first four years, Roberto did everything in his power to annoy me, aided by the fact that in his mother's eyes, he could do no wrong. He barged in on me while I was getting dressed, tipped Ribena on to my homework, and asked me, wide-eyed with pretend innocence, why

I didn't go to see my mummy when he stayed with his daddy. When I was sixteen I forced Dad to let me go to boarding school, and a few years after that, Roberto and I finally learned to tolerate each other.

These days, he and Julie largely devoted themselves to sponging off the family. Twenty-eight years had passed since I met Roberto, and Sue was still inclined to indulge his every whim. Roberto and Julie infuriated me but, in the name of family harmony, I generally tried not to let it show.

'Right, then,' I said briskly. 'Got to go, Dad. I'll get a cab from the station.'

'Are you sure? We can always . . .'

'Nope. I'll just turn up on Friday night. Bye.'

So I was going to be sharing my news not just with my father, but also with Sue, Roberto and Julie. There was no way I would be able to get Dad on his own for long enough to tell him privately, and Sue would wrench the truth out of him in five seconds anyway. I sighed, and turned back to the website. I continued my sentence. 'My dad wouldn't dream of taking control. I wish he would. I hope my stepmother might come through, because otherwise I'm on my own.'

CHAPTER 10

HELEN

1 February

I stared, transfixed, out of the train window. This was England. This was the strange, almost mythical land of my heritage.

I had heard about England at school, from the ex-pat girls and boys. They were so casual about it that it was hard to know, from listening to them, what it was actually like. I used to want to scream at them to tell me more. They were talking about a land that scared me and fascinated me, but they spoke, frustratingly, as if it was normal. I had an impression of England as a land of cool music, and dark frightening shadows. It was the country that had driven Mother away, never to return. It was the seat of an old empire, a weird, powerful place.

Yet here I was. I gripped the edge of my seat as I gazed out of the window. I could not believe I had done this. I stared at fields, at houses that were squashed up together. The cars already had their lights on. The sky was full of heavy black clouds. It was getting dark in England.

I told myself that I was not scared. I reminded myself that I was doing the right thing. I did not doubt my mission. I did not doubt it. I did not.

I was running away. Years ago, Mother ran away from England and left her child behind. Now here I was, running in the other direction, to bring the baby back. I was a long way away from anything that had ever made me feel secure and safe. I felt sick. I made a big effort to take some deep breaths. I told myself to live in the moment, to think only of the next thing I would do. I would stay on this train until it stopped, and then I would get off it. Tom was the only one who knew I was here, and lately he had done everything he could to stop me leaving.

'Just write her a letter,' he said, before I went to catch my train.

'But I can't,' I told him. 'Writing a letter would be no good. It would leave it up to her.'

He rolled his eyes. 'Your plan sounds nice, doesn't it, in theory. Make friends with her. Go to London. Meet her. Somehow bring her back here and present her to her mother. It won't work, Helen. I promise you, you won't pull it off.'

I snarled at him, trying extra hard to convince both of us. 'I will! I can do it! You don't think I can do anything, but I can!'

We ended up pulling each other's hair. I shoved him and he hit the ground. I told myself that he was jealous. He was jealous because he couldn't come with me. He was trying to play with my mind.

Mother and Papa seemed to believe me when I said I was going to Paris to stay with an imaginary school friend. They looked worried when they put me on the train, and they told me to use the credit card as much as I needed to. I was certainly planning to take them up on that offer, and at some point, I supposed, they would notice, from their bills, that I was in London, rather than Paris. I tried to savour the notion that, for the first time ever, I was about to surprise them.

Liz knew I was coming, but she didn't know exactly when. I'd made an enormous effort and forced myself to be breezy and casual about the whole thing, and sketchy with details, as if my trip to London was no big deal; as if it was not all about her. I knew that if I was going to appear in her life as a friend, I had to give the impression of having a life of my own. The last person Liz seemed to need in her life was the real me. She needed someone different, the person I pretended to be when we emailed each other. I was going to become somebody new, and I was going to get my sister to come to France before her baby was born. Mother would be enraptured: a daughter and a grandchild in one go. This was why I was here. This was what I was doing. I told myself, again, that it was an excellent plan.

As London got closer, I gripped the armrest so tightly that my fingers went white and my nails hurt. The cars drove on the wrong side of the road. Their number plates were clear and big, like a child would draw them. I tried to see people, but we passed by too quickly to see what the English looked like when they were at home.

I stared at lighted windows as the sky grew darker and we started getting closer to London. I saw occasional flashes of people's lives. I could convince myself to be interested in it all, if I wasn't going to have to get off the train and try to become a part of it.

I stretched my legs, and looked around the inside of the carriage. The train was a haven of stale air and anonymity. Nobody else seemed to be at all interested in what was outside the window. This was normal for them. They would think it odd that it was exotic to me. A woman was reading a book. However hard I stared at her, I couldn't work out whether she was English, or French, or something else entirely. A Frenchman shouted into his mobile phone, complaining about the lunch menu for an upcoming conference he was hosting. I listened, but failed to work out what sort of conference it was. His voice clashed with that of an Englishman in his thirties who seemed to be speaking to his children. 'Daddy be home soon,' he said soothingly, into his telephone. 'Daddy'll read you a story tonight.' I smiled at him, and looked away, embarrassed, when he caught me watching, listening, envying his children.

There were not many of us in the carriage, and I was certain I was the only one who was scared.

I missed Tom, and I was trying not to think that he might be right. I reminded myself again: I am not being ridiculous. I am not going to fail.

London was suddenly outside the window. It was big and dirty. There were billboards, advertisements for investment funds and Hollywood films that meant nothing to me. Other tracks ran alongside ours, and I found myself peering into another train, a smaller one which was packed with people. A couple of them looked straight back at me, unseeing. The other train was gone a moment later. I looked at streets filled with houses, and at roads, and at people, and then we pulled into Waterloo station, and we stopped. Everyone stood up, put their coats on, gathered their things and disappeared. They all, clearly, knew where they were going.

I hung back for as long as I could, putting off my first step on to British soil. I longed to go back and fetch my brother. Perhaps I could summon him, after all, later on. I had never been so far from him before.

When I put my foot down, a shiver ran through me. This was it. I was in England, and I had a job to do.

Nobody in the station glanced at me, even though I felt I looked weird. I was wearing my smart coat, but carrying a backpack, so I was neither a proper young traveller nor the rich girl on tour. That, I supposed, was me all over. I had never had a defined identity. Someone else would

121

have found that liberating. I wished I didn't want to belong.

I walked as purposefully as I could through the crowds, and took the escalator up to the main part of the station. It was five in the afternoon, and the place was alive with a shifting mass of people. There were definitely more people in this station than lived in our whole village at home.

The thought of home made me ill. I pictured the vines and the trees, the little roads with the same cars trundling along them all the time. Everything I despised about home suddenly seemed good, and I hated myself for leaving. As I passed a couple of payphones, I paused, trying to overcome the temptation to call the parents and Tom. Someone walked into my back, then stepped sideways and dodged past without even looking at me. She didn't say sorry. She didn't even tut or frown at me for being in the way. I didn't know why this was crushing, but it was. For some reason, I would have preferred a stream of abuse.

The station was brightly lit. Most people were wearing suits. I looked particularly hard at the women, trying to work out what I needed to do to pass as a Londoner, to make myself acceptable to Liz, first as a friend, and then as a sister.

It was hard to pinpoint anything I could do that would magically make me a local. I found a wall to lean against, by a shop, and shrugged off my backpack. It settled on the tiled floor, and I sat on it, leaned back, and sighed.

I had booked a hotel, but I had no idea how I was going to find it. This station was bad enough: there was no way I was getting on to the Underground train. I was too shy to put out my hand for a taxi. For some reason I thought everyone would be able to tell I was alien here. They would know I didn't belong. I knew London was supposed to be one of those 'melting pot' cities, and, indeed, the people rushing by me were intimidatingly diverse. All but me knew exactly where they were going and exactly how they were going to get there.

I stayed where I was, sitting on my backpack, and waited for things to calm down. I imagined that these people were all rushing for the same few trains, and that when the trains left, everything would be calmer, less intimidating. Yet the rush went on.

I took the piece of paper from my pocket. I needed to get from here to Norfolk Square, Paddington, London W2. On the map, it hadn't seemed very far. I looked around nervously, searching for someone to ask for directions. The women looked just as scary as the men, and I didn't dare approach any of them.

I stood up, picked up my bag, and walked out of the nearest exit. It was almost properly dark now. I set off down a street, at random. The city was swallowing me up. I couldn't get a grip on it. Changing trains in Paris had been fine. Paris was like Bordeaux. It wasn't busy. I had been able to get on the Métro, to ride to my stop, and to get off again, at the Gare du Nord. London was enormous and terrifying, and even though it should still have been daytime, it felt like night. The air was dirty, and cold. Everything was different, unfamiliar, and unfriendly. I turned corners at random, took side streets, walked purposefully with my head down. From time to time I risked a glance at the grey buildings that towered above me on either side. I passed a bar, and looked in through the bright, misted windows. It was crammed with people, all of them in suits, everyone shouting and laughing and drinking. Loud music followed me up the road.

Round a corner, I stumbled upon some real outsiders. Three of them were sitting under a railway bridge, their legs covered by an old sleeping bag. The smell of them took me by surprise. The only homeless person I saw in France was a man who stood opposite H&M with a cardboard sign, and who greeted every passer-by politely with a *'Bonjour, madame'*. These men were different. They were frightening. I stared at them. They were outlines in the darkness.

'Spare some change?' called one, as I walked past. I tried not to look at him, but couldn't stop myself. I stared. He looked young, but his face was grey.

'All right, darling,' added another, an older man with a beard. 'We won't bite.'

'Not till we get to know you a bit better,' added

the third, who could, in the gloom, have been anywhere from twenty to sixty. They all laughed.

I felt sick with fear. I plunged my hand into the pocket of my smart coat, and took out all the coins I had. I stepped gingerly closer to them, and dropped the coins on to the corner of the sleeping bag.

'There you are. Sorry,' I said, and turned and walked away as quickly as I could. I listened to my shoes clicking on the pavement. I hadn't got far before they started shouting at my back.

'What kind of money do you call this?' roared one of them. I thought it was the bearded one.

I half turned my head. I stopped and looked round. 'Euros,' I told him. I had a stash of British cash, but no coins. 'Sorry.'

'S'OK, love,' shouted the young one. 'We take euros!' They all laughed.

I hurried away, feeling stronger. I related the encounter to Tom in my head, triumphantly, as I carried on taking random turnings, crossing busy streets and trying to look like someone who knew where she was going. My backpack was pulling on my shoulders, and I kept hitching it up. After a while, I did up its belt, even though I knew it looked stupid over my coat.

By now, I was properly scared. I knew that I had to find my hotel. I knew that I wasn't going to find it by walking randomly. I was stupid. I didn't know what to do with myself. I hadn't eaten anything all day, and I was beginning to feel dizzy.

125

I headed down another street. To my amazement, there seemed to be a wide river in front of me.

'Is that the Thames?' I said, aloud, gazing at it.

'Sure is,' said a young man in a suit, passing me without breaking his stride. I gaped at him, and he winked.

I stood beside the riverside wall, and stared across the water. The Houses of Parliament were right in front of me. According to the big clock, it was quarter past six. To my right was the huge wheel, lit in blue. A bridge stretched across the river before me. Everything was lit up in the night. The lights reflected off the water.

Here I was, in London. I was cold and tired, but probably no longer lost. At the very least, I had the landmarks to work it out. I took a map book out of one of my rucksack pockets, sat down on the nearest bench, and looked around, searching in the light of a street lamp for the name of a street to look up.

Two young women sat on the end of my bench. They looked funny, because they both had frizzy brown hair, but one was very thin, and the other was very fat.

The fat one smiled.

'You lost?' she asked. I smiled at her accent.

'A bit,' I admitted. I wished I knew how to talk to people. I tried to think of something else to say. 'I've got to find my hotel.'

'Oh, yeah? But you're English. You sound English.'

'I'm half English, half French. This is my first time in London.'

'Half French? Yeah? We're Australian.'

'Are you? I thought so.'

'Yeah. Where's your hotel?'

I took out my purse and unfolded the internet printout. I put the purse next to me on the bench and showed them the address. The other girl, the skinny one who hadn't spoken, stared at me, sizing me up. She came to sit on the other side of me. She took the map book and flicked through it.

'Here you go,' she said, with a smile. 'There's your hotel. Norfolk Square, Paddington. But you can come with us to our hostel, if you like. It's in Earl's Court. Seventy quid a week. You'll pay that per night in a hotel. You'll meet loads of other backpackers and shit. Seriously, it's better than a hotel, because if you stay in some crappy hotel no one will talk to you. Come to the hostel, and you'll make heaps of friends.'

I thought about it. The girls seemed friendly. I wasn't used to human interaction, and I tried to imagine what it would be like if I went to their hostel. It would be horrible, I was certain of that. I pictured twenty bunk beds to a room, and grime everywhere. I imagined stinking toilets. I looked around me. London was daunting, and it was night. These women were friendly. It would be nice to have companions.

Both of them were looking at me expectantly. I had to make a decision.

Liz would not be impressed if I smelt bad, and if I hung out with penniless travellers. All sorts of people came to London with no money. I was frightened of the idea of them. I did not dare to live amongst them.

'I've already paid for the hotel,' I said quickly. 'Thanks all the same, though. I appreciate your offer.' I bit my lip, longing for the day when I would suddenly, mysteriously, know how to say the right thing, how not to sound like a stuck-up bitch.

They looked at each other, smiled, and shrugged. 'That's fine,' they both said together.

'Enjoy your trip,' added the skinny one.

I stood up. 'Thanks,' I said. 'You too.'

The skinny woman handed me the map book, and the fat one gave me my purse. 'Here you go,' she said. 'Now, you take care.'

I managed to hail a taxi. The driver knew the road I wanted before I'd even started to explain where it was.

It wasn't until I tried to pay him that I discovered that the girls had taken all my money. I had only just got here, and already I had lost two hundred pounds.

CHAPTER 11

LIZ

2 February

I gave the taxi driver a huge tip. I never normally overtipped, but this man hadn't tried to speak to me, and hadn't had the local radio station turned up too loudly. He hadn't taken a round-about route in order to charge me more money, and he had refrained from telling me to cheer up. Specifically, he had managed not to speculate that something or other might never be going to happen.

As I stood by his window, in the rain, I gave him an extra five pounds, for a ten-pound journey.

'Much appreciate it, darling,' he said, smiling. Then he ruined it by adding, 'Cheer up, hey? Might never happen.'

I glared. 'I liked you because you didn't say that,' I told him. I put out my hand to reclaim the tip. Already, the raindrops were dripping off my nose.

He shrugged and quickly put the notes away. 'Sorry, then. Forget I spoke.'

I strode up the short garden path to the front door, stamping through two puddles on the way.

My work skirt felt too tight, already, and that was with the button undone. My heels clipped on the paving stones, making me sound like a teacher on the warpath.

Dad and Sue lived in a terraced house in Haywards Heath. It looked like every other house in the row, but inside I knew it was a temple to eccentricity. The first clue was in the front door – the only purple one in the street, possibly in the town. I pressed the doorbell, and inside, I heard the strains of 'If you're happy and you know it, clap your hands'. To my intense mortification, Sue had installed this when I was fifteen.

'It brings a smile to the faces of visitors,' she had explained blithely. For the next few years, I hovered by the front window whenever I was expecting anyone, ready to fling the door open before they rang.

'When it was just me and Dad,' I remembered telling her, 'things like this didn't happen.'

'I know,' she said, wilfully misunderstanding me. 'You poor darling.'

Sue opened the door, and I smiled, pleased to see her reassuring, familiar face, praying that she would react well to my news. She had negotiated my teenage years adroitly, never pretending to be my real mother, skilfully treading the line between parent and friend. I welcomed her from the start. Having a mother figure made me instantly feel normal. I spent my primary school years miserably crafting a mother's day card each year with the rest of the class. I would conscientiously cut out flowers, and stick them on to the front of a carefully folded piece of card. I would write strange words like 'Mummy'. I would sign my name. On the way home, I generally threw my handiwork into a bin, for Dad's sake.

The day when I triumphantly bought my first ever mother's day card from the local newsagent was a milestone in my life. Sue and I both cried when I gave it to her. Dad looked on, bewildered. I thought about how nice it was, now that there was someone in the household who was able to express emotions, and cried even harder.

The only complaint I had ever had with Sue was the fact that she brought Roberto with her.

'Lizzy!' she said now, and gave me a bony hug. Sue was wearing a floaty dress from Hampstead Bazaar, and her hair was long and dyed jet black. It was held back from her face with a row of sparkling slides. She looked witchy with her dark red lipstick and black kohl eyes.

'Come in, darling,' she said, and ushered me in. 'Your father's in the sitting room.'

I followed, my heart suddenly thumping. I walked carefully, operating in a heightened reality. I was bruised from my confrontation with Kathy. I knew that Dad and Sue were kinder, but I cared about their opinions more. They could easily hurt me and the baby with their reactions. I needed them to be on side.

Sue was still being extra careful around me

because of the Steve situation. I steeled myself for the task ahead: I needed to tell them my latest dramatic news, to convince them that Steve was not the father, and to refuse to tell them who was.

Right now, nobody knew it but me, Kathy, Anna, medical professionals, and the forumites. Now, it was going to become real. Jem and Helen had been helping me to try to straighten out my plans, but the more time I spent on logistics, the worse it became. I would, of course, take all the maternity leave I was entitled to on reasonable pay, which seemed to be more complicated than I was expecting, but as far as I could work out, I could have nine months before they stopped paying me. After that I would try to go back to work for four days a week, if school would let me.

'Swallow your pride, Liz,' Jem had written yesterday. 'Get as much as you possibly can from your ex.' I liked both Jem and Helen because they didn't write in text speak. I didn't think I could have been friends with either of them if I'd had to trawl through 'u' and 'm8' in their messages. 'I know it's hard. I'm there myself. Do it for the baby.'

I knew that I had to do it. I dreaded Rosa's reaction, but I had to tell her. I remembered her, in the last few moments of our time together. I vividly recalled the horror on her face, and her growing disgust at what we had done. I remembered, all too clearly, the way I had felt. I struggled to tell myself that, if this was her baby, it would mean that our night together had been, in a strange way, positive. I hoped that, if it proved to be necessary, we might both get used to the idea in time. I hoped that, in time, she might want to help support her child. I hoped she might want to get to know him, or her.

I hadn't told anybody about Rosa. All I had said was that it was a careless one-night stand, and that I was doing my best to trace the man concerned.

'In that case,' Helen had responded (to my response to Jem's response), 'you need to work on the basis that you might not be able to get him involved, and you need to make the numbers add up yourself.'

The trouble was that, try as I might, they didn't. My salary had always seemed to me to be modest but adequate. Steve had recently stopped paying his half of the mortgage. That was bad enough. I had looked up nurseries on the internet, and was astonished to discover that I was going to be charged about fifty pounds per day. It was barely going to be worth my while working, and I had no idea how I was going to get to grips with tax credits and benefits. And, assuming that I could just about cover the essentials, what was I going to put in my purse? How was I going to clothe the baby? What was I going to eat? The baby was going to have to be breastfed for years, because I wouldn't be able to nourish it any other way.

I stopped for a second, and attempted to imagine myself with a baby at my breast. It was impossible.

Helen's response had been immediate. Even though she was young, she seemed to have her head screwed on.

'Write it all down,' she'd written. 'If your mortgage is too expensive, move house. If you're in London, what about moving out of town? You're a teacher – there's always going to be a job for you. You mentioned once that your dad lives in Sussex. Is that far from London? Would it be worth relocating so you could be near him? I don't have any experience of any of this yet myself, but grandparents can apparently be the best form of free childcare. Here in France they look after their grandchildren all the time. If you really can't have any contact with the father, then family has to be the best option. Could you make that work?'

That message had brought me up short. She was right. I needed to face this. There were seventeen years left on the mortgage, so my outgoings weren't going to ease off until this foetus was old enough to support itself. Unthinkable as it was, I might have to try to set myself up in Haywards Heath. I might have to ask Sue and Dad to look after my baby.

'PS,' Helen had added, 'I'm in London right now. I got here yesterday.'

I wondered whether, if we met, she would say

'congratulations'. That was all I wanted to hear. I was desperate to hear it from somebody.

I duly located my father, in the sitting room. It was a friendly, familiar room, and it had not changed significantly in many years. The floors were wooden and scarred, the sort of floorboards that had never been supposed to be exposed. No one had bothered to sand them down before varnishing them in the most amateurish way possible. I clearly remembered Roberto being paid for this task, in his early twenties, as an excuse for his still living at home. There were candles on every available surface, and there was a lot of purple. On one wall was Sue's framed copy of the Desiderata, while another bore a Tibetan thangka that Sue and Dad had brought back from a walking holiday in Nepal, and a third, bizarrely, still carried a framed copy of Roberto's A-level certificate. I smiled at it. Roberto was thirty-three, and Sue was still proud of his B in geography and his C in maths.

Dad stood up from the sofa, which was a perfectly normal blue one covered by a star-spangled purple throw. As he hugged me, slightly awkwardly as ever, a wave of exhaustion broke over me. It always did after work, particularly on a Friday. I was interested, when I could be detached about it, in the way I ricocheted between extremes. Suddenly, I could barely stay on my feet. I sat down quickly on the sofa, leaned back on a blissfully soft cushion, and closed my eyes. Then I opened them again, certain that I really would fall asleep if I carried on. Dad and Sue were both looking at me. I saw the concern in their eyes.

'It's OK,' I told them. 'Really. But there is something . . .' I stopped myself. 'Where's Roberto?' I asked, politely.

Sue beamed. Over the years, she had managed to convince herself that Roberto and I were special friends.

'They've gone to the deli,' she said. 'To get special provisions for the weekend. They were going to go this morning but, somehow, they didn't seem to make it. They were doing . . . other things. I don't know exactly what. We're not privy to all their doings, are we, darling?'

My dad nodded, then shook his head. I caught his eye, and our old, unspoken understanding passed between us.

Dad looked old, though he was only sixty-two. He had been entirely grey for years, and now he seemed to have lost more of his hair every time I saw him.

Dad had accepted Roberto into our lives years and years ago, without ever saying anything about becoming a stepfather. This was in contrast to Sue, who had worked incessantly on her relationship with me: she took me clothes shopping, taught me to enjoy coffee, and showed me that, contrary to my expectations, sage tea really did cure a sore throat. I was surprised, when I met Sue, to discover that there was someone in the world who thought I was interesting enough for all that.

Meanwhile, Dad and Roberto more or less ignored each other. As far as I could tell, they still did.

Dad had never said anything much about my mother, either. Years ago, he gave me the precious photograph, and that was it. I knew that he still thought about her, that he still missed her, but he seemed to have shut all of that away, and nobody would ever have guessed it.

I knew that he had an opinion about his freeloading stepson moving in as frequently as he did. I had caught him looking extremely happy, the previous summer, when Roberto and Julie set off to start their new lives in Milan, home to Roberto's father. They went in a flurry of excitement and fantasy, even though neither of them spoke Italian.

'Anyway,' Sue continued. 'How about a drink while we wait for them? Liz? G&T? Glass of wine?'

This, I knew, was my moment.

'Actually . . .' I said. 'I *won't* have a drink, *because* . . .' My heart started pounding, and I was wide awake. It was about to become real, and official.

A key turned in the lock, Sue rushed away to open the door, and the moment was lost.

Roberto was in front of me, tall and stocky with a noticeable belly. His hair was in a ponytail, and

I noticed for the first time that it was thinning. Julie hovered behind him, mousy blonde and slight. The deli snacks were unveiled, and suddenly Roberto was putting a glass of champagne into my hand.

'What's the occasion?' I asked weakly. 'Are you getting married?'

Julie looked at me. 'Not likely,' she said quietly. 'I'm still married to the one before.'

Roberto frowned at her and shushed her with a look. He cleared his throat.

'*This* is the occasion.' He looked around, making sure he had everyone's attention. 'I'm really glad you're here, Lizzy, because Julie and I have an announcement to make.'

Julie was looking at the floor, her cheeks pink, smiling her wishy-washy smile.

I longed for it to be something else. I knew it wasn't.

'We were going to wait,' he said, with a smile playing around his mouth, 'but we can't, so here it is: we're having a baby!'

Ten minutes later, I put my champagne down, untouched. I was about to make the most unwanted and superfluous announcement anyone had ever heard.

'Actually,' I said, loudly. 'Actually, I've come here for a reason. Because I need to make an announcement as well.' And I told them.

Nobody knew what to say. Julie glared at me. I glared back. Apart from everything else, I knew that she had stolen my free childcare.

I slipped out of the room. I would get on Dad's computer, and arrange to meet Helen. Suddenly, she seemed to be one of the few people I could rely on, and I hadn't even met her.

CHAPTER 12

MARY

1969

Mary was sodding miserable. She had been miserable for months. In fact, she could pinpoint the beginning of it to the day.

On 17 April, she went to work as normal, ignoring the niggle at the back of her mind. Her job was dull – she was a member of the typing pool – but she enjoyed it. She liked the girls she worked with, and she was always aware of how lucky she was to be alive in the modern age. She lived in a tiny bedsit carved out of a big stucco-fronted house in Hove, and shared a kitchen and bathroom with five other girls. All six of them went to work. She listened to music, and she cooked whatever she wanted, whenever she wanted it. One day, when she could save up enough money, she was going to go travelling. She would go to Kathmandu and Afghanistan, romantic, exciting places that were far, far away from everything she had ever known. She was desperate for adventure. She was twenty. In her parents' generation, any woman of twenty who worked, and who, therefore, was unmarried, would have been getting close to being on the shelf. Not Mary. She thought she might like to get married one day, but it was not going to be any time soon, and in the meantime she was having plenty of fun.

On 17 April 1969, her boyfriend was Billy Greene. She'd met him at a party and had lusted after him at first sight. He was smoking hashish when she first set eyes on him, and he was wearing a psychedelic shirt with a long pointed collar. He was tall, with a fine, sculpted face, and he looked glorious. They had been hanging out together for a few months now. She was even considering going on the Pill. Mary knew that Billy was not The One, because he was dull underneath the clothes and the music and the drugs. He surprised her, when she got to know him, by being conventional.

'We should go on one of those buses,' she told him, leaning against his shoulder in a room full of people, breathing in a haze of smoke. 'Like Rose's brother did. He went to Kathmandu.' She loved the sound of the word. Sometimes, at work, she would whisper it to herself, again and again. Kathmandu.

Billy pulled away from her with a frown.

'Kathmandu?' he repeated, incredulous. 'Whatever for?'

Still, the fact that she had a boyfriend who would never be her husband made her feel deliciously modern and rather naughty. Billy would do for the moment. She was saving for her bus ticket.

That was how she felt on the morning of 17 April. At lunchtime, she went for a quick walk around Brighton to do some shopping. The sun was shining and the sea air was fresh and cold. It blew the cobwebs away, and at some point during the walk, she began to admit a few things. At the greengrocer's, she thought about the Tampax that she'd been carrying around in her capacious handbag since . . . well, for a long time. As she walked through the Lanes, gazing unseeingly into shop windows, she realised that she'd been expecting the curse last weekend, and that she'd missed it the month before as well. She hadn't had it since January. She hadn't noticed, because she hadn't wanted to. If anything, it had been mildly convenient.

By the time she got back to the office, Mary was trembling.

'This can't be happening,' she muttered. 'It isn't happening. It isn't.'

'Everything all right, dear?' asked Miss Manning.

'Yes,' Mary lied. 'Of course. Fine. I'm just . . . feeling a little bit unwell.'

Miss Manning was generally kind, and she liked Mary. 'You don't look well, dear,' she said, sympathetically. 'I'll tell you what. Finish that letter, and then why don't you go home early? Go on. Off with you.'

Mary looked at her gratefully. She dashed

through a letter demanding final payment from a client, handed the letter and carbon copy to Miss Manning, and fled. Various girls looked up as she dashed past, but for once, Mary avoided their eyes. She normally liked the social aspect of her job, but today she wanted to be alone.

She knew it. She supposed one went to the doctor and so on at this point, but she didn't need to, because she knew it for certain. And there were two extremely stark options that had opened up before her. *Am I brave enough?* she asked herself. And: *which is more frightening?*

Thus, six months later, she was sodding fed up. Everything had been snatched away. She should have tried her luck with a termination, but, when it came to it, she hadn't dared. Her parents were old-fashioned and very religious. She had always heard that abortion was evil, that it was murder. She simply had not been able to go through with it. She'd been stupid. In fact, she had fucked things up for good. What would a couple of hours of discomfort, a bit of bleeding, and, possibly, the odd twinge of guilt have been, compared with this?

Instead, she had told Billy. She watched him closely, knowing that his reaction would show her what her real options were. To her horror, a slow smile spread across his face. Billy, it transpired, was actually *pleased*. Now that she'd had time to think about it, she supposed he could afford to be. Nobody was going to make him give up his job. He wasn't going to have to stay at home with a squalling infant. He would not abruptly find himself metamorphosed into a housewife, his dreams, ambitions, plans and hopes all turned to dust. Billy could have it all, because Billy was a man.

They got married as quickly as they could. It was a small ceremony in a registry office. By then Mary was four months gone, and she had to clutch her bouquet of lilies strategically to disguise her growing stomach. Their families had been there, and a couple of friends each (hers: Cilla from the house, and Rose from work. His: Paul from the office and his best friend Martin). She chose orange lilies, after studying a book of flower symbolism, because they symbolised hatred and disdain. She dressed in a cheap pink dress that clashed with her flowers, with an ugly, big-buttoned jacket, a pair of round-toed shoes, and nylon stockings. She'd toyed with the idea of bare feet, flowers in her hair, and a short beaded dress, but that would have implied happiness, and she wanted to project her mood. Despite her efforts, everyone said she looked lovely, because nobody could ever say anything else to a bride.

As soon as she was Mrs Greene, she had to give up work because of the baby. She'd told all the girls that it was a shotgun wedding, and her predicament was met with a mixture of horror and envy.

'Come back and see us,' said Rose, and she promised she would, while knowing that she wouldn't. Her bedsit was immediately re-let to a girl who called herself Primrose, who was doing a secretarial course. Primrose was seventeen, with long, blonde hair, and plenty of jewellery, and the one time they met, Mary hated her. She hated the fact that Primrose had the world at her feet, and she had nothing.

She and Billy bought a little house, in the centre of Brighton, with some help from his parents. Billy worked for a small firm of solicitors nearby, and he instantly assumed that Mary was his chattel. She had known he would. She was expected to keep the house spotless, to cook his breakfast, lunch and dinner, to wash and iron his work clothes. He came home, if he didn't go to the pub after work, and sat down with his newspaper. He was a stranger to Mary, and it took her no time at all to begin to hate him.

Now the baby was due. Mary cried all day, every day. She was dreading the arrival of her wretched unwanted child. Every kick made her angry. Her dreams of seeing the Himalayan mountains were dust. All she had was an old copy of *National Geographic* with pages of Nepal in it, and she spent her days staring at it, willing herself into the pictures, into the temples and the markets and the clean, snowy mountains so far from everyone and everything she knew.

She still had her savings, and they were carefully hidden from Billy, just in case.

She sat in her little sitting room, both hands on her swollen belly. Her feet were resting on the small table, for the swelling, as instructed by the doctor. Tears rolled down her cheeks, but she barely noticed them any more. Mary knew a few women with children, but she didn't like any of them. She hated the way their lives were dedicated to the service of others, as if the women themselves were the least important people. Hadn't they heard of women's lib? And now look at her.

She should have got rid of it, for all their sakes. She had tried, throughout the pregnancy, with gin and hot baths and staircases, but nothing worked. Still, she could have taken the plunge and dropped out entirely. She could have had a bastard child, looked after it herself. Got a job as a waitress or something, and taken it travelling. Yet she hadn't; she had caved in. She had done what her parents' generation would have done. She was furious with herself.

She didn't want the baby, but she hoped it would be a boy. If it was a boy, at least it would have opportunities. If it was a girl it might just end up with an unwanted pregnancy, a brick wall. Like mother, like daughter.

She'd been having tightenings for a week or so now. Without even realising it, she was clasping her belly with each one, and they were getting stronger. Mary swallowed. This might be it. A wave of nausea broke over her, and she was barely on her feet before she was sick all over the leather sofa, part of the suite that her parents had given them as a wedding present. The sickness, she knew, was dread. These were contractions. The baby was on its way.

Mary opened her mouth and screamed. Nobody had even hinted that it might be this way. The fact that it was called 'labour' was the closest she had come to a warning. The doctor had talked of tightenings, contractions, and discomfort, and she hadn't given the process much more thought than that. He made it sound like a minor inconvenience. It did, she supposed, make sense that a big object coming through what had been a small gap would cause pain, but this was not pain. This was tearing, unremitting agony of a kind that Mary had never suspected was possible. This was payback for all the bad thoughts, for all the gin and the knitting needles. This was celestial condemnation. Someone up there hated her as much as she hated him. She was going to die. She begged for it to come soon.

Billy was somewhere in the hospital, shut away in a smoky room with the rest of the fathers. Mary was being tended by a midwife who frowned when she screamed, and a doctor who came in from time to time, and who wanted to be somewhere else. Her legs were in stirrups. She had been shaved on arrival. She knew that there were plenty of ideas around, that you could stand up and walk around, get up off your back, squat during labour, but when she tried these, it turned out she was not allowed. All the same, she kept trying to get up, to ease the pain by shifting positions. The midwife just pushed her back down. They gave her gas and air but it made her vomit everywhere.

During each contraction, she stared at the clock on the wall, and watched as time speeded up and slowed down. The labour rooms were on the thirteenth floor, and she could see the street lights coming on all over Brighton. Afternoon became evening, and night, then the sun rose and she felt sure she was no further on than when she had arrived. When she craned round, she could see the sea from the window, but the midwife didn't like that. She wanted her to concentrate. The street lights went off. Rain began to fall, and then the sky cleared. It was a watery blue by the time the woman shouted at her to push. It was a stupid thing to shout: nothing Mary could have done would have stopped her body pushing. The pain was better like this. Every ounce of her strength went into the primal business of ejecting her offspring. In between, she panted and waited. Suddenly, on one push, the midwife announced that she could see the head. The doctor appeared. They both told her to push. She swore at them, loudly, and felt the exquisite relief of a body slipping out of her.

'It's a girl,' the doctor told her, with a vague smile. 'Congratulations, Mrs Greene.'

A girl. Poor cow.

When the baby was handed to her, cleaned up

and wrapped in a pink blanket, Mary looked at its little face, crumpled and cross. She wondered, in a detached way, at the fact that it had grown inside her, with its angry fists bunched up ready for a fight, its eyebrows knitted together, its toes and everything. It had all been put together by her own body, and she had never even meant to do it. She waited, hopelessly and cynically, for the rush of love. It didn't come. She had known it wouldn't. This creature, she felt, had nothing to do with her.

'Sorry, baby,' she whispered. 'Mummy doesn't love you. Try Daddy.'

The midwife smiled. 'Now, shall we put Baby to the breast?' she asked.

Mary pulled her gown around her. 'No,' she said firmly. 'Let it have a bottle.'

Billy said they had to name it after the Queen, because that was what his parents expected. Once, Mary might have fought for a more interesting name, fought against the attitudes betrayed by Billy's statement, but by this stage she didn't care. And so it was that Elizabeth Greene arrived in the world: small, red, cross, and loved, perhaps, by her father.

CHAPTER 13

LIZ

6 February

I went for the scan on my own, because I had no one to go with me. I had to take an afternoon off school, and this provoked Kathy into silent fury.

The hospital was functional, but grim. Paint was peeling, and I got hopelessly lost on my way to the scanning room.

The midwife had told me to drink plenty of water before the scan, but when, finally, I was called in, the sonographer touched my abdomen and sent me away to the loo, with a roll of her eyes. She smeared me with some cold gel, and set to work.

The room was dark. I stared at the screen. At first it looked like nothing. Then I heard the sound of the baby's heart, and the swooshing of its home. Grey pixels moved around. The sonographer pushed the scanner hard into my belly, and I was suddenly afraid for the baby. Even though I could hear its heart, I was afraid it had died.

'See?' she said. She looked at me, and pointed to the screen. 'Here it is.'

I stared. Suddenly, what I was looking at fell into place. There was a huge head. There was a tiny body. The body had limbs, which were flailing around. It actually looked like a baby. I was looking at my baby.

She was busy taking measurements. 'All looks all right so far,' she said cheerfully. I couldn't take my eyes off it.

'So, how many weeks pregnant am I?' I asked, trying to keep the tremor out of my voice. I willed her to say 'eighteen'. If she said eighteen, it was Steve's baby. If she said fourteen, it was Rosa's.

She took her time before she answered. She was squinting at the screen.

'Oh,' she said, apparently registering what I had said. 'Oh, fourteen weeks exactly. Giving you a due date of August the seventh. Is that what you thought?'

I left with three photographs of my strange little embryo. I felt, although I shouldn't, as if my life raft had been taken away. Rosa had got me pregnant. I sobbed all the way to the Tube. This was Rosa's baby. I was well and truly on my own.

CHAPTER 14

HELEN

9 February

I sat on the uncomfortable chair and frowned at the screen in front of me. I was trying hard to block out everything else. I could only write to Liz if I was in character, and, under the circumstances, getting into character was not easy.

'Hi there!' I wrote. 'Liz, I am so sorry to hear about what went on at your dad's. I was hoping that telling them might be going to make your life easier. But it doesn't seem that way at the moment! Don't worry, though. It will all work out, and just because your stepbrother and his wife are having a baby too, that doesn't mean anything. There's nothing to stop Sue helping you both out. Glad the scan went well.'

I sighed. Once I got going, it was easy to be jaunty and upbeat on email. It was easy to give mindless and obvious advice off the top of my head. It was going to be far harder to convince her face to face.

I only ventured out of the hotel room to do this. So far, I had spent most of my time in London trying to avoid people. My room was horrible, but it comprised the few square feet of London that I could call my own. The bed was lumpy. The walls were stained yellow with nicotine, and pock-marked, I thought, with cigarette burns. There were brown watery outlines all over the ceiling. The carpet needed replacing. I wondered how people lived like this.

When I pushed aside the dirty net curtains, I had a view of a brick wall, very close to my window. There was almost no natural light. All the same, light seeped in at night and kept me awake. Somehow, street lights and car headlights invaded my sleep.

I hated my room, but the rest of London was worse. It was awful out there – big and dirty and frightening. I cowered indoors, feeling that I was in a war zone. I simply did not dare to go out. Girls who had seemed nice and friendly had stolen my money, so I dreaded to think what everyone else wanted to do to me.

When I forced myself outside, there were people who stared at me, even though this was a big city and no one was supposed to be interested. I looked fearfully at them, but as soon as our eyes met, I stared down at the pavement in front of me, at the wide slabs of concrete. I went out when I had to, to buy expensive, tasteless fruit and, more importantly, to use the internet. The rest of the time I hid in my horrible room.

So far, the project was a disaster. I tried and

tried to psych myself up to get out and see the city properly. For days, I stayed indoors. Strange sounds came from other parts of the hotel. I tried to ignore them. From time to time, a smell would find its way to me. It would creep under the door and assail me. Sometimes it was a cooking smell; at other times it made me think of mould, drains or bodily functions. I became horribly familiar with the patches on the ceiling, as I lay on the bed and stared upwards, trying to convince myself that they weren't shifting.

I hated being on my own. I could not bear to be so far from Tom. I was pretty sure that Liz was my sister, but she didn't know it, and the whole plan seemed ridiculous. It would be far more grown up if I were just to tell her the truth. That way, it would be up to her to decide if and when she wanted to meet the rest of the family. Tom had been right. But now that I was here, I had to try.

If I told her the truth, she wouldn't want to come to France to meet the woman who abandoned her. She wouldn't want anything to do with any of us. That was certain. That was why I had to take her back myself. If I did manage to take her home with me for a 'holiday', we would, eventually, have a reconciliation. That was why I was here. That was why I could not do the thing I was longing to do, and go home.

The internet shop was a small, dark room with thin squares of brown carpet on the floor. I came here because I knew that I had to. The men who worked here looked at me. When I came in, they said, 'How are you doing?' and I nodded at them but couldn't say anything in return. I saw them talking about me sometimes, but as I was relentlessly boring and unfriendly, they were starting to leave me to it. One of them came in now.

'Morning,' he said. I looked round.

'Hi,' I muttered.

'How are you?'

'Fine.'

I frowned at the screen to show him that I wasn't talking, and he started chatting to his friend, talking about United and Chelsea and the Champions' League.

'Perhaps you should talk to Julie,' I improvised, on my email. 'It doesn't sound as if you really know her, but could she perhaps turn into a friend, if you're both having babies?'

I sat there and dispensed random advice for a little while longer. It was surprising how easy it was to sort out somebody else's life when you weren't involved. I could tell Liz what to do all day long, if I let myself.

Tom never bothered to write. Beyond an occasional, formal message in French, from Papa, Liz was my sole correspondent. I had, in the past, had other email friends, people I had met on various websites. The friendships always fizzled out. They had all ended either with me accidentally saying something that made my correspondent cut off all contact, or with whoever I was writing to suggesting I send a photo of myself topless. I had done it once, had taken a photograph of myself in the mirror with the camera and flash obscuring my face, just to gain a life experience and alleviate the dullness. My 'friend', who until then had been masquerading as a woman, revealed himself to be a man living in somewhere called Blissfield, Ohio, and immediately demanded a bottomless shot too. At that point I felt obliged to drop him, especially because Tom read his mail. That was uncomfortable, but at least I had someone on hand to talk sense, and to tell me I was gross. He was disgusted with me, as I was with myself.

The tragic thing was, sending that photograph was the closest thing I had ever had to a sexual experience.

Five days later, I woke up manic. This was the day when everything was going to change. It would be a cornerstone in my life, one of the most important days I would ever have. Liz and I were going to meet for coffee at half past ten. I had barely slept, going through imaginary conversations in my head all night long.

Liz was vulnerable, and the last person she needed in her life was the real me. She needed someone happy, strong, and capable. She needed good advice and unquestioning support. Somehow, I had to become the person she wanted me to be, even though I was somebody else entirely.

She had asked whether I would mind meeting her in north London. I had agreed readily, even though I had yet to brave the Metro system. Today, I was going to leave the Norfolk Square area for the first time. I was going to go to Kentish Town.

I dressed carefully. Yesterday had been a big day: I went clothes shopping, and I got my hair cut and dyed. Even though I bought clothes all the time in Bordeaux, in London it was different. I had clothes, but this city made me look like a loser, however hard I tried. This was causing me some despair, until I happened to pick up a magazine that someone left in the internet shop.

It was called *Heat*, and it was actually open on a page about clothes. When I looked closer, I saw that the page was called 'Steal her style', and that the woman in the picture was wearing an outfit that I thought I could buy. In fact, it was idiot-proof. Every item had a cheap version listed next to it, and the name of a shop. Even a moron like me could copy it.

I steeled myself, and ran over to a cab that was dropping someone off.

'Can you take me somewhere where I can find Top Shop, H&M and Office?' I asked shyly.

'Sounds to me like you want Oxford Circus,' the driver suggested, though he didn't sound particularly interested.

I managed to buy every part of the outfit surprisingly easily, even though English sizes were difficult for me. No one gave me a second glance because everywhere was so busy. I started to do some gawping myself, at a woman standing at the traffic lights yelling into a megaphone about God. She saw me looking and stopped and smiled. I had to walk quickly away.

After that I walked into a random hairdresser's, and handed them the magazine. 'Can you make my hair look like this?' I asked.

The woman looked at the picture and nodded. 'You want to look like Fearne Cotton?' she checked, with a small giggle. I nodded, clueless. 'Well, I think you could do a bit better than that,' she told me. 'I think you could do Nicole Kidman.' Two hours and one hundred and fifty pounds later, I barely recognised myself. My hair was blonde, properly blonde, like Marilyn Monroe's. It was still long, but there was a shape to it. When I shook my head, it swung around. I looked like somebody different.

I tied my hair in a scarf last night, because I vaguely hoped this would stop it going scruffy again as I slept. My fear was that the bleach would have made it fall out, overnight, every strand of it.

My outfit for the big day comprised a pair of skin-tight black trousers, a 'peasant style' blouse with small blue flowers all over it, a huge wide belt, and pale blue cardigan. When all of that was on, I ceremoniously removed the scarf from my head, and checked the mirror.

It was the first time I had seen myself in the

ensemble. I was unrecognisable. The girl who looked back at me was the woman I wanted to be. She looked smart and confident and ready for anything. She looked like someone who had friends, someone you could talk to. I put on my new 'cowboy' boots, and I loaded purse, room key, the copy of *Heat*, and printouts of all of Liz's emails into my new black bag. It was a big bag (apparently bags were 'big this season'). I would never fill it up.

I had written out a list of conversation topics. 'London,' it read. 'My experiences of – positive!! France – idyllic and good place to visit, maybe Liz will come sometime? Baby – excited – father?? Pregnancy – sickness? etc. Scan – ask to look at pictures. Hotel – rubbish. Need place to live.' I added that to the handbag. Then I left. It was probably going to take me a long time to walk to 'Matt's Place'.

It was a sunny day, and, after a while, I began to relax a little. My new look made me feel better. I was so focused on the meeting with my sister that I stopped worrying that everyone I saw was going to steal my money, or assault me, or blow me up. I decided that most people really did have lives of their own, and that they really truly did not care about me. A few men stared at me, but I pretended they weren't there. Gradually, I began to feel all right. I tried to talk myself into being the person Liz would need me to be. I tried to remember to smile. If I smiled at all times, she would have to like me.

Her nominated meeting place was one of those London cafés that didn't exist in France, even though, in England, they seemed to have French names. This one was called 'Café Lumière', though Liz had called it 'Matt's Place'. I knew I had the right café because, on the door, a home-made sign that looked as if it had been drawn by a child said, 'Please don't smoke at Matt's Caff. Thanks.' Flowers had been drawn in many colours of felt tip pen, all around the writing. Next to it there was another sign, in purple pen, which said, 'Help wanted, apply within.' Below it, in bright pink, were the words, 'We rarely close! 8–midnight.'

I pushed the door, trying not to tremble. I never took drama at school, because the people who did it were intimidating and didn't like me. So I wasn't much of an actress. Nonetheless, I attempted to drift carelessly past the people, around the pushchairs, to sit casually at a spare table. I looked at the man behind the counter, wondering whether he was 'Matt'. His bleached fringe was too long and hung into his eyes, but he probably liked it like that. He had a nice face. He caught my eye, and smiled. His face was babyish, a bit like Tom's.

'Be right over,' he called, above the mellow music.

I was ten minutes early, and I could see that no one in this room was Elizabeth Greene. The room

160

smelt of coffee and hot milk. I hated the coffee you seemed to get in Britain, the buckets of milk with a mild coffee flavouring. French cafés were smoky and scruffy, with rickety chairs and old Formica tables. In rural France, there were more men than women in any drinking establishment, and at least half of them would be sitting at the bar with a brightly coloured liqueur even if it was nine in the morning.

This place had a wooden floor, and armchairs and sofas which looked as if they had been arranged any old how, though I supposed that they hadn't. I counted four large pushchairs. With each pushchair was a glamorous woman wearing shiny lipstick, and a baby, several of them ingesting sludge while their mothers talked animatedly to each other.

I caught sight of my reflection in the window, and smiled at it. It was nice to see a blonde bomb-shell staring back.

Matt, if it was he, jiggled around as he waited for my order. I stared at the laminated menu. He stood over me, nodding his head in time with the music.

'Sorry,' he said, noticing me looking at him. 'Over-caffeinated.'

'I'd like a double espresso, please.'

He nodded. 'Good choice. I like a woman who drinks a proper coffee.'

I felt myself blushing. I wanted to say something back, but I couldn't think what it should be.

I watched as a few people arrived. When half past ten came, I was certain that she wasn't going to turn up. I saw a man with a laptop arrive and set up a little office at a table in the corner. A fat woman came in, then another woman with a pushchair. In my mind, Liz existed as a tall, willowy, beautiful version of me.

I was staring out of the window, waiting and hoping, when the fat woman came to the table. She seemed hesitant.

'I'm sorry to disturb you,' she said, 'but I don't suppose you're Helen?'

I forced a smile. She had frizzy hair around her shoulders, a broad build, and a stomach that definitely looked fat, rather than anything else. She was not glamorous, not at all, though she was carrying a nice red bag. I tried to believe that this was my sister, that this ordinary woman was the one upon whom everything depended. I attempted to quell my disappointment.

'Yes!' I said, sounding as enthusiastic as I could. I cranked up the enthusiasm as far as it would go. 'I am!' I gushed. 'I'm Helen, and that means that you must be Liz!' I stood up, unsure whether to kiss her cheeks, as I would in France, or to shake her hand, since we were in England. I decided to lunge for a cheek, and she tolerated it. Her skin felt dry.

We both sat down. I cradled my coffee, hoping my nerves weren't showing. I tried to tell myself that Liz was less intimidating than I had expected, and that this was a good thing.

162

'God, look at you,' she said. 'You're all young and slim and gorgeous. I love that top.' She sighed. 'I couldn't wear it. I wouldn't even mind if I looked pregnant. But I'm just fat.'

I frowned, unaccustomed to compliments. I knew what I had to say here. 'You're not fat. Not at all. But you're right that you don't look pregnant yet. That's why I didn't think it was you when you came in.'

'Yes, because I'm fat.'

'No you're not.' I paused. It was odd, when I knew so much about her from the forum and from emails, to discover that she was, in fact, a stranger. I hoped she didn't feel that way about me.

'How are you feeling?' I said, keeping up my dazzling smile.

'Fine,' she said, flatly. 'Fine, in a crap way. The nausea's eased off, but I'm still so tired. It's all I can do to put one foot in front of the other. Some days the first thing I do when I get up in the morning is count the number of hours until I can get back into bed again at night.'

I touched her forearm, then took my hand away before she thought I was strange. I thought that if I worked hard at it, I could probably get used to her being ordinary. I told myself firmly that she could still be amazing on the inside. She could still be the one who would make it all better. 'That sounds hard,' I said. I cast around for another question. 'Are they being nice at work?'

She raised her eyebrows. 'As nice as a bunch of

163

kids want to be to a single, pregnant woman who's nearly forty. I believe they mainly spend their time speculating over the identity of the father. They're desperate for it to be a colleague.'

'Is it?'

I knew instantly that I had said the wrong thing. Liz frowned and edged away from me a little. 'Don't you start,' she said. 'No, it's not.'

I nodded, biting my lower lip. 'Sorry,' I said. 'I didn't mean it. How about the colleagues? How are they being?'

She sighed. 'That was my colleagues I was talking about.'

I was puzzled. 'But you said kids.'

Liz breathed in, and then out. She sounded tired. 'That was a joke. Just then, when I said it was the colleagues I was talking about. Though it might as well not have been.'

I didn't quite follow.

'How about Kathy?' I tried, eager to move on. Liz had written on the forum that her friend Kathy had been horrible when she told her about the pregnancy, and I thought that they hadn't spoken since. I was quite pleased about that, hoping that it might make Liz receptive to my arrival.

'Kathy's fine. I believe. We still haven't spoken. We just crash around our part of the staffroom and pretend the other one's not there. It's very mature.'

She dropped her bag and summoned Matt with a wave of the hand. He came straight over.

'The lovely Lizzy,' he said, pushing his hair out

of his face. I wondered how often patrons found stray blond hairs in their coffee. 'What can I get you?'

'Coffee,' she said at once.

'And yet I thought you were off coffee?' he mused, screwing up his face. 'Last time, you threatened to vomit all over the table because you could smell someone's latte.'

'Things change. Second trimester.'

'Whatever you say. Are you having a serious coffee like your lovely friend?'

She looked at me, then at my coffee, a small smile on her lips. Then she shook her head. 'She's French. That's why. No, I'll have your milkiest, most childish concoction. For the baby.'

'You got it.' He looked to me, his eyebrows asking the question. I wished it was afternoon so I could order a proper, alcoholic drink.

'Can I have a glass of water?' I asked.

'Sparkling or still?'

'Tap?'

He sighed. 'Only because I like you.'

'And an espresso?' I wanted to please him, and he smiled at this.

'Deal.'

As the hour passed, I realised that I might be getting away with it. I thought I was just about managing to convince her that I was ordinary. Thankfully, each of our lives provided an easy and obvious talking point, and I only once consulted the list in my bag. She didn't see me doing it.

I asked about baby names, but Liz hadn't started thinking about them. 'That would bring it a bit closer than I want, at the moment,' she said. 'The scan was weird enough. I'm still getting my head around the fact that I have photographs of my foetus.'

'Do you have them with you?' I asked.

She laughed. 'No. You don't have to coo over baby photos for a few months yet, don't worry. I've got them by my bed.'

We talked about the different types of pushchairs visible in the café. Liz said she had a pregnant neighbour whom she saw from time to time, but that otherwise her only pregnant friends were from the forum. She said that she'd shut herself off from most of her old friends. I didn't understand why, but I was glad.

She asked me what I made of London. I lied shamelessly, again and again, and pretended to be energetic and excited. Then, with a flash of panic, I understood that she was preparing to leave. I needed to make sure I was going to see her again.

'I think I'll be staying in London for a while,' I said, looking at Liz and looking away again. 'And I can't really stay at the hotel indefinitely. I suppose I should find a flat.'

'You're living in a *hotel*?' she asked, looking aghast. 'Where? That must be costing a bomb.'

'Not really.' I described my nasty, cheap abode,

with its dirty orange counterpane and its stained bathroom. For the first time in my life, I was enjoying the sound of my own voice. 'It's the original room without a view,' I added. 'So, where do people like me actually live? Some Australian girls told me about a hostel, but I didn't go, and then they stole my money.' The further I got into my new character, the more I said.

'Don't you dare go to a hostel. You need a copy of *Loot*.'

'*Loot?*'

'It's an ads paper. Everything's in there.'

'I can get somewhere to live from a *newspaper*?'

'Well, how else were you planning to do it?'

'I don't know.' I sounded stupid, so I kept talking. 'Where do I buy it from? *Loot*, I mean. Is it expensive?'

She smiled. 'Cheaper than living in a hotel.'

'What do I do then? I buy the paper, I find an advert for a flat I like the sound of. Then what? Do I find somewhere that's empty and just live there on my own? What about furniture? Do I need to buy that, too?'

Liz was looking at me. 'Helen,' she said, 'how rich are your parents?'

'Um. You know. They do well.'

'I should think they do. And I know you're new to the city and everything, but really, you can't rent a flat on your own. You need to find a flat-share. Unless they're oil millionaires, in which case let's get them to buy you a pad in Hampstead and

167

I'll move in with you, or unless you want to live in Penge or something.'

'I don't know. Where's Penge?'

'OK. You don't want to live in Penge. Trust me. So you look under "flatshares", and you put a ring around anything that sounds good. Then you check where they are, very carefully, on the A–Z. Once you've narrowed it down, you ring up the ones you're interested in and make appointments to go and visit. And you take the one you like the best. You normally give a month's rent as a deposit. I'm sorry, I don't want to patronise you. I realise that I sound as if I'm speaking to a moron.'

'No. You are speaking to a moron.' I remembered to flash my smile at her. 'I'm not offended.'

'You've never lived away from your folks? Did you go to boarding school?'

'No. Papa drove me into Bordeaux to school every day.'

She was trying not to laugh at me. 'So you've had a bit of a sheltered life.'

'I came away because I wanted to change that,' I said, defensively. 'It got stifling. My mother means well, but she is a strange woman and I got sick of her standing at the window watching me all the time. I do have my own house on the vineyard, but I was still at their beck and call. Poor Tom, though. All on his own with them now.'

'Your brother?'

'Yes. Tom isn't like anyone else. Sorry. I know

it's not cool to miss your little brother, but I do. I wouldn't tell him, though. Have you got any brothers and sisters?'

'A stepbrother, that's all.'

'Oh yes, Roberto. Of course. Roberto and Julie. Who spoilt your announcement.'

She sighed. 'That's the one. You know, it feels slightly creepy that you know so much about me. How about you? Just you and Tom?'

I hesitated. 'Pretty much.' When I saw that she was about to ask what I meant, I carried on talking. 'Do you miss your mother?' I demanded. I regretted it at once.

Liz did not look pleased. 'Goodness,' she said. 'You don't mince your words. Can you miss what you've never known? I'm not sure. In a way, I miss her. I miss the idea of her. Built her up into a saint in my head, over the years.' She finished her coffee and pushed the cup away. 'Anyway,' she said briskly. 'We need to get you out of that hotel.'

I saw my chance, and grabbed it. 'Will you help me? Really? That would be fantastic. Thank you so much. I wouldn't be able to do it on my own.'

She sighed. I could see that this was not what she had meant at all. 'OK.' I watched her spoon the last of the frothy bubbles of her coffee into her mouth. 'Let's go and buy *Loot*. I'll help you pick out a few to look at.'

'I'll pay for the coffees,' I said eagerly.

She looked at me with a smile. 'Daddy's money?'

'It's the least he can do.'

'Then I won't refuse.'

We left the café together. So far, I told myself cautiously, so good.

CHAPTER 15

MARY

December 1969

Mary thought about running away, and taking the baby with her. It wouldn't work. She knew it wouldn't, because it was the baby she wanted to run from.

All the same, as it lay in its Moses basket, with its fists bunched up, she told herself that she might be going to grow to love it. If she suddenly woke up one morning feeling like other mothers seemed to feel, then she would take the baby with her. Whatever happened, she was not staying here, not with Billy Greene.

But she knew she was pretending. The baby was at the centre of everything. The baby was why she needed to go.

One Tuesday morning, she decided to go out on her own, to see what it felt like. The baby was four weeks old, and it was asleep as usual. It wasn't due a bottle for three hours. She closed the front door quietly behind her, and listened for a few seconds to check that it hadn't woken. Then she strode along the street, feeling transgressive. She felt that

171

everyone she passed could see that she had left an innocent child unprotected, so she looked down and tried to be inconspicuous.

At the corner shop, she bought a newspaper, a bag of apples, and a copy of *Private Eye*.

'Little one not with you today?' asked the woman behind the counter.

'No,' Mary told her. 'My mother's looking after her.' She made an effort, when she was talking to people, to say 'her' and not 'it'. She was careful to get it right today.

'Oh, how lovely,' the woman said, sounding rather bored. 'Make sure you make the most of your time off. You've earned it.'

Mary walked home slowly. She let herself in quietly. She had been out for twenty minutes, and the baby didn't seem to have stirred.

She warmed the bottle, and flicked greedily to the back of the magazine. 'Eye Escape' was the section she was looking for. She scanned the classified advertisements, and suddenly, there it was. It was only a few lines, but it was all that was needed. There was a bus to Kathmandu. There was a telephone number. There was a price: one hundred and twenty five pounds. She had that much saved already.

She put a chair next to the telephone, took the baby on to her lap, and started giving it the bottle. Then she dialled the number. A man answered.

'Hello?' he said.

She took a deep breath, and spoke clearly.

'I'm calling about the bus to Kathmandu,' she said.

CHAPTER 16

LIZ

21 March

Kathy leaned across me and picked up her handbag, which was at my feet. She brushed my arm, in passing, but said nothing. I looked pointedly away from her, at the pot plants. One of them had almost reached the ceiling.

'Bye, Sandrine,' Kathy said, poison in her voice.

'See you, Kathy,' Sandrine said, with a sigh. Although Kathy and I had not quite reached the point of asking Sandrine to carry messages between us, we were nearly there. I shook my head gently. I wasn't going to move from our corner of the staffroom. I wasn't going to apologise, because I had nothing to apologise for. We had been ignoring each other for weeks, like vindictive teenagers, or a miserable couple in the last stages of a dire marriage.

'Bye, Kathy,' I said, pointedly, to her departing back. She paused, then carried on walking without a word, without looking round.

I looked at Sandrine.

'I tried,' I said. I could feel the rage simmering,

but I was determined not to let it spill out. I would not give Kathy the satisfaction of a shouting match. I would not give the spectators anything new to gossip about.

In Kathy's eyes, I was a traitor. I had never quite realised the extent to which our friendship was founded on the fact that neither of us wanted children. I knew she had plenty of friends who were parents, and I was simmering at the unfairness of it all.

'You did try,' Sandrine said, and put a gentle arm on my shoulder. I wanted to shake it off, but was loath to alienate my one remaining friend.

'She won't change her mind,' I said. 'But I'm not moving from here. This is my chair and I'm fucking staying.'

'I know. She will change. She can't be so mad with a pregnant woman, just for being pregnant.'

'I hope you're right. But I don't think so. She'll never apologise. She might just start speaking to me again one day. I'm not sure I'll be saying anything back.'

Sandrine shrugged. I stood up, gathered my things, and left. The path to the staffroom door was, by necessity, a meandering one. There were chairs and bags and piles of books everywhere. I was aware of several pairs of eyes following my progress. My colleagues were still speculating incessantly about the baby's paternity. They thought that if they stopped talking the moment they saw me, I would never guess what they had been talking about. I watched two conversations screech to an emergency stop as I came close.

I paused at the doorway, struggling with myself. In the end I couldn't help it.

I turned round and clapped my hands. 'It's all right, everybody,' I shouted, staring particularly at the geography department. 'I'm leaving now. You can gossip about me with impunity. And to get you off to a good start, the baby's father is *not* in this room, and is *not* my ex-partner. OK? Go!'

And I left, fuming.

It was reassuring to be able to disappear into the central London crowds, and I tried hard to relax. I put a hand to my stomach, and briefly hoped that my emotions were not making the baby neurotic, or psychotic, or just plain miserable. I tried to think positive thoughts, to direct some good emotions in its direction, but at the moment that was hard to do. I was scared. I wanted to be in control of my life, but I was at the mercy of too many other factors, too many other people.

I had a bump now, a small but definitely pregnant stomach. I was proud, and it made me sick with fear. I often looked at myself, side on, in the mirror, and marvelled at the fact that this was me, and that I never expected that I could look this way.

I wandered towards the station without enthusiasm: I was supposed to be looking at a flat with Helen, when all I wanted to do was to go home, run a hot bath, rub my bump, and wallow.

175

My phone started serenading my fellow pedestrians with the strains of Beethoven's Fifth Symphony, which had seemed appropriately portentous and doom-laden when I decided to get rid of the Nokia tune, years after everyone else. I grabbed it from my big red bag, praying it was Helen cancelling. Helen was sweet, if naive, and I thought that she was probably a positive force in my life, but I had never intended to be her flat-hunting partner. I had an uneasy feeling that she had tricked me into it. I wasn't used to being tricked.

I didn't recognise the number, and answered warily.

'Where are you?' barked Steve.

'Why?'

'You know why.'

'I don't, actually.'

'Are you on your way home? You should be on your way home.'

I was suddenly alert. 'Why? Where are you?' I was approaching Victoria, and looked around carefully. There were people everywhere, most of them on the move. I stood by the clock that called itself Little Ben, and scanned the crowds. It was futile. I crossed the road, looking around carefully.

'Where do you think I am?'

'Don't you dare ambush me!'

'Why not?'

He was standing by the entrance to the Tube, holding his phone to his ear and looking hard at

176

everyone who passed. I stepped behind a tall man, and used him as cover for a few metres. Then I managed to pass on the other side of the Tube entrance, and headed, at a jog, on to the main station concourse.

Steve still had an effect on me. Seeing him standing there, wearing a nice grey suit, made my stomach flip. I was certain it was pheromones, rather than the baby. I didn't want to have any feelings for him. All my anguish had supposedly been mown down by the shock of the pregnancy. He was supposed to be nothing to me any more. The baby was supposed to be the important one now, and it was not his.

I stood in the middle of the concourse, surrounded by hundreds, thousands, of commuters, and pretended to look at the times of trains to Croydon.

He tapped my shoulder.

'Gotcha.' He was laughing, and not in a nice way.

'Oh, hello.'

'Saw you slipping past. You can't get away that easily.'

'Why didn't you stake me out at school?'

He was standing close. He smelt different. Steve had never worn aftershave, but he definitely had something of the sort on now.

'Oh, I was going to,' he said, gazing at me, then stepping back for a look at my bump. I was self-conscious as he sized me up. 'But my bike got a puncture, and I had to ditch it and get the Tube. Only just arrived. Thought I'd get you here instead, and it worked, you must admit.'

'Yes,' I said. 'It did.'

Steve raised his eyebrows. 'Do you have something to tell me, Ms Greene? Congratulations are in order, I believe.'

To my horror, I felt myself about to cry. This was the first time anyone had said the word 'congratulations', even in jest. I blinked hard. Steve, who knew me too well, squeezed the top of my arm, and gave me time to recover.

I had known this would happen at some point, but I could have done without it being today. At home, I had a handwritten letter that I had been planning to post. It explained, courteously and with some dignity, that I was expecting a baby, that I was on my own, and that it was not his. It had taken me a lot of time and tears to write it, and I wished I had actually posted it.

'There's a letter I've written to you,' I muttered. 'Yes, I am having a baby. No, it's not yours. I'm sorry I didn't get to you before the gossip factory did.'

He touched my shoulder, with unexpected tenderness. 'Liz,' he said. 'You don't have to do this on your own.'

'Yes I do.'

'You can tell me if it's mine. I'll do everything I can to help you. It might end up being an unconventional set-up, but that doesn't matter.'

I forced myself to look into his face. He looked sincere. I was desperate to say yes, to accept his help. For a fraction of a second, I considered doing it, pretending. No one would ever need to know the truth.

'I wish it was yours, Steve,' I said, quickly. 'But it's the result of a stupid drunken one-night stand. I've been trying to track down the father but as far as I can tell, they've disappeared. It was never someone I was going to see again. In fact, the idea of seeing them again makes me heave. We weren't exactly good together.'

Steve was looking at me, hurt and dubious.

'What is he – married?' he asked.

'Umm. Something like that.'

'Lizzy, I can't tell if you're telling the truth. Do you think that no father is better than a gay father? Is that it? I know I hurt you, but don't push me away out of pride. We can still do this together somehow. We were never going to have kids, but . . .' He tailed off.

I was angry again.

'No!' I struggled to keep control of myself. 'I wanted it to be yours. I wasn't completely sure until the dating scan. Even though I knew it probably wasn't, because of the circumstances, I still hoped it would be yours. That's how fucking bad things are right now. I'd rather have a baby with *you*, the twat who was too spineless to tell me that he was gay, the arsehole who brought a teenage boy *into my bed*, than be in my current situation.

And that is bad.' I stopped. All I could hear was the sound of feet rushing past.

'Yes,' he said mildly. 'It doesn't sound good.'

I looked at Steve and wished he would renounce homosexuality. Bisexuality would do, if he decided he wanted me again. I would take him back like a shot. For a moment, I wondered whether to tell him everything. Before I could decide, he grabbed my shoulder and gripped it tightly, almost violently. He looked fiercely into my eyes. People strode around us, seeing nothing but an obstacle in the line between them and the correct platform.

'Only you know,' he said, 'but I just want to say this, and you can't interrupt. If it was my baby, and by my recollections, there must be a chance that it could be, then you could tell me, and I'd help you out as much as was needed. With the money side of things. It would be weird, but I would do my best. I don't think I'd be disastrous. And if it isn't mine, and if you're sure of that, then of course it's none of my business what you did with yourself when I left. God knows I am in no position to lecture you on that front.' He sighed, and looked away from me, into the window of W.H. Smith. 'So,' he continued, 'assuming you're right and it's this mysterious, elusive chap who did the deed, rather than me, then I still won't do anything awful to you. I mean, if that is the case, then you must stay in the flat for a while until you get your-self sorted. I'm not going to rush you.'

I frowned. 'What do you mean?'

'I mean the flat.'

I felt stupid. The ramifications of what he was really saying began to dawn on me.

'I'm paying the mortgage now,' I said quickly. 'I'll work it out and pay you back your deposit and everything you've paid while you lived there.' As I said it, I knew that this was not what he meant. Sure enough, he smiled a slippery, handsome smile.

'Lizzy,' he said softly. 'We paid five grand each as a deposit. I've been having a look at what's on the market. They go for 300K, minimum. Take off what's left of the mortgage, split the value, and we're looking at seventy grand each. More, probably. It's insane.'

'I have to magic seventy grand out of thin air to buy you out?' I was holding myself together, but only just.

He laughed softly and shook his head, as if this were nothing, a trifle. 'Not out of thin air, no. It's right there, in bricks and mortar. It's good news for you, too, Lizzy. Sell up, cash in, and put it down as a great deposit on a new place.'

I opened my mouth to reply. I wanted to shout. I wanted to tell Steve I hated him. I wanted to push him to the ground and kick him. I wanted to rope in a bunch of passing commuters to beat him up. I wanted to shout 'fuck' and 'prick' and all the swear words I knew. In the manner of the kids at school, I wanted to spit 'Your mum', a perennial favourite insult in the playground.

181

Instead, I controlled myself, and spoke icily. 'I can barely pay our mortgage on my own as it is,' I said stiffly. 'With half the equity and the same mortgage, I won't be able to buy anywhere decent. I'll still need two bedrooms.'

He shrugged. 'You'll find something. Further out of town, maybe, but you'll do it.'

'Cheers,' I said, and walked off. Every step was an effort. Every ounce of civility cost me dearly. The worst thing was the fact that I knew he was right. The flat must be worth a lot. Half of it was, indeed, his. Of course he wanted it. It was his money.

I was exhausted beyond anything I had ever known. And I was a coiled spring. I was desperate to scream at somebody.

I was at the top of the steps to the Tube when my phone rang again. It was an unfamiliar central London number. Again, I answered warily. This time, I thought, it had to be something good.

'Hi!' she trilled. 'It's me! Are you still up for looking at the flat? Because I'm in Victoria and I thought you might be around here too.'

I took a deep breath.

'Look, Helen,' I said, slowly. 'Today has not been a good day for me. If it's OK by you, I think I just need to go home and do nothing for a while. Let off steam.'

'Oh, but Liz.' She was petulant. 'You did say. It won't take long. How am I supposed to know what to do, without you there?'

'Helen.' I was trying to lay down the law, but I was too bloody tired to do anything. 'You're an intelligent woman. You can tell if it's what you want or not. Can't you? You can guess whether you'd like to live there.'

'No I can't. Remember, I come from a chateau. I don't know what you have to put up with, living in a flat in a city.'

'Go back to your stupid chateau, then. Or change the appointment. We can go at the weekend if you really think you need me there.'

She hesitated. Seconds ticked by.

'OK,' she said, sounding subdued. 'That's fine. Of course we'll do that. Are you at Victoria? You *sound* like you're in a station.'

Every fibre of my being was crying out for rest.

'Actually,' I began. My mind leapt ahead. I would tell her I was on a bus, nearly home. 'I'm on a bus,' I began.

'Oh, wow! I can see you! You're by the steps to the Tube! That's great! Don't move.'

I looked around, wondering how two people had staked me out on one station, within half an hour of each other. Then the adrenaline kicked in. I turned and ran down the steps, pushing through crowds and thankful that, at five in the afternoon, it was going to be easy to lose myself in the commuting masses. Helen was a limpet, and I didn't care that, if I ran away, I would never see her again. She was the least of my worries.

My Oyster card was in my bag. I ran towards

183

the barriers, searching for it. I felt, and cast aside, masses of school work, Rennies Rapeze tablets, tissues, gloves, a pregnancy book. No Oyster card. Instantly aware of the frustration of the people behind me, and the likelihood of outright violence, I stepped aside, opened my bag, and starting searching it in earnest. I looked at the ticket machines. There weren't many people around them. Perhaps I should just buy one. I decided, instead, to run through the barriers after someone else. I stepped forward, and felt myself pulled back, by the coat.

'Here you are!' she cried. When I looked round, exhausted, ready to cry, and slightly guilty, she was smiling her inane grin. She looked thinner than the last time I saw her, and a bit grimy. I had never seen Helen without that odd smile on her face. I imagined her staring at herself in the mirror before she left her shitty hotel, muttering, 'Come on, Helen! Sparkle!' The woman sparkled without pause. It was disconcerting.

'You thought I was down here!' she said slowly, grinning stupidly. I sighed, and didn't contradict her, even though we both knew it was untrue. 'Don't worry about the flat,' she added, as if none of this had happened. 'You're pregnant. Let me take you out for some food, or something. Have a drink. One glass of wine? Or I'll come to your place.' She was looking and sounding reasonable, but I was shattered. 'I'll cook a meal for you at your home. Or we can go to the National Gallery, or on the

London Eye. Come on. Let's get in a cab and go on the London Eye!'

I could barely speak. A glass of wine sounded tempting. It would be the first official one of my pregnancy. If 'Papa' was paying, I could handle that.

'Can we just go somewhere for a drink, then?' I asked, relenting. 'I could, actually, use a drop of alcohol.'

Half an hour later, we were in the café at what used to be the National Film Theatre, though it seemed to have been rebranded and made much shinier since I'd last visited. I was not quite sure how we had ended up there, beyond Helen's inexplicable desire to get close to the London Eye. The bar was busy, but we found a table, and we looked out at the river.

'Maybe we could see a film,' she said, brightly. The strange glint in her eye had not gone away. 'A French one even?'

I was annoyed with myself for being easily led by a teenager. 'No,' I said, grumpily. 'I don't want to.'

'That's fine.' She looked around. Her hands were shaking slightly, and she was drinking fast. She had bought a bottle of wine, and while I was nursing my one small glass, she was topping hers up every couple of minutes. 'Who are all these people?' she asked, quickly. 'Are they film buffs and things? Do you think? I mean, they look like they could be. Look at that man – he's got little round glasses like John Lennon.'

'Mmm.' I roused myself and tried to address her question. 'Some of them are probably film students.'

'And professors, I reckon. And maybe directors and things.'

'Maybe.'

'Do you think actors come here?'

'Probably. A few.' I yawned.

'So, shall we get some dinner? Or do you fancy the big wheel? Is that the kind of thing Londoners never do? Parisians never go to the Eiffel Tower.'

'No, I don't fancy it at all. I think I'll go home and make myself a sandwich. I can get a bus over there.' I pointed at Waterloo Bridge, and imagined myself flopped out on the bus. I could manage that.

If she let me go now, without complaining, it would be all right.

'Oh, but Lizzy,' she whined. 'I really, really want to treat you. What about the Oxo Tower? Or the Eye? Go on. Let's look at London together from up in the sky.'

I drew in a deep breath. Then I stood up. I could not stop myself. Most of my fury was for Kathy and Steve, but Helen was in front of me.

I watched her expression change.

'How many times can I say no?' I asked. Then it all came out. I was much nastier than I should have been. 'Will you fuck off?' I found myself yelling. I pointed at the door. 'Go on! Fuck off. That's the door, there. I don't want to see you. I don't want to look at stupid flats with you. Find

186

yourself your own hellhole to live in! Or stay where you are, with a view of a wall.' People were staring, and I was only just getting started. 'I don't care where you live, Helen. I don't know you. You're not my friend, I'm not your friend, and guess what? I don't want to be your friend. I've got things going on you know nothing about. Nothing! I can't find Rosa, Steve wants his money, Kathy hates me. Roberto and Julie have stolen my family. Then you turn up, grab me at the ticket barriers when all I'm trying to do is go home on my own, and you start off with the "Oh, let's go on the Eye! I want to treat you!" Why don't you take your daddy's money and buy yourself another friend? I don't need you. I don't want to see you, ever. You can't make friends on the internet. It isn't like that. *Leave me alone!*'

I paused for breath, and found I had run out of things to say. I looked at Helen's face, and then away again. Her mouth was open but, luckily for both of us, she was silent. I felt better, in a strange way. Before anything else could happen, I picked up my bag and left the café as quickly as I could.

CHAPTER 17

HELEN

21 March

When Liz stormed out of the bar, I just sat there. I sat still and I felt nothing. I wondered why I wasn't upset.

People had teased me before. They had talked about me behind my back, called me weird. Teachers had told me off. Mother and Papa had been exasperated with me, all my life. Nobody had ever shouted at me like Liz just did. No one had told me to fuck off. But I felt nothing. I sat calmly and finished the bottle of wine. After a while, the film people stopped looking at me.

When I stood up, I was wobbly. I made my way carefully to the door. I passed a man who said, 'Hello, darling,' but I ignored him. Men said that quite a lot, if I dressed up. I only dressed up if I was seeing Liz. Otherwise, I wore anything that came to hand. I never washed those clothes, and I didn't bother to wash my hair either. There was no point, if I wasn't seeing Liz. I was only here for her.

As I reached the glass door that led into the Film Theatre, it swung back into my face. I put out a hand to stop it, but it was heavy and hurt my wrist. In that moment, everything became unbearable.

I sobbed, without meaning to. It was loud, and sounded like someone coughing, or being sick. A few people were milling around, and the nearest ones looked at me. I walked up to someone. It was a young man, with hair that stood up on end.

'Can you tell me the way to Waterloo?' I said, as steadily as I could. I took no notice of the tears that were pouring down my cheeks. I was unable to stop a loud gulp.

He looked embarrassed, but pointed me in the right direction.

'I hope you feel better soon,' he added.

'Cheers,' I said, because that was what Londoners seemed to say.

I often cried in London. I cried because I hated it. I cried because I couldn't work it out, because I couldn't belong here. But I pulled myself together to see Liz. This was the third time I'd met her, and it was over. I had failed. I was useless. No wonder my own mother couldn't stand me.

I ran to Waterloo, desperate to go back to my flawed, familiar home, to the place where I belonged. The station was there, where he said it would be. There was an escalator that went down to the Eurostar, and I jumped from step to step, desperate to hit the bottom. I was still crying when I reached the front of the ticket queue.

'Can you sell me a ticket all the way to Bordeaux?' I sniffed. 'Can I go tonight?'

I hated her. She was my sister, but she was horrible. I hoped she was ashamed of herself. She would see how mean she was when she realised that I had gone. She was driving me out of London. That was how dreadful a person she was. I would write to her, when I got home, and tell her the truth. Then she would see what she had done.

All my stuff could stay behind. The hotel people would find it, one day, and they could keep it or sell it or burn it or something.

I got as far as passport control before I realised.

'Is there any chance,' I asked the man, 'that you'd let me through without it? I'm English and French, so I don't really need one, do I?'

The man looked at me. 'Back in the day I might have let you through,' he said. 'But we can't do things like that any more. Snowball's chance in hell, love. Sorry.'

'Please?'

'No chance.'

I tried to think. 'I'll do anything you want.'

He looked at me oddly. 'Tempting as that offer is . . .'

By the time I got back to Paddington, I was calming down. I spoke to Tom, and told him exactly what had happened.

'Stick it out,' he said.

'I can't,' I sobbed. 'She hates me. She said so.'

'She didn't say she hated you. She told you to fuck off, admittedly.'

'Several times.'

'Yes. But she's pregnant, she's in a situation that's so stressful that we can't imagine it, and she was tired. You pushed her too hard. You should have stood back and let her go home. You shouldn't have run after her at the Tube.'

'I know,' I sobbed. 'I know that now. But she was running away from me. Running away from me!'

'It's all right, H. Find yourself somewhere to live. Do it by yourself. That'll show her. You know you can. You've learned to get around London, haven't you? So you can do this. Arrange to bump into her at some point in the future. I promise you, she'll apologise. She will.'

Tom had always been the silly one. Now, suddenly, he was the fount of all wisdom. He had been convinced I was on a wild goose chase, but now he was helping me with it. I supposed, in the same way that it used to be easy for me to give Liz obvious advice, he could see the situation more clearly from a distance. He could see that I was managing, in my own way, and he thought I could do it. I tried to take some strength from that.

I decided that I would try to stay a little bit longer. London was big enough for both of us. I was not going to stay at the hotel. I would find myself somewhere else to live, and I didn't care where it was. And I would watch Liz. I would watch her all the time. She would not shake me off. I was going to stick this out.

CHAPTER 18

MARY

February 1970

She felt that she never slept any more. It wasn't usually the baby waking her. She just didn't manage to fall asleep. Everything was wrong. She had fallen into the wrong life, and she needed to get out of it. She desperately searched for ideas. It was the fact that she was stuck that kept her awake.

She was going out without the baby, quite often. Nobody knew. So far, the baby had always been all right. She wondered how she was going to feel, one day, when she came home and found a fire engine outside. The trouble was, she didn't care enough.

One February night, she lay rigidly still, and stared at the orange light of the street light outside, the pattern it made on the ceiling. The bedroom was a box, a prison. She was shut in there, with Billy, this stranger, snoring beside her. And Elizabeth, her tiny jailer, shifting around in the little bed, farting occasionally and making little sucking noises that she was supposed to find sweet.

Everything was supposed to be getting better. She had her daughter. She was a mother, and nobody was interested any more. Her parents, and Billy's parents, had a granddaughter. People were vaguely disappointed on her behalf that Elizabeth wasn't a boy. She didn't care, one way or the other. She told people often that she hadn't particularly been hoping for a boy. That was true, in its way. She hadn't wanted a girl, either. A kitten would have been fine.

Billy seemed to be working harder than usual. It felt that way, anyway. The days were strange grey things that lasted for ever. Because she didn't sleep any more, she felt that she lived in a half-night, whatever time it was. The baby slept quite a lot, in a cot next to the bed, but it woke up for a bottle every four hours or so, and in between, Mary just lay there, trying to find a way out, thinking of Kathmandu.

She knew she was unnatural. She couldn't begin to tell anybody about the way she felt. Everything was wrong and she was evil. Nobody knew that she was in the wrong life. No one could tell how she was feeling about this baby. The baby was her own flesh and blood – she knew that, in her mind, but she couldn't feel it. She couldn't feel anything towards it except resentment. She hated it more, every day. It was a horrid little bundle that made demands on her day and night, that insisted on overriding whatever she wanted to do. It cried when she was trying to nap. It took half an hour to cry itself to sleep in the cot, and sometimes the neighbour on one side banged on the wall, and at other times the other neighbour came over to tell her to rock it to sleep instead of leaving it to cry.

Mary told the neighbour that the baby still cried if it was being rocked, but in fact she never tried it, because she was scared of herself. She was beginning to realise that if she carried it around, she was going to give in to an unspeakable urge. Sometimes she had to stop whatever she was doing, to freeze and wait for the feeling to pass, because she knew that if she didn't, something awful was going to happen, and the baby would die and she would go to prison.

As she lay in bed, she tried not to think about her alternative life. If Billy hadn't got her pregnant, she would have gone travelling. She would have left him, and he wouldn't have cared, and she would be in Afghanistan or somewhere by now. If she ever escaped this life – and although she couldn't, she was going to – then she would never have sex again. If she never did it again, she could never be trapped like this again. If she only had herself to think of, she could do anything. She lay in bed and cried silent tears as she tried to work out how old she would be when Elizabeth left home, and how long it would be before Billy had an affair, and whether she would be able to get a divorce and leave the baby behind, and if so, how soon she would be able to do it.

She had £125 in an envelope. The magazine was under the mattress. The bus was due to leave in April. She was going to send off for her ticket, post an envelope full of cash. She was going to do it, as soon as she dared.

The alarm woke her, so she must have drifted off. She rolled away from Billy and pretended to be asleep as he got up and dressed in the shirt she had somehow managed to iron for him (the iron and the baby together were dangerous for her, and she could only trust herself to do it when Elizabeth was asleep, in a different part of the house). She was aware of him pacing around the room, and heard him pause by her side of the bed, and she wondered whether he could tell that she was awake. Was her breathing all wrong? Were her eyes too tightly shut?

He only stopped for a moment, then continued out of the door. Without looking, she knew that his shirt was open, that his tie was hanging over his shoulder, and that he was going to the bathroom to shave. She knew that he thought his wife should get up before him, to cook him a filling breakfast. For the moment, the baby was so young that she could get away with 'resting', but soon, she knew, he would start to pressurise her. Soon she would have to do it properly: she would have to spring up out of bed like a housewife from ten years ago, cook breakfast for her husband, wave him off to work, and devote the day to housework and the baby. This was her personal version of hell.

They were in the 1970s now. Things were supposed to be changing. There was a street in Lambeth where everyone was squatting. There was France across a tiny stretch of sea, there were mopeds, and there were people of her own age drifting around, free. There was music and there were cigarettes and there were fabulous things to wear. But scratch the surface, and there was no revolution. As a woman, she was still expected to stay at home and subsume herself. She was still nothing.

And so there was a terraced house, in a street near Brighton station. There was a man who had transformed himself from casual hippy boyfriend to boring old-fashioned husband, a man who seemed to dote on the baby, but who could barely think of a word to say to his wretched wife. He was sinking into the life his parents led because he had no idea how else they could do it. He could see how miserable his wife was – even Mary could see that he was concerned about her – but he couldn't do anything. He lacked the vocabulary, emotional and literal. As the weeks went by, Mary watched Billy becoming frustrated. She didn't care. She couldn't find it in herself to care about anything. The bus was her only lifeline. She had to be brave. She had to do it.

She lay in bed and listened to him downstairs. He had the radio on, a dull drone that was imparting the news of the day in a masculine monotone. She couldn't hear what it was saying, but she knew vaguely what it would involve. Nixon, Wilson, Rhodesia. It all washed over her these days.

She pictured him. He had shaved, buttoned up his shirt, and tied his tie. He was eating toast, slightly burned, that he had made under the grill himself. It was covered with slabs of butter and an inch of marmalade. His hair was tidy, swept into place with a wet comb. Billy had caved in and cut his hair before their wedding, under parental pressure. Once, Mary had liked the way it curled over his geometrically patterned collar. Now it was brutally short at the back and sides, and a little longer on top. His eyes had seemed gentle to her. Now they were panic stricken, and his face was closed, and he looked just like everybody else. His shirt was white. His suit was dark grey. He was twenty-six, but he might as well have been forty. The only concession to the boy he had been a year ago was a slight flare to the suit trousers.

He was picking up his briefcase. The front door opened. From upstairs, Mary sensed his hesitation.

'Bye, love,' he called softly.

She rolled over. As he banged the door shut, the baby started to stir.

CHAPTER 19

HELEN

15 April

The best way to watch her was by sitting at the station. If I got there early, at about seven, I could sit with the boy and wait. He didn't mind.

'Hiya,' he said today, and he patted the pavement next to him.

'Thanks,' I said, and I sat down, leaned back against the grimy wall, and looked at him. 'How are you?' I asked politely.

He shrugged. 'Better. Better with the weather.'

It was sunny, and not at all cold. I was pleased, because I'd got very cold some days, sitting with David. He stayed there when it was raining, and when it was icy, and even, once, when it hailed. He never asked me why I came to join him, and I never asked how he got there in the first place.

'Why don't we go into the station?' I asked, the first time it rained.

He snorted. 'You're joking! Do you think we'd last five minutes in there?'

'Why wouldn't we?'

'They'd chuck us out. Don't you even know that? You haven't been doing this long, hey?'

At first, I thought he might try to steal things from me, or ask me for money, but he didn't. He didn't seem to care about anything at all.

I began to examine everyone who came past. It was hard work, at this time of day, because there were too many of them, and hardly anyone stopped to look at us. Some did, and quite often women would give me money. They looked at me with funny 'poor you' expressions on their faces. I always gave it all to David, because he didn't look as if he had a credit card from his father.

Liz came at five to eight. When I saw her, I pulled my baseball cap over my face, and looked down at the pavement.

'There she is,' David hissed. He raised his voice. 'All right, darling? Spare us anything, love?'

Liz stopped, fumbled in her pocket, and chucked us a pound coin. I kept staring at the pavement, even though I knew she was trying to look at me. This was always the dangerous part. She moved on quickly, and I got up, smiled a goodbye to David, and followed her into the station.

I hated her and I was glad that Mother had left her. But at least I was keeping an eye on her, and, on the positive side, she had taught me how to use the Tube.

I went with her to her school, which was in a place called Pimlico. As soon as she went through the gates, I turned round and wandered away. That was my work done, for today.

I walked and walked, and ended up in St James's Park, asleep on a bench. When I woke up, there was a newspaper in a bin, next to me. It was *Loot*. I knew that this was the place to look for a flat-share, and so I picked it up, just out of curiosity.

CHAPTER 20

LIZ

21 April

'See you later then, darling,' said Anna. We kissed each other's cheeks, and I watched her saunter over the road, back home. She lived almost directly opposite. I was pleased that I'd knocked on her door and invited her for coffee. The fact that I had a pregnant, local friend made my life immeasurably better.

I bounded upstairs, ready to attack the flat. My flat was annoying me. It annoyed me with its infidelity, with the fact that it stubbornly resisted being mine alone. Until I found seventy thousand pounds, half of it would be devoted to Steve.

I pushed the vacuum with a grim determination. No dirt, dust or grime was going to survive this campaign. I was on a mission to make the place spotless. I would make it pay for the fact that it still belonged to Steve. The housework had been neglected for months. It would be neglected no more.

The radio was on, at a high volume. When I switched it on, on the dot of eight o'clock, every station wanted to tell me about a car bomb in Baghdad. It had taken several minutes to locate loud dance music from the nineties. The music took me back to an era when nothing had really mattered to me. It was an innocent era, both for me and, I thought, for the world. Back then, we were worried about the rainforests. The very idea made me nostalgic. Now we were worried about survival.

As I went on, I almost began to enjoy myself. Cleaning was turning out to be rather therapeutic. I patted my baby, who jabbed me back, and redoubled my efforts.

When the floors were clean, I got to work on the junk. As I worked, I decided that the cluttered bohemian aesthetic was outdated. When I could, I would get rid of the bits of mosaic and the black candlesticks. I would change the overly exuberant pictures on the walls. I would paint each room in tastefully neutral colours, perhaps frame some Hopper prints. The red walls in the sitting room gave me a headache. This was like a student house. I would make it different, better. The sitting-room walls, for instance, would be transformed if they were a pale green. The kitchen would look much better white than it did in blue and yellow. This flat needed to become my home, mine and the baby's. Not Steve's. Not a place where two silly, deluded people had wasted the best years of their lives with a love that turned out to mean nothing. It needed to be a grown-up place, somewhere that would shelter a funny little family.

I was aware that my ideas of what a home should look like had been formed entirely by cheaply made television programmes. This was depressing. It was sad to realise that I didn't have an original idea of my own, but I would do what I could.

The realisation that I couldn't change a thing hit me in the stomach. There was no way I was going to be able to afford to do anything so frivolous, ever. Every penny counted, from now on, and I was going to have to move house, so I could give Steve his money.

By the time I reached the spare room, I was fuming. I was often fuming, these days. Occasionally it worried me, but mainly I liked it. It gave me the strength to carry on. I pushed the door open with some trepidation.

'It wasn't meant to be like this,' I wailed aloud as I surveyed the junk. For the past six months, whenever I found anything I didn't want to look at or deal with, I had thrown it into the spare room. There were a lot of bits and pieces that belonged to Steve. There were clothes that no longer fitted me. There was a heap of Steve's post.

'It was meant to be different,' I whispered. I patted the baby. 'You were meant to be his.'

I cleared a space and sat down on the floor. For a moment, I allowed myself to be weak. I put my head in my hands and sniffed. Then I stopped.

'Pull yourself together,' I told myself crossly. That was what I would have said to a fourteen-year-old girl snivelling in a class. It worked on them, occasionally.

There was something odd under the bed, and the whole room smelt weird.

Nervously, I went closer. It took me a while to realise that I was looking at the green, powdery remains of two pumpkins. They had been silently disintegrating in perfect tandem with my life. It took three plastic bags, and much retching, before I was rid of them. The carpet would never completely recover.

The rest of the Halloween paraphernalia was scattered around the tiny room. I couldn't remember throwing it in there, but I supposed I must have done it in a rage, sometime after the dreadful night. There was a half-burned Halloween candle stuck on top of the curtain rail. Drink must have been involved, or I would never have thrown it so far.

I bagged up Steve's things, binned his pants, socks, and odds and ends, and put the rest of his clothes aside to take to the charity shop. I threw away the stupid witch's hats. I snapped the plastic Halloween-themed champagne flutes. I was mortified all over again when I recalled the way I had chased the boy, Miles, out of the flat, thinking he was a girl.

Years ago, in a different lifetime – a lifetime of heterosexuality and growing old together – we had painted the spare room walls purple. I had regretted it ever since. The day we did it, I looked at the finished effect, and shook my head.

'It's rubbish,' I announced. 'It's dark and spooky. Bad things would happen in here.'

But Steve shook his head. 'It's funky,' he told me firmly, and I shrugged my shoulders, as if in agreement, because I didn't want the hassle of changing it.

Now I decided that I could probably afford a tin of cream paint to make it nice for the baby. It was a small room, but it would be sunny, sometimes, when I changed the colour. When I half-closed my eyes, I could picture a cot in the corner. It was impossible not to be excited, at odd moments like this.

In the meantime, I was trying to be realistic. I was facing an enormous financial crisis, and I needed to use whatever means I had available to claw back a bit of cash from this flat. It was not a nice idea, but I was going to have to face it.

I tidied up my own bedroom, which took a long time. There were clothes and cups and crumby plates everywhere. I held the picture of my mother for a moment, and stroked her face with my thumb. I would have given anything for a memory of her, for the concept of a mother's love. I pushed away the bitterness, the sense of rage at the unfairness of it all. Perhaps now that I was having my own baby, the pain that I had so carefully hidden away for all my life might go away. It had taken me until I was twenty-six before I could even manage to have my dead mother's photograph on display. I had propped up her grandchild's scan pictures next to her. I wondered whether she had any idea.

I made the bed, pulling out all the creases and lumps, even though I knew no one would see my bed but me. Nobody, apart from the baby, and my poor mother, would see it for years. I tried not to dwell on that unpleasant truth.

CHAPTER 21

HELEN

28 April

I was still living in hostels when I went to see the flat in Kentish Town. This, I thought, was a masterstroke. It had been right there, the first one I looked at when I took *Loot* out of the bin in the park. 'Small bedroom with single bed and wardrobe,' it said. 'Kentish Town. Sharing with two females and one male.' I ignored the rest of the advert, the bit about washing machines and bills, and went to a phone box to arrange to have a look at it.

I arrived early, as I didn't have anything else to do, and sat down to chat to David for a while.

'Sorry, mate,' he said, after a bit, 'but no one's giving us anything with you sat here.'

I realised he was right. I was dressed as I hoped an appealing flatmate might look, in a pink cotton top and a pair of tight jeans, with high heels. They almost hadn't wanted to serve me, in Whistles, as I looked like a homeless person when I wandered in, but I persuaded them with my poshest English voice. I'd even had my hair done again, so I was properly blonde, and rootless, for the first time since That Night with Liz.

I gave David a ten-pound note, and kissed his cheek. I regretted that part straight away, as he smelt bad. I knew all about smelling bad. That morning, I'd queued for ages for a shower.

The flat was round the corner from Matt's café. I checked the patrons carefully through the window, then went in.

Matt was standing there, dressed all in black, looking at me and nodding.

'Have a good look before you make your decision,' he said. 'An excellent strategy.'

'I was just seeing if I knew anyone in here.'

'And you do that from the outside?'

I shrugged instead of answering. There was something else I wanted to talk to him about.

'You know that sign in your window?' I began.

A week later I was sitting at the kitchen table, in the flat, in north London. The kitchen was the only communal room in the house, and as well as an old table and four chairs, a sofa was crammed in by the window. Battered old kitchen units and an ancient cooker ran down one wall, and I didn't think it was big enough for one person, let alone for Angelika, Ewa, Adrian and me. Luckily, I never cooked. That took some of the pressure off.

I lived in a flat. I lived in London. I was so excited that I said it out loud to myself many times every day.

I sat at the table and opened a letter. I knew who it was from, because he'd told me to expect it, and I knew what it would say. All the same, I was nervous. I scanned it. Everything was there.

'Oh, Helen, Helen, Helen,' I said. It was funny that I was talking to myself, out loud. That was the kind of thing I did, these days. Now that I lived in a flat. Actually, it was the kind of thing I'd done when I lived in hostels, too, except that I'd done it more. 'Oh, Helen,' I said, again. I leaned over and banged my head on the kitchen table, for comic effect. I giggled again.

'You OK?'

Adrian was standing in the doorway, smiling. He was the nerdy one. I knew this because that was how he had introduced himself. 'Hello,' he'd said. 'I'm Adrian, the nerdy one.' I think he meant that he worked in computers, for some big dull company. He wore glasses with invisible frames, so it looked as if he balanced two metal sticks on his ears for no particular reason.

I wanted to shrink away, but I steeled myself and stayed in character. The only way I was getting through this sudden change was by acting. For every moment of every day, I was in character as a kooky, happy French girl. If I pretended hard enough, I could almost believe I was someone else. It was getting easier as I went along. There was a strange sort of cachet to be had from being French. I hadn't expected that.

Adrian was nothing to me, so I had nothing to

lose if he thought I was an idiot. The same applied to everyone in Great Britain, apart from Liz, and I hadn't seen her for thirty-seven days.

I blessed him with my sparkly smile.

'Yes thanks,' I told him. 'I'm fine.' I tried to think quickly. What, I wondered, would the adorable foreign flatmate in a Hugh Grant film say at this point? 'You'll have to excuse me,' I improvised. 'I'm just . . . I'm coming to terms with the fact that I seem to have accepted a job, and I'm not at all sure I want it!' I laughed my new, tinkling laugh. This, I thought, was good. It was less scary for him than anything else I could have said.

I pushed the piece of paper across the table.

'Mind if I . . . ?' Adrian asked, and I shook my head, still grinning. He sat down. He was tall and lanky, and his light brown hair was bushy and rather wild. His breath smelt strongly of tooth-paste: I could almost name the brand, from across the table.

I struggled to understand his voice, because he was from Birmingham.

'. . . Pleased to offer you the position of wait-ress, immediate start,' he read. 'Café Lumière? Up the road? Handy. What's the problem?'

'Well, in a way you could say that there isn't one.' I giggled 'They had a sign on the door saying "help wanted". I went in and asked. Matt gave me a form to fill in and now I have a job.'

He laughed. 'And a job is precisely what you've been after. So the headbanging is because . . . ?'

I ran through a few potential answers in my head, as quickly as I could. Because I've never had a job before. Because I am amazed and incredulous that I have succeeded at something. Because now, soon, Liz, whom I love and hate, will have to speak to me again and I'm scared.

Because I know I will mess it all up and be fired within a week and I don't want the nice barman to hate me.

The last sounded all right.

'The headbanging, Adrian, is because I've never had a bar or waitress job before and I'm sure I'll get everything wrong and that the nice man will fire me.' I looked at him and realised that he didn't want to know that I thought the manager was strangely handsome and that he made me nervous, so I carried on, quickly. 'It's my friend Liz's favourite bar,' I added. 'So that's good.'

'And of course it's a local for us,' he said, looking casually into the windowpane and straightening his tie. 'So I'll come and order a bevy or two off you as well. And I promise not to complain about the service even though I'm sure French girls have no idea how to pour a decent pint.' He smiled, and I saw that this was a joke.

I was getting by. This was the only way I could survive in London. I was partly modelling myself on the popular girls from school. These girls had never spoken to me, but when they were around people they wished to impress, particularly boys, they shone and sparkled and giggled. They twirled

211

their hair around fingers and looked up, like Princess Diana, through their eyelashes.

I tried it now, to take my character further. I twiddled a strand of hair, and chewed my lower lip, as I looked at Adrian with what I hoped were wide, appealing eyes.

'That would be nice,' I said, attempting a sweet voice. 'Moral support would be lovely. It's a very busy place and I'm not at all sure what to expect. I know I'll screw it up. I mean, you know how new all of this city life is to me.'

He looked at me with something strange in his eyes. *He likes me*, I realised. *This stupid act is actually working*. I wanted to tell Tom, straight away. It's easier than we imagined it could possibly be. It works on Adrian. Now I just have to make it work with Liz.

'You'll be fine, Helen,' he said, and he actually reached out and touched my arm. 'They'll love you. You're so bubbly. You'll make a brilliant barmaid. *And* you're French.'

The flat was dingy and cold, but I'd known it would be. It was cheap, and it was in exactly the right location. I was spending so much on clothes that I felt unable to put an expensive apartment on Papa's credit card bill as well. Although they wanted me to go back to France, I felt sure he wouldn't mind footing the bill for a roof over my head.

I was living on a nondescript street of big old houses, in an upstairs flat, with Adrian and two

Polish girls I never saw. I was glad I had missed winter here because all the windows rattled in the breeze. I'd had to tape a long woollen scarf round the side of the window frame in my bedroom, to insulate it enough for me to sleep. My room was beyond tiny. If there was a lesser denomination of bedroom than 'small single', it would have been that. It could have been a kennel. I suspected it was supposed to be a cupboard. Apparently whenever one of the flatmates moved out, everyone moved up a room. This was the new person's room, the initiation rite, and it was always occupied by the most recent arrival. The door didn't open fully because the bed was in the way. The room was exactly the length of a single bed, and less than double its width. I was glad I didn't have much stuff. What I did have was kept in a nasty old wardrobe with peeling varnish, which blocked the end of the room and part of the window.

I could walk from here to Liz's place in six minutes, and I often did. I stood outside, a little way down the street, and made sure there was a car I could hide behind if she came out. Sometimes I would spend half an hour out there, just watching. In thirty-seven days, I had seen her more than thirty-seven times. I hadn't tried to speak to her, because, like Tom said, I was leaving her alone.

As soon as the first credit card statement arrived, the parents noticed I was in London. At first Papa

213

had threatened to come and fetch me, but I'd laughed at him (which was easy to do by email) and said that, in a city of ten million people, he would never find me (and he wouldn't have, because he wouldn't have come to look for me sitting outside Kentish Town station looking like a homeless woman). Then he said he would cancel the credit card. I asked if he would really abandon his only daughter, penniless, in Europe's biggest city. Yesterday, Papa sent one of his gruff emails.

'*Ta mère espère que tu vas bien,*' he lied. Mother didn't hope I was OK. He probably did, but only in the same way that he hoped the grapes were growing all right, or probably less. She didn't care. He was always pretending it was her who cared. If she'd cared, she would have contacted me herself, which she hadn't done one single time since I'd been gone. I was annoyed to be ignored by our mother on one side, and by Liz on the other, when I was only trying to bring the two of them together. I knew that they would thank me one day.

I imagined that day, constantly. No one had appreciated me before, but Mother and Liz were both going to thank me for this. It would be the greatest thing I had ever done.

I had almost forgiven my sister, though it was hard work. Every time I saw her leave her flat, every time I watched her walk to the Tube, I felt our connection more strongly. I was angry about the way she had spoken to me, and the anger was festering rather, but I knew I would be able to put it aside, because she was my sister, and sisters quarrelled and then made up.

Unfortunately, I looked rather like Mother. Liz, luckily for her, must have been the spitting image of William Greene. I wondered whether Liz had a photograph of Mother. If she did, would she notice that the stranger she had met on the internet, and yelled at, nastily, in a room full of film critics, bore a strange resemblance to the mother she hadn't seen since babyhood? It was, I supposed, unlikely. I didn't want her to guess. It wasn't time.

'What's your mother like?' I asked Adrian, suddenly. He was pushing a teabag around a cup of milky water with a spoon. He looked up, surprised.

'Mum?' he said. 'She's a hairdresser.'

'What's she like?'

He smiled. 'In what way?'

'Is she nice? Does she care about you? Is she friendly? Can you tell her anything?'

He laughed. 'That's a funny old list of questions.' He counted them off on his fingers. 'Yes, she's nice. Yes, she certainly does care about us. She'd send me food parcels, given half a chance, and she still does us stockings at Christmas.'

I interrupted. 'But doesn't Father Christmas do that?'

He frowned. 'Pardon?'

'Joking.'

'Right. Well, yes, she's friendly. She'd love *you*, for instance. What was the other one? Can I tell her anything? Well, let's put it this way: there are many things I've done that I have no intention of ever telling my mum about. I think that's healthy, isn't it? Why do you ask?'

I waved a hand. 'She sounds nice. Mine's hard work. That's all.'

Adrian drank his tea quickly, and struggled into an overcoat, even though he already had a suit jacket on and would, I thought, have been perfectly warm enough like that.

'Sorry to hear that,' he said. 'Righty-ho. I'm off. The world of work beckons.' He winked at me. I wasn't sure why.

I smiled at him again. 'Have fun.'

'Yeah, right. Fun. That's one word for it. What are you up to today?'

'I'm going out. I'm meeting someone for lunch, and probably doing a bit of shopping. Although I'm nearly out of money, so I shouldn't really. Not if I want to pay the rent this month.' I savoured these words. Talking this way made me sound normal. A few months ago I would never have imagined that I was in any way capable of living in London and paying rent.

'Go on. You only live once.' He paused. 'You know, I was going to ask if you wanted to meet *me* for lunch, but you're already busy.' He looked away. I followed his gaze. He was looking at the

216

hood of the cooker. I looked back at his face. 'But one of these days,' he continued, 'if you're free, you could mosey on down to Tower Hill, if you were at a loose end, and we could grab a sarnie or something?'

I twiddled my hair and beamed. 'Sure.'

He left with a smile on his face. I refilled the cafetière, and decided that I would never meet Adrian for whatever a sarnie might be. The very fact that he seemed to like me made me despise him.

I decided to walk to Liz's school. It would take ages, but that was good. She always took the Tube, but today I had all morning, and so I would go on foot. I wasn't following her, because she was already there. I closed the front door behind me, and double-locked it carefully. I set off down the road, walking briskly, looking ahead, trying to be a Londoner.

In France I felt like an overgrown child with no social graces. I was a haughty, spiky girl who lived with her parents and had no friends because it was easier to keep aloof. In London it turned out that being skinny was good. I knew that already, in a way. France, after all, is the home of women who have black coffee for breakfast and cigarettes for lunch; whose thighs are as thin and frail as most people's arms, and whose clothes hang straight down from bony shoulders and hips. But in the part of France that I knew, those women were older, and they had helmet hair and three inches of make-up. I may have been thin, but I had never equated myself with those odd creatures.

Now that I had moved into a real flat, I was dressing in clothes from the magazines every day. As long as I acted as if I wasn't lost, I rarely got into strange encounters. In fact, these days, I smiled at everyone, and everyone seemed to like me, particularly men. I smiled and edged away from comments I didn't understand, which mainly came from strange men.

I tried not to feel self-conscious, because I was wearing a very short green dress, with a pair of thick black tights, a wide belt, and a beret. I felt ridiculous, but tried not to show it. *Grazia* magazine, after all, said that this outfit was 'indispensable for the Euro-chic look', and I thought that this was exactly what I wanted.

I walked with my chin up, my mouth forced into its customary smile. David was outside the Tube, and I stopped to give him a five-pound note.

'Fuck it,' he said. 'You look different. Again.'

'I know. Thanks for being nice to me.'

He looked at the money. 'Thanks for being nice to *me*. Come back any time.'

David and Adrian were my only friends. I kept walking, strutting, wishing that I'd worn my scruffy clothes, because nobody took any notice of me at all in my jeans and tatty fleece. I could blend in anywhere.

I passed a young man in a turban. I looked at him out of the corner of my eye, fascinated by his headwear. I saw him look back, his eyes flicking down to my legs. He was wearing a long-sleeved T-shirt, and it said on the front: 'Don't freak! I'm a Sikh'. I looked at it, slightly puzzled, and looked away. Then I looked again.

He stopped.

'What?' he asked.

I looked down. 'Nothing.'

'Oh, the shirt?' he said, and smiled. 'Yeah, it is rather 2005.'

I nodded, baffled, and started walking again.

I walked through some rough areas, looking straight ahead, and approached King's Cross. Suddenly, people were everywhere. They were all around me, walking fast, hurrying to the station and away from the station. Some of them looked like they were selling drugs. Some were going to work. I passed the British Library and wished I could go in, because if I worked in there, I would be successful in some way. I saw some women who might have been prostitutes. The people were white and black and Asian, and none of them took any notice of me at all. I kept my head down and wove through the crowds, crossed the enormous, terrifying road with a lot of other people, and carried on my way. You could lose yourself in a city like this. You could be anybody. I was settling in London. I wished that I had lived in a huge city all my life.

★　　★　　★

It was an understatement to say that Liz's school was not like the International School in Bordeaux. These buildings were built from dirty red bricks, with dark slate on the roof, and high, arching windows. The grounds seemed to be dotted with boxy extra classrooms. I stood outside the gates, and stared. This was truly intimidating. I thought that lessons were still going on, because it was quiet, and I felt like an intruder. I was absolutely excluded here. As soon as I looked at the main building, my stomach clenched, and I was fifteen.

I stood out here often, and I always felt this way. Today was different. Today I was feeling good, so I was going to take it further.

The playground was concrete, with some old lines delineating some sort of games pitch that had been half worn away by children's feet. I plucked up my courage, and walked slowly in, living my own private nightmare. The moment my foot touched the concrete, I had to swallow bile that leapt into my throat. Irrationally, I was certain I was going to be consumed by the school, to be made to go to lessons, to be the odd one out in the corner of the classroom, alternately ridiculed and ignored.

I rethought my plan, and hurried back to the gates. When I got there, I wasn't sure what to do.

'Go away!' said Tom, at once. 'What the hell are you doing there? She might not like it if you jump out at her when she's at work.'

'I just want to see where she teaches,' I said

sullenly. 'The inside, I mean. I won't let her see me. I'm cunning. You know that. I watch her all the time and she has no idea. I'm brilliant at it.'

'You wish. You're loopy.'

'I'm not.'

'Are too.'

'She's our sister, that's all. I need to know all about her. For the project. So that if it doesn't work out, at least I can tell Mother everything.'

Just to show him that I could pull it off, I went in. I attached my smile, tossed back my hair, and strode across the playground.

I never fitted in at school. It had not worked for me. I had never known what to say. Occasionally someone gave me a chance, or a new girl attached herself to me before she knew better. When this happened, I would try my best to hang on to the potential friend, but it never worked. They always hurried off to join the crowd, and laughed about me from a distance. Everyone else had the indefinable quality that I lacked. I had no idea what it was. Still, apparently these days I seemed to be better at getting away with it.

School, to me, meant being alone and trying to pretend it was because I was a loner. Tom never had my problems. He had hundreds of friends. Everyone wanted to be with him, to be in his gang. He hardly even seemed to notice his popularity. He took it for granted. He had also never mentioned the fact that I existed outside all the little groups of friends in my year. I wanted him to think that I preferred my own company. I needed him to believe that I was that way because I was bored by the rest of them, with their fashions and their cliques. I never knew whether he believed it, or whether he could see through me. I had no idea whether he knew that I was desperate to be friends with the rest of them, but that I could never find the right words to say.

Now, all of a sudden, I was back at school. Not only that, but I was probably trespassing.

A black boy came out of a side door, and sloped across the playground. He looked around, furtively. I looked straight ahead and walked more purposefully towards what looked like the main entrance. I knew I was shaking, and thrust my hands into my big pockets to hide my fear.

'All right?' asked the boy. I looked over to him. He was about ten metres away from me, and had pulled his hood aside to look at me. I nodded.

'Yes, thanks,' I answered, trying to keep the tremor out of my voice.

He smiled a slow smile. 'You a teacher then?' he demanded, looking me up and down. I was conscious of my hemline.

I shook my head. 'No. Well, probably not.' I improvised. 'I might get some work as a French assistant.'

He laughed. 'Yeah? First sexy Sandrine and then you? I like their methods, I have to say. I like their methods.'

I knew I shouldn't say it, but I did anyway. 'Do you know Miss Greene?' I asked primly.

He was looking at me hard, and I was uncomfortable. He must have been at least three years younger than I was, but he was a lot bigger.

'Lizzy Greene?' he asked. 'Yeah. I know her.'

'You like her?' I said, trying to copy his London accent. 'Is she . . .' I nearly said 'cool', but suddenly feared the word would reveal me to be its opposite. 'Is she OK?' I asked, neutrally.

'Oh, she's OK. She's OK, man. You know she's having a little baby?' He looked at me. 'Hey, I bet you know who's the daddy!'

I bit my lip. 'I don't, actually. Probably her ex, though.'

'So how do you know her? Because of Sandrine?'

I nodded. 'That's right. Because of Sandrine.'

He looked back at the building, and seemed anxious to head off. 'Well, good luck, Miss. I wish I still did French, for sure.'

As I edged closer to the school, a high-pitched beeping noise began to sound. I jumped, and looked around, scared. I had been identified as an intruder. I was about to flee as fast as I could when, abruptly, people were everywhere. Pupils poured out of the doors. I forced my way in, relieved to be invisible now that there were bodies all over the place.

The floors inside were Formica tiled. The building smelt of school, of officialdom and paper and bodies. There were teenagers everywhere. I stuck

223

to the sides of the corridors. I wanted to run away, and it was only by reminding myself that I was twenty years old and that nobody was going to corral me into a group of bitchy teenagers that I managed to keep going.

I almost walked into a miserable-looking girl who was slinking along slowly, trying, like me, to be invisible, while everyone else thundered around, their conversation echoing off the gloss-painted walls.

'Hello,' I said, recognising a fellow outcast. 'Where's the staffroom, please?' I wondered, as I said it, what I was doing.

The girl looked at me for a moment. She had attempted to put on make-up, but her mouth just looked as if she had been drinking red wine. Her skin was white and pasty, and she needed to wash her hair. Her shoulders slumped as she considered my question. After a few seconds she seemed to reach a decision.

'That way,' she whispered, pointing in the direction I was already going.

'Just that way?' I asked. She could have been me, five years ago. Looking at her made me feel confident. She could barely bring herself to speak. 'Or do I have to go anywhere when I reach "that way"?'

'Get to the front hall,' she muttered, looking down at her shoes. 'Door on the left.'

'Thanks. That's really helpful.'

'Yeah, sure.'

'I mean it.'

'Right.'

'Really.'

'Mmmm.'

She sidled off, looking miserable. I was filled with a new energy. This was exciting. I was in Liz's world and every detail of it mattered. I looked around, drinking in everything about Liz's day-to-day life. She walked in these corridors. The danger of being there thrilled me.

I was alert as I edged along the corridor. I found the 'front hall', checked it from round the corner like somebody in a detective thriller, and established that it was free of Liz.

The children I passed were looking at me, and I knew I hadn't dressed properly. I should have tried to look sensible. As it was, my bottom was almost on display, and everyone stopped to stare, to wonder who had come to school without a skirt on.

I could see a heavy wooden door with a sign saying 'Staffroom' on it.

I strode over, feeling weirdly invincible, and raised my hand to knock. Then I lowered it. I had no idea why I was here. If Liz saw me, she would freak out. She would scream at me again. I was ready to run. For some reason, though, I stayed.

Teachers rushed past, in and out of the staffroom, and none of them even looked at me. I stood to one side and watched. It was good to know where my sister was, when she was at school.

After a few minutes, a slim black woman wearing a huge cardigan and a long floral skirt stopped next to me, with a little frown.

'Can I help you?' she asked, clearly unable to place me as either teacher or pupil.

I was scared, yet grateful. 'Um, I'm not sure,' I said, rolling back on to my heels. 'I'm looking for—' I stopped myself. 'Sandrine,' I substituted, at the last moment.

She peered at me, looking curious. 'Are you? Don't look so worried. I think Sandrine's around. Are you a friend?'

'Not exactly.' I was mortified that she thought I looked scared. Hurriedly, I smiled. 'A kind of friend of a friend, I suppose.' I made a leap of faith. 'Sandrine teaches French, doesn't she?'

The woman frowned again. 'Yes.'

'Well, I'm French. I wondered if she might need a language assistant or something.'

'You don't sound French.' She looked me up and down. I was cripplingly aware of how short my dress was, and how tight. 'You look it, though.'

'I'm bilingual. French father, British mother.'

At this, she smiled. 'Impressive. So you're not a sixth former? I must admit, that's what I thought when I saw you. I'm Kathy. Maths teacher. I'm a friend of Sandrine's. She hasn't got the budget for an assistant, and it's not up to her, anyway. But come on in and we'll have a look around for her.'

I was giddy. This was Kathy, the woman who

had told my sister to abort her baby. I was right inside Liz's life. I was paying her back for being mean to me. Kathy seemed nice, and I decided Liz was probably exaggerating. In fact, I felt a kinship with Kathy. We had both fallen out with the same person.

As I was about to step, with some trepidation, into the staffroom, the door flew open, and Liz stepped out. She was frowning, and staring straight ahead. I gasped, and hid behind Kathy, who stepped backwards and trod on my foot.

'Sorry,' she said, turning with raised eyebrows. She looked at Liz's departing back. Liz had not even glanced at either of us. Instantly, the danger was over. 'Some people.'

'Right.' I couldn't say anything about Liz, because I didn't want Kathy to know that I knew her, let alone that we were family. I couldn't even hint to Kathy that I knew everything that had happened between them.

'Still, the atmosphere tends to lighten in here when she's out. So, welcome to our happy haven.'

I followed her, almost on tiptoes. The big room was messy and busy. There were adults everywhere, some in suits, most of them dressed semi-formally. There were notices all over the walls, including five or six posters about the Iraq war, a row of mainly unhealthy pot plants along the window sill (though one was flourishing and had grown almost up to the ceiling), and chairs pulled into clusters. At first nobody seemed to notice me, and then, after a few

227

seconds, I saw that some of the men were looking at my legs.

'Yeah,' said Kathy, as she pushed past a man in his twenties who was wearing a suit and a purple tie. 'She's got legs. She's French.'

He looked anxious. 'Not a sixth former?'

'No, you're safe. Ogle away.'

'Cheers.'

I smiled at him. He smiled back. A few people chuckled, and someone wolf whistled.

By the time we found Sandrine, sitting in a corner sending a text message, I had formulated my plan.

'Sandrine,' said Kathy. 'Hi, darling. Listen, this is . . .' She turned to me. 'What was your name?'

I thought I had better lie. 'Isabelle.'

'Right. This is Isabelle. She's half French. She says you've got a friend in common or something. OK, chick? Must dash.'

Kathy left us. Sandrine was truly glamorous, in a way that I only pretended to be. Her hair was expensively cut and coloured, and her clothes and make-up were more grown up than mine. She was like Juliette Binoche.

'*Tu es française?*' she asked, smiling. 'Do we share a friend?'

I nodded, and slipped into French. 'I'm not sure. Are you Sandrine Dupouy?'

She smiled and shook her head. 'Not quite. Sandrine La Salle.'

I put a hand to my mouth and looked mortified,

which was not difficult. 'Oh, I'm so sorry,' I said quietly. 'I thought you were someone else. A friend of my sister's I was supposed to look up in London. Sorry.'

To my surprise, she believed me.

'Hey, don't worry about it. Have a seat, anyway. How long have you been over here?'

We chatted for a while, and I was pleased, because I knew that Sandrine was Liz's friend, and had stayed friendly with her after she fell out with Kathy. I was, however, extremely nervous. As we talked, I couldn't stop my leg jiggling about. After ten minutes, I could stand it no longer. I stood up.

'Thanks for being so friendly,' I said, politely. 'I'd better go now, and let you enjoy your hard-earned break.' I looked towards the door. Liz could come back at any moment. I was suddenly certain that she was on her way. There was no way I was going to be able to explain myself if she saw me.

'Sure. Here, this is my card. Give me a call or a text sometime if you like. I can't give you any paid work, but if you could come along sometime to chat to the kids . . . ?'

I smiled. 'Of course. Thank you.' I couldn't wait to get out. For a second, I seriously considered leaping through a part-open window, landing in the playground, and running. Instead, I started to edge towards the door.

'Take care.'

'Bye.'

I looked down as I walked, longing to be out of this room. As I passed, the young man in the purple tie touched my arm.

'Hello,' he said.

I looked at him. 'Hi,' I replied, and carried on walking.

'Hi. I'm Ben,' he offered. He was smiling, and I knew we had an audience.

'Isabelle,' I told him. I wished I really was Isabelle.

'Are you working here, or what? I teach geography.'

'No, I'm not working. Sorry, but I have to go now.'

'That's a shame. Will you be back?'

'Probably.' I looked to the door, terrified. 'Nice to meet you, Ben. Sorry. Bye.'

I walked away, ignoring him. I caught a few smiles between other teachers, but I tried not to look at anyone in case they spoke to me. When I was nearly at the door, it opened.

Elizabeth Greene came in. This time, she scanned the room. I turned quickly to the wall and pretended I was reading a poster.

'NOT IN MY NAME,' it said. 'Come and demonstrate against the WAR CRIMINAL Bliar. HANDS OFF IRAQI OIL.' 'Don't attack Iran,' read the one next to it. My heart thumped. I clenched my hands. She was less than a metre behind me. I was paralysed. I couldn't breathe. I heard her footsteps passing. She hesitated. I tried to think of a plausible explanation, but my mind was blank. I could hear her breathing. I clenched my teeth, my stomach, everything. I closed my eyes.

When I thought she had gone, I looked cautiously to where she had been, then walked straight out of the door, and closed it gently behind me. I had never felt this excited before. The whole experience had been strangely exhilarating.

CHAPTER 22

LIZ

8 May

When the buzzer sounded, I surprised myself by being ready, and surprised myself more by being in unusually good spirits. I lolloped downstairs.

Dad and Sue were on the doorstep. Dad's eyebrows were raised: this was their default position. He was always ready to be mildly surprised by something, and I had no idea what it was this time. Possibly, my visibly pregnant stomach. Sue was beaming at me, and holding a bunch of gerberas.

I stared across the road, distracted, briefly, by a figure over there. When I looked, though, there was no one. That had happened a few times lately. I shook my head. Then I noticed that Julie was standing behind Sue, trying to look as if she wasn't there. She looked as if she wanted to see me about as much as I wanted to see her.

'Hello!' I said gruffly, pushing back my hair. I had not invited Julie. I didn't want her in my house. My mood swung abruptly from sunny to stormy. I was livid at the idea that Sue wanted me to be friends with her just because we were both having babies. I almost said as much, but bit it back.

'Hi, Dad,' I said instead, giving him a kiss. He hugged me close, which was unusual for him, and I was touched. 'Hello, Sue!' I continued, knowing that I sounded too enthusiastic. 'Wow, those are gorgeous flowers. Come on in. Oh,' I added. 'Julie! This is a nice surprise.' I glared. At least I had my own home, precarious though it might be. At least I wasn't sponging off my in-laws, and not just because I didn't have any. I radiated that fact to her through the medium of the scowl as I ushered her past me, into the hallway, and watched her back follow Dad and Sue through the door to my flat and up my stairs. She was waddling. I hoped I didn't waddle. I did my best to walk elegantly, like a model.

When I caught up, closing doors behind me, I found the three of them standing in the kitchen. Dad was nodding to himself and looking around. Sue had already found a vase for the flowers; it was my only vase, a purple and pink striped one that she gave me years ago. Julie was sitting down. I gave her a hard stare, and she avoided my eye. She looked as miserable as she always did. I looked at her middle, critically. Her bump was bigger than mine, though she was due three weeks later. Her hair was loose and lank and, while her nose was red, her face was pale. I was pleased to see that she wasn't blooming either. Anna was in full, lustrous bloom, and that was quite bad enough.

'Well, you look absolutely lovely, Lizzy.' Sue knew she had to be the one to speak, because nobody else was ready to say anything. Suddenly, I wished that it was just Dad and me here. We would have been able to talk. He had always reassured me.

Sue continued. 'In fact, you're blooming. Don't you think, darling?' she added, nudging Dad. Sue was wearing purple glittery eye shadow. She took a candle from her handbag and lit it. 'For peace and concentration,' she said quietly. She put it on the table, next to the vase. A sickly smell instantly permeated the room.

'Well, very much so,' Dad muttered, looking around the room for someone who might rescue him from pregnancy talk.

'We brought Julie with us,' Sue added. 'Because the two of you have so much in common. It's wonderful, these two little souls arriving in the family at the same time. And of course you two girls don't really know each other yet, but the babies will be cousins. It's about time you had a good old natter.'

I wondered why Sue was doing this. I knew she had mixed feelings about Julie. No woman in the world could ever be good enough for Roberto. I looked hard into her face, narrowing my eyes until she half smiled and turned away.

'Liz!' she said.

I drew in a breath. I knew I was horrible, but I couldn't help it.

'I wanted to see my dad,' I said rudely. 'If I'd wanted to be friends with Julie, I'd have rung her up and said so. If she wanted to see me, she could have done the same.'

'Oh, how tempting,' Julie muttered. I ignored her.

'But you just have to interfere, don't you? You can't let me do anything my way. My baby's going to come second to your grandchild, and to add insult to injury you're trying to turn us into the fucking Waltons. Now that Julie's here, she'll have to stay, but for Christ's sake, Sue, why do you always have to do things like this? You're not even my mother.' I said it quite calmly, and was pleased that I was managing not to shout. All the same, I was incensed.

Sue had been waiting for me to finish. 'Oh, for heaven's sake, Lizzy. Listen to yourself!' She looked at Julie. 'This is what I had to put up with when she was a teenager. All the time, I tell you. Look, we know you don't mean it. You can say what you like to me. It's water off a duck's back. But you owe Julie an apology.'

I huffed a bit. I looked at Dad. He rolled his eyes at me, which meant that he agreed with Sue.

'Don't mind me,' Julie said quickly. She stood up. 'I'll just go. That would be the best. I'm not going to stay where I'm not bloody welcome. I'll see you at home.'

Sue and Dad both looked at me. I sighed.

'Don't go, Julie,' I said. Then I tried to say it again, as if I meant it. 'Sorry. Please don't go. I'm horrible at the moment. I'm so moody. I made three children cry at school last week. I've lost all my friends. I lost one the other week by going off on one when she hadn't done anything. I didn't mean to be nasty. Look, sit down. Have a drink.'

She didn't look at me. 'I'd really rather leave,' she said, in her usual monotone. 'I'm not some stupid charity case, you know. I don't actually want to be Liz's friend.'

Sue shook her head. 'No. You're staying,' she said. 'Let's get everyone a drink. Have you got any incense? The right incense would calm us all down.'

I looked at Julie, and caught her trying not to laugh. That was good enough. I sat down next to her.

'There's some nice lemonade in the fridge,' I said

'Good for growing babies,' Dad said hurriedly. He busied himself getting drinks. Dad had always been surprisingly skilled in the kitchen when he put his mind to it. He used to impress my school-friends by whipping up bananas, ice cream and chocolate powder into everyone's favourite milk-shakes. When he remembered, he would cook dinner for the two of us and it would be better than anything we had at restaurants. When he forgot, I fetched myself a bowl of cereal.

'Two glasses of lemonade,' he said, passing them to Sue, and he looked around to see what else he could do.

'Thanks,' I said, addressing him, beyond Sue. 'Sorry,' I added, talking to Julie. I swallowed my pride. 'Sorry, Sue,' I added. I hated apologising to her. I was thirteen all over again. I reminded myself that I needed to apologise to Helen, too. Anna thought I shouldn't bother, because she said 'she sounds like baggage and no good', but I knew that I had been in the wrong. If Helen had just turned up on the doorstep or something, I would have been reasonably pleased to see her, but then again, I supposed she didn't know where I lived.

'That's OK,' said Julie, with a little tut. 'Hormones, I guess. We've all got them.' She was being distant, and all of a sudden I wanted to be her friend, after all.

'How are you doing, Julie?' I asked, as brightly as I could.

She leaned back. 'Bollocks, really,' she said, in her usual monotone. 'I don't know about you, but I've got piles like you wouldn't believe.'

I was taken aback. 'Oh,' I said. 'I've escaped those, so far. Lucky me. How did your twenty-week scan go?'

'Yeah, s'all right,' she said. 'Everything in the right place, they said.' She looked up and raised her eyebrows. 'Saw a willy.'

'You're having a boy! That's great.'

'What about you?'

237

'I didn't find out. The scan went fine though.' I had to leave it at that. The second scan had broken my heart. I looked at my baby, and was felled by a sudden deep longing for my own mother. The glimpse into the abyss of my loss – the loss of the only person who would have looked at me and felt like I felt, seeing my baby – had knocked me out, and I was not sure I would ever recover. It had also confirmed the dates. There was no chance that Steve had fathered this baby.

I decided not to share any of this with Julie.

'So, what do you think you're having?' asked Julie, without much interest.

'Umm. A baby?' I felt years away from giving birth. 'Dad, are you all right over there? There's pasta in the fridge and a tomato sauce in the pan. Not very original, I'm afraid.'

'Fine,' he said, with a cheery smile. 'Never better. Leave it to us.'

I shrugged, and capitulated. Being looked after was an unusual and comforting experience.

Strangely, I managed to relax for the first time in months. I pretended the sauce was homemade, even though I'd bought it in a little plastic tub from Waitrose and added cream for authenticity. I was not sure why I was lying about it, but everyone said it was delicious, and that made me feel good. I knew I was pathetic, and I knew I ought to start to cook properly, but I could never be bothered. I should have been shopping at Lidl, not Waitrose. My finances had the illusion of being shaky but fine, but I was like a cartoon character who has run off the edge of a cliff. Everything was about to crash to earth.

I drank two pints of water in quick succession, while Dad and Sue had wine and Julie finished the lemonade. The kitchen smelt of Sue's candle, and pasta, tomatoes and melted cheese. Slowly, I relaxed. It was good to have company. I realised that these people, who all shared a home with each other, had no idea what loneliness was like. They had known it, but they didn't any more. They ate together every day. Steve and I had done that, and now I fended for myself, and so, possibly, did he.

I still thought about him all the time. That was my guilty, pathetic secret. I was carrying a transsexual's baby, and pining covertly for my gay ex-boyfriend. I thought I would concentrate on Julie and try to forget about all that.

'Are you going back to work?' I asked. I realised I knew nothing about her. '*Do* you work?' I added, trying hard to remember whether she had ever talked about a job.

'Yeah, I work for a couple of hotels in Brighton,' she said, 'but it's only casual. You know I'm an accountant?' I nodded, although I didn't. 'Well, I do their books. But I'm self-employed so I get no maternity leave and certainly no one's going to be paying me for not working. I haven't really got my act together to work properly. I've just been doing what I've had to to get enough money for the two of us to get by.'

I looked warily at Sue, who was pathologically averse to any perceived criticism of her only-born.

'Is Roberto working?' I asked, quietly and innocently. I saw Sue look at me, and quickly look away again. She had not forgiven me for being rude, and now she was watching me hawkishly.

'Yes,' said Julie, and I thought she was wary too. 'He's got some shifts at the local retail emporium.'

Sue butted in. 'We can't all be teachers and accountants,' she said, in a gentle manner that belied the underlying ferociousness. 'So yes, for the moment, Roberto's helping out at Sainsbury's. It's just as a stopgap, just until he gets himself straightened out. He's doing it to make sure he's supporting his son.'

'Good for him,' I said, as casually as I could. I hoped I didn't sound sarcastic.

Soon afterwards, I addressed Julie across the table.

'Can you come upstairs for a moment?' I asked. 'I need a second opinion on the spare room walls.'

'The walls?' She heaved herself up. I looked at her trousers, which were surprisingly nice.

'Are those maternity jeans?' I asked. 'Where are they from? I've looked everywhere for good ones.'

'They're bollocks,' she said. 'They look OK, but they cut into my crotch like you wouldn't bloody believe.'

As soon as we were out of earshot, I turned to her.

'How are you getting on with Sue?' I demanded. 'Living with her! It must be hard when you're carrying her grandson.'

Julie looked miserable. I was beginning to see why this was her default expression.

'Tell me about it,' she said, in a dull voice. 'Nobody could ever be good enough for Bobby, you know that. Least of all me. And I know that once the baby comes, no one but Sue will know how to look after him. I feel like an incubator on legs. Like when he's born I'll be expected to hand him over and crawl off into a corner until next time, because my work will be done.'

'Aren't you guys going to get your own place?'

We arrived in the spare room doorway. 'Oh, look,' she said. 'This is purple. It makes me feel quite at home, living at Sue's. The House of Purple, I call it. If we got our own place I'd do it beige throughout. I see purple when I shut my eyes at night these days. Purple with silver stars.'

'I think I'm painting this one cream. For the baby.'

'Don't you want to know the sex? Then you could do it blue or pink.'

'I don't think I'm ready for that. If I knew the sex it would mean I had a son or a daughter tucked away in there. For the moment I'd just rather call it "the baby".'

'Fair enough.' Julie seemed to take a deep breath.

'Look, I'd love us to move out. Obviously.' She paused for a moment, close to tears. 'It goes without saying that there's nothing I would like more than that. I hate being the spare part, and I don't think they realise half the time that I'm even there. No one cares what I think. Well, your dad's great, but Sue rules the roost. Anyway, Bobby says no to moving out. He says we can't afford to, but it's not actually that. I can easily earn enough money to pay the rent on some little flat in Haywards Heath. He could stay home with the baby. Or Sue could help out. But Bobby doesn't want to do that.' She looked at me, and smiled a tense smile. 'Can you believe that? My boyfriend has no interest in cutting the apron strings. He prefers his mother to me.'

'But you moved to Milan together last year.'

'Mmm, and his dad was an arse. But honestly, I think he missed his mum. I think that's one of the many reasons why we didn't stick it out. Milan was amazing, but we were so far out of our depth. We didn't speak Italian. Bobby's dad wanted the two of them to be off chasing beautiful girls together. We were never going to stick it out.'

I thought about this. 'Sue and Dad's is just a little terraced house. Surely Roberto can see that you need more room?'

'No,' she said in her deadpan way. 'Apparently it's fine. Three bedrooms: one for them, one for us, and a room for the baby – what could be better? So, this one'll be a good room for the baby, won't it? When it's cream.'

I decided to try out my latest idea. 'I might get a lodger,' I told her.

Three rooms opened off the tiny landing: my bedroom, the little bathroom, and the spare room.

'It would have to be a lodger you know pretty well,' said Julie. 'I mean, you'll be living on top of each other.'

'I'm desperate for cash.'

'Be careful.'

'I know.' I sat down on the spare bed, and turned to her. 'I can't really think how I can possibly find a lodger who's guaranteed to be sane and easy to live with and non-psychotic. I'm telling myself that most people are relatively normal, and I'm going to advertise it and hope for the best.' For a moment, it seemed funny that we were here, in a small room, with our swollen bellies. 'And as for you,' I told her. 'You are going to need to force a move, you know? Because otherwise, Julie, I promise that you will be living with your mother-in-law for ever. Sue would never turn Roberto out, and Dad wouldn't make her. The only person who's going to make anything change is you. So you have to.'

'But how?' She walked over to the window and looked down at the street. 'I wish I was like you,' she said quickly. 'I wish I was brave enough to think about striking out on my own. I used to be. I never used to care about the consequences, not about what anyone thought. But I'm not brave any more. I know I can be blunt, but that's just an act. Roberto's a bit of a shield between me and the world.'

I walked over to her. She was biting her lip and staring out of the window. Again, I thought I saw movement outside.

'Was there someone out there?' I asked her.

'Yeah, there's a woman. She's gone now.'

'You said you were still married,' I remembered. 'Is it to do with that?'

Julie sighed. 'Yes, I'm married. Sue absolutely hates it, but I mention it from time to time just for the hell of it. I don't think Bobby's bothered. He understands.'

'Understands what?'

She pushed out her lower lip and blew upwards. A lock of hair flew up, then settled haphazardly on her face.

'Terry,' she said quietly. 'Even saying his name feels a bit disloyal.' She shrugged, and looked towards the open door. I closed it. 'We were very young when we met. Eighteen. That was thirteen years ago. He was the big, muscular guy in the corner of the nightclub. The one everyone wanted for the slow dance. I, believe it or not, was the most exciting girl in Leatherhead. There's an epitaph for you. The rest was history.'

'Until?'

'Well, we got married pretty quick because we were so grown up and mature,' she said drily.

'Terry was in the army. Still is. For about three years I was excited about being a forces wife. You have to understand that my friends were doing hairdressing courses or buggering about with McJobs, for the most part. So I was the winner, fair and square, when I snagged my sexy soldier and got to invite everyone to the wedding. We moved around a few bases. I hung out with the other wives a bit. It was dull as all holy shit. Terry got posted to Northern Ireland and I decided I'd had enough.'

'So you dumped him?'

'From a safe distance. Brave.'

'But you never got a divorce?'

She sighed. 'That's right. Terry, it turned out, has some issues. He's in Iraq right now. He's volatile. I worry about him. I'm not supposed to think about him because I'm with Roberto now and I'm pregnant.'

'And Terry knows that?'

She winced. 'Mmm. Not so much. He knows I'm with Roberto. I haven't told him about the baby. When I say I'm worried about him, I'm afraid that he'll lose the plot. Not that he'll go on a rampage, but that he'll do something to himself.'

'But you're going to tell him at some point.'

'You'd think so, wouldn't you?'

I was amazed, and intrigued, to discover that Julie's life was as messy as mine. Apart from anything else, until two hours earlier, if I had considered her at all, it would have been as the most boring person I knew.

'You're going to get a divorce?'

She sounded firm on this. 'Yes, but not until he's back from Iraq. It took ages for us to split up when he was in Ireland, because he thought I was being mean to keep him on his toes. I tried to convince him that I wanted out, but he'd wear me down and we'd suddenly be "trying again". We were on again, we were off again, he hated me for abandoning him when he needed support, and accused me of having no idea what he was going through out there. Which was true, but I did have enough of an idea not to want a piece of it. Lots of letters. I loved him, I didn't love him. He was all I'd ever known. In a way it was all quite exciting. Dramatic.'

'And?'

'In the end we agreed it was doing neither of us any good, so we decided to take a break. That was five years ago. We're hardly ever in touch and as far as I'm concerned the marriage is just a piece of paper I haven't managed to tear up yet. He doesn't want a divorce while he's out there living in hell, and I can't argue with that.'

'So how did Roberto come on to the scene?'

She smiled. 'I was at my lowest ebb, and there he was. A man with no career ambitions, a man who was never going to take me further afield than his dad's apartment in Milan. I didn't have the strength for any more fighting, and I didn't want to have to agonise any more. Roberto was never going to go to war. So, Roberto it was.'

I wasn't sure whether I was meant to ask, but I did anyway. 'Do you love him?'

She looked at the door warily.

'Yes, I do. When I met him, I was bowled over by how gentle he was with me. We would just hang out, talk, go to the cinema. It was exactly what I needed. There were no dramatics. And where we are at the moment, it's just a blip. I know I'm going to have to get us out of it, because there's no way I'm going through a nasty split again, and particularly not with a baby involved. So I'm going to stick it out with him, no matter what. I've made my own bed, I suppose.'

'And do you still love Terry?'

Julie smiled wanly. 'That's not something I can ever allow myself to think about.'

We looked at each other and laughed. 'Don't you wish you could get drunk sometimes?' I asked her. 'Wouldn't it be great if we could sneak off together to a bar and spend the rest of the afternoon getting off our faces, to make it all go away for a little while?'

'I bloody wish that all the sodding time,' Julie replied, fervently. 'And I spend a lot of time wondering what in Christ's name I'm doing bringing a baby into this world anyway.'

The spring was warmer than usual, and when we went out after lunch, it was actively pleasant to be walking around the streets of north London. I loved it when it was like this. The trees were in the process of unfurling their leaves. The paving stones seemed wide and clean. The people we passed did not look as if they were mired in unbearable misery. We strolled from middle-class suburbia to gritty urban landscapes that alarmed Sue (though she made a point of not showing it), and back again. I signalled to Julie to occupy Dad, and hung back next to the window of a New Age shop that had recently opened. This was in a row of shops that was in the process of being nicely gentrified. The random, scruffy places that had been there four years ago – pound shop, betting shop, dodgy burger bar – had been replaced by a dippy greetings card shop, an interior design consultancy, and this, the incense-scented horoscope emporium.

'Those candles look nice,' I told Sue. 'Look, they're zodiac ones.'

'Oh, yes,' she said, immediately interested. 'Look at them. We should pick a couple up for the babies. So nice that they'll both be Leo, if they arrive on time. Nice strong fire sign. Very loyal. Do you remember when you were young, I bought you your star chart? You were furious because you didn't want to be Cancer. You thought I'd done it to upset you, and under the circumstances, of course . . . It was stupid of me. I didn't think. But no one could complain about being Leo. In fact, have you thought about it as a boy's name? Or perhaps Leonora, for a girl?'

'Not really. We will talk about names, I promise, but not yet. I haven't given them a moment's thought.' Dad and Julie were well ahead of us, so I started walking again. 'Look, Sue,' I said. 'I'm sorry about what I said earlier. I actually like Julie a lot, and I never realised that before, so thanks for bringing her.'

She smiled. 'Good. I hoped you would. She's a meek little thing, but she's nice, in her way.'

'But Sue, are they really going to live with you? With the baby? Is it a good idea? I think you need to have a word with Roberto.'

She turned to me. Her eyebrows, which were always elegantly plucked, rose. 'Roberto? Why?' She was instantly defensive and suspicious.

I spoke quickly. 'I'm only saying this because I don't want things to go wrong. But I'm afraid that he's going to lose Julie if he doesn't get his act together. Julie wants her own home. You must understand that. You wouldn't have moved in with Dad's parents, would you?'

'But we're nicer than them. Not meaning to speak ill of your grandparents.'

'Oh, speak ill. Go ahead, be my guest. You know what I'm talking about, all the same. If Julie left, she would take the baby. Sue, you and Dad *have* to kick them out.' I looked at her face, and carried on quickly. 'You know I love Bobby. He's my brother, to all intents and purposes. I want him to be happy. But that means Julie being happy too. And that means you have to make him set his family up away from you and Dad. It's too easy for him, being with you.'

Sue shook her head emphatically. 'No, Lizzy. You're projecting. You wouldn't want to live with Steve's family, that's all.'

I glared. 'Steve is not the father.'

'Oh yes, of course. Sorry.' I hated the fact that no one believed me. 'But anyway, they like being with us. And we like having them. We're like one of those family units in African villages, all piled in together, all mucking in, looking out for each other.'

'But you're *not*,' I said. 'You don't live in an African village. You live in Haywards Heath, in a terraced house. Roberto needs to get off his fat arse, and he needs to move into a family home for him and Julie and their baby. Even if it's a tiny rented apartment. They can still be close to you. Think of it as their hut, still a part of the circle. Bobby loves being with you. Julie loves you all too, but she needs her own place.'

Sue looked at me. I saw her ferocious side.

'What has she been saying?' she demanded.

'Nothing bad,' I said hastily. 'She just doesn't want to feel like a guest for the rest of her life. She's only thirty-one. Seriously, she's heading for an ultimatum. And she thinks he's going to choose you.'

Sue looked pleased for a moment. 'Yes, I see that there is that danger.'

'I know you love him. But can you try to tell him to build a new hut? For his own sake?'

She opened her mouth to argue. As she spoke, I turned away. Suddenly, I could not hear a word she was saying. There was someone on the other side of the road, walking in my direction. As she got closer, I became more and more certain that it was her. I stared. I felt the blood pounding around my body. I was terrified, and excited.

'Hold on a second,' I managed to say to Sue.

'No,' she said, sharply. 'I haven't finished.'

I crossed the road. The woman stopped, and looked me up and down as I approached. I reached out to touch her arm, then withdrew my hand.

'Rosa?' I asked, even though I knew it was her.

CHAPTER 23

MARY

April 1970

O nce she had bought the ticket, she felt
wonderful. She was an evil, unnatural
woman. She would be condemned by
everyone. She was cutting herself off both from
her birth family (there was no chance of her
mother and father speaking to her again, not after
this) and from her new family. She was losing her
parents, her husband and her daughter, all in one
go. Nothing she had ever done had brought her
anywhere close to this exhilaration.

She planned it meticulously. She could not
possibly mess this up. It was her only chance, and
she was going to take it.

The grey days, the tunnel, had finally become
too much. Her life – bottle-feeding the alien
creature, devoting herself to housework, lurking
inside this house that she hated – was over. The
little trips to the shops by herself were never
going to be enough. They gave her a tantalising
glimpse of what freedom would be like, but they
were not freedom. Often, nowadays, the baby was

crying when she got home, which made her guilty. She thought the neighbours were going to work out what she was doing. She was going to do it properly now. She had a seat on a bus, and it was going to leave from Victoria, and she was going to go east, and east, and east.

It was hard for her to quantify exactly why she was desperate. She had never tried, had never spoken to another person about it. She had not stopped to analyse it herself, not until now. The baby was nearly six months old. This, in the eyes of the world, meant that Mary had to be out and about. By now, she should be used to motherhood. The baby was supposed to be sleeping through the night, so Mary had no more excuses for not being the perfect mother. She ought to be down at the shops, chatting to other young mothers. She should be going to coffee mornings and Tupperware parties, comparing babies with new friends and sitting by the beach talking to her daughter, waiting for a gurgled response.

Instead, she lurked indoors. She barely felt able to put one foot in front of the other, and she had stopped making an effort, had stopped even bothering to get dressed, unless it was to go out alone. She answered the door to the milkman, to the religious callers, to the neighbours, in her nightdress, even in the afternoon. People were talking, tutting and muttering about her. She watched the women walking past, pausing in front of the house, inclining their heads and judging her, sotto voce.

She stood behind the net curtains and stared back, wondering whether or not they could see her.

Now, she was going to give them something to talk about.

The bag was packed. It was a small bag, because, on her own, she was hardly going to need a thing. She had taken her toothbrush, toothpaste and cold cream. A couple of changes of underwear and one spare outfit were all the clothes she would need. She had her ticket. She was going to be at Victoria station tomorrow, at ten in the morning. She'd saved all her housekeeping money for two months, and Billy had noticed (she had asked him for shopping money several times) but had never tackled her about it. That money was going to buy her a new life. When she thought about it, she felt she was growing wings.

The baby stared at her. She stared back. It smiled. Mary could see, objectively, that Beth was sweet. She had fat red cheeks, and had grown a head of soft yellow curls. Her eyes were bright blue, and everybody said she was adorable. It was all Mary could do to change her nappies. Then she had to wash them. Then she needed to hang them out on the line, or drape them around the house if it was raining, which it generally was. Often they never quite dried, and that meant she ended up ironing one dry, while the baby lay, bare bottomed and cold, on its changing mat, and kicked its legs crossly, and tried to roll over, and then yelled. When that happened, Mary looked at the iron in her hand, and looked at the baby, and ran out of the room.

She checked the time. It was ten past five. Billy was almost always back before seven. She was nervous about this part of the plan. She had practised and practised for it, walking out on her baby even before she realised what she was doing. But now she faced reality, and she knew that Billy might be stuck at work in some flukish meeting until nine or later. It seemed that, after all, she could not leave this baby on its own. It would be scared and it would cry and cry and no one would go to it.

Something inside her was pleased. She might not be absolutely inhuman, after all.

Half an hour later, Mary knocked on her neighbour's door. The woman answered it, and looked surprised.

'Oh, hello,' she said, peering at Mary and smiling slightly. 'Nice to see you out and about.'

Mary nodded.

'And this is your lovely little girl. Hello, Betty.'

'Beth.'

The woman leaned forward and took Elizabeth's hand. 'Hello, little Beth!' she said, in the voice that women inexplicably used for speaking to babies. Mary had never tried to copy it, because she knew she wouldn't be able to do it. 'Well, aren't you a precious cherub!' She looked at Mary. 'It's nice to see you, Mary. Make the most of her, won't you? They grow up so fast. My boys are nine and eleven now. Nine and eleven! Would you like to come in?'

Mary spoke quickly. 'I'd love to another time. I'm really sorry but I wondered if I could ask you a favour? I've just had a call from my father, and my mother's ill, and it sounds quite serious.' She checked the woman's face. She had already composed her features into an 'oh, I'm sorry' expression, and Mary could see that this was going to work. 'She needs me to go at once, and I'm not allowed to take Beth to the hospital. My husband will be home in an hour or so. Would you mind the baby? She's had her bottle, and she's got a clean nappy on. I'm so sorry – I know we don't even know each other very well. I'm afraid I've been a bit too wrapped up in motherhood to be a good neighbour.'

The woman held out her arms for the baby. She was beaming. 'Oh, I'd be happy to, dear. You just run along and look after your poor mother.' She looked at the baby. 'Bethy will be perfectly safe with me. For as long as you need.'

Mary gave the baby a quick kiss on the top of its head, and retreated.

She had already left Billy his note. She hadn't taken a lot of time over it. It said 'Billy – sorry. I just can't do this any more. Beth is next door. Don't look for me. Look after her. Mary.'

Now, she carried her bag stiffly as she hurried down the hill to the station. This was the danger point: if he came home early, this was where they would meet. But they didn't. Mary bought a ticket to London, and boarded a train, placed her small bag of worldly goods in the luggage rack, and found herself a corner seat. She heard the whistle blow, and looked up, to the hill to her right, knowing that she was closer to her daughter now than she might ever be again.

The train pulled out of the station. As the platform slid away, Mary wanted to jump for joy. The fog lifted. She was on her own, and this time she was going to stay that way. She didn't care what they were going to say about her, because she wasn't going to hear any of it. She was going to have an adventure, and it was going to last for the rest of her life. She was going to Kathmandu.

She was free.

CHAPTER 24

LIZ

8 May

Rosa looked at me. She looked down at my stomach. She looked uncertain, then suddenly smiled. Her eyes weren't smiling: she was wary of me.

'Hey,' she said, a hand on my shoulder. 'Hello, Liz. Look at you!'

She looked different. She was dressed in jeans which emphasised her slim legs, a burgundy blouse, and a silk scarf. I realised that when we met before, she had been terrified at everything that lay ahead of her. Now she seemed to have relaxed.

The sight of her affected me more than I wanted it to. I recoiled, and swallowed, then made myself smile. This was the encounter I had been seeking. I would rather have been anywhere else in the world.

I wondered how drunk I must have been not to have noticed, when I first met her. The structure of her face was masculine, but her long hair hid the sides of it. She was not particularly tall, and she was slim. I could see that her body shape had changed. I thought about how brave she must be, to be doing all this, making herself this vulnerable. I liked Rosa. The last thing she needed at the moment was the thing I was about to throw at her.

'You look great,' I said.

She looked scared, but she tried to brazen it out.

'So do *you*,' she said, with a smile. She put a hand on my stomach and rubbed it. 'Could this be the same woman who was bemoaning the fact that Prince Charming had buggered off? So to speak. With a boy? The girl who confidently predicted that motherhood was never going to beckon?'

I looked down. 'Well . . .' Her hand was still on my bump. We are a family, I thought. Here we are, together. It was a weird thought. Rosa was a stranger, but I had a closer link to her than I did to anyone.

'So I'm assuming he came back,' she said, talking quickly. 'I had an inkling that he might. Decided not to be gay after all? Got it out of his system? Gave you the baby to force you to forgive him? Seen it all before.'

I was chewing my thumbnail. When I glanced over the road, I saw that Dad, Sue and Julie had stopped and were waiting for me. I thought they were out of earshot, but wanted to be certain.

'Guys?' I called to them. 'Why don't you go to the café? Matt's place, on the corner? We can get a coffee. I'll be there in a few minutes.' Then I looked back to Rosa. Her eyes were wide, begging me to agree with her hypothesis.

I steeled myself. It would be far too easy to agree that Steve was back. This was the only opportunity I was going to get.

'Actually,' I told her, 'I've been trying to track you down.' My heart thumped. I clenched my fists.

We looked at each other. I opened my mouth to spell it out. She put up her hands to stop me. She took a step back and her face was suddenly contorted. I realised, in that second, that Rosa was both vulnerable and strong. I was afraid.

'You're lying,' she whispered.

'Why would I lie?'

'I don't know why. But it isn't true. It can't be.'

'What can I say? The baby's due on August the seventh. You do the maths.'

She drew herself up. I tried to remind myself that I hadn't done anything wrong. She looked as though she would either cry or hit me.

'I don't want to do any maths,' she said, staring into my face so hard that I put a hand up to shield myself.

'And I don't want to fight,' I said, as levelly as I could. 'I'm not going to. I've been looking for you for months. I didn't do this on purpose. Neither did you. It happened. You have the right to know. I wanted to tell you the facts, as a courtesy.'

'Matt said you were after me.' She took two steps back. 'That is exactly why I haven't been into his establishment lately. He didn't mention your condition.'

'That's unusual. So you just didn't want to see me?'

'No, I didn't. I didn't want to remember. I was afraid you might want to do it again.'

'Jesus.'

'What?'

'Rosa. When you ran out on me . . . you were ill. Not from tequila, either. You were disgusted at yourself, and at me. You thought I'd taken advantage of you, and I probably had. I was so drunk that I could hardly see. But all the same, I made it happen. I wanted it to be bad for me and bad for you. I haven't told anyone that it was you. I've lost all my friends because I've sealed myself away, because I don't want to talk about what we did. I can't tell you how much I wish it was Steve. But it isn't.'

'Mmm.'

'So,' I said, hoping I sounded more controlled than I felt, 'I'm giving you my phone number. Think about this because I know it's a shock. If you want to see the baby or anything after it's born, give me a call. If you want we can do a DNA test. I imagine that's what it'll take to get you to believe me. And Rosa, I'm not asking you for anything. Not unless you choose, at some point, to be fully involved, and that's your decision.'

I had practised that speech, and was pleased with myself for delivering it calmly.

I scrabbled in my bag, found a pen and a crumpled receipt, and managed to write 'Liz Greene' and my phone number. When I held it out, Rosa didn't move. She was looking at the ground, her face frozen. I forced the paper into the pocket of her jeans. Suddenly, she smiled a vicious smile.

'Careful, darling,' she said, nastily. 'Don't get too close. You'll get me all excited.'

Then she patted me on the stomach again, and walked off. I stood still and stared after her. She walked briskly, without looking back. I knew that she knew I was watching.

'If you want money,' she yelled, without looking round or breaking her stride, 'you can go fuck yourself.'

I heard the catch in her voice. I sat on someone's doorstep and cried.

CHAPTER 25

HELEN

8 May

I looked one way, and then the other. I had to move quickly.

The long-haired woman was coming straight towards me.

'If you want money, you can go fuck yourself,' she shouted suddenly, without pausing. I could see her face. It was twisted into a bizarre expression.

Down the road, Liz said, 'Rosa.' She didn't say it loudly.

I could hide, I thought. I could run out into the road, and hide on the other side of the van. I could just stay here and watch her, and if Rosa looks at me, I could pretend to be fiddling with the back of the van, as if I owned it. Or I could get a bit closer and try to work out who she was. Liz had mentioned Rosa before. I needed to know what was going on.

I walked into her, on purpose.

She spun round, and stared at me.

'Watch it!' she muttered, and turned away, frowning. She was a strange-looking woman and

I was certain that I had never seen her before. I wanted to ask why Liz was asking her for money, but I wasn't sure how to go about it.

'Sorry,' I said. 'Um, do you know the way to Café Lumière?' I added.

'Corner,' she said, without breaking her stride. She pointed, without looking.

'Thanks.' I walked with her, even though she was going the other way. I had nothing to lose. 'Was that woman asking you for money, then?' I added.

The woman stopped. She looked as if she wanted to hit me, and I cowered, sure, for a second, that she would. I leapt mentally ahead, and wondered whether Liz would come to help me, and if she did, what she would think of my being right here, in the middle of her drama.

'Oh, fuck off,' she said, and I didn't dare say anything else. This lady was obviously horrid, and I was pleased that Lizzy was fighting with her. It was always good to see Liz in a confrontation with someone else. It proved that she was just hot-headed, that nothing was really my fault.

I waited for Rosa to get a good twenty metres ahead before I followed. I didn't look behind me, because I was sure Liz was staring at the woman, and I didn't want her to realise that the person between them was me.

She wouldn't, from my back. I was dressed in 'spring's classic capsule wardrobe', which meant that I was wearing a white blouse with puffy sleeves, and a miniskirt with flowers printed on it. My legs were bare, even though it was too cold. I wanted to start getting them brown. They were covered with unsightly goose bumps. My hair was very blonde, but shorter than it had been last time Liz saw me, because after the staffroom incident I'd decided I needed a disguise of sorts. Then, it had gone halfway down my back. Now it rested on my shoulders, and I was holding it back from my face with a pair of sunglasses, ready to flip them down as an extra disguise, in case she saw me watching her. If I felt a bit hidden, it was easier for me to keep an eye on her.

Liz had told those people to go to Matt's, and my shift was starting in twenty minutes. This was it. I went into a phone box, put my glasses down over my eyes, and spoke to Tom.

'Wish me luck,' I said.

'Yeah,' he said. 'You'll need it, I reckon.'

'I don't think she cares about me any more,' I told him. 'In a good way, I mean. I don't think she really hates me. I didn't do anything to make her hate me, did I? She's a flawed character, but you can't choose your family, can you? She fights with everyone, from what I can see.'

'You'll be OK if you play it properly. Careful, though. I wish I was there to hold you back. Be cool. Don't get in her face. Make her think it's her idea. She did wrong, so be cool with her.'

I moved from one foot to the other, and back again. 'I know. It's hard. I so desperately want to tell her that she does have a mother, after all. Whenever I see her, I want to shout, "We're sisters!"'

'You'll scare her off. Promise me you won't.'

'Yeah, I promise.'

'Off you go then. Remember, cool, calm and collected.'

'Tom?'

'What?'

'Do you still have crazy half-hours?'

'No,' he said. 'Not really. They stopped. Hey, I think the parents are missing you.'

'They could always contact me.'

'I'll tell them.'

'Don't bother.'

I walked in, looking straight ahead, three minutes before the start of my shift. It was much cooler in the café, and I regretted my bare legs. I wished I had time to run home for a pair of tights. I could have been home and back in ten minutes, but I didn't ask, because Matt was obsessive about time-keeping. He ran the place on his own most of the time, and only had the occasional evening off if he managed to persuade his brother, Joel, to take over. Joel was a bearded stockbroker and I never knew what to say to him.

I always made sure I was at work on time, because I was not at all good at my job, and time-keeping was the only bit I could get right. It was odd to have obligations like turning up at work on time, because I had got used to doing what I wanted to do, when I wanted to do it, but in a way I liked the structure, and I loved the fact that I had a job at all.

I looked around surreptitiously. Liz and the people I presumed were her family were at a table by the window. I didn't look at them. It was hard, because if he was her father, that man was almost my stepfather. And the woman was a few degrees away from being my mother. I kept myself rigidly under control, and managed not even to sneak a glance. Tom would have been proud.

I ducked behind the counter, tied my hair in a little ponytail, and smiled at Matt.

'Well, well, well,' he said. 'The lovely Helen. Just in the nick of time.' He looked me up and down. 'Looking gorgeous today, if one's allowed to say so.'

I tried to deal with Matt in a sophisticated and worldly way, but I hadn't quite worked out how to do it, so most of the time I smiled and laughed my special laugh at him. He was alternately flattering and nasty, and I had never met anyone like that before. I hoped he couldn't see how he confused me.

'Can I run home and get some tights?' I asked brightly.

'No,' he said, and he glared at me. 'You want tights, you put them on before you come. Not too much to fucking ask, one would have thought.'

'Sorry,' I muttered, looking at my shoes. I put

myself into bubbly mode and attached my smile. 'So, Matthew! What needs doing?'

He set me to work cleaning one of the coffee machines. This was a relief as it gave me a break from doing sums in my head, and from trying not to spill beverages. Waiting on tables was turning out to be harder than it looked. The coffee machine was chrome, and I was able to stare at Liz's reflection while I worked. I didn't learn much. Even when I'd cleaned it, I couldn't see anything but a blurred profile.

Nobody from her table ordered any more drinks. They didn't even look around. I wondered whether the other pregnant woman was Julie. She was a tired-looking woman wearing boring old clothes. A few weeks ago, I could have been described in exactly those terms. Yet she was twice my age and heavily pregnant.

It was a pleasant novelty to me to feel superior. On top of everything else, I had youth on my side.

I made numerous cups of coffee and tea, opened bottles of beer, and poured wine for the afternoon's customers. I managed to do almost all the adding up on my little calculator. If I concentrated hard, I could convince myself that I was starting to enjoy my job. When I let myself panic, it all went wrong, but today I was rigidly controlled, and was even remembering to breathe. I liked living in my gritty flat with the puppyish Adrian and two girls I rarely saw. I liked the fact that Matt paid me.

'Is it pay day?' I asked him, as we converged at the coffee machine.

'Do us two lattes,' he said, and he patted my bottom.

'Could I sue you for that?' I asked, genuinely curious.

'Yeah, but you won't. And yes, one wage packet hidden under the counter, all above board, tax and everything.'

I beamed. These would be the first wages of my life. I had already received plenty of tips, most of them from men. The tipping thing surprised me, because in France, nobody did anything more than rounding the bill up to the nearest euro. Last week a man gave me a ten pound tip, and all I'd done was pour him a beer.

As time went on, people like that were beginning to make me uneasy. The unease started two weeks into the job, when a smart-looking man drank beer all evening with his friend, stared at me without stopping, stayed behind when his friend left, gave me an enormous tip, and hung around outside while we closed up.

'Hello,' he said, as I stepped out into the darkness.

'Oh,' I said. 'Hello.' I didn't know why he was there, or what I was supposed to say to him. I started walking, and he walked with me.

'Shall we go somewhere for a drink?' he asked.

'But everywhere's shut.' It was not, with hindsight, the best response.

'Do you live nearby?'

'Um, yes.'

'Perhaps you would invite me in for a coffee?'

I started to panic at that point. I had no idea how to get rid of him. I thought about going home and asking for Adrian's help, but I thought that maybe I shouldn't show this man where I lived. I looked at him sideways. He had to be in his fifties and I wondered what he wanted with someone as inexperienced and clueless as me.

I turned and started off back to the bar.

'Forgot something,' I said.

He smiled and looked at me as if he was pleased with me. 'Oh, yes?' he asked. 'Got the keys, have you?'

We walked in silence, and I was scared he was going to grab me. When we got to the bar, I pressed the buzzer for Matt's flat upstairs, holding my finger down on it.

'What?' he demanded down the intercom.

'Matt?' I said. 'Can you come down?'

The man looked angry.

'Why?' Matt asked.

I tried to be brave but I was hopeless. I tried to tell the man that he had me all wrong, that I was not that sort of girl, mainly because I didn't know how to be that sort of girl. A part of me wanted the adventure, wanted to do whatever this man was after just to see what it was like, but the rest of me didn't dare. Even now that I lived in London, there were things I didn't dare to do. I was pathetic.

Matt sized the situation up easily. 'Fuck off, mate,' he said, sleepily. 'Leave her alone. She's not interested.'

'Jesus,' the man muttered. 'She only had to fucking say so.'

He left, and Matt turned on me, wide awake.

'For Christ's sake, Helen.' He was furious. 'You've got to stop giving these people the fucking come-on! That guy's a sleazeball. Luckily for you, he's nothing worse. I see you doing it. You smile at them, you flash your legs. I'm surprised more of them haven't tried it on by now.'

I looked at the ground. 'Sorry,' I said. 'I don't mean to.'

'Just fucking stop it or you're going to end up in one hell of a lot of trouble. OK?'

I knew it would happen again, because I still smiled at everyone. If I stopped smiling, I was afraid I would go back to being myself, and then everything would fall apart, because I wouldn't be able to do anything.

I pretended not to watch Liz getting up and walking over to the counter. I busied myself frothing milk while she stood and waited patiently for my attention. I watched her reflection in polished chrome.

'Hello, Helen,' she said when I had to turn round.

'Oh!' I knew I was doing a bad job of pretend surprise, but I ploughed on. 'Oh, Liz! Hello!'

271

She smiled, though her face was red and puffed-up. In spite of everything, I was angry with that horrible woman who had made her cry.

'Hello,' she said again. 'So, you're working here?'

I felt I had to explain. 'Matt had a sign up.'

'I remember.'

'I needed a job so I applied.'

'Look, I'm sorry. You felt you had to pretend not to see me when you came in. That's a crap situation for you to be in. I'm sorry that I was so horrible to you. A lot of other things had happened that day and I took it all out on you.' She looked at me, a nice, friendly look. 'You were only being nice. In fact, you were being lovely. Can we start again?' she asked.

I counted to five before I replied. 'Yes,' I said. 'Sure. Of course we can.' I fought to keep the hundred watt smile off my face. 'I understand.' I was being as cool as I could manage.

'You're sure?'

'Of course I'm sure. Are you after any more drinks?'

'No, I don't think so. I just came over to talk to you.'

'Is this your family?' I was dying to ask her about Rosa, but I couldn't.

'Mmm. That's Dad and Sue, and Julie.'

I looked at my reverse-stepfather and wondered if I could term him my 'pets-father'. That was a funny way of making him a stepfather in reverse, but I couldn't tell it to anyone but Tom.

It was nice to be able to look at William Greene properly, after the sneaked sidelong glances I'd been giving him for fifteen minutes.

He was old, but looked kind and friendly. He had changed since Lizzy's baby photos were taken: it was mostly the hair that did it, but he had lost weight, too. As I looked, he caught my eye and smiled. In fact, I would never have recognised him.

Sue looked like a good witch. She had one of those faces that belong to people who have thought happy, kind thoughts for their entire lives. This was the woman who had replaced my mother in William Greene's life, and in Lizzy's life. It looked to me like a good swap. In fact, I was jealous. If this man had been my father, and if this woman was my mother, then Liz would still have been my sister and I would have been a balanced, functional human being from a loving and normal home. I thought I would, anyway.

I managed to play it cool until they left. Liz came over again, after her stepmother had paid the bill, and said, 'So if you're working here, does that mean you live nearby?'

I tried to be cold. 'Yes, I am, actually. Around the corner. Norbert Road. I got it out of *Loot*, like you said. It was the one with the sanest flatmates and the cleanest toilet. Where do you live again?'

She gestured with her head. 'Over there. Did you know that?'

I shook my head. 'Actually, maybe. I think I knew you lived in Kentish Town. I haven't heard of most parts of London, so that probably made it jump off the page at me. Plus I'd already been here, to the café I mean, so I knew the area a tiny bit.'

She nodded. 'We're practically neighbours. Maybe we'll run into each other sometime.' Liz smiled and stroked her bump. It was visible – it was large – and this reminded me that I had to bring her to France before the baby was born, or all my efforts would count for nothing. That probably meant that, now that I had been cool, I needed to be nicer. I should start to reel her in.

'That would be great,' I told her. 'I'd love that.' She turned to leave. 'And Liz?' I said, impulsively.

'Mmm?'

'It's really nice to see you looking so well. You know where to find me. I'm here, most of the time.'

She grinned. 'Nice to know there's a friendly face in the neighbourhood. Cheers.'

We shut the café at midnight. When the floor was clean and the glasses put away, I poured myself a glass of white wine. It wasn't great, but it was open, and it was cold.

Matt dimmed the lights, and leaned on the counter. I looked at him, surprised. He was well-built, and not much taller than I was. Today, his bleached hair had thick black roots. He was dressed all in black, and I noticed that I could see the outlines of his muscles under his T-shirt.

'Do you go to the gym?' I asked, randomly. 'When do you manage that?'

He smiled. 'Good line,' he said. 'I do press-ups every night and every morning. Thanks for noticing. And to return the compliment, how do you stay so skinny? You must be part of the size zero culture that everyone seems to be obsessed with.' He pinched me, and I backed away.

'I'm not size zero,' I told him quickly. 'And I was just born this way. Anyway, you don't help, keeping me running around with a tray of coffee all day long. How do you do this all the time, without falling asleep?'

'It's called work. And I have a secret weapon in the struggle to get through the working day. Do you want something else with your wine?'

'Like what?' I asked primly. 'A snack?' Then I smiled. I liked Matt and I couldn't help but show it.

'No, Helen. Not a snack.'

I thought he might be going to kiss me. Instead, he took something from his jeans pocket. I watched in puzzlement as he unfolded a piece of paper, and took a credit card from his wallet. I couldn't think what he was about to pay for. A pizza delivery, perhaps? As he moved the contents of the paper around carefully with his bank card, I realised what was going on.

'Are those drugs?' I asked, reverently.

He laughed. '"*Are those drugs?*"' he mocked. 'You're sweet, you know that?'

'Am I sweet? Is that good?'

He looked at me, and I blushed. 'Yeah,' he said. 'It's fine.'

I watched him at work for a while, noticing the way his brow furrowed in concentration. He pushed his fringe back, apparently irritated by it at last. Then he rolled up a twenty-pound note and held it out to me.

'Here we go,' he said, proudly. 'Would you like to be my guest?'

'What is it?'

'What is it? Here's a clue. It's white powder and it comes in lines.'

'Not heroin?'

'Are you really so innocent? Is this an act? Because it's a cute one. Helen, this is coke. Everyone does it. Come on.'

Matt put his hand on the small of my back, and showed me what to do. I put the rolled-up money up my nose, shut the other nostril with my finger, and sniffed. The chemicals hit the back of my throat, and I swallowed hard.

He took the note out of my hand. 'My turn,' he said.

While I watched him, my head started to spin. I got up on a bar stool and gripped the counter. The surge of bliss almost knocked me over. I was suddenly, absolutely and utterly happy. I looked at my bare legs. They were beautiful. I was gorgeous. I was happy and gorgeous and I lived in London and everything was going to work out perfectly.

Matt grinned. 'You look cheery.'

I opened my mouth. He pulled me to him, and kissed me.

It was four o'clock when I started to walk home, and my bare legs were freezing. I ran between street lamps, from one pool of light to the next, giggling. I talked loudly to Tom, though he didn't answer. I carried on the conversation I had been having with Matt, although in fact there had been two conversations going on at the same time, most of the time. As well as that, we had kissed a lot.

The kissing was a first for me. We hadn't actually had sex, but I didn't think we had been far from it. Matt had touched me in ways that I had only imagined before. I wanted to do that again, when we were sober. I thought we probably would. I imagined him being my boyfriend.

'I live in London and I've got a boyfriend,' I said aloud. I wondered whether I actually needed a sister at all.

I was happy, happy, happy. All those solemn warnings about the evils of drugs had been a plot to stop me discovering how amazing life could be, how exhilarating it all was. I hoped this feeling would never wear off. I wanted it to last for ever. I wanted to do it all again, and again, and again.

As usual, I took the long route home so I could pass Liz's house. I skipped by on the other side of the road. Then I stopped, and stared up at the windows. I had been doing this for long enough to know that the big window belonged to Liz's bedroom, and the smaller one was in a different room. She and Julie had been in there earlier.

Now the curtains were closed, and there were no lights on. I fought a strong impulse to ring her buzzer and tell her everything.

'Go home,' Tom said. He was shouting. 'Go home!'

I rolled my eyes. 'OK,' I told him. 'Off we go.' And I decided to hop all the way back.

When I got in, I considered waking Adrian and asking him to have sex with me. I didn't do it, and that, I knew, was good.

CHAPTER 26

LIZ

4 June

The woman was called Nicky, and her voice was soothing.

'And hold it for a count of ten,' she intoned. '. . . eight, nine, ten. And relax.'

Pregnancy yoga was far easier than I had expected it to be, and I was relishing every moment. I had assumed that, like normal yoga, it was going to involve holding agonising postures while my muscles shrieked to be left alone. Instead, I had just stood with my legs apart and reached up towards the ceiling for ten seconds. This much I could manage.

The class was in a big old house that smelt of polish and incense. There were activities going on in several of the rooms. This one had wide floor-boards and large windows. There were seven of us in the class. The others were intimidatingly gleaming and well turned out. I stuck to Anna and got on with the exercises. I was annoyed to discover how inferior I felt when suddenly surrounded by women with clip-on bumps and skinny thighs. They all seemed to know each other, and I caught snatches of conversation about whether one needed a doula, and who was going to 'do Gina Ford'.

We ended with relaxation. I lay on my left side, as instructed, and relaxed everything from my toes upwards. 'The neck. Feel the tension slide away,' Nicky breathed. 'And the face. Your mouth . . . nose . . . eyes. Let the eyes stay loosely closed.' There was a quiet snore from across the room. 'And try to stay this side of the sleep barrier,' Nicky added hurriedly. 'Now. This is a good time for you to be with your baby. Talk to him, or her. Say hello.'

'Hello,' I whispered, though it came out louder than I had intended, and there was a ripple of quiet laughter. 'Hello, baby,' I said, in my head. 'I'm sorry, baby.' I knew my eyes were full of tears, but there was nothing I could do about it. I thought about my innocent child, and the fact that he or she was often the last thing on my mind. I imagined the life I was going to give it. It would go to nursery while it was still a baby, and while it was there it would doubtless be cared for by feckless sixteen-year-olds who nipped out for fags every ten minutes. We would struggle for money all the time. We would never be able to go on foreign holidays, would never see the Pyramids or queue to examine Mao's corpse in Beijing. This baby's father was a woman who didn't believe a word I said, and who thought I had as good as raped her at the conception.

280

And yet. My father was a good man, and he would help us. My stepmother would do everything she could, even though I knew I had annoyed her lately. Julie and I seemed to be friends. Anna and I were getting on well, and her baby was going to a local nursery too. She was due to give birth in three weeks, and I was terrified, both on her behalf, and because once her baby was born, mine would be next.

I put a hand on my stomach, and the baby stretched a limb out to meet it. I rubbed it. Moments like this, rare as they were, made me feel that nothing else actually mattered, that all the rest of it was a detail.

'Mummy's here,' I mouthed. I was already this baby's entire world. For the moment, it loved me unconditionally, because I was its mother. I let myself consider the possibility that we might be going to be all right, in spite of everything. Then Nicky told us to sit up gently, and I came back down to earth. Although all the usual worries flooded back in, they were slightly more distant than usual.

I gazed at Anna, too wrapped up in the blissful moment to say a word. I was aware of the other women in the room standing up, putting their shoes back on, and leaving. I reached for my own shoes. They were ballet pumps because summer had started pleasantly early. While I pulled them on, I tried to get my thoughts together sufficiently for me to speak.

'Everything all right?' asked Nicky, who was tiny and sensible-looking, with short hair and a pale face. She looked concerned.

I nodded. 'That was a bit too nice,' I told her, wiping my eyes. 'I'm on my own with this pregnancy. It's a scary thing. I never relax like that.'

'It does you good,' she said. 'Sorry to rush you, but I have another class now. Do come back. I look forward to seeing you next week?' She said it as a question, and I nodded.

'Definitely.'

Anna was looking at me and laughing. 'Didn't I say that you'd like it?' she said as we walked down the front stairs together. It was pleasant to walk into the sunshine, and I hoped that my sleepy happy feeling would continue. I looked sideways at Anna. My seven-month pregnant stomach looked large to me, but Anna's full term one was far more impressive. The black dress she was wearing covered it like a tablecloth, and seemed to end a metre or so in front of her. Her black hair reached all the way down her back. Everything about Anna was gorgeous: she was one of those people who are made to be pregnant.

'You might not be here next week,' I told her. 'You look like you're about to burst.'

'Yeah, cheers for that,' she said, laughing. 'Jeremy said to me last night, "There's no way that's coming out naturally." I mean, thanks. Cheer me up, why don't you?'

I waved a hand. 'You'll have a great birth.

You've been going to yoga, after all. It's funny because before I was pregnant I thought the idea of childbirth was petrifying, but these days, that's the one part I don't care about. I read people's birth stories on the forum – I read them obsessively sometimes – and you do read things like, "and after four days of labour they said I wasn't progressing and so they gave me a section", but I just assume it'll be fine. You know? It's a day or so – how bad can it be?'

'I know. Me too. Forget about labour. It's the bit where they let you keep the baby that worries me.'

'Tell me about it.'

We strolled towards Matt's place. I had seen Helen in there a couple of times lately, and I was regretting ever having been so horrible to her. She was unremittingly kind to me, and I needed people like that around.

I was pleased to see that she was working today. She was wearing a skimpy red dress, with her hair in an eighties-style high ponytail. The trouble with Helen was that she could carry anything off, and she often seemed to have no idea of how sexual she looked. Today, she seemed tired.

'Hi, Helen,' I called as we came in.

Anna looked at her. I saw that she was screwing up her face, trying to place her.

'Hello,' Helen said. She looked at Anna, shrugged, and looked away.

'I've seen you around, I think,' Anna said suddenly. 'Do you hang out near Lizzy's house?'

Helen nodded. For once, her manner was vaguely confrontational. 'Yeah, I live nearby. Why?'

'I live opposite her.'

'Well, what can I get you to drink?'

Anna still looked puzzled, so I ordered fizzy water for us both. Then I introduced them. Anna said all the right things, but without enthusiasm.

When Helen had gone, she said, 'That girl spies on you, I think. I've seen her watching your house. She hides behind our car.'

I shook my head. 'No, she really does live nearby. I feel bad about her, actually. I was awful to her, months ago, and it wasn't her fault at all. I yelled at her. Told her to fuck off, and everything. She was in the wrong place at the wrong time.'

'What did she do?'

I smiled. 'She was too nice. As you can imagine, we can't have that.'

Anna nodded seriously. 'Quite right. You need more people like Kathy and Steve in your life. More bastards. Get rid of those who are nice! Remind me to be mean to you from time to time.'

I sighed. 'I'm getting on a bit too well with Julie, you know. It's probably time I offended her again.'

Sitting with Anna and talking about pregnancy was a luxury. The fuzzy yoga feeling took a long time to wear off, and for once, I was uncomplicatedly happy. I knew it was difficult, but I felt I would be all right. I told Anna about the spare room, about how I had painted it cream and bought some cheap bedlinen. I took the signs I had printed up out of my bag, and showed them to her, nervously. Helen came over to have a look, a tea towel in her hand.

'What's this?' she said. 'Room to let? Where?' She looked at me. 'You're renting out a room?'

I nodded. 'I don't feel great about it, but if you could see my bank statements, you'd understand.'

'Seriously? You're renting out your spare room?'

'I have to. I have to claw some money where I can find it, till the baby's born.'

'Do you want me to stick one up in here? But are you sure? You could end up with anyone.'

'I know.'

Anna touched my arm. 'Liz, she's right. Are you sure? Your bedroom is right next to the bathroom, and this person will be sleeping across the landing and sharing your toilet and everything. Is that really what you want?'

My worries came back, and I shook my head. 'No, of course it's not.' I saw Helen glancing quickly at Matt, who was busy at the counter.

'I have to go,' she said. 'Or the beast over there will shout at me. But, Liz, can we have a chat? Later?'

When Anna left, to go shopping for pushchairs with Jeremy, I decided that I didn't want to move. I stayed at the table and phoned Julie. She sounded exhausted.

'Hiya,' she said. 'Let me just go up to the room

285

a sec.' I heard her feet treading heavily on the stairs. 'Better. Jesus.'

I kicked back. 'How are you?'

She was speaking quietly. 'I've been better. I'd definitely say that I've been better, but thanks for asking.'

'Come and live in my spare room.'

'I would.'

'Well, if you ever need to escape . . . I've started to advertise it. It's just to get a bit of cash. I've got no idea who might end up in there, and I'm shitting myself.'

'Yeah, be careful.'

'Everyone says that.'

'Only have a woman, for one thing.'

'I'd worked that one out.' I looked around, hoping to signal to Helen that I needed another glass of water. 'So, what's happening?'

She lowered her voice. 'I'm public enemy number one. Not to your dad. Sue and Roberto are fighting hammer and tongs, and every now and then they get together to blame me. Um, Roberto's not over the moon with you, either. Sorry.'

I waved my hand, although she couldn't see me. 'I can handle him. What happened?'

'I was brave. I said I liked his family a lot, but I didn't want to live my life under their roof. I was as calm as I could be about it. I said we needed a home for our family, and I said that if he wasn't coming with me, I was going to go without him.'

'Good work.'

'Shit. I was so scared. It felt like the wrong thing to be saying. We're a family. We want to be a family. I don't want to flounce off and have the baby on my own. Sorry,' she added. 'I suppose I'm not as strong as you.'

'Don't be sorry. I didn't want to do it on my own either. And I didn't even have the chance to do any flouncing. So, he didn't take it well?' I picked up my glass and drained the last few drops of water. Helen was at the counter, flirting with Matt.

She laughed, a brittle laugh. 'He honestly seemed to have no idea what I was on about. You'd have thought I'd never mentioned it before. He kept saying, "But it's good here. We've got every-thing we need. What's the problem?" Then when he realised that I was serious, he said I was a crazy woman, and stormed off, to complain to Mummy.'

'Which made it worse?'

'Yeah. He was livid that she was on my side, as he saw it. So we had a proper fight. He said I wanted to go to Iraq and get back with Terry. I told him he was a fat lazy pig. I guess I may have used your name as back-up.'

'OK.'

'So meanwhile Sue is trying to calm everyone down. She says that if we want to move out, she won't be upset. She says it's normal to want your own home when you're starting a family. Then she holds forth about African villages, and how we're not living in an African village but in Haywards Heath. She says we can get a flat and it'll be our very own mud hut. She *then* says that it was you who put her straight on that.'

'So Roberto is in a rage at me?'

'I'm afraid so.' She sounded scared. 'And Sue's being off with me, although she would never admit it. Right now I just want to get out of here, but I feel I have to stick around. I'm working later, thank God.'

'Julie,' I told her, 'don't worry about me. Believe me, I have my problems, and Roberto in a temper is the very least of them.'

As soon as I hung up, Helen came over.

'Hey,' she said. 'You OK?'

'Fine. Any chance of some more water? The baby seems to be drinking me up.'

'Of course.' She looked around. 'I'll get you a big bottle. On the house. Don't tell Matt.' She ran over and fetched it straight away. 'So, I was going to talk to you about something.' She looked nervous as she sat down opposite me. 'If that's OK. I don't want to put any pressure on you, though.'

'Go on.'

'It's my flat. I live with three people, and the girls are fine. They're Polish. I hardly ever see them, actually, with the hours I work and the hours they work.'

'Right.'

'But the guy. Adrian. He's nice enough, at least

I thought so at first. You see, I sometimes get into sticky situations because I send out the wrong signals. I know that. Matt tells me. But I'm starting to feel uncomfortable.' She looked down, blushing. 'A couple of times I've caught him outside the bathroom when I've had a shower. The door doesn't shut properly, you see, so he could be watching through the crack. He probably wasn't, but . . . Then the other day I came home and I'm sure he came out of my bedroom, in a hurry, when he heard me coming in. And I think my underwear drawer had been, um, rearranged. You see, I'm quite obsessive and I fold all my, um, knickers.'

I felt my jaw drop. 'Helen, that's awful! Have you told the others? You have to confront him.'

She wrinkled her face, still smiling. 'Well, I'm not very good at confrontation,' she said. 'As you know. So I was thinking more of moving out. I could always leave a note saying what my reasons were, or something.'

I felt responsible for this. If I had come flat-hunting with Helen, like she had asked me to, I would definitely have spotted this weirdo and I would certainly have stopped her moving in with him.

'You should talk to him,' I told her. 'Let him know he can't get away with it. And you should move out as well. You're a long way from home. You don't want to be living with someone like that.' I pictured Adrian as a creepy-looking man in a knitted waistcoat, living in a flat full of women, tiptoeing around sniffing their knickers.

'And now,' said Helen, 'you say that you're looking for a lodger . . .'

I didn't know what to say. 'Right.' I tried to think quickly. Helen was tense and she put on a front the whole time, but she was harmless. I was in no position to be fussy.

'Well,' I said. 'That's an idea. You haven't seen the place. Why don't you come back with me now, and have a look at the room? If you like it, I don't see why you can't have it.' I looked at her. She was grinning, and for once her smile looked genuine. 'It'll be nice to have you around,' I said.

There was a sudden shout from the bar.

'Girl!' Matt yelled. 'Honestly. I keep a girl around here, and she never comes when I call.'

Helen giggled, her face dimpling. 'Looks like I'm needed,' she said happily. 'I'll come over later. I know which house is yours.'

I was left speaking to thin air. I said it anyway: 'Don't let him speak to you like that! The tosser.'

CHAPTER 27

HELEN

12 June

'Lock the door, and come here,' Matt ordered. He liked bossing me about, and I liked it, too. It made me feel good in a way I could not really describe.

I locked the café door, changed the sign to 'closed', and savoured the walk back to my boss. This was part of our Saturday night, now.

'Here.' He pushed a glass of white wine across the bar. I picked it up.

'Cheers,' I said. I was tingling with anticipation. Matt didn't have a drink himself. He just watched me sipping mine. There was something nasty, and exciting, about being watched. This was how some customers made me feel, when they asked me to have a drink with them, or when they talked about me, staring and laughing. With Matt it felt safer, but still dangerous.

'Come here,' he said. I took another sip, walked to him, and let him take me in his arms and kiss me. He pulled at my dress, and I let him undo it, and then stepped out of it.

I had never told Matt that he was the first man I'd kissed, and I wondered whether he had guessed. It had probably never occurred to him that anyone could be twenty, and that inexperienced. He still thought it was funny that I hadn't recognised cocaine.

He pulled away, and took out the charlie (as I was self-consciously calling it) from his pocket. We always had a line each, at this point, and then we talked for several hours. That was my favourite part. Before the coke, I wanted to have sex, but afterwards I just wanted to talk. Matt liked me to sit there naked, in front of him. Sometimes he got me to lie down, and snorted his coke off my body. I liked that. But he never actually tried to have sex with me, and part of me was relieved. Part of me was frustrated, but mostly I was glad. I was scared of the whole idea.

I sat next to him, naked, at the bar, and smiled as he looked at my body. I remembered how I'd sent a photograph of my tits to the stranger on the internet, and wondered whether I was an exhibitionist or something. I liked being looked at, and I was a bit surprised that I wasn't ashamed of my body. Matt liked it. He complained that I needed to eat more, though, because he said there was nothing to grab hold of.

He carefully made the lines for us both, and we snorted them together.

It took all my will power, on a Saturday night, not to tell Matt about Liz and Tom and Mother and everything. I often started. Sometimes Tom's voice started up in my head and made me stop. Tom was convinced that I was going to screw everything up. I half expected him to turn up in London to check up on me. I often wished he would. Instead, he wrote me letters, pages covered in neat black handwriting which set out my mission. He reminded me that I needed to be in France with Liz by the end of June, and told me again and again that I must not tell anyone at all what was going on. His letters arrived every few days.

And, in fact, it was easy, because Matt asked me questions, but didn't listen to the answers.

'So, what's the story with you?' he said now. 'What brings Helen to London? What goes on, out there in France? What are you really about?'

As usual, I overcame all my better judgement, and started to tell him, my words falling over each other. 'It's my family,' I said eagerly. 'I shouldn't really be saying anything, but it all started when Tom and I were looking through some of our mother's things, ages ago. And it was very strange because we found . . .'

I realised that he was talking over the top of me.

'I went to France, you know,' he was saying. 'On the French exchange. Ah, yes. We were on a coach. You remember what it was like, a bunch of kids on a coach? Who'd want to be the teacher in charge of that lot, hey?' And on he went, and on I went, too, telling him my secret, if only he had stopped to listen.

As usual, he didn't invite me upstairs to his flat. I wondered why he didn't. Perhaps he had a wife up there or something.

'Off you go then,' he said, when hours had gone by and we were beginning to droop. 'Get some clothes on, woman.'

I was always surprised at how suddenly it stopped: once it began to wear off, my spirits plummeted. I needed to lie in bed for twelve hours before I could reasonably see another human being. I felt gloomy and bad, and I hated myself. I hated myself passionately. I loathed myself. I made myself sick.

'See you Monday,' I said.

'Don't be late.'

'I'm moving tomorrow,' I reminded him, as I unlocked the door to let myself out.

He barely looked up. 'Oh yeah. Do you want any help?'

He sounded so unwilling that I forced a laugh. 'No, I'm fine. You have a rest.'

'Cheers.'

I crept into the flat, closing the door behind me as quietly as I could. Nobody knew that I was moving out. I knew that I should have told them, but I had decided to leave a note instead. That could wait. If I wrote it now, I would mess it up. I messed everything up. I was going to mess it up with Matt, with Liz, with Mother. I was certain of it.

I was in no mood to do anything but lie down and close my eyes. Somehow, although it was Sunday, I would find a way of moving all my things out without Adrian asking me what I was up to. Perhaps I would go to Liz's with a small bag. I'd come back and do the rest, and leave the note, on Monday.

I fished the keys Liz had given me out of my pocket. Every time I looked at them, or felt them, I felt a small sense of triumph, but now it was elusive. I knew I had done something that was good for the project, but I could no longer feel it.

I undressed, but couldn't be bothered to find a T-shirt. Instead, I climbed naked into my single bed, pulled the duvet around me, and thought of Matt. I stared at the ceiling for a long time before I fell asleep.

There was a gentle, but persistent, rapping on the door.

'Who's it?' I managed to mumble. My head was thumping and I wanted to die. The world was bleak and miserable.

'Only me!' Adrian poked his head into the room. 'Jeez, I'd forgotten how small it is in here. Do you want a . . . Oh! Sorry.'

I rubbed my eyes. 'What?'

He was out of the room already. 'I'm sorry, Helen,' he called from behind the door. 'I was going to ask whether you wanted a cuppa. It's a quarter to twelve, that's all. I'm going to be cooking some lunch in a while. Can I tempt you with one of Sainsbury's finest chicken breasts, and some mash? I may even throw in a vegetable. Girls seem to like that sort of thing.'

I realised that I had been lying, naked, on top of my duvet. I was sweating slightly, and the more I woke up, the worse my head felt.

I wriggled under the covers. 'Um. I feel a bit shit,' I muttered. 'Um, but a cup of tea would be good. Thanks. Actually, coffee. And a big glass of water.'

'Coffee and water coming up. Bit fragile?'

'Mmm.' I could hear him clumping around in the kitchen, which was next to my bedroom. Coffee would be bad for my head, but I didn't care. It would make me feel rubbish in a more bearable way. I wondered whether caffeine and cocaine were related. Their names were alike.

'Adrian?' I shouted, suddenly.

'Yes?'

'Real coffee! Not instant!'

'Your wish is my command, O Mistress.'

I sank back on to the pillow. I was supposed to have gone by now, but I couldn't even muster the energy to get some clothes on.

CHAPTER 28

LIZ

13 June

I was tense as I waited for my new lodger. Letting Helen move in was a mistake. It had been impossible to say no, but I wanted a stranger. I wanted a nice student nurse, or similar. I wanted my lodger to be someone who would lead their own life, who wouldn't want to be a part of mine. Still, it was too late now.

The windows were open and a warm breeze was fluttering the sitting-room curtains. I was sitting on the edge of the sofa, absently stroking a poking-out baby foot, and waiting. I could hear distant music.

Her bedroom was ready. There were only a few purple patches on the walls. I'd bought a cream duvet cover. All the spare room clutter was now in my wardrobe and under my bed. I'd allocated her a kitchen cupboard and half of the bathroom shelf. I told myself, again, that she was fine. She was a nice girl whose only fault seemed to be that she was too keen. When I had fallen out with her, she'd been new in London and probably

297

clinging on to me as the closest thing she had to a friend. Now she had a job, and, as far as I could see, she appeared to be going out with Matt.

'She'll be different, now,' I told the baby, with a stroke. 'She won't drive us mad, and anyway she knows she has to move out when you're born. And you're due to be showing up in eight weeks.'

When the buzzer sounded, I was relieved. She rang it once, then twice, and then three more times in quick succession. She had a set of keys, but I supposed it was only polite to ring, the first time.

'Steady,' I said, into the intercom's handset, and buzzed her in.

I went down and opened the flat's front door, at the bottom of the stairs.

Roberto was standing there, nose to nose with me, and he did not look happy.

'Leave my family alone,' he said, before I was able to begin to collect my thoughts.

I tried to smile. 'Not the person I was expecting,' I said, and ushered him up the stairs. It was depressing to have to deal with this. For the first time, I wished I hadn't got involved with Julie. 'What can I do for you, Bobsicle?'

'Shut up.'

I had been dealing with Roberto for twenty-six years and I knew that the thing that made him furious was being patronised.

'How's my favourite little brother?' I asked in a baby voice.

He frowned. 'Stop it.'

We were in the kitchen. He spun round to face me. Roberto had always been thickset, but recently he had grown the sort of belly you saw on news items about the 'obesity epidemic', cut off at the neck. I decided to go on the offensive, and patted it.

'Sympathetic pregnancy?' I inquired. 'That's sweet. When's yours due?'

'Shut up.'

I opened the fridge. 'Beer? Actually we haven't got any.'

'Nothing.'

'Tea? Coffee? Juice?' I looked in a cupboard. 'Gin? Vodka? A dribble of tequila?' I shuddered at the tequila. I could almost taste it at the back of my throat.

He looked at me. 'Tequila,' he said, seeing that it had some sort of effect on me. I filled a shot glass. He took it, clearly not intending to drink it, just intent on getting at me in any way he could.

'OK.' I sat at the table and motioned for him to do the same. 'Go on, then.'

He huffed importantly.

'Lizzy,' he said. 'Right.' His voice was gruff. He looked down at his drink, tipped it from one side to the other, and swirled the liquid so it almost splashed over the top. 'Look, I know you're pregnant and everything. Which apparently means you get to say and do what you want and no one can pull you up on it.'

'But? There's a big "but" coming, isn't there?

I know it.' I smiled. 'And you should know about big butts.'

'Why? Why do you do it?'

I knew what he meant. 'Why do I do what?' I asked.

'Why do you fucking interfere? We were getting along just fine, all of us. I'd even say we were pretty happy. A baby on the way. Julie and I were going well. She comes to visit you for an afternoon. Suddenly, she wants us to move, she wants me to get "a proper job", she wants a home of her own. Julie's always been a lovely laid-back girl, but all of a sudden she needs material things. She wants *stuff*, and I have to provide it. If she doesn't get it, she's going to be out of the door before you can say apron strings.' He looked at me with distaste. 'Apparently that's a phrase you've used.'

'I think it was Julie who said it first.'

'Meh.'

I tried to look as if I didn't care.

'Is that it?' I asked, lightly. 'Is that Roberto Does Angry? Meh?'

He glared. 'Don't push it. And you spoke to Mum, too, and fed her something about African villages. You *know* that saying shit like that gets to her. I know she wants us there, and I know she's dying to have the baby under her roof, but you seem to have got her to say she'll take "a step back" and that she doesn't care if we leave. Apparently we should be building our own mud hut.'

'She does care. But she knows I'm right. She knows I'm right because she wouldn't have wanted to live with her in-laws. In the case of my dad's parents, she *definitely* wouldn't.'

'Yeah, I think we lived with *my* dad's parents for a while when I was a baby. That wasn't the most fun for her.' He looked at me and his anger flared up again. 'But it's different! No one can mind my mum and your dad. They're not exactly demanding.'

'They're not to you.' I watched as he picked up his glass, and drank the shot in one go. 'But Julie already wanted to go, Bobs. And you know that because she'd already said so. And then I was the only person she felt able to talk to about it. Yes, I encouraged her. Because it was what she wanted. So shoot me.'

'I wish.'

Neither of us said anything. I picked up the bottle, and refilled Roberto's glass. He emptied it again, and stared at me challengingly. I was beginning to feel nervous. I hoped Helen would arrive soon.

'So you think Julie's going back to Terry?' I asked, after a while.

'Yeah, cheers for bringing that one up. Appreciate it. She says not but I reckon so. I think that's her plan. In fact I think it's a plan you two have cooked up together.'

'Oh, don't talk crap.'

'I don't know what else you've said. All I know

301

is that she wants out, all of a sudden, and since she does, in fact, have a husband busy being heroic in a war, I guess that's where she'll head.'

I laughed. 'To Iraq? You think Julie's going to go to Baghdad? To Basra? I hear Fallujah's pleasant at this time of year.'

'Well, all I can say is that I wish you'd left it all alone. You have no idea how much trouble you've caused. So, thanks for everything. Yes, she's married to a soldier. Yes, I have a crappy job in a supermarket, and yes, I live with my mother. Yes, I am useless. OK? We're agreed on that. Now, can we move on?'

I stared at him. 'I never knew you felt that bad.'
'Duh.

I shook my head. 'You're just trying to manipulate me like you do Sue. It won't work. Oh, poor little Roberto. You see, you don't need to be in the real army like Terry, because you're already Mummy's special soldier boy.'

At this Roberto jumped up and walked towards me. I was scared, because I knew he was a bit drunk and I knew that I had pushed him. I put my hands on my stomach, to protect my baby. He reached out, and grabbed me by the shoulder. His fingers dug into my skin. I stepped back.

'Bobby,' I said, and now it seemed urgent. 'Bobby, you have to go now. You have to go home. You can see that.'

He paused. I held my breath. Roberto had been in fights before, and although I hoped that he was just trying to scare me, I wasn't sure. His grip tightened. I wanted to push him away, but I didn't dare to move my arms away from my baby.

He took a step closer and I shrank away from him. My back was against the wall. He leaned over, so his face was far too close to mine. When he spoke, it was in a hiss.

'Leave . . . my . . . family . . . alone,' he said.

I nodded, furious with him for doing this to me, but too scared to do anything but agree. As I nodded, my nose hit his. I tried to look at his eyes, but he was too close to me, and I just saw a blur of eyes and stubbly skin. I tried to pull back but my head hit the wall.

I waited, knowing that if he was going to hurt me, there was nothing I could do. We were face to face, far more intimate than we had ever been before. His breath stank of alcohol.

A door slammed downstairs, and he pulled away suddenly. As soon as he released me, I shoved him hard, and caught him off balance. He stumbled and fell on a chair.

'Fuck!' he yelled. He rubbed his bum.

We looked at each other. I dared to smile. To my immense relief, Roberto smiled back.

'Cheers for that,' he said, his eyes wide. 'See, I'm going to be the one with bruises now. Julie will ask me what happened, and I'll say I fell downstairs.'

'Say you fell on top of a chair,' I suggested, relief surging around my veins. 'Tell the truth.

Tell her you were physically intimidating someone because you'd lost the mind games. That'll make you a hero.'

We looked at each other.

'Sorry,' I said.

'Sorry, too,' Roberto muttered, in exactly the same voice he'd used as a child, on the rare occasions Sue had forced him to apologise to me. He didn't say anything else. Instead, he turned and headed down the stairs without looking back.

CHAPTER 29

MARY

1971

Mary chose a corner of the hut for her bed. Most of the others were sleeping on the bus, but she wanted to be out here, in the stone building with the wonky floor. The two Dutch guys who were also bedding down in here were already out cold, next to the glowing embers of the fire. Mary would have slept in here anyway, even without them. She depended on no one, these days. She would never owe anyone anything. That was the way she liked it. This was why she was so happy. Her head was pleasantly fuzzy from the hashish.

The inside of the hut was pitch dark, apart from the soft light that came from the last of the sticks they had burned. She curled up in her sleeping bag. It had been a magical evening, up near the Tibetan border. They had cooked over the fire, sung along to Bob Dylan songs thanks to an Australian couple and their guitar, and, to her slight surprise, Mary was still ecstatically happy. She kept expecting that this would wear off, that she would find herself miserable again, or pining for the baby, or guilty. But it wasn't happening.

Nobody here knew that she had a child. She hardly ever thought about her, and when she did, she knew that Elizabeth was better off without her mother. She gave thanks every day for the fact that she had managed to effect an escape, after getting so deeply into the wrong life.

She had cast off her shackles. Most of her fellow-travellers had had no shackles to begin with. She thought she was the only one among them who was literally running away. Running away was by far the greatest thing she had ever done. She thought she might stay in Nepal for ever. She would find a way to make some money, somehow. She would find a way to live. She had seen Buddhist nuns in Kathmandu, their hair shaved close to their heads, and she had admired the focus and the serenity on their faces. Although she felt humble before them, and knew that she would struggle to live like they lived, she felt that one day, perhaps, she might try to join their number. If she had a plan, which she didn't, Buddhism would be it.

It was a cold, clear night in the Himalayas. *The Himalayas.* The sense of wonder would never wear off. Al, the bus driver, said he had only just started running trips to Tibet, or as close to Tibet as you could get. The bridge that marked the border between Nepal and Tibet, or China, was about a mile away. Nobody was allowed to set foot on it without travel papers to get into China, so instead Al and his people camped by this old hut, and imagined the magic of Lhasa, back when it had been a proper mountain jewel, before the Chinese came. Mary was ignorant of many things, but she was learning fast. She knew exactly who the Dalai Lama was, for instance, and had spent half yesterday afternoon standing as close to Tibet as she could go without being shot, shouting, 'Long live the Dalai Lama!' and 'Free Tibet!' at the border guards. To everyone's disappointment, the guards had stayed completely expressionless. They were frighteningly smart in their green uniforms, and most of them looked younger than Mary was.

'Do they even understand what we're saying?' she asked Al.

He shrugged. 'They catch your drift,' he told her. 'They get your sentiment.'

'So why do they ignore us?'

He laughed. 'Doing a job, Mary. This is the fourth time I've been here, and they've yet to crack a smile, or even a frown.'

The night got colder, and the hut had no glass in the windows, no door in the doorway. She wriggled closer to the dying fire, and tried to wrap her hair around her neck, like a scarf.

She had seen France, Italy, Yugoslavia, Bulgaria, Iran, Afghanistan, Pakistan and India on her way here. She still found it hard to believe. She had seen all those countries, had persuaded border guards to give her visas, had made friends and learned to smoke, had bounced along in the bus, singing. She had eaten whatever food there was, and her money was lasting better than she had expected, because everything was so cheap. Sometimes the bus broke down, and to her amazement, nobody cared. Everyone knew it would work out in the end, and it always did. They all just sat there and waited for the next vehicle to come along, and for somebody to give the driver a lift to a mechanic, and they assumed that the spare part would be available and that the bus would be fixed. And it always was.

It was dawn when she woke. Birds were singing, and the Dutch guys were stirring on the other side of the cold fire. Mary stayed where she was, snuggled down into her sleeping bag.

Slowly, the others began to emerge. Jennifer, who was from New Zealand, stepped down from the bus, yawned, and started her stretching exercises. Mary heaved herself up and went to join in. She enjoyed stretching, and she enjoyed the idea of it just as much. She liked being the sort of person who could say, 'I do my stretches every morning. It clears my head for the day.' Mrs Greene, wife of Billy, mother of Elizabeth, would never have said a thing like that. She would never have been friendly with Jennifer, who had blonde hair down to her waist and tanned legs that she kept on display all the time.

'So, Mary,' said Jennifer, as they touched their

toes. The backs of Mary's legs burned with the effort. 'Where do you go from here?'

Mary thought about it. 'Nowhere, I hope. I'm staying in Kathmandu as long as I can. I don't want to go anywhere else, ever. I might join a convent, actually. Buddhist.'

'Oh, really? 'Cos I was thinking about Goa. They have the most amazing full-moon parties on the beach. What do you reckon? We can hitch to the border and get a train across India.'

Mary looked sideways at Jennifer and smiled. She dismissed the thought of money. It would work out.

'I reckon that sounds good,' she said, thrilled at the very idea of the train ride across India.

Jennifer unfurled herself and reached for the sky with both arms. 'So you in? We can always do the ashram thing later if you want to get spiritual.'

'I'm in.'

They went down the hill a little way and bathed in the hot baths. The *tatopani*, as Mary made herself call them. That was what the others called them. It was the most incredible place to bathe. The baths were concrete structures, and water flowed into them from a hot spring, then gushed away down the mountain in a waterfall. Mary lay back and looked up. She saw the endless blue of the mountain sky. This was freedom.

CHAPTER 30

HELEN

12 June

I ran to the corner of the road and sat on a low wall, and leaned forward, my head in my hands. That man was Roberto. Liz had been kissing him. I had seen her. Her back was pressed up against the wall, and he was standing in front of her, and they were face to face, mouth to mouth. She was kissing her own brother, with her bump of a baby squashed between them.

Roberto was her brother. It was like me kissing Tom.

I tried to breathe deeply. I managed to disappear down the stairs as quietly as I'd arrived. I was certain she didn't know that I knew. Neither of them had seen me. When I'd tiptoed nervously up the stairs, they were so wrapped up in each other that I could have danced the macarena around the room and they wouldn't have noticed.

I still felt like shit. My stomach was full of chicken breasts and mashed potato that Adrian had made with margarine. All it tasted of was chemicals, and I was homesick, desperately homesick, for Mother's

310

Sunday lunches. The occasions may have been dry and formal – though all that would change when Liz arrived, because she was going to bring my family to life – but Mother knew how to cook. She would never have pureed potato with anything but butter. I wanted my family. I wanted to be in France. My sister was having an affair with her own brother, and I wanted to go home.

But I could not go home. Liz was messing up her life more every day. She needed me. I was immensely relieved that I was moving in, because she could not look after herself any more. I was going to be there, to look after her. That was my mission.

I sat there for a long time. The man I was certain was Roberto hurried past, heading, I assumed, to the Tube, to go home to his pregnant girlfriend. He didn't glance at me. He walked fast, and he was frowning. Although it was a warm day, rain started to fall, gently. The paving stones were splattered with water. After a while they were a darker grey entirely.

When I was completely ready, I went back to the flat. This time I rang the buzzer. I should have done that the first time. I should never have thought I could just march in there, with my lovely new set of keys.

Liz was subdued. She showed me the room, and I used all my strength to keep myself from bursting into song. I stood on the threshold and tried not to smile too much. I was here. This was my bedroom, and I lived here, and it was in Liz's flat. I lived with my sister.

'Hello,' I said in my head. 'I'm Helen. I share a flat with my sister.'

It was everything I had ever wanted. I was here. I had won.

I stared at the single bed. Liz's bed was on the other side of the landing from here, a couple of metres away. We were sleeping together, essentially. That meant she trusted me. I was the one person in the world who got to share her space.

There was a cream duvet on the bed, and a metal clothes rail against the wall, and there was a set of shelves and a little bedside table. It was the most wonderful place I had ever lived in my life. I propped the photograph of Tom and me, when we were little, against the wall. I hung up tomorrow's outfit on the rail. I put my scrapbook under the bed. That was everything.

'Where's the rest of your stuff?' asked Liz, suddenly back in the doorway again.

'At the other place,' I said casually. 'I'll fetch it in the morning. I'd like to hang around and settle in, if that's OK.'

'Let's go and fetch it now,' she said. 'I'd like something to do.'

I looked at her knowingly. You'd like something to do, I told her silently, because you don't want to think about the fact that you're sexually involved with your brother.

'Let's not,' I said with a smile. There was no way

312

I could let her come face to face with Adrian. 'For one thing, Adrian's home.'

She looked grim. 'Good,' she said. 'I'd like to meet him.'

'Please don't. I've sent a letter to the landlord because I'm allowed to give a month's notice, but I haven't told the flatmates that I'm leaving. I don't want to tell them.'

'Helen, you have to be grown up about this.' Her mouth was set. 'Adrian's been "behaving inappropriately", as they say at school. You have to confront him. I'll back you up. Come on. This is the perfect moment.' She reached out and took my hand. I was holding my sister's hand. 'We'll do it together. I'll do the talking. Believe me, I am just about ready to lay into someone. You don't have to do anything. Just stand there and nod from time to time.'

I stared at her. I wanted to say something about *inappropriate behaviour*, about how she, of all people, should know that when she saw it. I wanted to scream, 'I saw you!' I wanted to tell her that I was ashamed of her. But I didn't.

'You have to let me do this my way,' I said, hoping I didn't sound sulky. 'I'm getting my stuff tomorrow. I'll mention his behaviour in the note I leave, if you like. Then the girls will see it too.'

She picked up her keys. 'Oh, come on. Let's do it now. I'm dying for a fight.'

I stepped back. 'No,' I said.

We looked at each other. It might have been the

first time I had looked at her without smiling. I felt crap. I felt crap because of Adrian, and because of Roberto. I felt crap because stale cocaine was coursing around my system, poisoning me and making my head throb. I felt crap because I kept thinking about Matt. I was pretty sure he wasn't thinking about me. After half a minute or so, she shrugged.

'It's your life,' she said.

I sat on my bed and looked around. I was actually here. I basked in my own brilliance. I couldn't wait to speak to Tom. I had wheedled my way in. I had done it, and my next concern, rather an urgent one, was to get her to France. I counted my cash, and went downstairs, smiling again.

'This is the deposit,' I said, counting out three hundred and fifty pounds, and handing it to her. 'And this is the first month's rent.' I counted another three hundred and fifty. 'There you go. Now I officially live here. Do you want me to sign a contract?'

I was so happy that I was surprised all the lights didn't spontaneously come on, lit up by my cleverness.

She smiled. 'No, Helen. That won't be necessary.' She flipped the banknotes with her thumb. 'Thanks for this. I could get used to it.'

'Do get used to it.'

She looked at me. 'I can't get used to it. That will have to be the baby's bedroom at some point.'

Liz was subdued, as she should have been, so

I pretended to be as well. We spent the evening watching mindless television. Watching it together, the television set we shared.

'Who's Rosa?' I asked, at one point.

She looked round. Why?'

'You mentioned her once. You said, "I can't find Rosa." I could help you find her if you wanted.'

She shook her head. 'Don't worry. I found Rosa.'

We both went to bed early. I lay awake and marvelled at what I had done. Before I opened that box in Mother's wardrobe, I had never done anything interesting with my life. Now I felt I could do anything. I heard Liz going to bed. I could even hear the pages turning as she read a book.

Everything was different here. The flat smelt homely. My sheets seemed to be included in the price, and they were chemically fragrant. The carpet was clean. There was a see-through curtain at the window, and the light from a street lamp outside was illuminating my bedroom, in yellow. I had rarely had a good night's sleep in London because of all the light that trickled in around the windows. In this room, it poured through the wispy curtain.

It was the middle of June. The baby was due in August. I had to move on, quickly, to the next part of the plan.

I stared at the light and thought about it. If I listened hard, I could hear Liz breathing. I was in.

CHAPTER 31

LIZ

20 June

'Look at this!' I showed my new trick to Sandrine. I leaned back in my chair and carefully balanced a cup of tea on my stomach. I took my hand away, and it stayed there.

Sandrine applauded. 'Well done,' she said. She looked at me, slightly strangely.

'What?' I asked.

She paused. 'I'm just wondering,' she said, her head on one side, 'whether you are all right? Are you all right? I worry about you, Lizzy.'

I forced a laugh. My due date was approaching too rapidly, and I worried about myself, too.

'No,' I told her, firmly. 'I can cope. I have my family.' I was still angry about Roberto's aggression, but I hadn't told anyone about it, and I hoped that I would soon be able to forget it. 'And I have enough friends to keep me going. And now I have a flat-mate. It's going to be fine.'

'Are you sure?'

'Yes.' I shook my head, because I really meant 'no'. I gathered up my things. 'Do you want to go for a drink?' I asked. 'Not that I'm much of a drinking partner, but it would be nice to see you.' I looked around the shambolic, yet secretly organised, staffroom. 'Out of this place, I mean.'

She sighed. 'I'd love to. Let's do it. Unfortunately for me, I'm supposed to be going to the cinema later, or I'd have taken you out for something to eat.'

'A date?' I laughed. The idea of a date was alien.

'Oh, gosh, nothing like that. It's that French girl, Isabelle. Did you meet her? She came in to talk to the A-level students once or twice. Skirts up to here.' She indicated her crotch. 'The boys loved her and the girls wanted to be her. But she's turned into a bit of a drag. She seems a bit homesick, and I can't seem to manage to drop her.'

I thought about it. 'Did I meet her?'

'You'd remember if you had. Come along to the movie, by all means.'

I shook my head. 'I'd just fall asleep. But let's go for that drink.'

We caught a bus to Oxford Circus, and from there we walked (I waddled) to Soho. From time to time I paused, with a shooting pain across my stomach. The pain was gone as soon as it arrived, and I knew it was my penalty for being unfit. I was breathless by the time we arrived, but pleased with myself for having exercised. I was pleased, too, that I was managing to keep up a trivial conversation with Sandrine. We discussed Kathy and her tentative softening towards me. We talked

317

about when and whether I should extend the hand of friendship back towards her.

'She can't ignore you,' Sandrine said, 'now that you're like this.' And she patted my stomach. I tried not to wince.

'I might make her wait till after the birth,' I mused. 'Because she's been so horrible for so long.'

Julie had called me the day before.

'I don't know what you said to Roberto,' she told me. She paused, then carried on when I didn't tell her. 'But it worked. You won't believe this, but he's been out looking at flats!' She sounded different. Her hangdog tone had melted away, and she seemed younger.

'Oh,' I said, trying to inject some pretend excitement into my voice. 'That's great! You must be over the moon!'

'Yes, I am. I owe you. He won't tell me how you did it.'

I paused. 'It was nothing.' I remembered Roberto backing me up against the wall, using his bulk and his strength to win the fight. It seemed that I had won, after all.

'And I had a letter from Terry. He wants to give the marriage another go. Can you believe it?'

'What do you say to that?'

I heard the smile in her voice. 'I say *no*, of course! I've written him a letter. I should have done it months ago, but I suppose I was never completely sure of Roberto. And now I am, thanks to you.

Now I'm setting everything straight. I've told Terry about the baby, and he's just going to have to deal with it. He's a big boy.'

When we arrived in Soho, I was sweating. I could feel the damp patches under my arms, and I hoped that my size, my 'condition', might stop it being quite as disgusting as it should have been. My feet were aching. I knew my face was red.

'Can we sit indoors?' I said. 'Somewhere with air conditioning?'

Sandrine nodded. 'Sure. Let's go to the cinema café. They do gorgeous cakes.' Sandrine loved the word 'gorgeous'. She said it was her favourite word in the English language.

The café at the Curzon Soho was busy, but I stood close to the most comfortable-looking seats, a little sofa, and stroked my belly and complained loudly about my exhaustion until the people stood up, awkwardly, and let us have their place. As I tried to smile my thanks, several lightning flashes shot across my bump simultaneously. I clutched my stomach and tried not to let it show on my face.

Sandrine smiled. 'Nicely done.'

I settled back and stretched my legs out. After some deep breaths, I felt normal again.

'You have to milk the benefits. Because they are few and bloody far between.'

'You won't say that when you've got your baby.'

'Try me.' But I knew she was right. I had no

concept of what it was going to be like to hold my baby in my arms, but I knew I would not reject it. I just knew.

'What time are you meeting the crazy girl?' I asked.

She looked at her watch. 'Half past six. That gives us an hour and a half. What are you having?'

I leaned my head back, on to the edge of the sofa. It was slightly too low, so I pulled myself upright again. 'Would it be weird to have a glass of wine and a piece of cake? A small glass of wine? If I don't drink it all?' I looked around. 'Will I be lynched?'

Sandrine was on her feet. 'You have to have water with it. Then it's fine. I may not have children, but I'm French, and we know about these things.'

I was going to stay and meet Sandrine's French assistant friend. I was probably going to go to the film with them. It was a French film, and it seemed to be about a man who was being spied on by someone with a video camera. Right up until she was ten minutes late, I was going to stay. Then, suddenly, I fell asleep. This was happening a lot.

I dragged myself to my feet and held tightly to my aching belly. 'Sorry,' I said. 'If she turns up, I hope you have a good time.'

Sandrine grimaced. 'I might have a better one if she doesn't. I don't know what it is about her. She's hard work, in a way that other people just aren't.'

'Anyway, I have to get home. I just have to go to bed. I hope Helen's out tonight, because I can't speak to anyone. Bye.'

I got home to find that Helen was, indeed, out. I was thankful as I stumbled into the bathroom. I was going to be in bed at eight o'clock, because that was the only thing I could possibly do.

It took my brain a while to register what my eyes were seeing. The words echoed around my mind before I took in what they meant. Red. Red was all right. I liked red. Blood. Blood was not so good. In my knickers. That had to be bad. That was something I had not seen for a long time.

I was bleeding. It was fresh, red blood. There was not a lot of it, but it was there, and that either meant that I was miscarrying, which would mean a stillbirth, or it meant something else was wrong and the baby would be born prematurely. I was thirty-two weeks pregnant. This, I was certain, was not good.

I stared for a while, and wondered what to do. I had no idea where Helen was, and wondered whether I should phone Matt and see if she was there. But I didn't trust Matt enough to launch myself into his hands. I felt disconnected, vague. I walked into my bedroom and picked up the photograph of my mother. My poor mother. I looked at her, and at the baby in her arms – at myself – and, for the first time in many years, I began to cry. I longed for my baby, longed for it to be all right, and stared into the pit that I knew would await me if it was not. Nothing else that had happened to me this year – nothing that had ever happened – would mean a thing if I lost my baby.

I needed to do something. I could feel that the blood was still coming. I wondered whether the pains I'd had earlier had been contractions.

I looked out of the window, and saw that a light was on over the road.

I picked up the phone and punched in a number. 'Anna?' I said.

It was frightening to arrive at Accident and Emergency. It was terrifying that I didn't have to wait. I had never met Jeremy, but he took charge. He spoke to the woman on the desk, and suddenly I was in a wheelchair. I hated that. They pushed me along corridors and took me up in a lift. The walls were painted a sickly green.

'Who thought that would be a good colour for hospitals?' I asked.

'Shhh,' said Anna, and she patted my hand.

'You shouldn't be here,' I said, looking at her enormous bump. 'You should be resting at home.' I craned my neck to look at Jeremy, who was a pale, freckled Englishman in complete contrast to his wife. 'And you shouldn't be here either,' I told him. I felt inwardly hysterical, and I couldn't stop my voice from catching. 'You should be at home, relaxing with your wife. It's Thursday. No one should be at a hospital with a woman they've never met before. Not on a *Thursday*.'

Jeremy shook his head. 'Hey,' he said. 'Anna's talked about you a lot. She worries that you've only got some loopy girl in short skirts for company. Anything we can do. Really.' He smiled. 'Thursday or not.'

'Oh, God, I'm losing my mind.'

Anna patted my hand. 'Shhh.'

I lay back and felt detached as things happened to me. I felt like an observer, watching dispassionately as I was hooked up to a monitor, as my blood pressure was taken, as I was told to put on a hospital gown.

The nurse had to push Anna and Jeremy aside to check the monitor.

'Well, baby's heartbeat's lovely and strong,' she said cheerfully. 'So that's one thing not to worry about. Now, do you think you could have felt a contraction?'

'I don't know,' I told her. 'I had some pains earlier. But they weren't like I'd expected contractions to be. They were sharp. Sudden. And they only lasted half a second.'

'Sounds more like you've been overdoing it,' she said. She felt my bump with strong, experienced hands 'Baby's head down, but not fully engaged. It's fine for him to be head down at this stage. It doesn't mean anything.'

I stared at her. 'Him?'

She laughed. She was a competent woman in a blue uniform, and I was glad to be under her care, even if she was telling me my own secrets.

'Oh! Sorry. I just tend to say "him" because I think it sounds nicer than "it". I don't have any inside knowledge, don't worry. Didn't you find out, then?'

'No.'

'Good idea. There aren't many surprises left in life, after all, are there?'

I thought about my life. 'There are a few.'

'Well, I'll check your cervix, and then if everything's in order and *if* we can get a sonographer, then we'll take you downstairs for a scan.'

It turned out that my cervix was 'impeccable', which seemed to me to be a nice thing to be told when you're tearful and hysterical on a warm Thursday night.

'That's not opening any time soon,' the nice nurse assured me.

'So – the bleeding?' I didn't dare to be relieved.

'Oh, there are a few things it could have been. A small blood clot is the most likely. It happens more often than you'd think.'

I sat up. 'Can I go home?'

The nurse looked at Anna and Jeremy, who were still sitting in the room, sharing a big bottle of water. Anna's head was resting on Jeremy's shoulder.

'Your friends can go home. You'll need to stay in tonight, just to be on the safe side. For once, there's a couple of spare beds in ante-natal. The nurse on duty tomorrow can monitor you again in the morning and then, assuming all's well, we'll let you out.' She smiled. 'For the moment. At least you'll know the ropes when you come back, but I don't expect that to be for another eight weeks. I really don't.'

I slept surprisingly well. The hospital was rundown, the ward was busy, and there was a woman in the room who was having increasingly noisy contractions. In spite of all this, I had relinquished control, and this gave me a strange sort of peace. I woke up at half past six, when the light was flooding in, the nurses were clattering around, and everyone seemed to think it was a reasonable time to start the day.

'Oh, fuck,' I said, speaking vaguely in the direction of the woman in the next bed. 'I've got to go to work today.'

She looked at me, wide-eyed, and shook her head. 'You're in hospital. You don't have to go to work. That's the *whole point.*'

I got home at eight, feeling weirdly rested. I was ready to shower and change and get to the Tube as quickly as I could.

Helen was standing at the top of the stairs. She looked like a child, in tiny shorts and a vest top. Her arms and legs were so skinny that her knees and elbows bulged out.

'Where have you *been*?' she demanded. She sounded petulant.

'Oh,' I said. 'Sorry, maybe I should have let you know. I was at the hospital.'

She turned away. 'Well, actually, I know that now,' she said. 'But you could have left a note or something. Honestly, I've been worried sick.'

I didn't have time for this. 'Sorry,' I said again. 'But how did you know?'

'Anna told me. But are you all right? Seriously? I was so scared you'd had the baby. Or something.'

'No, I'm fine. And now I need to go to work.'

Helen stared at me. Although her face was pretty, there was something hard about her. I thought that I had preferred her when she used to smile inanely all the time.

'I can't let you go to work,' she said, in a monotone. 'There's no way. You have to stay at home. I'll stay with you. I won't go to work either. Matt will understand. I'll look after you, all day. You don't have to lift a finger. Stay in bed. I'll wait outside on the landing, so that I don't annoy you. You can have a little bell to ring if you need anything.'

I laughed, though she was unnerving me. 'No, honestly. I'm not delicate. I'm fine! It was just a clot of blood. It's gone now. It was actually nothing. They only kept me in because they happened to have a bed.'

'Lizzy! A blood clot is *very* serious. Everyone knows that. People *die* from blood clots.'

I started up the stairs. 'Not this sort,' I said. 'This was a small lump of blood, completely harmless, that came from the placenta. It was nothing to do with the baby, and it was nothing to do with deep vein thrombosis. The baby was never in any danger, and nor was I. I feel quite energetic. And I'm going to work.'

I was nearly at the top of the stairs. Helen stepped back. I could almost see her mind ticking over.

'Oh,' she said, after a few seconds. 'Sorry. OK. That's fine. I didn't meant to hassle you. I was trying to help. I was trying to think what would be best for you.'

I felt bad. I could not fall out with her again, not now we were living together. All the same, I was tempted. There was something about Helen that brought out the worst in me.

'No,' I said. '*I'm* sorry. I shouldn't have snapped. It was a worrying evening and I have to go to work. I really do. We'll have a proper chat at the weekend.'

She smiled her old, manic smile, nodded, and went into her room.

I got home after a hard day at work. I was hot, sunburned after a lunchtime sandwich in the park, and starving. Helen was in the kitchen.

'Hello!' she trilled, beaming. 'I've got a surprise!'

I looked around the room. 'I can see that. Helen, if you're cooking dinner, I love you.'

'I know it's only early, but I wanted to leave it for you, because I'm working this evening.' She took a bottle out of the fridge. 'Non-alcoholic champagne,' she announced, flourishing it. 'Sparkling grape juice, to be precise. In fact my dad would go mad if he could see this. Look, it has the word "champagne" on the label, which I think is technically illegal. Have some now. Sit down.'

I sat down, grateful. Helen opened the bottle.

'You look like quite the expert,' I observed. 'Do you do that at work? I hate popping corks.'

She grinned. I liked it when she smiled properly. I didn't often get a sense of the real Helen.

'I'm crap at it,' she said. 'This one's a lot easier.'

'Probably because it's made for children.'

'The other day I had to open one at work. I was trying to hold on to the cork with the tea towel, like Matt said, but I let go and the cork hit the ceiling, then flew back down and landed in a woman's drink. Which fell over, and the glass smashed, and spilt red wine everywhere.'

'Matt was pleased?'

'He said he's docking my wages for the two drinks, the broken glass, the dent in the ceiling, and the woman's dry-cleaning bill. I have no idea whether he's joking.'

'He is joking. If he's not, refer him to me.'

'Thanks, Miss Greene.'

I looked at her. 'Are you and Matt an item?'

Helen smiled, and suddenly she looked like a girl in love. 'Mmm,' she said, with a giggle. 'Sort of. I'm not really sure. We've never talked about it.'

'He should be nicer to you.' I took a sip, and

waited for her to say something. Instead, she looked worried. She was pacing.

'There's something else,' she said, quickly. She put an envelope on the table. 'Open it in a minute. I'm off now. Working at five. Your dinner's in the oven. You need to switch it off at six but it'll keep warm for as long as you want. It's fish pie, I hope that's all right. I read on the forum that fish is good for the baby's brain and for its eyesight. Salad's in the fridge and the dressing's in the door. There are strawberries and cream for pudding if you want them.' She practically ran out of the house.

I picked up the envelope with some trepidation.

CHAPTER 32

HELEN

21 June

Matt finished making the two lines. I screwed up my face.

'No, thanks,' I said. His head jerked upwards.

'What?' he said. He was angry. 'We always do this. Don't be stupid.'

I shook my head. 'I need a clear head this weekend,' I explained. I pulled my T-shirt off, over my head. 'You do it, though,' I said, politely. 'And I'll still take my clothes off. I'll maybe have a drink instead.'

I was feeling nervous. This was the first time I had ever stood up to Matt. I didn't want to, but I had a strange feeling that it was what I needed to do. I wanted a clear head, and I didn't want to be his little slave. I thought he would like me better if I did my own thing sometimes. I had read an article about it.

'It's no fun if it's just me,' he complained. 'Come on. You normally can't get enough of it.'

I carried on undressing. Although he was hostile,

he was watching me closely. I stood up, naked, and smiled at him.

'Charlie makes me feel crap all weekend,' I told him. 'So let's have foreplay instead. What do you think? That would be fun, wouldn't it?' This was from the article, too.

He grunted. 'What's this all about?'

'It's about me having lots to do.'

'What? What have you got to do?'

'Family stuff.'

I was longing for the coke. I was desperate for the confidence boost. I was exhausted, because I'd been up all night. I was beyond tired. I was so exhausted that I was hallucinating. Today, I had been spooked by Tom, standing outside the window, on a sunny street in Kentish Town. He looked so real that for a while I thought that he was really there. I knew he couldn't be, though. I knew I was imagining him.

I looked back at Matt. He was dressed in black combat pants, as usual, with a black T-shirt. His hair covered half of his face. I wondered whether I had fallen in love with him. I wanted to drink and snort drugs and kiss him. But I needed to get Liz's answer more than anything else in the world. And I wanted to lose my virginity, because the fact that I hadn't was starting to annoy me. I was supposed to be going back to France soon, and when that happened, I supposed that I would leave Matt behind.

I had been awake almost all night. When I got

home from the cinema and found Liz wasn't there, I stared out of the window, up and down the street, until I saw Anna and her husband walking slowly back from the Tube. Although I didn't like Anna, and I could tell that she didn't think much of me, I rushed downstairs and out into the warm night air.

'Anna!' I said. 'Hello,' I added to her husband. 'Do you know where Liz is? Have you seen her?'

Anna managed to smile although she looked exhausted.

'We do, as a matter of fact,' her freckled husband told me, and he explained that she was at the hospital because she had been bleeding. He said that everything seemed fine now, but I didn't believe him. I wanted to go straight there, but they told me she was sleeping. Still, I couldn't sleep. I was so scared that she was losing the baby. That baby was my nephew or niece. It was Mother's first grandchild.

Matt stood very close to me. I was fiercely aware that he was clothed and I was not. I tingled. I was certain now that I was an exhibitionist. He put his hands on my waist. His hands were warm.

'What is this about?' he asked, softly. 'Is it one of those commitment things? Is that it?'

I had read about commitment problems. Commitment was to do with babies.

'No,' I told him. 'I don't want a baby.'

He laughed. 'Good! But do you want me to be, like, your boyfriend or something?'

'What are we at the moment?'

He smiled. 'Buddies.'

'Would you like to be my boyfriend?'

He was frowning and smiling at the same time. 'Dunno,' he said. 'I could try.'

'Seriously?'

'You're not supposed to. With people you work with.'

I gestured to my naked body. 'You're not supposed to do this, either, then.'

'Still. We could go out or something. If you wanted.'

'OK.'

'You're busy this weekend.'

I nodded. 'How about during the week?'

'Monday night? No one goes out on a Monday.'

'That would be fine.'

'I'll see if Joel can hold the fort.'

'Great.'

'So, do we shag now, or what?'

I started getting dressed. 'No. I think I'm supposed to make you wait till Monday, aren't I? Or the third date, maybe? I do read magazines, you know.'

I walked home feeling confused. A 'date' with Matt was a strange prospect. I had never been on a date, never been on anything close to one. Although we worked together all the time, I worried that I wouldn't have anything to say to him. And I thought relationships weren't meant to work that way. I was sure that normal people didn't get their first date after weeks of drugs and groping and nudity. Or perhaps that was exactly the way it worked. There was so much I didn't know. I decided not to mention it to Tom.

I soon forgot all about it. I had invited Liz to France, and I was about to find out what her answer was. This was it. The moment of truth.

There was a note on the kitchen table.

'Had to go to bed. Thanks for a wonderful dinner. And for the tickets. Let's talk in the morning. L x'

I could hardly sleep, once more, for wondering what she meant.

In the morning, I felt tired. I dragged myself downstairs when I heard Lizzy getting up. I felt as if I hadn't slept for ever. Then, when I sat at the table, with a strong cup of coffee in front of me, Liz looked me in the eye and said no.

'It's lovely of you,' she said, 'and in many ways I'd love a break. But I do have to work, and after that scare, I think I'll stay around here, now. Until the baby's born.'

I tried hard not to show her how I felt. 'Are you sure?' I asked her levelly. I topped up both our coffees from the cafetière. I was drinking mine quickly, because I knew I was going to need litres of it to be able to function. 'I can't tell you how lovely it is, out there at this time of year. It's not too hot yet. But it's warm enough.' I looked out of the window, at the back of a house in the next street. 'London really isn't the same,' I told her. I tried to think of anything that might change her mind. 'Where I come from is just right for you now. There are trees and flowers, and it smells of herbs. And it's hot but in the shade it's perfect, and you can lounge around. Mother and Papa have a swimming pool. Honestly, you need to relax. A weekend away is exactly what you need.'

She sighed. 'It sounds delicious.'

'So come! It's only an hour and a half.'

'I don't fly. I don't take flights, because of the emissions. Sorry. I just don't feel I can. Maybe after the baby's born I could bring it out sometime, on the train.'

I knew she was fobbing me off. She had no idea what was at stake.

'You should come now. I've paid for the tickets, and everything. And the flight's leaving anyway, whether you're on it or not, so those emissions are out there no matter what.'

'Which is called the continuum fallacy, and it's not an argument. And Helen, I didn't ask you to buy them.'

We were at a stalemate. I said the only thing I could think of.

'Think about it,' I said, and I tried to sound as if I didn't care. 'The offer's open right up to the last minute.'

Liz went off to her stupid pregnancy yoga class with nasty old Anna. I watched them leaving, from my window. Anna's baby had to be due soon, but she looked as if she'd got a football up her dress. It didn't look natural. Liz, on the other hand, was padded all over.

I saw someone running away down the street. He was wearing a black T-shirt and shorts. He ran to Liz and Anna, and past them, and he was gone.

I phoned home, but he wasn't there. When I called his mobile, it rang with an English tone.

'Where are you?' I demanded.

'Why?'

'Tom! Where are you?'

'Nowhere special.'

'Are you in Britain?'

'Do you think I'm in Britain?'

'Yes I do.'

'Anyway. What's going on with Liz?'

'You know, if you are here, you're allowed to come and see me.' I swallowed. 'I have missed you, you know.'

'OK.'

'And we need to do some planning.' I told him what Liz had done to me, that morning.

'OK then,' he said when I'd finished. 'She'll be on the plane on Friday. You just have to make her life so hard, in London, that she's desperate to get on a plane and escape.'

I thought about this.

'I could tell Julie that she kissed Roberto.'

'Only if you can do it without anyone knowing it was you.'

'But I'd feel terrible if I told her. It would cause Liz so many problems.'

I heard Tom tutting at me. 'Don't get sentimental. We're doing this for the greater good. We're doing it to get our family back together. OK? Remember, those people are her *other* family. We're her real family. We're her birth family. Be ruthless.'

'Liz doesn't know I saw her. I could maybe do it anonymously.'

'Go on, then. What else?'

'She's got really friendly with Anna. I'm not sure I could change that.'

'Do something about it.'

'This woman Rosa seems to be important.'

'Do you know anything about her?'

'She looks weird and she's scary.'

'So you can dig around. Anything else? What about the baby's dad?'

Tom made me realise that I needed to be brave. This was crucial. I pictured myself, arriving at home with Liz. I could see the expression on Mother's face when she realised what I had done. I glowed at the idea that our family was going to be reunited. Tom was right. I had to be ruthless to make it happen. Mother needed her baby back.

Cautiously, I pushed open the door to Liz's bedroom. It was messy, as I had expected. Liz made a mess everywhere she went. She was incapable of having so much as a drink of water without

337

leaving a trail of drips across the counter and a half-empty glass next to the sink. There were clothes on the floor, and cups and glasses on her bedside table. She didn't have a duvet, just a sheet, and it was twisted around itself, hanging half off the bed. I wanted to tidy up for her, but decided that I had better not.

There was a photograph on the table, an old one. I looked away.

I wasn't sure what I was looking for, but whatever it was, it wasn't there. I thought for a while. Then I went downstairs, to the sitting room, and switched on the computer.

I tried to log on to Babytalk as LizGreene, but I kept getting the password wrong. I tried three times before it shut me out. Liz's password wasn't Steve, it wasn't mother, and it wasn't baby. She was less predictable than I'd thought.

Then I quit my browser, opened up again, and clicked the 'password reminder' link. It was easy to open Liz's email, because she didn't have it protected at all. After a couple of minutes, the Babytalk email landed in her inbox. Her password was twix.

I hadn't been on to Babytalk for ages, which was a good thing. When Liz wasn't speaking to me, I had logged on regularly to check up on her but it had all been very boring. I did not miss that stupid website at all. It had played its role as a means to an end, but I had never met a duller bunch of self-obsessed people, and I was glad I didn't have to pretend to be interested any more.

Once I was logged in, I got to work quickly. In a few minutes, I had written a short, vitriolic post. I copied the link, and created a new Yahoo account. I chose a username that sounded as if it belonged to a different Babytalk member entirely: fluffball@yahoo.com. I remembered that the whingeing forumite called Fluffball used to sign herself 'Jem', so I filled in my name, randomly, as Jemima Jenkins. I checked Liz's email address book. Then Jemima Jenkins pasted the link on to an email, wrote, 'Honey, I thought you should see what your "friend" has to say about you,' and sent it off.

I erased the history, and shut down. Liz would be back soon.

When she got back, I made her a pot of herbal tea, gave her a bar of chocolate, stole her phone from her handbag when she wasn't looking, and went upstairs. I was on a roll; I didn't dare to stop this, because I knew that if I hesitated, I wouldn't be able to carry on. I was exhausted, and I didn't want to stop and think about whether what I was doing was wrong. I did not want to address the question of whether this was an acceptable way to treat a beloved sister.

First I looked up Steve's number, and copied it down. Then I sent a text to Julie, and deleted it from the 'sent' folder. The phone was back in Liz's red bag before she noticed it had gone.

'I'm off out now,' I said, trying to look and sound natural and carefree. 'Got some shopping to do.' I smiled my old smile, and Liz looked back anxiously.

'You OK?' she asked. 'I really do mean that I'd like to come to France another time.'

'I know. It's fine. I think I'll go home next weekend anyway.'

'Good idea. Will Matt give you the time off?'

'He already has.' I smiled at her. 'Guess what? He's getting Joel to mind the caff on Monday night and we're going out on a date!'

Liz grinned. 'That's wonderful news. How exciting for you. I can get my thrills vicariously now. You'll have to tell me all about it. I want all the gory details.'

I smiled. Liz's life was very wholesome, compared to mine.

'You don't,' I told her.

I bought several outfits. These ones were from expensive magazines, because I needed to feel extra confident if I was going to pull any of this off. I bought a fifties-style dress with a full skirt, and a pair of round-toed red shoes with a small heel. I got some new jeans, recommended for my body shape by *Elle,* and a couple of lovely tops from Agnès B. I had my hair done. I gave my credit card a workout that I knew would shock my father, but at least it would reassure him that I was still alive – though he would find that out

340

before the bill reached him anyway. He would, I hoped, agree that my clothes bill was a small price to pay for the reinstatement of a stepdaughter and a grandchild.

I smiled throughout my shopping, even when I was tired and anxious and so strung-out that I considered calling Matt and asking whether I could have some drugs after all. I chatted brittly to the hairdresser, telling her about my family in France and explaining that I hadn't seen them for months and so I wanted to look good for when I went back next weekend. I told her about my little brother and my big sister. I grinned without stopping. The woman nodded and said 'That's nice' a lot, and I was pleased.

I sat for ages with dye on my hair, flicking through magazines with trembling fingers. My nostrils filled up with the smell of bleach. I was pleased to stumble upon a page of dating tips. By the time my hair was finished, I knew that on a first date I ought to ask Matt about himself, and listen to his answers. I should not wear too much perfume, and I should not dress provocatively, or he would think I was tarty. I should meet him in a public place, look into his eyes, and laugh a lot.

I would do all of that, though I wasn't sure the bit about dressing in a tarty way could really apply to me, since I'd been stripping off for him every weekend for quite some time.

I walked back to Kentish Town, because I was too nervous to do anything else. I had, at the same time, no energy and far too much of it. As I crossed the Euston Road, however, my feet almost stopped. I stood still, in the middle of the dual carriageway. Cars thundered towards me.

'I can't go back yet,' I said to myself. A taxi sounded its horn, and suddenly I was alert. I ran to the pavement, aware that the driver was shouting at me. It was true. I was a stupid twat. But I really didn't want to go to the flat. I didn't want to be there when things started to happen.

I wondered what to do with myself. It was another hot, sunny day. They were saying it was a drought, and that water was going to be rationed soon. If it was this hot in London, I dreaded to think what it must be like at home.

I decided that I needed to see somebody. Apart from Liz, I really only knew two people in London: Matt and Sandrine. Sandrine had given me a scare a couple of nights ago by turning up to our meeting with Liz in tow, but I hid, and watched, and after a while Liz left. I wondered whether there was any chance Liz was with her now, worried about it, and decided to see Matt instead.

'You sad loser!' he yelled, with a laugh, as I walked in. I was hot and sticky, and felt slightly faint. 'What kind of a nutter comes to work when they've got the day off?'

I smiled and took a stool at the bar. 'The kind who wants to see her *boyfriend*.' I regretted it at once, and sure enough, Matt took a step back.

'Steady,' he said, widening his eyes at me. Then he laughed and patted my shoulder. I noticed he was still keeping me at arm's length.

'Can I have a glass of tap water?' I asked, looking as innocent as I could. Matt hated people asking for tap water. If somebody asked me for a glass of tap water, and Matt was within earshot, I had to smile and say, 'Water? Still or sparkling?' I could only give tap water if they specified it for a second time. Matt said that anyone that cheap and that brazen could have his fucking tap water, but they couldn't have his fucking ice.

He rolled his eyes. 'Get it yourself, you cheap tart.'

I went behind the counter and poured myself a pint glass of water. I added ice and lemon, for good measure. On impulse, I poured myself an enormous glass of cold Sauvignon, too.

The door opened, and two customers came in.

I recognised her at once. She was almost beautiful. Her hair was long and black and she was wearing a long tight skirt and a magenta T-shirt with 'You wish' written in diamanté across the breasts. I wished I was that confident.

I looked at the man next to her. He was shorter than she was, but he looked frightening. His neck was thick, his hair shaved to distract from the way that it was half gone, and he radiated aggression. I looked down as he looked at me.

'Do we order at the bar?' he asked, and to my surprise his voice was upper class to the point of parody.

'Yes,' I said, making myself smile again. It seemed I was working, and, indeed, I would happily relinquish my day off for a chance to observe Rosa at close quarters.

'Course we do,' she told him, and rolled her eyes. 'That's what you do at bars, isn't it?'

'I didn't know,' he complained. 'Just checking.'

'Just wanting to talk to a pretty barmaid, more like,' she said, and I watched them look at each other and laugh.

She looked at me, and smiled. I knew I wasn't imagining the suspicion in her eyes.

'I've seen you somewhere,' she said. 'Haven't I?'

I spoke quickly. 'In here, probably.'

'Certainly not. I haven't graced this establishment with my presence for a very long time.'

I kept my smile at full beam. 'Well, welcome back, madam.'

'Cheers, my dear,' she said, and sat down. All of the other customers were outside, frying themselves in the afternoon sun. Only this woman – Rosa – and her friend were sheltering. I listened to their exchange.

'Well?' he asked.

'White wine,' she said firmly. 'I'd prefer champagne, but I'm trying to wean myself off the habit. It's too decadent when there are people starving in the world.'

'Champagne it is,' he told her. 'The children of Africa won't begrudge it, just this once.' He walked towards me. 'Do you do it by the glass,

344

or are you going to do me for a bottle?' He caught my eye and smiled, eyebrows raised.

I was trying to work out whether I could turn this situation to my advantage. 'By the glass for the cheap stuff,' I said, 'and, er, by the bottle for the good stuff.'

The man sighed theatrically. 'All right. Would you bring us a bottle, please, my love?'

'Sure,' I said. I pushed a list towards him and, yet again, forced a bright smile. 'Which one?'

He scanned it. 'Jesus. Erm, we'll have the Moët, I guess. Which should be pronounced with the final "t" as Claude Moët, while French by birth, bore a Dutch surname.'

I nodded and wondered whether he would be cross if I rolled my eyes.

'Whereas his son-in-law, Pierre-Gabriel Chandon de Briailles, was French through and through,' I told him instead.

He stepped back. 'A well-informed blonde!' he cried. 'How did you do that?'

'Oh, my father's obsessed. He's a wine-maker and he'd love to make champagne. But he lives in the wrong region. Would you like two glasses with your Moëtt?'

He leaned in. 'To tell you the truth, love, I'd prefer a pint, but under the circumstances I think I'd better join the lovely lady.'

'Sit down and I'll bring it over.'

I took out the glasses, assembled a bottle and an ice bucket, and took a chilled bottle of Moët from the back of the fridge. I tried not to take my eyes off Rosa. I wondered whether she was a friend of Liz's or, perhaps, a friend of Steve's. Perhaps she was a former in-law.

It was clear that Rosa and this man didn't know each other. He was desperate to impress, and she was more nervous than she was letting on, her hand trembling slightly, her posture exaggeratedly relaxed. She crossed her legs, hanging a sandal from her big toe. When I got closer, I discovered that she was wearing a strong perfume.

I steeled myself to open the champagne. I hated that even more than I hated adding up people's drinks orders in my head when the bar was busy and everyone was waiting for me. I knew I was supposed to twist the bottle, not the cork, but I had yet to perform the manoeuvre successfully, and after my previous performance, I dreaded what might be going to happen. I tried to look confident as I placed the cloth over the cork, gripped it tightly, and clasped the bottle under my arm while I twisted it with my left hand.

The cork came out without a sound, and champagne emerged. I grabbed a glass from the table and managed to catch most of it. A good dribble, however, went on the floor.

'Well, *that* was blonde,' said the man. 'Are you charging me for that bit?'

I was relieved to have messed it up so little. 'No,' I told him happily. 'I'll deduct it from your bill.'

'Helen!' called Matt from the bar. I couldn't

look up, as I was still trying to pour it without it bubbling all over the table.

'Yes?' I asked. I quickly put my finger into the bubbles to pop a few, hoping no one would notice.

'You know the rule. Discounts come from your wages.'

'Well, since I haven't got any wages as this is my day off, I think we can call it quits.'

Despite my best efforts, Rosa's glass frothed over, and I wiped champagne from the table with my cloth, apologising again.

I rushed in and out, waiting on outdoor tables because I had to. Every time I came in, I watched Rosa and her friend closely. I watched them finishing the bottle. I watched as Rosa stood up and muttered something about the little ladies' room. She wandered over, smiling, and grabbed me as I walked past with a tray of pints. All of them spilt a little, but I thought I would get away with it.

'I know how I know you,' she said, twiddling her hair. 'You were hiding behind a car. You walked into me and asked about Lizzy.'

I was suddenly scared. I did not like being found out.

'Mmm, maybe,' I said, vaguely.

'Don't "maybe" me,' she said sharply. 'You know I'm right. Do you know Liz?'

I nodded. 'I'm her flatmate.'

Rosa looked confused. 'Then why the fuck were you spying—'

I spoke over her. 'She took a lodger in to pay the bills,' I told her. 'And it's me.'

'Has she said anything about me?'

I decided to try bluffing, to see what happened. 'Yes.' I looked into Rosa's eyes. I looked all over her face, and realised what it was that was odd about her. 'Yes, she's told me quite a bit about you, as it happens.'

Rosa took a deep breath and raised herself to her full height. She was exactly the same height as me. I was surprised she wasn't taller.

'In that case,' she said, 'please ask her to get in touch. We have certain matters to discuss. As you are no doubt aware. Here is my card.' She almost put it on the tray, then pulled it back and stuffed it into my pocket, instead. 'That tray is a disgrace,' she said. 'Matt ought to fire you.'

I wanted to say something back but I didn't know what. Rosa strode off to the loos. I poured myself another glass of wine.

'Do you know that Rosa woman?' I asked Matt when he came back in.

He chuckled. 'Sure I do. She used to come in here, back when she was a bloke.'

I was excited. 'Really? She really used to be a man? I wasn't sure if I was imagining it.'

'Nope. Ross, she was back then. That was a while ago. Then for a long time she'd come in women's clothes and demand to be called Rosa, even though she was clearly shaving and padding out her bra. I think she's gone the whole hog now.'

'Does she know Liz?'

He nodded. 'They were both in here on their own, a while back. Before you showed up, for sure. Liz had just been dumped. The whole Steve business went off – Christ, that was a weird one. I think Rosa was suffering some pre-op nerves, or something. They got chatting and ended up drunk as skunks. I practically had to pour them out on to the pavement at closing time.'

'They're friends? Was that the first time they met?'

'I think so. Never seen them together since. But Liz did come in after that, asking for Rosa, and Rosa's barely been in from that day to this. I'm not sure I've seen her at all, actually.'

I was trying to work it out. After some hard pondering, I had to admit that I had no idea what was going on, or whether there was anything I could do about it.

CHAPTER 33

MARY

1973

Going back on the bus was a different matter altogether. As Mary watched the countries passing by in the other direction, she found it hard to breathe. Pakistan, Afghanistan, Iran, and Turkey went by far faster than she would have liked. Suddenly, they were in Europe again. The roads were different. The loos flushed. And still they headed west.

She sat by the window and cried, silently. Her chest felt as if it had been crushed by a heavy weight. All the life force had gone out of her. Everything felt wrong. She was only going home to get a job for a while, probably in London. As soon as she had some cash, she would be back. This time, she thought she would hitch. She would go straight back to Goa, and she would take it from there.

The decision to return to Europe had happened suddenly. One minute, she had been living in a hut on Arambol beach with a man called Singaporean Clive, who made her laugh. Then, her money ran out. She had no cash at all, and neither did Clive, and anyway, he was getting bored. When he saw that she'd run out of money, he buggered off. She ate nothing for a couple of days. She asked around, desperate for a way to earn a few rupees. A hippy with a beard pointed her towards a man in Anjuna market. This man told her to take a package into Pakistan and deliver it to a man at a hotel in Lahore. He gave her two hundred dollars.

She did it. She walked across the border, and looked the border guard in the face, and she held her nerve. It was the bravest, most stupid thing she had ever done: only as she stood in front of him did she realise that she could be executed for this. She knew she could never do anything like it again, and so she found out about the bus, and she was going home.

They stopped overnight somewhere in northern France. Most people slept on the bus, because everyone was out of cash. In the morning, Mary stepped out under a slaty European sky, and started to do her stretches.

She looked around. France wasn't much, but it was better than England.

'I'm getting off,' she told the driver. 'That OK?'

'Got any francs?' he asked.

She shook her head and pulled her backpack off the bus. The driver handed her a ten-franc note.

'Consider it a refund for the ferry crossing,' he said. 'Good luck.'

She stood on the pavement, and waved the bus away. Then she looked around. An old woman was walking by, looking rather nervous at the sight of her. Mary supposed she did look unusual, now she was back here. Her hair was as long as it would get, and it straggled down her back. She was dressed in a kaftan, and although she was wearing shoes, they were stringy sandals from India. All her goods were in a canvas backpack.

She approached the woman anyway, smiling to show that she was harmless.

'*Bonjour,*' she said. 'Um. *Hôtel, s'il vous plaît?*'

CHAPTER 34

LIZ

22 June

I lay down on my bed, feeling happier than I had for ages. Yoga had been lovely. Anna was lovely. My baby was kicking like a small puppy. I was still half tempted by the idea of a weekend in France. Part of me was desperate to go, but I was trying to be sensible. I was nearly thirty-four weeks pregnant. My life was a mess. I was longing to go away, but I didn't want to put myself in Helen's debt. I was a grown woman, and I couldn't accept a minibreak paid for on someone's father's credit card. Helen didn't seem to be taking offence, and I was glad. The sun was shining, and it was the weekend. The yoga class had helped me to put most of my worries to the back of my mind.

I yawned. It was definitely time for a little nap.

Several hours later, I woke up to the sound of screaming in the street outside. Someone was yelling, barely pausing for breath. I jumped out of bed, picked up my phone, and ran to the window, ready to call the police.

When I looked down, I saw Anna, outside her

house, doubled over with pain. She looked small and vulnerable from up here, though she sounded like a cow being slaughtered. Jeremy was holding her arm and looking worried.

'Jaaaayy-soooos!' she shouted. 'Get me to the fucking hospital!'

I took the stairs two at a time, and galloped across to them in an ungainly fashion. I had no shoes on. It was pure luck that I was even wearing clothes.

By the time I reached them, an ambulance was pulling up.

'Anna!' I called, grinning. 'Is this it? You're having the baby!'

She didn't even look at me.

'Get her to fuck off,' she said to Jeremy, between screams.

I stepped back, confused.

A paramedic came to Anna's side and gently touched my elbow to move me out of his way.

'Jeremy?' I said. He didn't look at me. 'Jeremy, will you let me know when the baby's born?'

He looked at me, then away again. His lips were pursed. He shook his head tightly.

Anna was in the ambulance. He got in after her. I stood on the pavement, barefoot and bewildered, and watched them drive away.

As I went inside, through all the doors I'd left open in my excitement, the phone was ringing. I went up as quickly as I could, to answer it. As I did so, I told myself that Anna and Jeremy were just focused on the baby.

I picked up the receiver.

'It's Julie,' she said. She sounded cold, and sharp.

I yawned. 'Hello, Julie,' I said. 'How are you?'

'Oh, fine and dandy, thank you, Liz. Fine and dandy.'

There was a challenge in her voice. She clearly knew what had happened when Roberto visited, but she sounded as if she was blaming me.

'What's going on?'

'Oh, you know. The usual. Baby's kicking. Flat-hunting. Boyfriend carrying on with his sister.'

'Your boyfriend? Roberto?'

'Yes.'

'Carrying on?'

'Which is a polite way of putting it.'

'With his sister? As in . . . me?'

'Yes.'

I tried hard to process what she was saying.

'You think I've been . . . me . . . and Roberto?' I laughed. 'Julie, are you crazy? What are you talking about?'

Her voice was icy. 'Yes, I can quite see that you'd want to deny it now. Bobby's taking the same approach. Were you drunk when you sent me that text then? You really shouldn't do that. It's *very* bad for the baby. But *in vino veritas*, as they say.'

'What text?'

She sighed. 'The text you sent me. In which you confessed everything and said it meant nothing. Or have you forgotten?'

'I haven't forgotten because there's nothing to

forget. I don't have a clue what you're talking about.' I was so desperate to be believed that I knew I was sounding horrifically guilty. I tried to sound sincere. 'I haven't sent you a text for ages,' I added. I was sounding worse by the second.

Julie put on a false-pleasant voice. 'Would you like me to read it to you? Refresh your memory?'

'It can't have come from my phone. Go on, then.'

'Here goes.' She read it in a sing-song voice. '"Hi Julie. I have to tell you this because I feel so bad. Roberto and I kissed when he came to mine. We couldn't stop ourselves. It meant nothing. Sorry. Love from Liz."'

'I never wrote that.'

'You did. It came from your phone.'

'It can't have.'

'Shut up,' she said. 'I don't care what you've got to say now. I just called to say that that is the most disgusting thing I have heard in my entire life. So does Sue. So does your dad.'

I tried to hold back the tears that were springing to my eyes. 'But it's not true. It's someone messing around. Roberto's denying it because it's not true. I wound Roberto up, and he snapped a bit and pushed me against the wall. It got pretty scary. Then I shoved him. It was aggression all round. Nothing else.'

'Yeah, he says that too. You've done a good job of cooking up a story together. He says you pushed him over a chair. I bet you did. He likes a domin-ant woman.'

'You've got it all wrong. Somebody's—'

She hung up.

I was wretched beyond anything. None of this made any sense. I wondered whether I should call Roberto, but worried that, if he was with Julie, a call from me would make us look guilty. But if I didn't call him, that might look worse. Julie had told Dad and Sue. I prayed that they wouldn't believe her.

It was hard to do anything after that. I wandered around the flat, listless. I tried going back to bed, but I just lay there and cried. I was suddenly scared that the baby wasn't moving, but when I ate some chocolate, it jigged around as usual. I wished Helen was home. I desperately wanted somebody to talk to.

I began to reconsider escaping to France.

The week went on, and it got worse. On Monday, I noticed that Anna and Jeremy were home, and tried to talk myself into knocking at their door.

'Go on,' Helen said. She was fiddling with a handwritten letter that had just arrived for her. 'If they were a bit weird when you saw them leaving, that's only natural. They were getting in an ambulance. You can't blame them for not noticing you.'

'But it wasn't that,' I told her. 'Anna told him to tell me to fuck off.'

'Yeah, and she's, what is she? Mexican?'

'Venezuelan.'

'Yeah, exactly. So she can say things like that

357

because she feels like it. Latin women are tempestuous, aren't they, and she was in labour.'

I was not convinced. I watched Helen opening the letter and easing it out of its envelope.

'I went to yoga with her in the morning and she was fine,' I said. 'We had a great time and she even said she thought things might be starting. She was having mild contractions. We talked about it for hours.'

'So go and see her! She's the one with the new baby. It's not up to her to come to you, is it?'

I nodded. 'I guess you're right. Will you come too?'

Helen frowned, and put her letter down. 'Anna hates me. Are you sure?'

I felt pathetic. 'I just need some moral support. Just in case. I couldn't take it if they turned on me, too.'

We stood side by side on the doorstep, and knocked at their red front door. Anna and Jeremy lived in the whole house, not a flat, and I envied them.

Jeremy answered. I noticed him looking Helen up and down, in her tiny pink dress, before his eyes fixed on me and he frowned.

I handed over the flowers I'd brought. 'Hi, Jeremy.' I was speaking quickly. 'These are for Anna. So, the baby's been born?' He didn't immediately respond, so I carried on. 'Is it a boy or a girl? Did everything go OK?' I heard a funny, squeaking little wail from inside the house. It hit me in the chest. That was the sound of Anna's child. 'Can I come and say hello, or is it a bad time?'

Jeremy shook his head. 'It's a bad time,' he said curtly. 'Always will be, I'm afraid.' He started to shut the door. Helen spoke quickly.

'At least tell us about the baby,' she pleaded.

'Girl,' he said. He smiled in spite of himself. 'We've called her Gabriella Rose. She knows how to use her lungs, but she hasn't quite worked out the sleeping part yet.'

Helen grinned. I tried, but I couldn't work out why he was being horrible to me.

'Congratulations,' Helen said. 'Is she a good weight?'

'Oh, absolutely. She's a chunky little thing. Nine pounds two,' he said proudly.

Anna's voice came from inside the house. 'Jeremy? Who is it?' she demanded. He looked worried.

'Sorry,' he said, looking at Helen rather than me. 'I can't actually stay and chat. I'm not supposed to be talking to you.' At this point, finally, he looked me in the face. 'You can say what you like about people,' he said, 'but you can't get away with it. Maybe you were having an off day, or maybe Anna annoyed you. I don't care. We don't need people like you around us. Leave us alone.'

'But I have *no idea* what I said about them,' I wailed. 'I didn't say anything!'

Helen stroked my arm. She looked uncomfortable. 'It must be a misunderstanding,' she said.

'I know, but why? They're my friends. They took me to hospital. What am I going to do? Anna and I are both having babies. She was going to be my lifeline.'

'I'm sure she'll come around,' Helen said. She was obviously out of her depth, emotionally. 'Just give her a bit of time to get over the birth. If you haven't done anything, it can all be sorted out in time.'

I wiped my eyes. 'I guess you're right.'

'You know I am. And in the meantime, you've got me. You've got your family. You've got other people. Actually, that reminds me. There was a woman in the café asking for you on Saturday.

'Yeah?'

'Nice-looking woman. Used to be a man, Matt said.'

At this, I brightened. 'Rosa? What did she say?'

'She knew that I knew you. I guess from Matt.'

I was feeling cautiously happier. 'He's a terrible gossip, your boyfriend.'

'I know. So she asked if I knew you, and then said you should get in touch with her because the two of you have things to talk about.'

'Did she? Did she leave a number?'

'No. Matt might have one for her, though. I'll ask him.'

'She should call me. She's got my details. She knows I haven't got hers.'

Helen fiddled with her cup. 'What was it about, then? She seemed very keen.'

I smiled. 'It's a long story. I hope she gets in touch.'

'Try me.'

'Try you with what?'

'The long story. I'm a good listener.'

I considered it for half a second.

'Not yet,' I said. 'I'm not really ready to tell anyone. It all depends on what she's going to say to me.'

Helen looked at me for a while, then picked up our teacups, washed them up, and went upstairs.

'Got to get ready,' she said. 'It's date night.'

She went out half an hour later, looking far more subdued than normal. The long dress and cardigan she was wearing suited her far better than the sexy stuff she normally wore. These clothes covered up her bony arms and her matchstick legs. Her hair was silky, tucked behind her ears.

'You look lovely,' I told her. 'Seriously. You look absolutely beautiful.'

She beamed at me. 'Oh, thank you,' she said. 'I don't look frumpy, do I? Only I read something that said you shouldn't dress provocatively on a first date. I'm trying to do this properly.'

While she was out, she got a phone call. This intrigued me, because nobody ever phoned Helen.

It was a young man.

'Is that Tom?' I asked.

'No,' he said. 'It's Adrian.'

It took me a while to place him. I always thought of my ex-husband when I heard the name.

'From her old flat,' he prompted.

At this, I pulled myself together. I was spoiling for a fight, and this one would be perfect.

'Well, Adrian,' I said, 'I'm surprised that you've got the nerve to call. But then again, I know that she never spelt it out to you. She didn't dare. But she was on to you, Adrian. She knew what you were doing. *That* was why she moved out: you were spying on her. She *certainly* doesn't want to speak to you. Don't you dare call again. Understood? Or I will phone the police.' I waited for a response. There wasn't one. 'You see?' I asked triumphantly. 'You don't know what to say, do you?'

He cleared his throat. 'Er, you're right. I have no idea what to say.'

'So, piss off.'

He sounded strangled. 'But I don't have the faintest idea what you're talking about. I didn't spy on Helen. Did she say that?'

'Yes she did. In no uncertain terms.'

There was silence. I made myself keep quiet.

'Oh, fuck,' he said suddenly. 'I think I know what she meant. That Sunday. When she moved out. I popped my head round her door to see if she'd like a cup of tea. It was nearly lunchtime, you see. I was being friendly. But she was on her bed, and she didn't have any clothes on. I jumped back out

362

of the room pretty sharpish, but it obviously made her uncomfortable. I had no idea it had upset her that much. It was an honest mistake.'

I shook my head. 'Yeah, but I don't think it was just that. There were other things.'

'What other things? I would never spy on anyone. I had no idea that was why she left. I cooked her Sunday lunch. It's true that she didn't seem very happy, but I thought she was hungover. Then she vanished and we haven't seen her since. She didn't say anything in the note she left, just that she was leaving. We've filled her room. Got a new flatmate. I just wanted to make sure her direct debit was cancelled. Where is she? Is she at the café?'

'You cooked her Sunday lunch?' I tutted. The poor girl needed to learn to assert herself.

'Um, it sounds as if I owe her an apology. Can you tell her I'm truly sorry?'

I opened my mouth to respond, but decided to hang up instead.

CHAPTER 35

HELEN

22 June

I sat across the table from Matt, and played with my napkin. We were in an Indonesian restaurant. It was small and dimly lit, and although the tables were close together, it felt as if there was nobody else in the room. I wanted to appear highly sophisticated. I had never been to an Asian restaurant of any sort before. In France, I ate French food, provided by Mother, or I cooked for myself, which meant sandwiches and crisps, or nothing. Where I came from, there was French food, there was English Sunday lunch, or there was pizza. There were a few Vietnamese and Chinese restaurants dotted around rural France, but I had never been into any of them. None of my family had. It would not have occurred to us. Now I lived in London, and in London you could pick any country from the whole world, and get on the Tube and go to eat the food. We could have had Ethiopian, Malaysian, or Ghanaian food tonight. I chose Indonesian because I liked the word *Indonesia*. It sounded like somewhere I would never go.

Matt looked at me and smiled.

'This feels strange, doesn't it?'

I made sure I was looking into his eyes.

'Yes,' I told him. 'It feels like we're children in the world of the grown-ups. At least, I feel like *I* am.'

'I know what you mean. I feel that way a lot.'

The music was quiet enough for us to hear each other. It didn't really have a tune but it was nice, in a random-sounding way. I remembered that I was supposed to be asking Matt questions, and listening to the answers.

'So, Matt,' I said. 'Um, how long have you had the café?'

He looked at me in a searching way, then laughed. I wasn't sure why he was laughing.

'I've been open three years,' he said. 'Essentially, I've been working, without a holiday, with barely a night off, seven days and nights a week, for three long years. The financial thing's just about working out now, but honestly, it's a labour of love.'

'Is that why you do it? Because you love it?'

He nodded. 'You know, I do love it. I love seeing the same people all the time. I love chatting to them, finding out what's going on in the neighbourhood. I love it when they come back again and again. I really love it that I'm holding my own, in a town full of Starbucks and Costa and Coffees-R-Us emporiums. It feels good, you know, to go out on a limb for something, to go up against the big boys, and then to find that it works.'

I smiled. His happiness was infectious.

'So is that the plan? Keep Café Lumière going for ever?'

He leaned forward, his eyes shining in the low lighting. I looked at him, at his big dark eyes, his bleached hair that was always a little bit too long, his broad shoulders. I leaned forward, too.

'Actually, Helen,' he said. 'I have a proposal for you.'

I thrilled inside when he explained it. He wanted me to become his business partner. He wanted me to get some cash from Papa, and to set up a kitchen. He wanted me to work as hard as he did, cooking big English breakfasts, sandwiches and chips at lunchtime, and a small bar menu in the evening. Every day.

'Do you think I could do it?' I asked.

'Of course you can. You're French. You know about food. We'll go to the bank together, get a new business loan. We'll use the back room for the kitchen, and move all the crap from the back room upstairs into the flat. We'll get the kitchen kitted up according to all the health and safety bollocks, and put you in an apron, and off we'll go.'

'Are you sure?'

'I know you can do it. And I think we kind of work well together. Don't you?'

I smiled at him. 'Yes,' I said. 'I do.'

Our starters arrived. Matt had ordered for both

of us, as I'd never eaten food like this. I hoped he hadn't got me anything too spicy.

'Chicken satay,' said the waiter, and Matt gestured to show him that it was for me. I looked at it. It looked like chicken on a stick, but there was a gloopy sauce poured over the top. I wasn't sure how to eat it, so I picked up the stick and took a bite.

'Oh,' I said. 'Peanut. Actually, it's quite nice.'

Matt nodded. 'Nectar of the gods. Only two downsides to the plan. Number one, I like you to be out and about serving customers. You add a certain sparkle to the place that ain't there if there's just a stroppy git in a black T-shirt. Number two, and we've touched on this before, I know that you're not supposed to be emotionally entangled with colleagues. But I feel a little reckless about that. What do you think?'

I chewed my chicken. It was nice. I wanted to like it, and I found that I could, quite easily. I tried to be brave, to make him respect me. 'I think,' I said carefully, 'that as long as we both know what we're doing, that's fine. I mean, things like this, we won't have much time for them, which is a shame. But we'll still be able to do other stuff. The other stuff . . .' I hesitated. I had never in my life felt as alive as I did after work, when Matt and I kissed and got high, and touched each other. I didn't want it to end. 'The other stuff makes my life worth living, to be honest.'

Matt beamed as he topped up my wine. He topped up his own.

'Me too,' he said. 'So, do we have a deal?
We clinked glasses.

I gazed across the table. Matt made me feel different. It was ridiculous, but I felt sexier at this moment, in a long dress and a frumpy cardigan, than I ever had when I was running round the café in clothes that were so small that they barely existed. It was because of Matt. Perhaps, I thought, it was not actually essential to dress in a way that was designed to make every man like me. Perhaps I could cover up a little bit more. Maybe life was better that way.

I tried to remind myself that Matt was peripheral. He was not the centre of my life. He liked me so much that he wanted to spend all day, every day, with me. He wanted to go out to restaurants with me, too. I was giddy. I was happy. I didn't care about anything.

'You know I'm away next weekend?' I asked.

'And how am I going to manage without you?' he demanded.

'You might not have to. I might not go.'

'How come?'

I shrugged. 'I don't think there's anywhere else I want to be.'

He leaned across the table, and kissed me. I kissed him back. My stomach was in knots.

'Can I tell you something?' I asked quietly. Matt reached under the table and picked up my bare foot.

'Go on,' he said. He put my foot on his lap and stroked it. I shivered.

'I've never had sex,' I whispered.

He smiled. 'I did have an inkling,' he told me. 'Would you like us to remedy that?'

I was deeply, contentedly asleep when the alarm went off. My face was buried in Matt's pillow, and the duvet was on the floor. It was a hot morning, and I felt sticky.

Matt rolled over, next to me, and kissed my lips. I reached for him. I was delirious with happiness.

'Come here,' I said, and I pulled him closer. I felt like a different person today. Nobody had ever even hinted that sex would be like this. I had always assumed it was an ordeal, something to get out of the way. Now I knew differently. No wonder so many people were having babies.

Matt smiled and unhooked my hands from his waist.

'Got to get up,' he said, and he jumped out of bed.

I looked at him naked. His body wasn't exactly as I thought it would be, but I hadn't really known what to expect. He was muscular and stocky, and I could have looked at him for ever. I sat up in bed to get a better view as he did his press-ups.

'You could charge people money to watch this,' I told him, as his naked bottom went up and down, again and again.

'Oh, I do,' he panted. 'Whenever things get short here, I line them up along that wall.' He motioned to it with his head. 'And get a fiver apiece.'

'I could join in. They might pay more.'

'You do sit-ups next to me. We'll make a bomb.'

I thought he was joking, but I lay next to him and did some sit-ups all the same. I wasn't used to eating a big meal, like I had the night before, and exercising felt good.

I was extraordinarily happy. I felt that everything had fallen into place, overnight. I loved Matt, though I wasn't going to tell him so. And I had made a decision.

I wasn't going to go to France at the weekend. I was going to stay here and be happy, instead. I would open the kitchen, and if it went badly, I would do something else. I had never felt alive like this, never felt special before. I was going to tell Liz the truth. I would write to Mother and explain that Elizabeth Greene was in London, and that she was about to have a baby. I would stop messing things up for Liz, and I would try to mend what I had already done. I was going to be good. And I was going to have as much sex with Matt as I possibly could.

I went downstairs in my clothes from last night, and started getting ready for customers. There was normally a rush at eight, because they were all on their way to work.

'We should open earlier,' I told Matt, excited by the way that everything felt different between us now.

'Yeah, I've always known that really,' he agreed.

370

'If we were up and running at seven we'd do a good hour of takeaway coffees. It's just, where do you draw the line? I'm sure I could shift some cups of tea to clubbers at four on weekend mornings, but I'm not about to have a try. I spend every waking moment in this place as it is.'

He left me in charge, and went off to see some suppliers. At about nine, the rush died down, and I sat on a bar stool, in front of the counter, with a double espresso, and pretended to read a magazine while reliving the evening, thrilling at the memories. I was not a virgin. I had slept in Matt's bed. I was in love.

When someone came in, I jumped up and ran to the right side of the counter. Then I looked at my customer.

Everything evaporated. In a second, I was weighed down and guilty again. Bile rose to the back of my throat. My stomach heaved. I stepped towards the sink, sure I was going to be sick.

'Hi, Helen,' he said. I swallowed hard. He wasn't smiling.

'Hello, Tom,' I managed to reply.

I was overcome with the knowledge that, somehow, I had betrayed him. I told myself that he was my brother, not my boyfriend. I was a free agent. I had done nothing wrong.

I didn't believe myself.

Tom was wearing shorts and a T-shirt. He looked the same as ever, just slightly more tanned than the last time I had seen him. I didn't go to hug him.

I hadn't seen him for months. He had always been my best friend in the world. Now I wished he would go away. He reminded me too much of home, of the strange world we'd lived in, of everything I had left behind. I had missed him horribly until recently, but now I just wanted to get rid of him.

He sat on the stool I had just vacated. I stood in front of him, sipping my coffee. He inclined his head and raised his eyebrows, and, with shaking hands, I made him a cappuccino and pushed it across the counter.

When I saw his milky moustache, I managed to assert myself enough to form some words.

'Did the parents send you?' I asked him.

He wiped his face with the back of his hand. 'They paid for me. But I sent myself.'

'They let you come?'

'They trust me.' He looked at me hard. 'So, how's it going?' he said. 'Are we on for the weekend? I'm going back on your flight.'

I took a deep breath and looked down at the dirty floor. 'Actually,' I said, talking quickly, 'I'm going to stay here. Tom, you don't understand, but I can be normal here. I've finally managed it. I've got a life. I've got everything I've ever wanted. I'm happy. So I've decided to tell Liz the truth. We can tell her together, if you like. It's not fair of me to be messing things up just so she'll come away with me. You can tell Mother, if you like. Tom, it'll be better this way. Trust me. I'm your big sister, and I know.'

'That's no good, H,' he said, at once. He shook his head and his glossy hair moved. 'It's no good at all. You came here for a reason. The reason was to find Liz and bring her back to Mother. And that's what you have to do.'

'I want to do it another way. A better way. A grown-up way.'

'There isn't another way. There's the plan. That's it.' He looked, hard, into my face. 'I don't want to know about your love life, but if you're letting some man stop you, you're far more pathetic than I would have believed. Don't you want Mother to love you?'

I was stunned. 'Of course I do.'

'Don't you want to see her face when she realises what we've done?'

'Yes. Yes I do.'

He spoke urgently, with complete conviction. 'Helen, you've changed. I can't believe you've forgotten what this is all about. Bringing Liz to France is the thing that will make our family OK. Not just you. You're doing it for me. For Mother, and Papa. This is what will make us into a real family. Elizabeth has been missing for all this time, and we never realised it. She wasn't there and that was why nothing was right. If you don't do this – if you don't finish it off, follow it through – then I will never speak to you again, Helen. Never. Forget about Mother. If you don't do it, you will never even *see* me again. You think I'm a kid, but I'm sixteen now. I can run away from you just as easily as you can run from Mother. And I will.' He raised his chin and looked at me, the challenge in his eyes. 'Think about that.'

He left. I stared after him. I thought my little brother had lost the plot completely.

Matt came in.

'Whose is that coffee?' he asked.

'No one's,' I said, miserably.

'Clearly,' said Matt. 'Hey, Helen, are you OK?'

I nodded and smiled, and tried to act normally. The trouble was, I couldn't manage it. My sparkle had gone. For the rest of my shift, I went through the motions, but I couldn't get close to recapturing the morning's exhilaration. I smiled brightly, but my heart wasn't in it, and Matt could tell.

'Was it something I said?' he asked. 'Something I did?'

'No,' I assured him. I looked at him as he waited for an explanation, and I realised I had to provide one or he'd think I regretted everything. 'It's my little brother,' I managed to say. 'I heard from him. I think I'm going to have to go to France after all.'

Matt brightened up. He put a muscular arm around my shoulders. 'Hey,' he said. 'That's OK, isn't it? I mean, a weekend, that's nothing. You'll be back on Monday. Won't you?'

Would I be back on Monday? 'Of course I will,' I said, and I went outside to wipe some tables.

I kept busy until three, when I finished my shift. I couldn't bear to go to the flat, so I walked randomly for a while, not noticing anything going

374

on around me. I half hoped that Tom would show up again, because I thought he might be following me, but instead I found myself outside Waitrose.

I walked in, to get out of the sun. For a second, I stood still, letting shoppers pass around me. I closed my eyes and scrunched them tight. I felt a tear forming in the corner of my eye. I wanted to cry because, suddenly, I didn't know what to do.

I loved Matt, but I could only ever have one mother. I needed her.

I decided to distract myself by doing a big shop for Liz. Whatever happened, I owed her. She always said she liked Waitrose but she couldn't afford to go there any more.

I was mooching around, shivering at the chill on my bare arms, when my mobile rang. I picked up a random, expensive carton of fortified mango juice, and threw it into my trolley. Then I answered. I longed for it to be Tom. I was desperate to try to convince him again.

'*C'est Papa.*' He didn't sound happy.

'Papa,' I repeated. I stood on the bottom of the trolley, and skidded along in a kamikaze manner. 'How are you? How's Mother?'

'*Oui, ça va.* Look, Helen,' he continued. 'You have to stop spending our money. I'm sorry, but you do.'

I rolled my eyes. 'That's not fair.' They had paid for Tom to come over, even though he was supposed to be at school. They would rather spend their money on him than on me. He was right: they didn't love me.

'I'm sorry. We've never worried about money in the past, but this year is not going well with the wine, and sales are down everywhere. The drought is taking its toll and we have to cut back our spending. I have to say, *chérie*, that most of our spending comes from you. You have a job.'

I was cross. 'I have a job in a café! It doesn't pay well.'

'So you should think about a career. A real job.'

'I've got one lined up. I might be coming home at the weekend, just for a few days, OK? I've got a surprise for you and Mother.'

He was taken aback. '*Génial.*'

He did a good job of pretending to be happy.

I redoubled my efforts with the shopping. I threw in hummus and paté and Duchy Originals and anything that looked as if Liz would like it. It all seemed disgusting to me and I wondered, for the second time that day, whether I might be going to throw up. I bought two packets of eco-friendly nappies in the newborn size. I got Liz three different types of biscuit and an array of the Green and Black's chocolate she liked. I bought fruit and vegetables, fish and lentils. The bill was huge, and I paid it proudly with Papa's credit card. As I waited for it to authorise, I was suddenly afraid that he might have stopped it. To my great relief, he hadn't.

I didn't want to do the next thing, but I knew

376

I had to. Tom was right. This was my duty. I had done some research on the internet, and I had a vague idea of what I was going to say. It would not be pleasant. I hated myself.

There was a patch of grass round the back of Waitrose. I sat on the wooden bench, put all the carrier bags down around me, and took out my phone. I dialled the number I had copied down from Liz's phone.

'Hello?' said the voice.

'Hello,' I said crisply. 'May I speak with Mr Steve Leavis?'

CHAPTER 36

MARY

She stayed in France, and realised that she was quite good at languages. France was an interesting place. The best thing about it was the fact that it wasn't England. She bought a cheap moped that often didn't start, and found a job in the new Roissy airport, where she worked in a bar. They liked the fact that she could speak English, and they didn't mind that her French wasn't good.

It was exciting, working in an airport. She loved seeing people coming and going, having adventures, starting new lives. She often looked at them, at the ones who weren't business travellers, and imagined where they might be going, and why. She made up little stories about them. She lived in a daydream, much of the time.

Mary rented a little room in Paris and lived a different dream for a while. She survived on baguettes and cheap red wine. Nearly two years after Elizabeth's birth, Mary wrote her a card. She even changed some money into pounds to put inside it, but she could not bring herself to send it. She did the same a year later. She couldn't manage to think of herself as a mother. Even though she was often lonely, she wouldn't have gone back, not for anything. She did not regret running away, because there was nothing else she could have done, but she was beginning to feel desperately sad for Elizabeth.

In time, Mary's French became passable, then almost fluent. She lived frugally, and saved obsessively, planning her return to India. She had plenty of friends, and she didn't miss anything about her former life. Nothing at all. She was itching to get back on the road again.

Then things changed.

One autumn afternoon, she met her friend Chantal at the Louvre. Mary had lived in Paris for three years, but she had never been inside the Louvre, so Chantal had said they would go together, and meander around looking at whatever came their way. It was a misty day, with a chill in the air, and Paris looked perfect. Mary pulled her long woollen scarf around herself, and made sure her knitted hat was covering her ears.

Chantal had brought two friends with her. One was Nicolas, her boyfriend. The other was Nicolas's friend, Jean-Pierre.

Mary had had plenty of casual relationships over the past few years. But as soon as she set eyes on Jean-Pierre, in the Louvre courtyard, she was afraid. Part of her wanted to turn and walk away from him. She was scared because she knew, instantly, that they would be together. The sexual attraction was like nothing she had known before. She tingled all over when he looked at her.

He was not particularly handsome, and he was no taller than she was. His dark brown hair reached his shoulders. He was wearing a black coat, over jeans and a paisley shirt. On the surface, he looked like lots of other people she knew, but when he turned his big dark eyes on her, and smiled, Mary was giddy and terrified. Even before they spoke to each other, she was certain he was her future.

They looked at art, but all Mary saw was Jean-Pierre. They stood together in front of Fragonard, and laughed at the nude pink women, and a heap of cherubs reclining on clouds. Jean-Pierre shyly reached for her fingertips. She looked at him, and laughed.

Everything that hadn't worked in other relationships suddenly did, this time. Mary had never been drawn in by a man before. She had never stayed interested for very long. Now, the world around her shrunk until there was nobody in it but her and Jean-Pierre. They talked about music and philosophy, and India and France. They hardly ever mentioned England. And, to Mary's amazement, Jean-Pierre loved her. He adored her. He worshipped her. She was absolutely consumed by him. There was nothing else that mattered in the world. From time to time, she thought of Billy Greene, and of the way he had turned her into his slave. Jean-Pierre would never do that. He wanted to do everything for her.

'Come to Goa,' she said, as they lay, entwined, in her attic bed. 'You have to come, because I can't go without you. We'll live in a hut on the beach, and get our water from the well. We'll go to full-moon parties. You have to get the ferry to get to the parties. You just stand on the bank and shout for the ferry man. We can wear Indian clothes. Everything is different when you're wearing Indian clothes.'

Jean-Pierre was not convinced.

'If we go to India,' he said, 'I'll have to speak English.'

She shrugged. 'So? I speak French all the time, and I don't care.'

'But I do. My life is in France. Come south with me, Mary. We can make a life here, in France.'

She was dubious. She was itching with the travel bug, but Jean-Pierre had turned her life on its head. Because she loved him, she agreed to give southern France a year. After that, they would go East.

They settled down. They took over a vineyard, and bought it out. They made good wine. Jean-Pierre wanted children, but Mary said no.

She was terrified when she told him about Billy and Elizabeth Greene. To her amazement, though, he didn't judge her. He thought it was a sad story, but he said he had always wondered about the sadness in her eyes, and now he knew.

As the years passed, she was resolutely unable to regret her flight from poor, defenceless little

Beth, and so she knew she could never have another child. Jean-Pierre accepted it. She wrote a sentence on a postcard and sent it to Billy, asking if he wanted a divorce. Billy refused to have any contact with her, but his parents and his lawyer helped sort it all out. Mary asked her former mother-in-law, by letter, how the baby was. Mrs Greene did not reply.

Mary and Jean-Pierre were married in a small, happy ceremony at the local church. She was settled. She happily let go of her Goan dream, because in its place was a reality in which she was cherished.

When she was thirty-eight, she discovered that she was pregnant. She was hysterical with fear through the pregnancy, but when she laid eyes on tiny baby Helen, the strangest thing happened. She was knocked down by love. Everything that hadn't happened the first time did happen this time. It was like her meeting with Jean-Pierre, yet even more surprising. It was the most unexpected thing that had ever happened to her. She loved her daughter.

CHAPTER 37

LIZ

My eyes were closing. It was almost irresistible. I can't sleep, I reminded myself. I mustn't fall asleep. I must not. My head rocked forward, and there was nothing I could do to stop it. When my chin touched my breastbone, I jerked upright again, but couldn't shake myself awake. I felt my head beginning to descend.

The room was warm. I heard an insect buzzing by my ear. Had there been a breeze, I might have been able to stay awake. But it was getting hotter and hotter. The warmth of so many bodies was stultifying.

'Miss? Miss?'

A whisper of a giggle went round the room. I forced my eyes open a slit. As I remembered exactly where I was and what I was supposed to be doing, I was horrified enough to wake up properly. I looked for a waving hand.

'Yes, Charmaine?' I said, as briskly as I could.

'Can I have some more paper, please, Miss?'

'Mmm. Yes, of course.' I staggered from my plastic chair, and picked up an answer booklet. I glared around at the GCSE candidates, all of whom appeared to be laughing at me. Perhaps they would do worse in their exams now, distracted by a heavily pregnant, dozing whale. Maybe they would do better, thanks to the serotonin rush this giggle would have given them.

I handed paper to Charmaine, and to everyone else who raised their hands, which seemed to be everyone in the hall.

'All right, Miss Greene?' asked Davy Johns as I passed his desk. There was a flutter of merriment.

'No talking,' I muttered. I sat down heavily and felt immediately drowsy again.

The door at the back of the hall opened, and Kathy came in. I looked at her warily. She had been smiling at me lately, sympathetically, her head on one side. I was ignoring her. The clip-clop of her heels rang out as she walked through the silence to my desk. I looked at her hands, with perfectly manicured nails, as she put a steaming mug in front of me.

I had never seen this mug before. It was shiny and new, without any of the usual chips and stains of staffroom drinkware. It was shocking pink, and the writing on it was black. 'I'm not fat,' it said, on one side. I turned it round. 'I'm pregnant,' it said on the other.

She smiled as she put it down. 'Present for you,' she whispered. 'New mug.'

I sighed. It was a relief to have her back. I touched her hand, and she squeezed back. I was overcome with a feeling of enormous relief. Other people might hate me, but at least I had Kathy back. I could forgive her, easily, for everything.

'Sorry,' she whispered. I nodded. That was all that was needed.

A ripple of laughter started up as the children nearest to the front read the mug. Kathy and I both gave our scariest stares. When the sniggers continued, she clapped her hands.

'Shut up!' she shouted. 'Silence, or you're all resitting in September.'

'Thanks,' I whispered.

'Thought you might need a caffeine boost,' she whispered back. 'We all fall asleep in here, and you look like you should be at home, dozing, with your feet up.'

'I'll see you later.'

'That would be nice.'

I raised the mug to her. 'Cheers.'

She winked and left the room, dispensing icy glares right and left as she went.

I sighed, forced my eyelids to stay open, and tentatively sipped the brown liquid. It was lukewarm and stale, and had clearly been in the staffroom pot for at least an hour, but I was grateful. With any luck, it would get me through the next hour of GCSE history. Then I would be free to leave. In two weeks, the summer term would end, and a month after that, my baby was due. This was terrifying. I was just about used to pregnancy, and now it was going to stop. I was going to enter the bizarre new domain of parenthood, and this one lasted for ever, not for nine months.

The thing that was driving me crazy at the moment was the constant injunction that I should 'make the most of your freedom while you've got it'. Colleagues told me this. Anyone I met who had children said it. Even Matt, whose life consisted of working all the time, grabbing Helen's bum, and taking drugs, had said it. Sue and Dad had both said it, in the past. I had not tried to contact either of them since Julie's call, because I was too exhausted to deal with Julie's ridiculous accusation. They had not contacted me, which probably meant they believed her.

A woman had stopped me on the street on my way to work that day. She'd put a hand on my bump, which had made me flinch.

'Your first?' she had asked.

'Yes.'

'Well, you make the most of your freedom while it lasts!' she'd said.

I wanted to scream at them all. How could I make the most of being heavily pregnant on my own, in a heatwave? In what way could I milk some unimaginable drop of luxury and ease from my current situation, as a working single woman who seemed to have alienated everyone I knew, to the point where my own father didn't seem to be speaking to me? I appeared to have Kathy back, but that was scant compensation. All that the world seemed to be saying to me was a loud: 'Ha ha ha, it's going to get worse.'

I stared at the rows of teenagers. Some of them I knew. Others I didn't. Of the ones I knew, some of them I liked, some I didn't. Some were good workers and would go far. Others were lazy, bored, unhappy. All of them had been babies, not so long ago. All of them had gestated, like my baby was doing now. They had flailed about, hiccuped, kicked and squirmed, and their mothers must all have been impatient and scared to meet them. And here they sat, wearing a comprehensive array of odd fashions, sucking pens and scribbling semi-legible musings on the Second World War. I watched impassively as an earnest-looking boy was shocked as his biro exploded in his mouth. As soon as he recovered from his blind panic, he wiped his mouth on his sleeve, leaving dirty black streaks on a white shirt. Then he jettisoned his pen on his spare booklet, popped a Polo into his mouth, and looked around, increasingly alarmed, for a new biro. I took pity on him, and took him one of my pens. He looked up, younger than he realised, and smiled the grateful smile of a little boy. For some reason, I was close to tears.

I whiled away the rest of the hour looking at the children and trying to decide which one would be most like my own baby. At quarter to four, I said 'Ten minutes to go,' loudly, and ignored the muttered 'Shit' and 'Fuck' that rustled around the room. At four, I told them to put their pens down. At half past four, I walked out of the building, into the unrelenting heatwave and central London.

There were people everywhere. There were always people everywhere. Children clustered outside the school in groups, mainly getting out of my way when I barged imperiously through. The sun beat down on the top of my head. I felt sweaty, smelly. Everything was hot and grimy. I wanted to be at home, sitting in my bathtub, holding the shower head over my head, anointing myself with cool water.

'Hey, Liz.' He fell into step with me, smiling his menacing, calm smile. 'How was school?'

'Steve.' I wasn't sure what to make of this. 'What are you doing here?'

He looked casual in shorts and a cotton shirt. Steve was the sort of man who carried shorts off with aplomb. *Of course he is*, I reminded myself. *He's gay*.

'Came to say hi.'

'You could use the telephone. People often do that.'

'But I needed to see you.'

My heart sank. I could not imagine why Steve would need to see me, unless he was about to make me put the flat on the market, or magic up a fortune to buy him out.

'Well, if I'm not going home, I need to sit down.'

'Yes, I needed to sit down, too.'

I looked at him. 'What do you mean? You needed to sit down? When?'

He smiled back. 'When I got a call from the CSA.'

'The CSA?'

'Here.' Steve stepped out and flagged down a passing black cab. It stopped, and I hesitated before I got in.

'Where are we going? What are you up to? I can't afford cabs any more.'

'It's on the house. St James's Park, mate, cheers.' He got in and reached out a hand for me. 'We're going to sit under a tree and talk a few things over.'

We sat in silence. The driver took one-way streets and got us there quickly, working against the traffic. The tension between us was impossible to ignore.

The park was heaving. I waited for Steve to pay, looking at the bleak front of Buckingham Palace and noting that my life would probably be worse if I lived there, but in a different way.

'The Child Support Agency,' he said, picking up where he'd left off twenty minutes earlier. We walked slowly. 'You know who they are. You must do, because you told them I was your baby's father, and that you needed maintenance payments.'

I gaped. 'I did not.'

Steve kept walking. I had to run slightly to keep up. 'So how come they called me? Of course you did.'

'But I didn't.'

'Lizzy, I wish you'd just be upfront. I said that if I was the dad, I'd do my bit. I meant that. But you said I wasn't, and now you've told these guys that I am. Are you trying to screw me for money, or what?'

I shook my head. 'You're playing a game with me. What's it about? Is it about money?'

'No. *You're* playing the games. You want my money, but you don't want me involved. You want to stay in my flat—'

'*Our* flat,' I cut in.

'In our flat. And you want a nice little slice of my income. But you don't want anything to do with me.'

I shook my head. We walked on in silence. The atmosphere between us was poisonous. I was silently furious with Steve, for doing whatever it was that he was doing. When we reached the park, I was exhausted. I waddled over to a patch of grass under a tree, and plonked myself down. The park was filled with a mixture of tourists and newly released workers. It was crowded, and as far as I could see all the benches, and every square inch of shade, were taken. A skateboarder passed us at top speed. Steve leapt, unnecessarily, out of his way. I smirked.

'Oi,' he said. 'Less of that.' For a fraction of a second, it was like it used to be.

'Steve,' I said. 'I didn't call the CSA. I promise. If you think I'd do that, you must think I'm completely, utterly mental.'

He lay back on the ground and looked up. I followed his eyeline and stared at the layers of leaves above our heads.

'The notion had crossed my mind.'

I lay down next to him. 'The CSA are famous for screwing up, aren't they? Did the person you spoke to give you a case number or something? I'll ring them now.'

'She didn't leave any details, actually. Just said it was advance warning and if we couldn't sort it out between ourselves, she'd be back in touch.'

'That sounds a bit odd.' I shrugged. 'Then again, I don't know how anything works, these days. I can barely get myself a matching pair of shoes, most mornings.'

I called directory inquiries and wrote down the number they gave me.

'How's your life?' I asked, impulsively, before I dialled.

Steve propped himself up on his elbows. He was wearing a white shirt with a round collar, and it was sporting several green stains.

'My life?' he asked. He looked at me warily. 'Do you really want to know?'

I was practically inhaling Steve's company. I had missed him so much, and I wanted to know every-thing about him, no matter what it was.

'Yes,' I promised. 'I'm not trying to trip you up. I want to know. Tell me.'

He still looked unsure. 'It's really good,' he said. He checked my reactions. 'I feel like . . . well, myself. I am truly sorry for putting you through the mill. But this is who I'm meant to be.'

'Do you have a partner?' This was the most surreal conversation I had had for a long time.

'No. There are people from time to time.' Suddenly, he couldn't help smiling. 'But it's the freedom. I don't want a partner. I don't want a marriage. I won't be trotting down the aisle in a white frock any time soon, or ever. I'm just me. This is how it was supposed to be.'

I took a deep breath. 'That's great.'

He looked at me. 'That's very big of you. I'm not sure that I'd have been able to deal with it if the situation had been reversed.'

I laughed. 'Of course you would. If you were still straight and I ran off with a woman, you'd just ask to watch.'

He opened his mouth to protest, and I cut him off by calling the Child Support Agency.

When I got home, I felt as if a weight had been lifted. The man I spoke to had no idea what I was talking about. He had no record of either of us. I'd insisted on passing him to Steve, to be sure he believed me.

'Who called me then?' he asked afterwards.

I shrugged. 'I don't know. And I don't care, either. Someone made a mistake along the way.'

He looked at me closely. 'Be careful, Lizzy. This all seems a bit weird to me.'

I agreed that it did, and persuaded him to forget

about it. I didn't have time to dwell on matters like that.

I desperately wished this was Steve's baby. Even though it wasn't, he had tentatively suggested that he might be a presence in its life. That made me strangely happy. We would be unconventional, but it might still work. I still loved Steve, which was bad, but I liked him too. I wanted my baby to know him. He was concerned about me, and he wanted to know all about Helen and where I'd met her. I didn't dare tell him we'd found each other online, so I said something airy and vague, and he looked at me suspiciously, but let it drop. And Kathy was back as well. Perhaps, after all, things were looking up.

The house was empty. I went upstairs, to change out of my work clothes. At the top of the stairs, I paused. Helen's bedroom door was ajar. I knocked on it.

'Helen?' I said, but I knew she wasn't there. I pushed the door slightly. I was not sure why I wanted to look in there. I seemed unable to stop myself. This, after all, was my spare room. I told myself I was thinking about baby furniture. If Helen was working this evening, she wouldn't be home until well after midnight.

I stood inside the room feeling like an intruder. It was meticulously tidy. The bed was neatly made, without a crinkle. Helen's many fabulous outfits hung on the clothes rail, and the rest of her clothes were folded neatly on shelves. There were a couple of books on the desk, one in English and one in

French. I picked up the French one. It was familiar. In fact, I had seen Sandrine reading the same thing last week, in the staffroom. 'Anna Gavalda,' I said to myself. She must be a popular author. I put it down.

Another book was poking out from under her bed. Although I knew I shouldn't, I reached out and picked it up. It was a scrapbook, a nice one. Each page was a different colour. And, as I flicked through, I realised that each page featured an outfit, cut from the fashion pages of different magazines. Each outfit had been carefully cut out, and glued on its own page. Above it, Helen had neatly written the magazine's name, and the date. The first page was 'Heat Magazine, 4 March'. The picture showed Fearne Cotton (unfortunately I had watched enough bad TV over recent months to let me recognise her) dressed in tight black trousers, a white top with blue flowers on it, and a blue cardigan. Underneath it, in Helen's neat writing, was a list. At the top of the list were the words: '9 March, "Matt's Place", first meeting with Liz. 8/10'. She had, it seemed, worn the ensemble twice more after that.

I flicked through. The book was nearly full. I began to realise that everything on the clothes rail, everything on the shelves, was catalogued in this book. On the last page was the long dress and cream cardigan she'd worn when she went out with Matt, but in the picture Sienna Miller was wearing them. Helen had recreated the look entirely, even down to the 'banana pumps' on her feet. That outfit had been given a resounding ten out of ten, and considering that she'd stayed out till the following evening, and returned subdued with an enormous Waitrose shop, I wasn't surprised.

I looked at the dresses and skirts hanging on her clothes rail. I looked back to the book. Everything was there.

There was a pile of handwritten letters, still in their envelopes, all addressed to Helen. I didn't want to read them, but having got this far, I felt I might as well. I wondered, vaguely, who was writing to her. Helen was the only person I knew who conducted correspondence through the medium of the Royal Mail.

All the letters had London postmarks. Against my better judgement, and giving darting glances towards the door, I peered inside one of them. It was tightly packed with neat handwriting.

'Your brother, Tom,' it said at the end.

This was odd, because Tom was supposed to be in France. I wondered what he was doing in London, and why Helen had never told me he was here. I wondered why he hadn't called her, why he hadn't come over to see her.

I looked at the envelopes again. I had known it all along, but now I noticed.

I didn't want to jump to conclusions. But Tom's handwriting and Helen's handwriting were very similar indeed.

CHAPTER 38

HELEN

29 June

Liz was looking at me. I didn't like the expression on her face, so I smiled and whistled and started spraying the kitchen surfaces. I hummed. I jigged around. I created my own world. If I kept myself busy enough, I might be able to forget what I was doing.

'You know that guy,' Liz said. 'Adrian?'

I waved my hand dismissively, and thanked my lucky stars that Liz had too many other things going on to bother to take up the cause of his perverted behaviour.

'All in the past,' I said. I attempted to whistle the tune 'Happiness'. Matt liked to play that in the café, because he said it was the most sarcastic song ever written.

'He called the other day.'

I stared at her, then looked quickly away and tried to put on my casual demeanour. 'He called here? The cheeky sod. I'll get Matt on to him.' Adrian was the least of my worries, but I did feel bad about him.

'Uh-huh. I'm sure Matt would leap into action to defend your honour.'

I thought she was being ironic, but I wasn't sure. I tried to picture Matt getting righteously upset on my behalf.

'What did he want?' I asked.

'He wanted to tell you they've filled your room. You can stop paying.'

'I'd already stopped paying. I sorted that with the landlord. Silly Adrian. How did he know I was living here? Where did he get the number?'

'He didn't say.' She smiled, a bit of a mean smile, I thought. 'Maybe Matt told him. Matt is, after all, quite the expert at spreading news around the neighbourhood.'

'Matt wouldn't.' I thought about it. 'Although he must have done. Perhaps it was Joel.'

'Helen,' said Liz. 'Adrian seemed very confused.'

I wanted to change the subject. 'Oh? Do you want a cup of anything? Coffee, tea? Biscuit? I might make some biscuits today, actually. My mother makes them and they're always nicer than shop-bought ones.'

Disappointingly, the idea of homemade biscuits failed to divert her from her course.

'He said he'd barged in on you accidentally when you were naked.'

I rallied myself. 'Accidentally? My arse.' I decided to try my bright smile. 'Which is exactly what he got a good look at.'

'He's very plausible, isn't he? Anyway, I told him

where to go. Told him not to contact you again or I'd call the police.'

This was what I had feared. I owed Adrian a big apology. Perhaps when this was over, when I came back to London to run my kitchen, I would try to explain it to him.

'Did you?' I said. 'Thanks, Liz. So, chocolate or raisin biscuits?'

She was still looking at me as if I might be mad.

'I like your skirt,' she said.

'Thanks.'

'Where's it from?'

'Um.' I looked down at it. It was from *Heat*, but that wasn't what she meant. 'Zara,' I told her. I swung round. It was a full skirt, and when I swung my hips, it made me feel like a flamenco dancer. 'I like it too.' I smiled as hard as I could, to convince her that everything was all right. Today was the day. I desperately hoped that I was going to be able to do what I needed to do. It had to work. The stakes had never been so high.

I had decided that Tom was right. I had to do it, had to force her to come back this weekend. I couldn't drop the plan, because it wasn't about me. It was about Liz and Mother. I longed to sit Liz down now and make her listen to the truth, but I couldn't. I would have done it in an instant if it wasn't for Tom. But Tom was unstable and erratic, and I didn't want to lose him.

I opened cupboards, looking for flour and sugar

and things like that. I knew Liz was watching me, so I started singing again. She didn't stop staring.

'Helen?' Liz asked, after a while.

'Mmm?'

'Tell me about Tom.'

After a few seconds, I realised that I was breathing too loudly. I was making little 'huh' sounds on the in breaths, so I made an effort to stop it.

'What is there to tell?' I asked, rhetorically. I smiled my big, starry smile. 'He's my little brother. Sometimes a pain, often my best friend.' I paused. 'A bit like you and Roberto,' I added.

I watched her reaction. She had not said anything to me about Roberto or Julie, and I was cross with her about that. I could see, though, that it was not easy for her to admit that she had got off with her brother. It was a horrible thing to have done.

'Where is he at the moment?' she said.

I snatched up my bag, and checked my phone was in there.

'Going out,' I trilled. 'Need to get ingredients.' I started jumping down the stairs before she could say anything. I sang 'Happiness', quite loudly, all the way down the street.

The Steve call had backfired. He and Liz were now, apparently, the best of friends. I half expected her to tell me they were falling in love all over again. Just as bad was the fact that Kathy had given her a mug, which, in Liz's eyes, made up for the fact that she'd told her to abort the baby. That part made me furious. I had put in a lot of groundwork with Sandrine, just to keep my bases covered, and it was extremely difficult to stay in character when I was talking French, because I always felt as if I was talking to my father. I had never thought I would need Sandrine, but now I was beginning to wonder whether there might be a way in which I could use her.

I was almost in despair. I tried to speak to Tom, but he wasn't answering. I looked around. He was probably lurking somewhere, watching me. I had no idea where he was staying, what he was doing. I knew he didn't want to talk to me now, because he knew I would persuade him that if we did this my way, things would work out better. I wondered how the dynamic had changed. Not long ago, he had done whatever I told him. Now he was calling the shots, and I was torn in two.

There was one big gamble I had decided to take today. It was a very, very long shot, but I thought there was a chance that I might have put the pieces together.

She sounded surprised. 'You're the *who*?' she asked. Her voice was softer than I'd remembered. I was briefly sorry to be doing this to her.

'CSA,' I said. 'The Child Support Agency.'

'And you want *who*?'

I paused so I could pretend to consult a piece

of paper. 'I want somebody called Ross McAndrew. Madam.'

'Well, there is no one of that name in this household, I'm afraid. Why do you want him?'

I was prim. 'I'm afraid I'm not at liberty to divulge that information.' I was pleased with that. It sounded nice and official. It was what the woman at Liz's telephone banking had said to me a few days earlier.

'But you're the Child fucking Support people.'

'I'm sorry, I need to speak to Mr McAndrew.'

'Can you hold on one moment?'

She put the phone down with a clatter, then picked it up again.

'Yes?' said an aggressive voice. 'This is Ross McAndrew.'

'Mr McAndrew?' I said. I struggled with a giggle, successfully. 'I'm terribly sorry to disturb you, but it's concerning information we have that you have fathered a baby due to be born shortly. The baby's mother is a . . .' Again, I pretended to be consulting my paperwork. 'A Ms Elizabeth Greene. She is concerned that you are not acknowledging the fact that you are the baby's father, and she wants us to make sure she gets financial support from you.'

There was a gasp, followed by a stream of violent swearing.

'I'm sorry,' I managed to say. 'I must ask you to modify your—' And I was cut off.

This, I sincerely hoped, would do the trick.

★   ★   ★

401

I wanted to see Matt, but I wasn't working, and he was, so I thought I should probably stay away. I longed to see him, but I was trying hard to be cool. I thought I might go round later in the evening, and see if he invited me upstairs. Meanwhile, I needed to stay away from Liz, or I was going to crumble and tell her everything.

Sandrine lived in south London, which was annoying, but I got there in the end. I buzzed three times before she answered.

'Yes!' she said.

'*C'est Isabelle!*'

She didn't say anything. After a few seconds, though, the door opened, and Sandrine stood before me, wearing denim shorts and a pink tunic. She looked slightly pissed off at my appearance, but I pretended not to notice that. It wasn't hard to persuade her to come out for a drink.

I knew I needed to tread carefully, to remember to be Isabelle. Everything was at a delicate point and if Helen and Isabelle were connected at this stage, it could all unravel. Part of me hoped that it would.

'There's a nice pub on the corner,' she said. She was looking at me a bit oddly, I thought. People did that. 'But I can only do one drink, OK? I've got a lot of marking to do. Lesson preparation. Coursework to sort out. You name it.'

'Of course. But a drink will help you relax as you do it.'

'You think?'

'Of course.'

Sandrine always seemed to treat me with a kind of aloof irony, but I didn't care. She had no idea why I was really there. I wasn't interested in her at all. That would have surprised her, if she'd known.

We talked about boring things for a while.

'What does your sister do?' she asked me. I was suspicious.

'I haven't got a sister,' I told her. I was quickly trying to work out why she was asking, whether she was on to me.

'I thought you said you did. Didn't you confuse me with Sandrine someone else, who was a friend of your sister's?'

'Um.' I chewed my lip. 'Er, no. The sister of my friend, that's what I said.'

'OK. Well, do you have a boyfriend?' she asked me.

'Yes!' I told her, relieved. 'I do! He's fantastic. He's called . . .' I quickly tried to think of a name for him. 'Tom,' I said, then wished I hadn't. 'We went to an Indonesian restaurant. I didn't really like the food, though. It was too spicy.'

She laughed. 'How very French of you.'

I finished my wine and poured some more. I topped up Sandrine's, though she had hardly drunk a thing.

'Isn't it?' I said. 'So I said that next time we should go to a French restaurant, but he said they're boring, and then he spent about an hour telling me that the wonderful thing about London is the world cuisine. He said British food may have a bad reputation, but the fantastic thing about a multicultural society . . . blah blah blah.'

'He's right, though.'

'I know. And I actually liked the chicken satay. I just wasn't keen on the main course. Nasi Goreng? Anyway, how's work? What's going on?' Before she could say anything, I said, as if it had just occurred to me, 'What about that nice woman, Kathy? The one I met that time?'

Sandrine nodded, and sipped her wine. 'Oh, Kathy. Thank God, she's doing well. She's made friends again with Liz – remember, I told you about her? So I'm not caught in the middle any more. Actually, it's great. I'm so pleased for Liz, because she's not having a good time at the moment, and now she's got Kathy back. She's got a bit more support.'

I was curious. 'Doesn't she have support at home?'

'Well, no, she's on her own and having a baby. She lives alone.'

'Does she?'

'Yes. Well, she's got a lodger, but she's a bit loopy by all accounts. She's only got her to pay the bills.'

'Doesn't she like her lodger?' I forced the words out. 'That seems a shame, to share your home with someone you don't like.'

'Oh, I think she likes her well enough. But she's young, and I suppose she's never going to fill the gap left by Steve. She's still incredibly cut up about that. She swears it's not his baby, but we all know that it is. She's just too proud to say so, because she doesn't want him to come back out of duty. Which I suspect he wouldn't do anyway.'

This was an interesting theory, but a wrong one. I wanted to hear more.

'Shall we get another bottle?' I asked. It was empty, and I was light-headed.

'What about some food?' Sandrine asked. 'You know, you're a terrible influence. I come out for one little drink before I do all my work. Now we've had a bottle and you're intent on getting some more. If you didn't know how to pick the good stuff off the wine list, I'd be at home with a red pen in my hand by now. As it is, I'm going to have to eat something, to absorb the wine.'

We both looked at the menu. It was crass; full of junk food and fried things. I was going to do much better food than this when I had my kitchen.

I knew that Sandrine wasn't at all drunk, because I knew that I'd had all the wine. I could tell that she just wanted food because she was greedy. I smiled tightly at her, and went to the bar, which I surveyed with a professional's eye.

'Well, hello,' said the barman. He was ugly, but I smiled.

'Hi, there,' I said. 'Another bottle of the French Sauvignon. And a chicken salad and chips. Cheers.'

I wasn't going to eat anything. I preferred to drink.

* * *

405

By the time I got home, Liz was in bed. I crept around the kitchen, looking for signs of anything that might have happened, but it all seemed normal. I could hear her snoring upstairs. My head spun, and I had to sit down for a moment while my stomach lurched. I recovered enough to pour a large glass of water and take it upstairs. I sat down on my bed, then jumped up. I reached the bathroom just in time, and was violently sick in the loo. The splashes went all over the floor.

I was relieved and annoyed. I still felt drunk, but it was better to have the vile liquid out of my stomach. Next door, I heard Liz stirring.

CHAPTER 39

LIZ

30 June

There were clouds scudding across the sky. I watched them from my sitting-room window. As I looked, Anna came out of her front door. She was pushing a big, old-fashioned pram. I watched her setting out for an early morning walk with her baby, and tried to work out what was happening. Mainly, I thought, I was losing my mind. I stood and stared, and she looked nervously up to my window. I raised my hand to wave, pathetically, but she looked quickly away. She seemed to stalk off. I could see from the slightly self-conscious way she was walking that she knew I was watching.

I was desperate to see baby Gabriella, but I didn't dare knock on their door again. I had racked my mind to work out what I could have done to merit this, but I couldn't think of a single thing. I hadn't talked about Anna to anyone. I hadn't done anything.

Strange things were happening. I was beginning to worry about Helen, and felt guilty that I wasn't looking after her enough. I was tempted to go and read her letters from her elusive brother, but I knew I shouldn't, and so far I was managing not to. Sandrine had said that French people all had the same handwriting, and that was all the explanation I needed. I vowed to be friendlier to her, because, more than she realised, it was Helen who kept me going.

I had the morning off, because of school exams. The baby was jumping around, and I patted it. That, at least, was a comfort. I thought of Steve and me, lying under a tree in the park. For a while, then, I had been all right again. He patted my bump and I revelled in the closeness. To passers-by, we had looked like a family.

Instead, I was on my own. Sandrine was going to be my birth partner, because I had no one else to ask. She lived on the other side of London. I knew I might end up with Helen holding my hand instead. A part of me liked the idea, but the rest of me knew she was not dependable enough.

She had come home late last night, and was noisily sick in the bathroom, then, I noticed, failed to clean it up. A vomity bathroom was, in a sense, the least of my worries, but all the same she was not really the person I wanted by my side as I gave birth.

When my mobile rang, I was still gazing, in a trance, at the black clouds. They filled the sky and, even indoors, the atmosphere was hot and sticky.

I answered it nervously, and then sighed with relief and sat down.

'Hi, Dad,' I said. He was the person I most wanted to hear from, in all the world. I had left him two messages, at work, and the fact that it had taken him three days to call me back did not bode well for my present status in the family.

'Lizzy.' He said it fondly, indulgently. No one else understood our relationship. Roberto thought he was boring. Everyone else thought we hardly spoke to each other, that we were distant and that, because I was motherless, I was pretty much an orphan. Only Dad and I knew the truth.

'How are things?' I asked. I took a deep breath, ready to fight my corner.

'Oh,' he said. 'Um. Well, as I think you know, there has been rather an upset.'

'What's happened? Are you at work?'

'I am. I got your messages and I was about to telephone you anyway. You see, Julie rather ran off. Roberto went to find her, on Sue's insistence. We haven't heard from either of them for a few days. Sue, I'm afraid, is getting rather frantic. Um, you haven't seen either of them, I suppose?'

'No, I haven't. I spoke to Julie a week ago.'

'Yes, I think we knew that.'

I couldn't bear this. 'Dad, this is ridiculous! It's stupid. Julie thinks there was something between Roberto and me, and there *just wasn't*. I have no idea where she got that text from or whether she was making it up. But it's not true. He's my brother. The very idea makes me sick. You know that, don't you?'

He sighed. When he spoke, he sounded relieved.

'Well, of course I do. And Sue does, too. Roberto seems to be alternately blaming you for apparently sending such an odd message, and Julie for refusing to believe him. He's not happy. But you know that we would never believe such a thing.'

I took a few deep breaths. 'Yes,' I said. 'I do know that. Thank you.'

'However.'

'However what?'

'Um, it's just that Sue, well, she's seen the, the message thing on Julie's phone. It does have your number on it. And when Roberto repeatedly says that you've got an agenda, that you're causing trouble for them because of jealousy or some such nonsense, then I'm afraid Sue rather . . .' He tailed off. I knew what he meant.

'So Sue's mad at me. Not because she believes this crap, but because she thinks I'm trying to split them up, because I'm torn apart by jealousy of their perfect lives.'

Dad almost laughed. 'It doesn't sound plausible, particularly, does it? I try to reason with her, and she will come round. Just give her a few days.'

I was crestfallen. 'Oh. Really? I was hoping I could come down for the weekend. Things are bad here. I do wonder whether I'm going mad, or whether I'm imagining things. Could I come? I can talk to Sue. I'm sure I can convince her.'

I listened to my father, my only true relative, trying to let me down gently.

'I don't think that this weekend would necessarily be a good idea,' he said, after hesitating. 'Sue is really very . . . distraught. In your condition, you don't need to deal with that. Next weekend. How about that? I'm sure she will have seen sense at that point.'

I bit back tears. 'Things are strange for me here,' I said. I wanted him to say he was catching a train after work and coming to see me.

'Then you must call whenever you need to,' he said firmly. 'And now I'm afraid I have to ring off. Try not to worry about anything, Lizzy. You have my full support. Nobody believes that nonsense apart from Julie. You're having our grandchild, and that is the only thing that matters.'

'*Your* grandchild,' I said grumpily. 'Not Sue's.'

I went to work, the storm still gathering overhead. I hoped it would rain. Everything was dried up and dusty, and we needed water. I hoped the clouds would burst overhead and soak me. It would wash away everything bad, would cleanse me and let me start all over again.

It didn't. The electricity buzzed around me. The hot air was choking me. The Tube was hellish, though empty, and everyone at school was bad-tempered and uninterested. I only had to go in for an hour. It was not in the least bit worth bothering, but at least it gave me something to do.

The staffroom was almost empty.

'It's funny,' Sandrine was saying to Kathy, 'because

411

in a way she's annoying, but in another way I like her. But I wish she hadn't done it. Christ.'

'Wish who hadn't done what?' I asked, sitting down gratefully, and rubbing my bump.

'Wish that Isabelle hadn't shown up on my doorstep yesterday and forced me to go out drinking.' She looked up. Her eyes were bloodshot. 'God only knows how she feels today, because I feel like holy shit. Seriously, I had to do a sixth form induction for next year's French students, and I could hardly say two words. My head. You know?'

'I can vaguely recall that feeling,' I said. 'I don't think I'll ever be able to do that again. What did you drink? You sound like the sixth form yourself.'

'I know. Wine. Nice wine, too. It's not like we were on Bacardi Breezers or anything. But she just kept ordering it. She didn't eat a thing. She tells lies about stupid things. She drinks me under the table. She's insane.'

Kathy looked up from her paperwork. 'Self-medicating?'

'Without a doubt. And here I am, thirty-two years old, being led astray by some child who thinks alcohol is cool because it makes you feel, like, really amazing and different. And that food is, like, really gross, because starving yourself is a sign of self-control. She is an anorexic, I swear.'

'Well, you're with us now,' I told her. 'You're among grown-ups. My only eating disorder is the fact that I can't shovel enough food into my mouth in the time available.'

Kathy snorted.

'Ain't that the truth?' I looked at her, eyebrows raised.

'For me as well,' she clarified, hastily.

'Do you both want to come over after work?' I asked impulsively. 'Come to dinner? Helen filled up the kitchen with food for the five thousand. I haven't had the heart to tell her that, even in my condition, I'm going to have to throw three-quarters of it away. She went crazy in Waitrose.'

'Can I fill up on carbs?' asked Sandrine. 'And don't you dare try to get me drunk.'

Kathy looked at her. 'And don't you bring that wayward girl with you either. She's trouble.'

'I should introduce her to Helen,' I said. I had a feeling that I dismissed, because it was impossible. 'Two French girls, short skirts, drunk in London. Separated at birth.'

Sandrine shook her head. 'Your flatmate sounds like a nice girl. This one is manic, and she runs entirely on alcohol, not food. Isabelle would never be able to do big supermarket shopping.'

I left at lunchtime, with a pile of paperwork to get through at home. By the time I got back, I was wishing I hadn't invited them. I was going to need to give myself an energy surge. I told myself it was fine. I could sit back and let them assemble something to eat. All I really wanted was a cold shower and a long, long sleep, one that would ideally end in my waking up and discovering that all recent events had been a dream.

There was a familiar figure sitting on the doorstep.

I tried to smile when I saw her, because I knew that her visit was a positive thing. All the same, I didn't think I had the energy.

As I got closer, she pulled herself to her feet and started walking towards me. She was smiling, but when I looked at her eyes, I knew I was in trouble. She didn't look back at me. She kept her gaze averted, looking at the wall behind me.

'Hello, Rosa,' I said. I tried to smile. I thought about access and birth certificates and money. Her mouth was tight as she walked slowly towards me. She stopped when she was close enough for me to hear her voice. She kept a good couple of metres away from me.

'How could you?' she asked the wall. Her tone was conversational, but there was an unmissable menace beneath it.

'How could I do what?' I asked mildly. I hoped my dread of whatever was coming was not as obvious as it felt.

Rosa looked at me, briefly, then flinched and stepped backwards. She looked at the paving stones beneath our feet.

'Well,' she said. 'Let's see. Can you think of anything you might have done? Any phone call, perhaps?' She looked at my huge stomach, and looked quickly away in clear distaste.

'Helen said you were asking after me,' I said, feeling lame. 'I thought that was good.'

She took another step away. 'It *was* good. At the time, it was good. I was trying. Do you know how weird all of this is? I'm a woman. I'm a woman on my passport. In every sense, I'm a woman. And that is all I've ever wanted. I'll never be a mother, I know that, but to have you swinging your fat belly about like this, after that night . . .' She shook her head. 'My whole life is about being Rosa. This is my future. I had no traces left of the way I was before. And then you hit me with this.' She glanced at my stomach again, and away. 'With parenthood. I've hardly slept since you told me. It's ruined everything. You couldn't have done a worse thing if you'd tried.' She took a deep breath. 'But I told your lodger I wanted to see you because I wondered whether we could turn it around, make it into something good.' She looked down at the ground, her face closing over.

'Something good?'

She didn't look at me. 'I'll never carry a baby. But I met a couple of trans-women who had families already, and they're the happiest women. Their children had to get their heads round the fact that dad was now another mum, but apparently kids are OK with that sort of thing. And that's what I was thinking about, when I gave that girl my card.'

'She never gave me a card. She said you hadn't left a number.'

'She was lying. I put it into her pocket myself.

I was going to put myself on the line. Ask whether you'd mind your baby having a second mother.' Suddenly, Rosa roused herself. '*But*,' she said heavily. 'None of that fucking matters any more, does it?'

There was something wearyingly familiar in this situation.

'But of course you can be the baby's other mother,' I told her. 'What else did you think I wanted?'

Rosa's fists clenched and the muscles in her arms stood up. I stepped back, but she wasn't looking at me. She seemed to be turned completely inward.

'What else could you have fucking wanted?' she said, enunciating each word. 'You know what you want. Money. Cold, hard cash. Do you recall making a telephone call to the Child Support Agency? Ring any bells?'

My heart sank.

'Not this again,' I said, and I was too tired to attempt to work it out.

'You said you weren't going to do that. You specifically said it.'

'I know I said it, and I meant it, and I haven't done it.'

'Don't you dare lie to me.' Her face was contorted, and I could see how hurt she was. She was simmering with fury. 'If you'd said I could be in the baby's life, we'd have sorted something out. I'm not rolling in cash, but I'd have done what

I could. But the worst thing? The very worst? The thing that makes me hate you for ever? You gave them a name that is *not my name*.'

She was close to the wall, and suddenly she lifted her fists and slammed them hard on to the bricks. She did it with such force that I jumped back. A piece of cement fell to the pavement. Rosa stretched her hands out, looking at them in surprise. Blood was smeared down the outside of her fists. She turned away from me, in on herself. She was throbbing with energy, with hate and anger. I reached a hand out, then took it back.

'I wouldn't do that,' I whispered, edging away.

'Not to my face.' She started walking, slowly and then faster, down the street. I followed at a safe distance.

'Not to anyone. I didn't do it, Rosa. I *swear.* I didn't do it.'

Suddenly, desperately, I wanted Rosa to believe me. I wanted her to like me. I wanted her to respect me. I knew that she was on the edge of physical meltdown, but I wanted her to look me in the eyes, and so I chased her. She was oblivious as I ran up behind her, but when I reached her, she took one look and jumped out of the way as if I might launch myself upon her, or attempt to repeat the miserable seduction.

Until now, I had never given much thought to the fact that, just as Rosa was becoming a woman, I had confronted her with unarguable proof of her virility. I watched her struggle to deal with it, and

I was afraid, not for myself, since she could hardly bear to breathe the same air as me, but for her. The force of her blow to the brick reverberated inside me, and I knew that she was capable of great violence.

'She's saying I imagined the fucking phone call,' she muttered, stepping backwards, getting as far away from me as she could.

'I'm not saying that,' I said weakly.

'I just dreamed a call on my fucking mobile from some woman asking for *him*!' She spat, and I thought that I could see her assuming a character to get her through this confrontation. 'I didn't think this of Lizzy. I never imagined she could turn out to be such a lying, cheating, money-grabbing *bitch*.'

'But I didn't do it!' I said, and I tried to take her hand. She pulled away and started walking backwards away from me. I walked towards her. 'Rosa, this happened with Steve, too. He said he had a call from them, and when we called back, they knew nothing about him. He said someone was setting me up.'

Rosa shook her head. 'Oh, it doesn't really matter to you, does it?'

To my horror, she turned to the nearest parked car, and abruptly began to rain blows down upon it. She thumped it with both of her damaged fists, and I watched the dent in the roof get bigger and bigger. Then she started kicking. A passer-by stopped on the other side of the road, and gaped. I watched the man get a phone out. I knew he was calling the police, and I wanted to get away. I couldn't bear to be a part of anything that would surely follow.

Rosa's face was screwed up with misery and concentration. I didn't dare touch her. I started to retreat.

A black cab drew up next to me. The door opened.

'Liz!' Helen shouted. 'Get in! Come on!'

I weighed up the situation for half a second, and jumped in. Helen, who was sitting on the tip-up seat, slammed the door behind me.

'Blimey,' the driver said, equably. 'She wasn't too happy, my love, was she?'

I sank back on the seat. This was definitely not how things were supposed to be.

CHAPTER 40

HELEN

30 June

We barely spoke. Liz kept looking at me. 'Thanks for the rescue,' she said. Her face was blotchy and red. My plan had worked very well indeed, because now that she was in the cab with me, I knew I was going to get her to France.

All the same, she was looking at me in that strange way. I hated it. I hated everything about today.

'We'll just go round the corner, shall we?' she said. 'We can hole up somewhere and go home in an hour or so. When Rosa's had a chance to calm down, she might feel better. And if she's going to be in trouble about that car, I want to help her out. I think I can get her to see sense, you know. I think things will be OK. I just have to get her to . . .' She tailed off, lost in her thoughts.

'No,' I told her, with a big smile. This was the last push. I had to force myself to go through with it. 'Well, I'm sure things will be OK, when you

420

make a fresh start next week. Don't you get it? Liz, you really, really need a break. You need to leave all this behind for a few days. So we're going to France.' I took the tickets out of my bag. 'Remember? The flight leaves at three. Which should be just about right.'

Part of me had hoped this wouldn't work out. But I had got it right. Rosa was the baby's dad. It was lucky for Liz that she had a new family now, because her old life was a mess. Right now, she desperately needed to meet her mother. That would make everything better. Tom was right. This was what I had to do, for her sake.

'But I can't really go to France,' she said, as we carried on driving south. 'I haven't got anything. Passport, or clothes, or anything.'

I smiled. 'Yes you have.'

'What do you mean?'

'I mean, I saw what was going on outside, and I was getting ready to go to the airport anyway, and so I thought you wouldn't mind if I nipped into your room and collected a few things for you. Just some clothes and your passport.'

'Oh,' she said. She looked puzzled. 'Really?'

I smiled and stroked her hand. Then I took my hand away. I was never sure how physical to be without being weird.

'It's all right,' I said. 'You can relax now. Just relax for two days. It's what you need.'

'We're not really going to France,' she said, as

the taxi crossed the river and carried on south, towards Gatwick.

'We are,' I told her.

She gave me a scare at Elephant and Castle.

'Excuse me,' she called to the driver, and she tapped the glass divide. 'Excuse me, but could you let me out? Anywhere is fine. Thanks.' She looked at me. 'Lovely idea, Helen, but I really need to go home. I have to try to straighten this out.'

It was lucky that I had primed the driver in advance.

'Sorry, love, but there's going to be a surprise for you,' he said. 'The young lady here said you might ask to get out, but she says it's important that we get you to Gatwick. I wouldn't ask any questions, if I were you.'

Liz tried again, a couple of times, but her heart wasn't in it. I knew that if she'd wanted to, she could easily have made him stop. She complained about carbon emissions a few times, but she tailed off.

'What was all that about?' I asked, when I was confident that she wasn't going to try to rush off. 'What on earth was Rosa doing to that car?'

She shook her head. 'You don't want to know. And if you do, I'm not telling.' She looked at me. 'Did she give you her card?'

I shook my head. I couldn't stop jigging my leg up and down. She was unnerving me. Her body language was strange. She was closed off, when

422

she should have been crying on my shoulder. I worried that I had made things difficult for her, had pushed it too far. I would make it up to her, after the reunion. Then she would understand.

My phone rang. I answered.

'You putting in an appearance?' asked Matt. 'Or what?'

'I told you, I'm away this weekend.'

'You said you weren't going.'

'I know. But then I said I am going.'

He didn't say anything for a while. 'When did you say that?'

'Two nights ago.'

'At what point?'

I looked at Liz. 'Just after a rather pleasurable point.'

'What did I say?'

'I don't think you were up to saying anything.'

'You slipped that one by me, you minx. So I won't take it personally, but what happened to not wanting to be anywhere in the world but with me?'

'Sorry,' I told him. 'That still applies. It's other stuff that's come up. Family things. I'll tell you when I get back.'

'You know, I was thinking, it's great that your family live in France, because it means I don't have in-laws to deal with.'

I thrilled at this. 'In-laws?' I saw Liz looking at me, and I wondered, for one stupid moment, whether she was jealous of us.

We ended with Matt telling me, in a low voice,

exactly what he would do to me on Monday, when I got back. I squirmed in my seat, and tried not to respond.

Liz was half smiling. 'Things going well, then?'

'I've never done anything like this. I think I love him, although I'm trying not to tell him so.'

'What were the family things you were talking about? We're not going to walk into some big drama, are we?'

I shook my head. 'No. Don't worry. My family doesn't do drama.'

A few minutes later, my mobile rang again.

'You're a terrible influence,' said Sandrine. 'Jesus. I felt like shit this morning. I still do. I'm going to dinner with Liz, and I wish I'd said no.'

I was glad to be able to speak French to her. I hoped Liz wouldn't understand a word of it.

'Oh, me too,' I said. 'Actually, I didn't feel too bad. I vomited most of it up when I got home. I felt fine this morning.'

'It's because you're young.'

'Who are you going to dinner with?'

'Liz, and Kathy.'

'Hey, Sandrine?' I said. I didn't care any more, because my work was done. I looked at Liz and spoke quickly. 'I don't think so. Liz is going to France for the weekend. She's not home. Try her.'

When I hung up, Liz was narrowing her eyes at me.

'Do you know someone called Sandrine?' she asked. 'Did you say "Liz"?'

I gabbled. 'Yeah, the woman who looks after my parents' house in France. I said I was coming with Liz. Because you weren't going to come, and now you are.'

I could tell that she wasn't convinced.

'Did you tell your parents' housekeeper that you threw up last night?'

I smiled, and nodded.

'Helen?' she asked, slowly. 'Do you ever go by the name of Isabelle?'

I shook my head. 'Why would I do that?' I said.

Liz stared out of the window.

Gatwick was jammed with people going on holiday, and with people coming back. It wasn't even the school holidays yet, but the crowds were out in force, nursing pink tans, or carrying brief-cases. We melted in. We could have been anyone.

The bit we went into was utilitarian and dirty. I pushed Liz on to an escalator, following a sign that said 'Departures'. I was on the step below. She looked down at me.

'Why did you pack my bag?' she said, staring into my eyes. 'How on earth did you manage to turn up in a cab like that?'

This made my insides clench up. I had to brazen it out.

'I was looking out of my bedroom window,' I said carefully. 'I saw that Rosa was being horrible to you. Like I said, I was about to go to the airport anyway, so I thought the best thing I could do was to rescue you and take you with me. When she was hitting that car, I thought she might turn on you next, or the baby.'

I saw that she was sceptical. I gave her a push so she walked backwards off the top of the escalator. She looked as if she wanted to go back down, but I took her arm, walked her around the corner, and guided her on to the next one. She turned to face me again.

'Did Rosa ring the bell earlier? Why didn't you let her in?'

I had an answer prepared for this one. 'She buzzed and asked if you were there. I said you were at work, and she didn't say anything else. I thought she'd gone. Ten minutes later, I heard voices on the street and I realised she'd been waiting.'

'At which point you found my passport, packed my bag, slipped out of the front door, and went down the road and hailed a cab? Rather than coming to help?'

I forced a smile. 'I had no idea what was going on. I didn't want to intrude and, to be honest, I was a bit scared of the way she was looking and I thought we might both be better off with a getaway car. Anyway, you and Rosa were quite a way down the road then, and I didn't "hail" a cab – I'd already ordered it.'

'Yeah,' she said, slowly. Then she smiled. 'I'm sorry, Helen. Look at you. Look at what you're doing for me. I shouldn't be so ungrateful. I have a shocking habit of turning on the people who least deserve it. Thank you for coming to my rescue. Thank you for taking me away for the weekend. I'm lucky to have you. I do know that, really.'

I smiled back. 'That's fine. You've got a lot on your plate. Anyone would be a bit grumpy.' I covered my mouth with my hand. 'Not that I'm saying you are!'

She smiled back. 'A change of scene is an incredible prospect. I have to say, though, that I hate the thought of flying. Can't we go by train instead? I haven't flown for years. I shouldn't be doing it.'

'But you've got a ticket, and the plane's leaving. I won't annoy you, I promise. Let's buy some books before the flight, and you can just lie in the shade and read all weekend.'

She turned round and stepped off the escalator herself. As we followed the signs for the North Terminal, she walked close to me.

'I don't think I'm even *allowed* on a plane, though.'

'You are. When they ask how many weeks pregnant you are, you just have to say twenty-six.'

'But I'm thirty-five.'

'We know that. They don't. Look, pull your cardigan round your stomach and stand behind the check-in counter. They won't notice. I couldn't get you a doctor's note, I'm afraid.'

She looked at me, puzzled. 'Of course you couldn't. Why would you try?'

I didn't tell her that I'd been to the surgery and asked for one on her behalf. I thought she might think that was weird.

We came out on to a big concourse, and I searched quickly for the right sign. When I spotted it, I pulled her along by her sleeve. She didn't even try to pull back. She just followed.

Tom was behind us. He thought I hadn't seen him.

CHAPTER 41

LIZ

30 June

I was desperate to get away. My life had fallen apart around me. I didn't know if I was doing all these things and blocking them out. I couldn't think how else it could possibly all be happening. It seemed that every time I sorted out one mess, another one appeared from out of the blue.

I was pretty sure that Helen was the only person who was truly on my side. I envied her life. She thought it was hard, but while she was busy disdaining her parents, and waiting tables, and giggling about her first boyfriend, I was struggling with a future bleaker than anything she could imagine. She was responsible only for herself; I was constantly chilled by the knowledge that my messed-up world was the only place my baby would know. Being with Helen, with someone who had the world at her feet and didn't even know it, sometimes lightened my burden. She annoyed me, often, but I thought that this probably said more about me than it did about her.

The idea of leaving the country, even for a few days, was so welcome and perfect that I could not possibly resist it. I didn't even have to do anything. I was in a taxi, on the way to France, and the whole trip had fallen into my lap. I felt annoyed with myself about flying, because I'd thought I was strong and principled, and in fact I was caving in the moment things got difficult. On the other hand, I was fed up with being the one with principles when everyone else leapt on a three-pound flight to Estonia for the weekend just because they saw it on the Ryanair website, and then boasted about it at school the following week as if it was a clever and impetuous thing to have done. This was my only opportunity to escape for a few days. I decided to take it, however imperfect it was. I made a conscious effort and relinquished control. The moment I did so, I felt better.

I sat back in the cab, and looked at south London going past the window. If Helen's home really was a chateau with a pool and a vineyard, then I didn't care about anything else. I had held her hand in London, had looked after her and given her somewhere to live, and now she was doing something for me. She was young and naive, but that was how it should have been, because she was twenty.

And so I was thrilled to be escaping, relieved to be running away. I sat on the plane and looked out at the sea, and then at France, below me. I kept the newspaper open to hide my bump. No one had even asked about my pregnancy.

Helen was nervous. She didn't say much on the flight, which suited me. I was having Braxton Hicks contractions, my stomach hardening every five minutes or so. I knew they weren't real contractions. My body was trying to slow me down, yet again. I remembered the bleeding, and decided that, as soon as I saw the famous swimming pool, I would lie down with the books I'd bought at Gatwick, and do absolutely nothing. I was going to try to forget everything but my baby. I would empty my mind like at yoga.

I turned to Helen. 'Will Tom be there?' I asked.

She stared at me, looking puzzled. Then she seemed to shake herself.

'Um, yes,' she said. She frowned. 'Well, he ought to be there.' She looked around the inside of the plane, as if she might see him there.

When I stepped on to French soil, I was instantly overcome by exhaustion. I was so tired I could hardly see. My mind filled with the broken and damaged relationships I had at home. I thought about Steve, and Anna, and Dad and Sue. I thought about Julie and Roberto, and the other friends I hadn't seen for months. I had cut myself off from many of my friends, first because I was ashamed that Steve had left me for a man, and then because I had behaved so badly with Rosa. I hadn't wanted to tell anyone that my baby's father was a woman. But weird things happened every day. It wasn't a thing to be ashamed of. In fact, if I accepted it and told people when they asked, it would make them interested in me again.

'What did you say?' asked Helen, sharply.

I looked at her.

'I didn't say anything,' I told her, although I wasn't sure whether I had or not.

She smiled. 'OK,' she said. 'Sorry.' She took my hand, then let go of it. Helen was always doing that. 'Come on,' she said. 'Let's go and have a holiday.'

I shook myself and tried to send the negative thoughts away.

'Yes,' I agreed. 'Let's do that. I've never needed a holiday so much in my life.'

'I promise I won't annoy you,' she said anxiously.

I laughed. 'You annoying me is the least of my worries, Helen,' I said, and she squeezed my arm.

It took us no time to get through passport control and customs, particularly since neither of us had checked in a bag.

Helen went straight to a cashpoint.

'My card doesn't work,' she complained. 'That's not right. I'll try again.'

When it still didn't produce any cash, I took some out of my account, and we found a taxi. Helen negotiated the fare in advance, in fast French, and I stared out of the window, hands on my taut abdomen, as the unfamiliar city of Bordeaux gave way to countryside. The vegetation was brown and yellow. The roads were dusty. There were flies everywhere. We passed vineyards that were well-irrigated, their leaves green and shady, soaking up the sun. Each time, I wondered if it was Helen's home, but each time we carried on going. Helen chatted to the taxi driver for a while. I tried to tune in, sometimes, but quickly gave up. She sat in the middle seat, pressed up to me closely, even though there was a big space next to her, by the window. I supposed it was easier for her to talk to the driver this way.

After forty minutes, Helen said something, and we pulled in between some old, stone gateposts. I stared ahead, through the windscreen, as we rounded a corner, and a chateau came into view. It was like a painting.

It was grand and beautiful, built from pale stone, with rows of windows winking in the sun. The evening sun made it all glow gold. Everything was casting long shadows. The drive was gravelly and dusty. There were two cars parked outside, both of them modest but shiny. Helen had told me she lived in a chateau. I'd had no idea that she really meant it.

'Helen,' I said. 'This is incredible.'

She shrugged, but smiled.

'Yeah,' she said, and for once, she looked genuinely pleased. 'I've missed it, actually.'

While I paid the driver, she bounded up the stone steps, looking like a princess in her floral dress, and banged on the door with a big brass knocker.

She shook her hair out, over her shoulders, and looked round at me. After a few minutes, the door swung open. A woman stood there. She looked at Helen, and then at me. Then she smiled.

CHAPTER 42

MARY

Mary's life as a mother, in southern France, surprised her every day. She found herself drawn into baby Helen's world, obsessing over every tiny thing her daughter did. She watched her as she learned to sit up, tried to crawl and then toddled along. They walked around the vineyard together, holding hands. She told Helen about Nepal and India, and promised her that one day, they would go back, would sleep on the beach and draw their water from a well. Helen was too young to understand, but Mary wanted her to know that she was included in her dreams.

She felt horribly guilty about Beth. She had done this before, and failed, and now she was trying again, and getting it right. She knew she was not a natural mother, but she knew, too, that she was good enough this time. More than that, though, she adored Helen in a way that she had never allowed herself to adore Beth. That was the thing that made the difference. Helen touched a part of

Mary that she'd never realised she had. Helen made her feel complete.

She was a beautiful child, and not only in the eyes of her adoring parents. Her hair was white-blonde, and her eyes were a piercing blue. People stopped on the street, all the time, and told Mary how lovely her daughter was. She was so happy that when the three-year-old Helen asked for a baby brother or sister, Mary managed to convince herself it might be a good idea. She could do it, now. Even though she was too old, at forty-one, she decided that it was worth a try.

Jean-Pierre was delighted. Mary worried ceaselessly, but she was pregnant within a few months. When she looked back on it, she was sure that she had had no premonition of doom. That was something she imposed on herself, with hindsight.

Everybody was excited when she had a boy. Jean-Pierre gave a case of wine to everyone in the village. Tom had a crumpled, imperious face, and a loud cry, and was quite different from his sister. To her relief, she loved him just as much. She would look at him, sleeping in his crib. 'My son,' she would say. 'My son.'

Mary found herself at the heart of a nuclear family. Married parents, a son and a daughter – and all that at an age when she could have been a grandmother. She could never have foreseen it. She still wanted to travel, but the world was changing, and for the moment she was content to be where she was. She hadn't felt that way since Goa.

For the moment she was tired and content, happily ensconced in France with her babies. She watched footage of John Major's election victory in the news, and she knew she could never go back. She was pleased with the way things were for her here.

Helen held her baby brother proudly on her lap, clasping him tightly around the waist, squinting into the sun. Mary snapped a photograph, and another, and another.

Two days later, the spell was broken. Mary had never known, had never wanted to know, the French for cot death.

CHAPTER 43

HELEN

30 June

I could feel the blood pounding around my body. My legs were shaking and I kept clenching and unclenching my fists. I was scared, and I was happy, and at the same time I had a strong feeling of dread. I could not stay still. I wanted to be with Matt.

Tom loitered in the drive, by the taxi. I pretended he wasn't there.

When I saw Mother, I wanted to cry. I had never been away from her in my life, and now I was back. It had only been a few months, but it felt like years. There was something about the familiarity of her – her slight body, her long hair, her flowing dress – that made me, bizarrely, want to hug her.

She managed to appear almost pleased to see me.

'Helen!' she said, and she pulled me close and rubbed my back. This was quite unlike her, and I reciprocated gingerly. 'Papa said you might be coming, but we didn't know when to expect you. Oh, how lovely to have you home again.' She pulled back and looked at me. 'But you're too thin! How much weight have you lost? You were tiny before, and now there's nothing of you. You look like a skeleton. We need to feed you. I knew you wouldn't be able to look after yourself.'

'I'm fine,' I said. I looked round. Mother was watching Liz walking over to us. The taxi disappeared down the drive in a cloud of dust. Tom was jogging away towards my little house. 'This is Liz,' I said, and I watched Mother hard to see whether she would guess.

I felt bad about Liz. The things I'd done had got out of control. I'd never meant to make it that bad for her, and I was praying that when she found out the truth, she would see that I'd had no choice: it had all been a means to an end.

Mother set off down the steps to meet her.

'Hello,' she said, warmly. 'I'm Mary, Helen's mother.'

'Hi, Mary,' said Liz, and there was an awkward moment when Mother went to kiss her on the cheeks and Liz was clearly not expecting it. They laughed it off and came back towards me.

When I looked at them together, I wanted to jump up and down and shout with joy. I had done it. She was here. They were together. This was the reunion. I was the only one who knew it. I savoured my secret. I tingled with anticipation.

'Welcome,' said Mother. 'Helen told her father she was hoping to bring a friend. But I had no idea you were expecting. When's your baby due?'

Liz smiled. 'In the middle of August.'

'Oh! Not long! I'm surprised they let you fly! You did come by plane? When Helen left, she went on the train.' Mother looked at me. '*And* she told us she was going to Paris.'

I shrugged. 'I got there and had an urge to go further. Check out my heritage.'

I looked at them both closely. Neither of them suspected a thing. I blocked out all the bad thoughts, and made myself concentrate on the positive. Whatever else happened, I had done a good thing. In fact, I was delighted, and proud of myself in a way I had never been before.

I wanted Liz to stay in my cottage, but Mother insisted on making up a room for her in the house. I supposed Tom would be in my spare room, anyway, so Mother was right.

'Can you believe it?' she asked Liz. 'You can see how much space we've got here. And yet she insists on living in a shed. She could have had her own wing, but no, she had to get out from under our roof. I suppose it's natural.'

Liz smiled. 'You've got one child at home, though, haven't you? Or is he away too?'

Mother froze. 'Um,' she said. 'No, I think you've got the wrong end of the stick there. There's just Helen.'

My pulse quickened. I shut the bad things out, again.

'You can put Liz in the pink room,' I said quickly. I stepped between them. 'That's got the nicest view. You can see across the vineyard to my house. Mother, did I mention that Liz is my landlady in London? I rent a room from her in Kentish Town.'

Mother took this in.

'Really?' she said. 'Thanks for looking after her, Liz. She's always been a bit of a law unto herself. It's nice to think that she's been with you. Did she eat anything at all?'

'I thought she did, yes,' said Liz. 'She's been a godsend. I'm on my own, and Helen's a great lodger. She even does the supermarket shopping, more often than not.'

'I lived in Brighton, myself,' Mum said. 'Up until I came abroad without looking back.'

'Oh, I know Brighton!' Liz told her. 'I grew up in Haywards Heath, so Brighton was always the place we went to for teenage kicks. I used to love it. All the little shops in the Lanes, and the fabulousness of sitting on the beach on a sunny day, drinking.'

I hugged myself and grinned.

Mother nodded. 'It's a good place to be when you're young. At least, it was for me.'

We had reached the pink bedroom. I was jigging up and down, trying to work out when I should share the news.

'It's seven o'clock,' I announced. 'Are we having aperitifs?'

Mother looked at Liz. 'You must be exhausted.'

Liz nodded. She was sitting on the bed, and she looked ready to collapse. 'I keep having these

Braxton Hicks,' she said. 'I think my body's telling me to stop.'

'In France they don't have Braxton Hicks contractions,' Mother said. I had no idea what they were talking about. 'In France, those are just called contractions.'

Liz looked alarmed. 'They don't feel like I'd expect real contractions to feel,' she said.

'Oh, don't worry! I had them for months with my first. Then I went a week overdue. It doesn't mean a thing, except that, you're right, your body's probably screaming at you to lie down. Why don't you come down at eight or so, and you can have a nice cold drink and something to eat, and then turn in for the night?'

I nodded my approval, thrilled that Mother had mentioned her first baby. With an effort, I restrained myself from blurting it out, on the spot.

There was still an hour to go until eight o'clock. I was so excited, so sick, that I had no idea what to do with myself.

My house smelt musty. No one had been in there for ages. It felt as if it was just as I had left it. The bedroom was bare and soulless. Clothes were hanging in the wardrobe, and folded neatly in the chest of drawers. I looked at my old clothes, and winced. I'd had no idea about style. The panic was beginning to mount.

'Tom?' I said.

All was silent.

'Tom, I'm here. It's me. You can come out. What are you doing?'

He didn't come.

'I did what you said!' I told him. 'I brought her here, for you. I wasn't going to and in a way I wish I hadn't, but we're doing it now. You have to talk to me. We have to decide what we're going to say.'

He didn't say anything. There was definitely no one in the house but me.

I forced myself to go to his bedroom. It was across the landing from mine. My hand shook as I pushed the door. It opened with a creak.

I half expected him to be lying on the bed, looking up at me with his big, lazy eyes. But the bed was not made up. There was nothing in the room but a dusty old bedstead and a small table. There wasn't even a mattress.

I shut my eyes and remembered this room as Tom's holiday room. It was his refuge from the main house, because he had needed one, just like me. Life with Mother and Papa suffocated him, just like it did me. He came to stay with me whenever he could, because we were partners. I pictured a plumped-up duvet on this bed, with a white cover. Two pillows with white cases. I imagined the windows thrown open, the sun pouring in. And Tom. I remembered Tom, in here.

'I don't know where he's gone,' I said aloud. I could hear my voice shaking, feel it trembling.

CHAPTER 44

LIZ

I lay down and closed my eyes. When I opened them, it was five to eight. I was desperate to roll over and stay asleep until morning, but I knew I had to be polite. Helen's mother, who was spookily identical to her daughter, seemed like a nice woman, and I couldn't just refuse to get up.

Exactly the right clothes were folded neatly in my bag. I imagined Helen rummaging through my bedroom. I didn't know how she had done it, how she had packed so well on the spur of the moment, but I was glad that she had.

There was a spotless little bathroom next door. I cleaned myself up, and went downstairs. Although I was only planning to eat for politeness's sake, I was feeling strangely relaxed. For the first time in ages, I was outside my normal parameters. I wasn't at home in Kentish Town, wasn't at school, or anywhere in London, or in Sussex. Those were the only places I went, these days. A few short hours ago, I'd been cowering away from Rosa, watching her smashing up a car because of me and the baby. Now I was in someone else's big old house, and for the moment

444

I had nothing to do. I was breathing more deeply, letting myself relax. This was a good place to be. All the same, as soon as I could make my excuses, I was going to go straight back to bed.

The house was vast, and I had no idea where to go. There was no sign of anybody. The entrance hall was surprisingly dark, and the furniture was big and old and beautiful. I went to an open door, and stepped through it nervously. There was a sitting room, clearly rarely used. It was a small, formal room with a sofa and chair that were both draped with sheets. I stepped back.

A man appeared behind me. '*Bonjour!*' he said. 'Hello!' He spoke English carefully. 'I am Helen's father. I am enchanted to meet you.'

I put out a hand, but he kissed me firmly on each cheek. He was a nice-looking man, with wild white hair and a friendly face.

'I'm enchanted to meet you too,' I said. 'Thank you for having me to stay.' He looked down at my bump, and we smiled at each other.

'Come and take a drink,' he said, and I followed him into a bigger, brighter room, which had French doors open to a gravelly area behind the house. Beyond that area, the lawn stretched away to the edge of a vineyard. He led me outside, and I saw that Helen's mother was sitting at a wrought-iron table, on a cushioned chair, holding a drink. Helen was there too. As I looked at her, I realised that she had to be anorexic. She was just bones. I had always believed her when she said she was naturally skinny. I felt sorry for her, and sad that I hadn't noticed before and tried to help her.

She seemed agitated, and she didn't look up as I came closer. The evening air was still, the sun casting long shadows. I saw that the table was set for a meal, with a big bowl of salad in the middle, and four places laid. I wondered whether Tom was still in London. He had to be: Mary had said he didn't live there at the moment.

Helen started hitting her chin repeatedly, hard, with her hand, frowning at the table. I had never seen her like this.

'Hello, Liz,' Mary said. She stood up, and pulled out an empty chair. I sat down heavily. I looked at Helen, then back to Mary. Nobody said anything for a minute or so. As I was about to launch into a random conversation to stop the awkwardness, Helen's father stepped in.

'My name is Jean-Pierre,' he said. 'And what will you drink? A little of our wine?'

I smiled. 'I suppose a little won't do the baby any harm. Is it your own? Helen's told me all about it. She says it's very good.'

He and Mary looked at each other.

'Does she?' Mary asked. She looked at Helen. 'Well, that's a first.'

Helen frowned. 'What do you mean?'

'You've never been at all interested before.'

'I have.'

Mary held up her hands in surrender. 'As you wish. Now, let's have a toast.'

Helen shook her head. She coughed. She banged her fists on the table. Everything rattled.

'Everyone,' she said clearly. 'Um, before that, there is actually something we need to drink to. There's something I need to say.'

I was embarrassed on Helen's behalf. I had no idea what her announcement was going to be, but I was certain that it would be something that was better left unsaid. I waited, wincing internally.

No one said anything. The cicadas were chirruping, and a couple of frogs croaked.

'Right,' she said, visibly pulling herself together. She was shaking: she looked terrified. 'Right. Mother. Papa. Liz. There is actually a reason why we're here. None of you realise it, but I've brought you all together for a reason. Particularly Mother and Liz.' She seemed to be forcing herself to speak. 'Mother,' she said. 'Your first child was called Elizabeth Greene. You abandoned her, thirty-seven years ago, and ran away to India. Liz – Elizabeth Greene – you're thirty-seven. And you've never known your mother.'

She let it hang in the air. It took me several minutes to realise what she was saying.

CHAPTER 45

MARY

Mary's first child wrote her a letter after Tom died.

It was the first time she had heard from her, and although she knew she should have been swamped by guilt and relief and hope and all sorts of other things, she felt nothing. Everything was grey. The world had constricted around her and she spent every moment fighting an urge to run away to India and live in a Buddhist convent, for ever. She would have left Jean-Pierre to do that, but she couldn't leave Helen. She couldn't do that again, and so she stayed, and tried to stay alive through one day at a time.

Many years ago, on Elizabeth's fifth birthday, Mary had managed to post the card she bought her. She dropped it into the box quickly, knowing that another fraction of a second would have changed her mind. She didn't expect to hear anything back, and Elizabeth never wrote. Equally, though, neither she, nor Billy, nor Billy's nasty mother ever told her to stop sending cards. So Mary kept on doing it, and then she added an annual Christmas card, too. Sometimes she felt she was mailing them off into an abyss, but she carried on, just in case. She hoped that, by sending a few lines, reliably, twice a year, she might not be a monster in her child's eyes. She knew that was futile. Two cards a year was the sign of a lax godparent, not a mother. It occurred to her that Billy might be intercepting the letters and telling Elizabeth that her mother was dead. It would not have surprised her.

Then, one year, he sent a change of address card. There was nothing personal about it, but Mary was deeply affected by everything it implied.

When little Tom was gone, there was nothing she wanted to do, no one she wanted to see. All she wanted to do was to run away, and she wasn't allowed to do that. She tried. Four times, she packed a bag. Once she got as far as the end of the drive.

It was Helen who kept her there, who forced her to stay in the house where the thing had happened, to give the baby clothes to a second-hand shop, to put the photographs away where no one would ever see them. Jean-Pierre refused to listen when Mary talked urgently, breathlessly, about the three of them going away together.

'We can't do that,' he said tightly. He was suffering, too, although Mary couldn't find the strength to comfort him. 'Our life is here,' he told her. 'Our business is here. We have a daughter.' He put his arm on her shoulder to leaven his words, but Mary pushed him away. She never slept. She paced the perimeter of their garden, marking the boundaries that kept her in.

Helen was an insult. She was full of life and energy, and she kept smiling and laughing. Her blonde hair shone in the sunlight. Her little face was chubby, angelic. Mary was viciously angry when she saw how easily Helen accepted the death.

'She's four,' Jean-Pierre said, holding Mary's shoulders, staring into her face. 'She has no idea what this means. How could she?'

Mary couldn't help it. She was furious with Helen's callousness, and with herself, because she had had three children, and now she had one. Helen was all there was. Mary knew she ought to have been nurturing her, watching her play, drawing comfort from her, and making Helen's world the best place it could possibly have been. She couldn't help herself: she pushed her away, figuratively, and literally, any time Helen came close.

One autumn night, while Helen slept, Mary sat down in a gloomy room and stared at the rain that was falling torrentially outside. She had a pen and a piece of paper, and after a while, she started to write. She wrote a letter to Elizabeth, because she wanted Beth to know what kind of a monstrous mother she had lost. She wanted to tell Beth never to miss her, never to regret anything, never to wish that her mother had stayed. Beth was twenty-two. She was older than Mary had been when she had

Billy Greene's baby. She was old enough to know everything.

Once she started writing, she couldn't stop. She put it all down on paper: she had never deserved Tom, not after what she had done to Elizabeth. She had been asking too much of God, or Fate, or of Karma. She told Beth that when she was younger, she had wanted to be a Buddhist nun. She said she wished she had done it. She said she wanted to do it now, with every fibre of her being, that the world would be a better place when she shut herself away in a convent with her hair shaved off. She told Beth about her time in Asia, about bathing in the *tatopani* springs until someone said the lepers washed there. She wrote and wrote. It got darker outside her window and the moon melted the clouds away and lit her with a ghostly light. When she had finished, she put the letter into an envelope, and stuck a random row of stamps on the front. She no longer cared what Beth thought of her.

Five weeks later, there was an airmail letter in unfamiliar handwriting. Elizabeth did her best to say the right thing to her bereaved, angry mother. That was how they started to build a relationship, of sorts.

CHAPTER 46

HELEN

My mother was staring at me. She was shocked, but in a good way. It had to be a good way. I stretched my arms out. I was still shaky, but I had done it. The sun shone on my arms, and thousands of tiny hairs glowed golden. I looked at Liz. She was staring down at her bump. She didn't look up at me at all.

Seconds ticked by. Cicadas and frogs voiced their thoughts, but nobody spoke.

'Liz, my mother is your mother,' I said, spelling it out, desperate for someone to say something. This was everything I had waited for. Everything I had done, I had done for this moment. Now it had happened. They were going to hug me. They were going to hug each other. People were about to cry. They would marvel at me. They would be amazed at my dedication, at my cunning, at my love for them both. I looked at Liz, then looked at Mother, and waited.

Of course, it was going to take a while to sink in. Of course, they might not believe it at first. I wondered where Tom was. He was the one who had done this, really. He was the one who had made me do it.

Liz was the first to respond.

'My mother died of cancer,' she said. Her voice trembled. She said it like a question. 'I was a baby.'

I could see that she was doubting everything she'd ever been told.

'No!' I hadn't meant to raise my voice, but I was so excited that I couldn't stop myself. 'No,' I said, more quietly. 'Your father *told* you your mother had died. That's all. He said it because he didn't want you to know that she'd left you. She left you, you see. I don't know why, but she can tell you herself. She went away, travelling.'

Liz was looking down. The evening sun shone on the top of her head.

'Helen,' she said. 'I can't believe I'm arguing with you about this. My mother is dead.' She swallowed. 'I've been to her grave.'

I knew she was wrong. I was bouncing in my seat.

'It was someone else's grave,' I explained. 'It was all a trick. She left you. Here she is.'

'Helen,' Liz said, and she looked at me for the first time. I held her gaze. In a moment, she would see the truth. I could see in her face that she was starting to see that I was right. 'Helen, I have no idea what you're on about. But I do know that I'm not the person you want me to be. I do know that.'

'You *are*. You're Elizabeth Greene. With an "e".

You're thirty-seven.' I smiled, encouragingly. 'We're sisters! I tracked you down because you're my sister. I'm sorry I didn't tell you before. I was desperate to bring you here. Now we have the family together. This is it. This is how we're going to be, from now on. Your baby has a whole other family, now. So do you. You understand, don't you?'

We both looked at Mother. Her face was pale.

'Helen,' she said. Then she was silent for a long time. I could see that this was an emotional moment for her. It was the biggest thing that had happened in her life. I was not surprised that she was overwhelmed. We waited for her to speak. The crickets were noisier than usual. I could hear a tractor, several fields away.

'Helen,' she said slowly. 'I did have a daughter a long time ago. I should have told you. Her name was Elizabeth Greene. It still is. You're right about that. But this Liz is a different person with the same name. Our Elizabeth Greene lives in New Zealand. She's a different person.'

My mind spiralled. 'You never told me!' I held tightly to the edge of the table, afraid I would fall. 'But this is her. I know this is her. She doesn't live in New Zealand. She lives in London. I know because I found her. And I brought her to you. I did it for you. I did it for us. For the family. Now that Liz is here, we're complete. Aren't we?'

Mother's hand was over her mouth. Papa leaned forward and topped up all our glasses. Mine was empty. Mother's was empty. Liz's was untouched, but Papa fitted a dribble more into it all the same. I tried to catch his eye, for some support, but he wouldn't look at me.

Mother kept opening her mouth and closing it again. I could see that she didn't know what to say. I decided to carry on speaking, to reinforce my point, but she got in first.

'We're never going to be complete, Helen,' she said quietly. 'Are we? I should have told you about Elizabeth. I know I should. I had an inkling that you knew when I found my box opened last year. But I had absolutely no idea that you would . . .' She stopped. I spoke quickly, before she could say any more.

'It doesn't matter now. Because I've found her for you.'

'You haven't, Helen. She lives in Auckland.'

The crickets kept up their racket. The house, the garden, the smell of the unrelenting summer made me sick. It all began to close in. I tightened my grip on the edge of the table.

'Helen?' said Liz. 'Here is the thing. Greene was my married name. I told you I was married for a few years, when I was younger.'

I kept fighting, because I had to be able to make it right. 'But you wouldn't take someone else's name.' I felt I was on firm ground, so I looked at her. Liz looked away at once. 'You definitely wouldn't keep it once you were divorced,' I said.

'My maiden name was Sidebottom. I couldn't

455

wait to get rid of it. There was no way I was taking it back.'

'Your dad isn't William Greene?'

My mother had her head in her hands. My father stood behind her, a hand on her back.

'Marcus Sidebottom.' Liz managed half a smile. 'He'd probably have preferred to be William Greene. But he's not.'

I closed my eyes. The golden evening sun was shining on half my face. I heard Mother and Liz starting to talk to each other, but I didn't know what they were saying, because there was a loud ringing sound in my ears. I stumbled to my feet.

If they were going to do this, to pretend that I had got it wrong, then I didn't want anything more to do with any of them. I still told myself that I was right. They were lying, and I needed to get away from them.

I stood up, and stepped away from the table. Then I looked at them, and this time, they didn't look like my family. They looked like an old man and an old woman, and a pregnant lady with a huge stomach. I looked at them, and I saw that everything was wrong.

I was afraid I would fall over. All three of them were staring at me with horror on their faces. I didn't want them to say anything, and so I turned and I ran. I didn't want to be a part of their world, and I didn't want to know what they would do next. I had nowhere to put myself. I switched off from all of them, like I used to do when I was young, and I ran away. I heard someone coming after me, and I thought it was Mother, but I shook her off. She couldn't touch me. I would never let her touch me. I closed myself off and ran, and ran, and ran.

When I came to the spot in the woods where Tom and I used to come on our walks, I sat on the tree stump and held my knees. I rocked back and forth. I didn't believe Mother and I didn't believe Liz. They hadn't had time to think about this at all, whereas I had thought of nothing else for a very long time. Everything I'd done, I'd done for this moment. I knew I was right. I wouldn't have gone to all this trouble if there was a chance I might have been wrong. I couldn't have done that. I just couldn't.

The whole world would look different if I was wrong. Everything would be hopeless. I would have failed completely.

I wouldn't be able to live with myself.

I looked around for Tom, but I knew he wasn't there. He had made me do this thing, and then he had gone, again. I was on my own. I looked up at the branches, dark against the evening sky. I imagined what it would be like to hang from the tree, to swing in the breeze. I wondered whether that would make them sorry.

CHAPTER 47

LIZ

We sat in the sunlight, and the horror of what she was saying hit me.

The sickening thing was that, for a couple of minutes, I almost let myself believe her. She was so certain. For a moment, I let myself reinvent everything. I let myself look at a world in which my mother had not died, but run away. In this world, my father was so bitter that he pretended she was dead. Even when I grew up and he met Sue, he stuck to his story.

In those few moments, I knew that if Mary was my mother, I would have nothing to say to her. The abandonment would have been worse than my real mother's death. Helen was certain she had pulled off an incredible feat that was going to bring nothing but happiness to all concerned, but she was hopelessly wrong. If she had done what she believed she had done, there would have been nothing but bitterness and recrimination ahead. And yet, I would have given anything to meet my mother. I wished Helen was right. I was glad she wasn't. I swung between the two states. I felt them both at once.

I made myself breathe deeply. I concentrated on the facts.

'Helen,' I said. 'Greene was my married name. I told you I was married for a few years, when I was younger.' That was a fact. That proved she was wrong. In a way I was glad. In another way, I was heartbroken. I kept glancing at Mary, trying to imagine her as my mother.

'But you wouldn't take someone else's name. You definitely wouldn't keep it once you were divorced.' There was a grim determination in Helen's voice. I couldn't look at her.

'My maiden name was Sidebottom,' I said. 'I couldn't wait to get rid of it. There was no way I was taking it back.'

'Your dad isn't William Greene?'

At this, I almost smiled.

'Marcus Sidebottom. He'd probably have preferred to be William Greene. But he's not.'

My mother was still dead. She had been dead for thirty-seven years, and that was not something that was likely to change. If Helen had been right, if my mother had left me and Dad to our own devices, and waltzed off to live in a castle in the south of France to have a new family, I would never have been able to forgive her. I preferred it the real way. I told myself this firmly. I was glad that my mother was Catherine Sidebottom, and I was glad that she was dead. I tried hard not to imagine the way things might have been otherwise. I had got over the loss years ago. I had never known her, and so I had never really missed her. I reminded myself of this.

Helen ran away. Both her parents stared after her. Her mother got up to follow her, and then Jean-Pierre looked at me in some bewilderment, shrugged, and followed them both. I waited for a while. I looked at the salad, but I wasn't hungry. I wished I could drink. After a while, I got up and went to bed. My mind was spinning. I needed to go home.

For the moment, I couldn't bear to try to piece together everything that had happened. I hadn't met Helen, by chance, on a website. She hadn't happened to come to London. We hadn't had a relationship that evolved gradually. It had all been part of her plan, ruthlessly mapped out from the start solely so she could bring me here and present me to Mary.

I spent all night staring into the darkness, seeing everything in a new light, feeling my increasingly strong Braxton Hicks contractions.

Early in the morning, I tiptoed downstairs. The house was silent and dark, many of its shutters closed. I didn't know whether Helen was here, or in her own house, or whether she was somewhere else entirely. I had no idea what state she might be in, but I was sure that it wasn't good. I wondered whether she might have tried to harm herself. I hoped that her parents knew how to calm her and control her. I was worried about her, because I knew that she'd meant well. But

I did not want to come face to face with her. I was making a conscious effort not to be angry until I was safely away from here.

I found my way to the kitchen, and switched on the light. It had a dim bulb, and the room looked sickly and yellow. Everything was meticulously tidy.

Although it was six o'clock, I was already hot, and my womb was tight. I knew that I needed to rest, for the baby's sake. I opened a few of the immaculate wooden cupboards, searching for a glass, but all I found were piles of plain white plates, and cups and saucers, and a stash of tins of tomatoes, chickpeas and green beans. Then I found wine glasses, and next to them, finally, some blue tumblers. I drank three glasses of tap water and realised that I was starving. There was a fruit bowl on the small kitchen table, so I took a banana and wondered whether it would be cheeky to open some shutters.

'You're up early.' It was Mary, looking at me with piercing eyes. She strode around the room, letting the daylight in and straightening things that weren't at all out of place. Her face was lined and haggard: she didn't look as if she had slept at all. 'Got everything you need?' she said briskly. She switched off the light.

I opened my mouth to ask about Helen. 'Actually,' I said, instead, 'could I have a cup of tea?'

She made tea for us both, in a pot. While she was making it, she kept looking at me. She was clearly distraught, but trying to hold herself together.

'It's nice to do this in the English way,' she said tightly, pouring a little milk into two cups. 'I hardly ever bother any more. Shall we go outside?' She left the room, tray in hand, without waiting for a reply.

I caught up as she strode across the lawn. The dry grass crackled underfoot. The leaves on the trees were shrivelling. Everything looked as if it were crying out for water.

She took me round a corner, and I saw the pool. It was an oasis in this parched garden. Mary's mouth was closed in a line. Her lips had vanished, the blood pressed out of them. She put the tray down, and held a hand briefly to her forehead. Her breathing was suddenly shaky, her eyes closed. I was suddenly scared. I felt certain she was delaying telling me something terrible.

'Where's Helen?' I asked, quickly.

After a few seconds, she inhaled deeply and looked at me.

'Liz, I'm so sorry,' she said, her words tumbling over one another. 'I don't know what to say to you. I mean, she's pulled you into this and it's nothing to do with you. You didn't need to be a part of it. you just happened to have the right name and be the right age. And I knew. I knew she'd found my box. If she'd just asked me, I would have told her, and that way, if she'd gone haring off, at least she would have gone to New Zealand.

At least she would have found the right person. Though what damage she could have done that way, I shudder to think. You know, while she was away, it did cross my mind to wonder whether she might be making inquiries, but because she was in London I never—'

I put a hand on her arm, and interrupted her.

'Mary,' I said. 'Stop. It's OK. Where is she? Is she all right?'

She stopped. We looked at each other. There was pain on Mary's face that I hoped I would never know.

'No,' she said. 'She's not all right. And it's not OK, is it?' she said. 'She's pulled you into this and it's not OK.'

'Well. No, it's not. But I can bow out of this now. I need to get home today. But where is she?'

She nodded vigorously. 'There's a flight at two or so. I'll get Jean-Pierre to make sure you're on it.'

'Thanks. And once I'm back, I can disentangle everything.' I looked at her, and suddenly decided not to share the list of things that, I was realising, Helen must have done. She had said it herself: 'I was desperate to bring you here.' She had pretended to be the Child Support Agency, twice. She had texted Julie from my phone, with a weird and random 'confession' that Julie had actually believed. I was strongly suspicious that she had done something to make Anna hate me, and whatever it was, she had done it effectively.

She'd even stood on Anna's doorstep with me and smiled sweetly at Jeremy, as he told me I couldn't come in.

'Where is she?' I said, again. I tried to shut my anger away.

'She's sleeping,' said Mary, sucking in her breath and looking anxiously towards Helen's little shack. 'I'm terribly worried she's going to do something stupid. We couldn't get a word out of her last night. She didn't even acknowledge we were there. We succeeded in dosing her up with enough sleeping pills to subdue a small elephant, but she didn't look at us or speak to us at all. I'm afraid we'll have to get the doctor out this morning. I don't know what to do with her. She scares me. She scares me witless.'

I looked at her, and she looked at me. For a moment, I felt that this flawed, scared woman really was my mother, and I felt a flood of warmth towards her. From the way she was looking at me, and my stomach, I thought she was thinking of her first daughter.

'Oh, Liz,' she said. 'I wish it was you.'

I sipped my tea. 'But you have Beth,' I said. 'You know her. That's what you said.'

Mary sounded distracted. She kept looking towards Helen's house as she spoke. 'Oh, yes, we exchange letters from time to time,' she said. 'It's all rather formal. She doesn't see me as her mother – how could she? She never will. I wouldn't expect her to. I try to handle things as best I can. But

464

I'm working blindfold most of the time. There's not exactly a template, is there? How does an estranged, runaway mother relate to the baby she abandoned? How, I presume, does the child deal with her anger – her hatred, in all probability? Sometimes I feel we'd be better off letting the relationship drop completely. I don't think any good can come of it. It's not a healing thing.'

'You don't want to meet her?'

'I've seen photos. That's enough. I'd dearly love to be her friend, but things don't work like that. I'm certain that, were we to meet each other, all her anger would come out. How can she not despise me? I ran away, and I never even regretted it. Not until a long time afterwards.'

I put myself in Beth's shoes. It would take a big person to forgive Mary, and to want to be her friend. I didn't say that.

'But Helen's the urgent thing,' I said instead, and Mary nodded vigorously. 'She needs help. What's the matter with Helen, Mary?'

Mary closed her eyes. She said nothing for a minute or so.

'Me,' she said, in a quiet voice. 'I'm what's the matter with her, Liz. I'm the worst mother in the world.'

'Of course you're not,' I said dutifully. 'But that's what I don't understand. I mean, you and Jean-Pierre obviously care for her a lot. She has two parents, unlike me, unlike Beth. And a stable background, an amazing home, a good education. She

465

has her brother. She speaks two languages. She's beautiful, and when she relaxes she can be lovely, and funny – and she has no idea of the effect she has on men. So, where does it all come from? The weirdness, the obsession, I mean?'

I watched Mary looking around, at the pale blue sky, the few birds skimming past overhead, the glistening water of the pool and the old tiles around it. I waited for her to say something, this woman who was not my mother. I could see that I had said something wrong, because her face tightened still further, and she seemed to close off from me.

'You said something yesterday about her brother,' she said, in a small, distant voice. She was looking, again, towards Helen's house. 'What do you mean?'

'I mean Tom,' I said. Mary said nothing, so I carried on. 'She talked about him a lot. She said he was her only friend in the world. He came to London, but I never met him. They wrote letters to each other . . .' I knew things were terribly wrong, but I carried on. 'She spoke to him on the phone. I heard her. She told me that he would be here, but I've been assuming he was still in London.' I looked at her. 'Tell me,' I said.

The early morning sunlight was making everything silvery yellow. The pool looked icy and inviting.

'We always thought Helen had some sort of imaginary friend,' she said, looking at the water.

'She's done it for years. She acted so oddly, laid extra places at the table, muttered things into empty space. She walked around the grounds having animated conversations with herself. But I never had the faintest idea that it was her baby brother. Oh, my poor girl.'

I didn't want to know the answer, but I asked the question, all the same.

'Why is he imaginary?'

Mary was starting to cry, and she was trying very hard to control herself.

'It's all my fault, Liz,' she managed to say. 'I'm a mess. I've been a mess since the moment I found out I was pregnant with Beth. I've done it all wrong. I wasn't a fit mother for Beth, because I spent the first six months of her life working out how I could leave her, and I haven't seen her since. I was not a fit mother for Tom – I can't have been – because when he was a few weeks old, he died. He died in his cot.'

I bit my lip, and clutched my baby with both hands.

'And I haven't been a fit mother to Helen, because after that, I didn't want anything to do with her. That, I imagine, is why she rushed off to find you. For years, I could hardly bear to look at her. She reminded me of everything I'd lost. And I didn't want to be too close to her, in case I lost her too. And I have lost her, I think. And the terrible thing – the thing she doesn't under-stand, however hard I try to tell her – is that it passed. I love Helen very much. I adore her, but she can't believe it, now. Perhaps it's self-defence. We both love her like nothing else in the world. She's all we've got. But it's too late, isn't it? She's been damaged.'

I nodded, and put a hand awkwardly on Mary's shoulder. She was stiff, but then she suddenly relaxed. She was sobbing in my arms, when Helen appeared.

'Hey, Mum,' she said. 'Pull yourself together.' She was trembling, and she looked tiny and frail in a small dress and outsized sunglasses. She looked as if you could snap her in half with a flick of your wrist.

Mary pulled away from me at once, wiped her eyes with the back of her hand, and went to Helen. I watched her reach out, wanting to take her daughter in her arms. I watched Helen push her away with surprising strength.

'Helen,' said Mary.

'What?' said Helen.

'Helen,' said Mary again. 'Helen, you know that Papa and I love you very much, don't you? We want to make everything better. We're going to help you with this. We're going to get through it together, as a family. I'm going to look after you.'

Helen shifted her tiny weight from one foot to the other. She moved incessantly, little movements of her hands and legs. She picked up a strand of her hair, and chewed it. She showed no sign of having heard Mary's words.

'Helen,' I said, and I stared at her. I was looking at her with new eyes, once again. A day ago, she had been my friendly flatmate. Now, not only was she someone who had wanted me to be her sister, but she was also somebody who had been so unable to accept that her brother had died that she reinvented him and took him everywhere with her. I supposed her coming to London and leaving Tom behind had something to do with her reaching adulthood. But he had followed her. It was all too much for me to take in. I felt desperately sorry for her, in spite of everything she had done to me. She seemed to notice me for the first time.

'Don't listen to my mother,' she said, in a quiet, urgent voice. 'To our mother, I mean. She's lying about the girl in New Zealand. She lies about everything, our mother. It's not Beth, it's Liz. It's you. I know it is, because I've just been on Google, and I can't find her in New Zealand, and the reason is, because she isn't there. It's just a lie. Just another lie. She doesn't want me to have a sister.'

I stood up and walked over to her. I desperately needed to convince her that I wasn't her sister, because otherwise I knew she would follow me back to London.

'But what about my name?' I took her hand, and made myself speak gently. 'Do you remember? I wasn't born Elizabeth Greene. Was I? You do believe me about that. Don't you?' I looked into her eyes. After a while, she nodded.

'I don't know about that,' she admitted. 'I don't know how that's happened. But I still feel it's you. We *are* sisters. Don't you think so?'

I looked at Mary's worried face, and decided to lie.

'Helen,' I said. I put my hand on her bony back. 'Helen, I'm afraid I'm really not your sister. Your sister is in New Zealand. Maybe your mother will show you some letters from her, later, or even a photo. Then you'll see. But we can be *like* sisters, if you want. I'm still glad I met you. And your parents are going to look after you now. And we can be friends. Would you like that?'

She looked at me. Her gaze was intense and unnerving. I tried not to look away. For a few seconds, she seemed to want to lash out, and then she closed herself off.

'But I don't want a friend,' she said. 'I want a sister.' And she turned her back on me.

I walked away. I felt emotionally battered, and I swallowed down my tears. I was so weary that I thought I could just lie down where I was, and sleep for a few hours. I told myself that this was not my problem any more. Tom had died many years ago. He was nothing to do with me. In a moment, I would go inside and pack my bag, and ask Jean-Pierre, who seemed to be abdicating responsibility very effectively, to call me a taxi.

For now, though, I found myself walking across the grass, towards the vines.

The soil in the vineyard was dusty, and the sun

470

was already hot. I walked between the rows of plants. The grapes were still small. The fields were huge. They just went on and on. I was seething. My life at home was a mess, and it was almost all down to Helen. I would go back now, sad and tired, and I could try to sort it all out. By the time the baby arrived, I might be able to have some semblance of a life.

I felt my loneliness more than ever. For as long as I could remember, there had been a mother-shaped hole in my life. Helen had thought she had the answer. In her cack-handed and damaged way, she thought she was on a mission to transform my life. I wondered at the way she had penetrated my world. She'd had an agenda, and I'd never suspected it. I had invited her to live in my home. All along, she'd been plotting to offer me up to her mother. Even if she had been right, Helen's plan could never have brought anything but misery. She was young, and she was screwed up, and she knew nothing.

It was only Tom who was stopping me hating her. The whole fact of Tom was unbearable. I knew that she had genuinely believed in him, and I ached for her.

I was heading wearily back towards the house, when I stopped. Something inside me popped. It was uncomfortable, but not painful. Then I realised that there was liquid running down my leg.

The first contraction came when I was halfway

471

back to the swimming pool. It did not hurt, but it was definitely a contraction.

I was alone, hundreds of miles from home, in a country where I only had a rough grasp of the language. I was in the middle of someone else's family drama. I was in labour, five weeks early.

CHAPTER 48

MARY

When Helen was seven, Mary looked at her, and suddenly she loved her again. It happened one morning as Helen was getting ready for school. Jean-Pierre was standing by the door, car keys in his hand, knocking back a third espresso and tutting as he waited for their daughter. Mary looked at Helen's serious little face, at the way she tied the laces on her school shoes with her forehead furrowed in concentration, and she was filled with precious, all-consuming love. She had forgotten what it felt like, the uncomplicated love a mother has for her child.

She smiled and touched Helen's shoulder.

'Can I help you with that, darling?'

Helen looked round and frowned.

'No. I'm OK,' she said.

Mary couldn't stop looking at her. This little girl, with her blonde hair and her fierce independence, was everything that she had. Helen picked up her school bag, ran her fingers through her straight fringe, and set off for the door.

'Can I have a kiss?' Mary asked.

Helen looked at her in surprise. Mary wondered whether she had really been letting her child go to school every day without a proper goodbye, and she decided she probably had. She held her tight, kissed her soft cheek three, four times. Helen wriggled and pulled away.

'Bye,' she said. She ran to Jean-Pierre, and took his hand and they left. Jean-Pierre looked back over his shoulder, and smiled at Mary.

He had been patient with her. He had stuck by her, in spite of everything. It was his steadfast love that had brought her to this point, where she felt ready to be a mother again. Tom was gone. She would hold him forever inside herself, and she would always ache. But she had someone else who needed her. Another baby: Helen. For three years, she had kept as far from her little girl as she possibly could. She regretted it, hated herself for it. Now she was going to do everything she could for her. She was going to try to make everything all right again.

Mary took Helen out on expeditions, just the two of them. She took her to cafés, bought her ice creams, went clothes shopping and let her have anything she wanted. They went to the beach together, the wide sandy beach that stretched for a hundred miles. They sat on the sand and looked at the sea. They made sandcastles, jumped over waves. It was a nicer beach than Brighton, by a long long way. She tried to tell Helen about Brighton, the beach where she'd once lived, the beach that was covered in stones. Helen wasn't interested, because she was completely involved in an elaborate sand structure she was building with her imaginary friend.

Mary kissed her peachy cheeks, first thing in the morning and last thing at night, and whenever possible in between. She told Helen about Nepal, about India, about how she had got off a bus in France and decided to stay, and about how she met Jean-Pierre. She felt she ought to talk to Helen about her baby brother, and she tried to do that, too.

Nothing she did seemed to make a difference. Helen allowed her to do whatever she wanted, but she kept a distance that seemed almost adult. She preferred her imaginary friend to her mother. She would not let Mary say a word about baby Tom, covering her ears and becoming agitated at the mention of his name. Soon Mary stopped talking about him.

She did everything in her power to be a mother again to Helen, and on the surface things were normal. She knew, though. She knew from the start: it was too late. And after a while, she stopped trying.

CHAPTER 49

HELEN

I couldn't do anything but shut myself down. I fought Mother off, because I couldn't stand to have her anywhere near me. All of this was her fault. She had failed and she was the worst mother in the world. Whenever she came close enough to touch me, I lashed out at her. I didn't want her to be my mother. I didn't want her anywhere near me. I was alone. My brother was dead, and my sister was on the other side of the world, and Liz, who had occupied my whole being, day and night for months, was turning out to be no one. The loss of Liz was almost as bad as the truth about Tom.

I had done it because I wanted them to love me. I'd fucked it up, and now they hated me more than ever, and I hated them, too. I looked around the garden, which was spiky and dry. I would inherit it one day. It would all be mine, because there was no one for me to share it with. I didn't think I could bear it. I didn't want to see any of them. I hated Mother. I hated Papa, because he should have been my ally and he never bothered to help me. I hated, hated, hated Liz. I hated her

476

most of all because she wasn't my sister, and now I had to forget her. I didn't want to be her friend, and I knew she didn't really want to be mine, either. She'd only said that to make me feel better and it hadn't worked.

I was on my own. I had been on my own all along. I sat on the prickly grass and curled up into myself, and every time Mother tried to come close to me, I kicked her, or scratched her, until she went away. Once I spat, and it went right in her eye. That sent her off, for a while. Matt wouldn't want to know me any more, because Liz would tell him what I'd done. And Matt was from Liz's world, and Liz's world wasn't my world, and it had never been my world.

When Papa came out, I turned my face away from him. He tried to talk, in a stupid soft voice as if I were a nutter or a baby, but I ignored him. I didn't even hear what he said. I turned in on myself, and blanked it all out, and soon I didn't even know what was going on at all. There were voices. More than before. There was a bit of commotion. I kept my eyes closed and wished myself away. I wanted them to grab me, to look after me, but they didn't. Nobody dared come close. They were pathetic. This was the test: if they cared about me, they would prove it. If they cared about me, they wouldn't leave me in a foetal position on their lawn, for hours. I wanted them to help me. I wanted them to help me, whether I liked it or not.

It took a stranger to do it. He picked me up gently, and I let him, because he wasn't them. He took me to a car, and I let him. He gave me a pill and a bottle of water, and I swallowed the pill and drank all the water.

'*Sage, comme une image*,' he said, not to me. I smiled. That was what French people said about babies. I liked being like a picture, unresponsive, inactive. I thought I might stay like this, for a while.

I stared out of the window. Mother tried to touch my leg from time to time. I stayed still and hard, like a statue. She was talking about Liz. I didn't listen.

We were going back into Bordeaux. I supposed they were going to put me away somewhere. Hand me over to somebody. Wash their hands of me.

As I watched the streets getting busier and the town appearing outside, I began to think that I had, in fact, known for a while that Liz was the wrong person. I just hadn't let myself notice it.

I knew it when I listened to Sue and Liz's father talking, in the café. She called him Marcus. I had pretended not to hear that bit.

I knew it when I went into Liz's room. There was a photograph by the bed. It was a picture of Liz and her mother, when Liz was born. That woman was not my mother, and no amount of staring could have melded them. That was why I looked quickly away.

Yesterday, I opened Liz's passport, curious. But

her middle name wasn't Rosemary. It said it was Jane. I shut it at once.

I'd never asked Liz much about herself, because secretly I didn't want to know. I wanted to be doing the right thing. Instead, I had got into the life of a stranger, and I had messed it up, on purpose, to make her need me. But it turned out that I didn't need her at all. She was the wrong one.

Mother was touching me. She was patting my arm, over and over again. I couldn't pull away, because I was already pressed up against the door. I pushed my cheek to the window. I liked the way it was smooth and cold. I shut her out. She was talking, in a quiet, secretive voice, close to my ear. I tried not to process her words, but I heard her say 'Tom'. When she said his name, I turned my head as far away as I could, squashing my nose against the glass.

It was autumn, and I was four. I didn't like the baby. I didn't like it that he took all the attention away from me. No one was interested in me any more, when there was a baby. And I had expected him to be like a doll, but he was ugly and he cried.

All the same, I liked the idea of him. I liked having a brother. I was pleased when they balanced him on my lap and let me grip him, tightly, around the middle. I liked it when he was sick, in milky pools that fell on the tiled floors and stayed there, congealing, until someone noticed them.

I was starting to get used to him, when he went away.

They told me gently. 'Tom's gone,' they said.

'When's he coming back?' I wanted to know.

I didn't believe them when they said never. If he had died, like they said, there would have been a funeral. There wasn't a funeral, and that meant he would come back one day. I knew it, and I was right. Old people died, not babies.

While he was away, Mother was sad. She never talked to me. She never played with me. She didn't want anything to do with me any more. Papa tried, but he was no good at it. I wandered around on my own, and I started living inside my head.

When he came back, I was seven. I was setting out on my walk, and suddenly, there he was, a little boy, running to catch me up. He had a scabby knee and the face of an angel. I waited for him.

'Hello,' I said.

'Hello,' he replied. 'Where are we going?'

'To the woods,' I said, and I took his hand. He let me guide him. 'You're Tom,' I said, as we walked down the path at the side of the vine field.

'Yes, I am.'

I was pleased to see him. He was three, but he could talk. We walked to the woods together. We talked about Mother and Papa. He already knew it all.

'I'm glad you came back,' I told him, as we sat down in a clearing and looked at each other.

He smiled. I was his big sister, and he loved me.

He was the only one. Although he never said it, I knew that if I told anyone about him, he would go away.

I opened my mouth, my face still pressed towards the car window. I screamed and screamed and screamed. I screamed until my voice started breaking up, and then I carried on. I blocked everything else out. The car stopped. I didn't notice what they were doing to me. I didn't care.

Hours later I found myself in bed. The room was pristine and white and creepy. I felt drowsy. I knew they had drugged me.

I would give in, for the moment. But soon, I would start to pretend. I would say what they wanted me to say. I would do what they wanted me to do. Soon, I would get out. I was on my own in the world. I had to look after myself, because no one else cared at all.

I began to make a plan.

CHAPTER 50

LIZ

I was on the delivery floor for days. My epidural was topped up again and again. They kept examining me, then shaking their heads in disappointment. I was not, it seemed, doing very well.

My French was rubbish, but I could get the gist of what they were saying. When they asked me harder questions, which seemed to concern my medical history and what the hell I was doing in France so close to my due date, I just shook my head and spoke to them quickly in my own language. After a few hours, a midwife was found who could speak English and I gave her a patchy rundown of my life. I missed out all the interesting bits.

At first I was in a dingy little room with a tiny television bolted to the ceiling. The wallpaper was bobbly and there was nothing to look at apart from the clock, which was behaving erratically. I had never felt so lonely. When I demanded pain relief, they took me somewhere else, to a shiny reassuring delivery room with every piece of equipment money could buy. First I got off my face on gas and air. That took the edge off things. I was not expecting to relax, but suddenly I started giggling. Then some blood test results came back, and I was allowed an epidural.

I sat on the edge of the bed, hunching my back, and tried to stay still through a contraction which hit me in the stomach like a ten ton weight thrown from close quarters. I managed to keep still, because I knew that there was a man standing behind me who had a needle in my spinal column. I felt the cold spreading through me, and suddenly, it was all right.

Time dragged by. I wanted some pain back, after a while, to stop me thinking about Helen. A few times I almost asked for Mary, but I managed to stop myself, because I knew I didn't really want Helen's mother by my side. By the time they said my father had arrived, I was naked, so I felt obliged to leave him in the waiting room. By that point, I knew I was doing this on my own. I was glad that Mary had managed to phone him, pleased that he'd arrived. If he was there, many hours must have passed.

If Dad had come to see me yesterday, when I'd needed him, I would have let him in now. If he'd come to see me yesterday, I didn't think I'd be in France. Because he had put Sue first, I made him wait. All the same, I was pleased that he was nearby.

I gritted my teeth and ran through some recent events in my mind. I thought I had pieced things together. I wondered whether Matt knew that I was, supposedly, Helen's sister. I imagined him laughing about it, confiding the details to selected customers.

None of this was real. I refused to believe I would soon meet my baby. I barely believed there was a baby. I could not conceive of its being born healthy, and after what I now knew about Tom, I was terrified of losing it.

I drifted, feeling the contractions faintly, allowing anybody to do anything they wanted to me. I had imagined my birth to be a haze of waterpools, scented candles, incense and soothing music. Instead I had a blood pressure band on my arm, and it inflated itself every few minutes. There was a monitor on a belt round me, constantly. I was lying on my back on a bed, and, to my surprise, I didn't want to be doing anything else. I resigned myself to staying here indefinitely, in a strange, constricted half-world.

It was light again when the woman did yet another internal and asked, in English, whether I wanted to push. I didn't, but I gave it a go, anyway. She went to fetch someone else, and I felt that pushing might be good, so I did it again. They came back and made encouraging noises, so I did it for a third time, and this time I felt it. Then I was possessed by it. My body could do nothing else but push. Suddenly, I was about to break in two. Then something slipped out of me, and it whimpered.

★　★　★

484

The midwife was holding up a baby, showing it to me. It was tiny, and red, and it had a full head of black hair.

I caught my breath. This was the thing that had been growing and kicking for all that time. It was a person, someone who hadn't existed in the world moments ago. I stared at it.

'It's a girl,' I said. I realised I was sobbing, but I stretched my arms out for my daughter. I cradled her close to me. She looked at me. When our eyes met, I saw that I knew her already.

'Oh,' I said to her. 'It's you.'

She just gazed back, searching and serious. Her innocence made me howl.

'Mummy's here,' I whispered, through my tears. I didn't want anyone to hear. 'Mummy's here,' I told my daughter. 'Mummy's here.'

They took her away to check her. I could see that they were concerned, because she was tiny, and premature. A female doctor with ginger hair checked her over. The doctor kept looking over at me and smiling.

She wrapped the baby up and handed her to me.

'She is good,' she said, in English. 'You feed her?' She pointed to her own breast, and I nodded.

I held her. The baby looked at me, and I knew that she knew it was me. She stopped crying when I took her. After a few attempts, she was suddenly sucking enthusiastically.

I was sitting up in bed, feeding my baby. I looked

at the clock. It was eight o'clock, but I didn't even know which eight it was.

'*Matin?*' I asked, pointing at the clock.

They smiled, and said yes. They wanted to know her name, so they could make her a wristband. A woman stood waiting for my answer, her biro poised above a tiny pink band.

'Eloise,' I said. The name came out of the blue. I'd heard a nurse saying it earlier and thought it was pretty. I could call her Ellie. The medical staff all smiled their approval. 'Eloise Catherine,' I said.

Then she was wearing a bracelet with 'Enfant GREENE Eloise' written on it.

Everything about her was perfect. She had tiny fingernails, which had grown inside me. Her eyebrows were surprisingly bushy. Her hair was black and smooth. I stared at the patterns in her ears. All the time I had been obsessing about the details, I'd had no idea that I was making ears. The world was a different place, and I was a different person.

When Dad arrived, I was in my own room. They said I had to stay for at least ten days, and Ellie had to be checked all the time, but I was allowed to keep her in the room with me as long as I fed her every two hours and pressed the buzzer if anything seemed wrong. They said my friends were paying the bill and that I could reclaim most of it later, from the British government, anyway. I presumed that Helen's family were my so-called 'friends' and decided I would happily let them pay.

Our room was pink. The walls were pink, the tiny en suite bathroom was pink, and even the baby's changing mat was pink. I realised that I was bleeding heavily, and, as the anaesthetic wore off, my stomach hurt more than it had when I was in labour. I didn't care. I wondered why nobody had told me that, as soon as I was holding my baby, everything else in the world was going to become irrelevant. They told me to have a shower, but I couldn't bear to leave her side, so I kept putting it off.

He was ushered in by a nurse.

'Lizzy!' he cried, and he came to sit on the bed. 'Lizzy, I'm so sorry you've been through this by yourself. Come here.' And he pulled me close to him. I managed to move my legs, with some effort. 'And who is this?' he asked, spotting her over my shoulder. His face was transformed. 'Oh, good-ness me. Who, indeed, is this?'

I grinned. 'This is Eloise,' I said proudly, and I picked her up carefully and showed her to him. She was sound asleep, and didn't stir as I lifted her. 'It's Ellie,' I said. I couldn't take my eyes off her.

'Welcome to the world, Ellie,' said my father, and we sat there, the three of us, in awestruck silence. I had my family, and I didn't want anything to change.

CHAPTER 51

Christmas

I was wary of the letter. It was bulkier than a card. I knew there was a folded-up piece of paper in there too. The last thing I wanted to land on my doormat was a handwritten letter with a Bordeaux postmark. I opened it, all the same.

As I scanned the closely written pages, I saw that Mary was being relentlessly upbeat.

'Helen's doing wonderfully well,' she wrote. 'We're so proud of her. She's put on some weight and got a job in one of the clothes shops in Bordeaux, where she really is in her element. She feels terrible about everything she did in London. She's very embarrassed about it and wants to write to you to apologise, but I wasn't sure how welcome that would be. I told her I would write first to make sure you wouldn't mind hearing from her. She is anxious to know that she hasn't left you any lasting problems. As am I: we all hope that you and your wonderful daughter Eloise are well and enjoying life, and that you both have plenty of friends around you.'

It went on and on like that. I wondered whether I was being cynical: I couldn't help assuming that Mary was seeing what she wanted to see. I looked down the pages for a mention of Tom. There he was: 'She's working through her feelings about her baby brother, which are, of course, very complex as he was extremely real to her for many years. This is a hard thing for all of us to understand. She's been to the grave, which was very difficult for her, and according to her therapist, Jean-Pierre and I should have taken her to his funeral, and brought her to his grave, all along. Then, apparently, that particular delusion wouldn't have happened.'

I shook my head. 'Of course it bloody wouldn't, you ridiculous woman,' I muttered.

It was still shocking for me to think about Tom as a tiny baby. In my head, he remained a lazy fifteen-year-old who was devoted to his big sister. It was horrible to realise that the Tom Helen had talked about had been an illusion, a ghost of someone who never grew up, who never even sat up or ate food. I shuddered and put the kettle on, still reading. Being thrust back into the world of the Labenne family was making me rather sick. Because all my anger at Helen was mixed up with shock and sympathy, I hadn't realised quite how much better my world was without her. Everything had been immeasurably simpler and more enjoyable since our return from France, but I'd been focused on Ellie, and had assumed that it was

489

mainly her doing. Having a baby was hard work, and I hadn't slept much, but that didn't matter at all. I was different, and my world was different, because she was in it: in this new world I was happier and less grumpy, and I didn't have time to sit and worry about things.

I smiled over at my daughter. She was sitting in her brand new high chair, a cheap one from IKEA, banging on her tray, looking up at me and grinning expectantly. I was still amazed at her, this little creature, who was vigorously, cheerfully, enthusiastically her own person. Before she was born, I had envisaged a weird and rather frightening hybrid of Rosa and me, but Ellie was something completely different. She had thick black hair, like Rosa, and I thought she had something of me about her mouth, but that didn't mean anything. She was Ellie: someone new.

I handed her a broccoli stalk and watched her turning it over with both hands, examining every millimetre before she held it upside down and sucked on it. On Anna's advice, we were doing something called 'baby-led weaning' which meant that I didn't have to mush everything up. I just handed pieces of food to Ellie, and she fed them to herself. I watched her, proud. Anna and Gabriella had been doing this for months, and I'd been desperate to join in for ages. We had started two weeks ago and, as I watched Ellie, I felt sure I had made a good parenting decision, for once. Julie had recently started spooning purees into

Jack's mouth, and I was sure that my way was better.

Jack had been born two months after Ellie, but because she'd been premature, and perhaps because Roberto was a lot bigger than Rosa, they were the same size. Jack was bald and enthusiastic, crowing with delight at the sight of anybody, particularly another baby. We went to see the family in Haywards Heath often, and put the babies side by side on the rug, looking in amazement at these two small people who would be the family's future. Julie and I were friends again, though she had been the hardest person to convince. In the end I'd had to get Mary to send Julie an email confirming that Helen said she'd walked in on Roberto and me and thought we were kissing, so had sent the text from my phone. As soon as she read that, Julie's face cleared and she nodded.

'OK,' she said. 'Sorry. Fair enough. Little Miss Nutcase does it again.'

From then on we were almost back to normal. Except that it was better than normal, because a week afterwards, Jack was born.

When Ellie and I arrived home from France, Anna had quickly forgiven me for Helen's post on Babytalk that denounced her, under her full name, as 'a crazy Mexican whore'. 'I couldn't see how that wasn't you,' she'd said, 'and I was so emotional with the birth and the baby, that I couldn't bear to have you near me. I always said that girl was trouble.' And she had.

Julie and I were both going back to work in the New Year. I was half dreading it, but half excited. Kathy and Sandrine had been to visit us often, and Ellie and I had been in to the staffroom to say hello, and instantly found ourselves swept into the part of the room I'd always overlooked: the Mummies' section. That, I found, was full of women who asked me exactly the right questions, and who were full of good advice. There were pictures by their children on the walls, and I'd never even noticed. I was looking forward to going back, and making some new friends. Ellie was going to a local childminder and I hoped that we would both cope. I had no idea what it would really be like, being separated from her, four days a week.

I looked at Ellie's fat little cheeks and watched her smearing broccoli pieces all over her face. Soon Adrian would be here, and we'd have a drink and head to the Tube, the three of us together, as if we were a family. This was something Helen and Mary would never know about. It was the good thing Helen had done. When Ellie was a couple of months old, and we were starting to settle into our new life, I'd called Helen's old flat-mate to apologise for accusing him of sexual harassment on Helen's behalf (no wonder, I reflected, that Helen had refused to let me confront him with her, when it had obviously been a strategy to get me to offer her Ellie's room). He'd suggested a drink, and to my astonishment

I now found myself with a boyfriend. He was ten years younger than me, and I wasn't picturing myself going up the aisle any time soon, but he was funny and sweet and he seemed to love Ellie almost as much as I did. Best of all, he wasn't Steve, and I didn't think about Steve when I was with him.

Yes, in a strange way, Helen had done me some favours. If she hadn't pretended to be the CSA, I wouldn't have had that afternoon in the park with Steve. Although I hadn't realised it at the time, that was when I started to get over him. We were friends now. He adored Ellie, and often said he wished we'd had children together. He had also said that I could stay in the flat for five years, because he couldn't bear to think of the baby without a secure roof over her head, and I'd accepted that offer with alacrity. I'd recently met his boyfriend, Pablo, and had liked him, in a grudging way. We were both moving on. I was feeling very grown up.

And if Helen hadn't sent Rosa to me, distraught and furious, then we wouldn't have started to sort things out between the two of us. Rosa, it turned out, was quite good at being a funny aunt figure to Ellie. She came to see us every week or two, and now that she had relaxed with me, we were almost able to laugh at ourselves and our bizarre little family. It was still early days, and I could not imagine a time when I would let her take Ellie out on her own, but the situation was already easier than I had ever imagined it could be.

Even Matt was doing well without her. He'd moped around, angry with her and with himself, for a few weeks, but he'd soon found another business partner, a Japanese woman who was about to open a 'fusion' kitchen in Matt's back room. I was looking forward to trying it out. They both seemed to be living in his flat, so I presumed that Helen was replaced in every sense.

I would reply to Mary. I would tell her nothing. I would tell her to tell Helen that we were fine and that she didn't need to write. I didn't want anything from Helen arriving in my home.

'A-rrrRah!' Ellie shouted, flapping an arm up and down in a bid for my attention. I leaned in and kissed her head. She threw her broccoli stalk at me. I picked it up from the floor.

The buzzer sounded.

'Hello,' I said into it. 'Hi, Adrian. We're doing broccoli. Come on up.'

I put Mary's letter into a drawer. Now, I was going to relax. I took the wine out of the fridge and got down two glasses. I was sure I was allowed to have one glass and still breastfeed.

He stepped into the kitchen, and hugged me tight. I knew he was making a face at Ellie over my shoulder, because I could hear her giggling.

'Merry Christmas, A,' I said, because I could never say the name Adrian and keep a straight face. For some reason it didn't remind me of my ex-husband any more. These days. I thought of Adrian Mole.

494

'Merry Christmas, Lizzy Sidebottom,' he replied.

I looked at him, and at Ellie, and I decided to forget all about Helen and her family. We were all so much better off without her.

EPILOGUE

HELEN

Next summer

The cab draws up outside a slightly battered wooden house with a blue sign outside that says 'Ponsonby Backpackers' in big white capitals. I thank the driver, still smiling, and heave my backpack on to my back. At least I look the part.

My hair is black now, because I am starting again. I have black hair, and I'm dressed like someone from the sixties, in a floating cotton dress with flowers all over it. I have flowery slides in my hair too. Mother told me about her travelling exploits when she was in between Beth and me, and she has inspired my style. She's made me more ambitious about my travelling, too. My legs are bare, because even though I knew it was winter here, I assumed it would still be warm enough. I might have to buy some jeans or something soon, because it's not warm at all. The air feels cleaner than it does in Europe, but the wind is positively cold.

The woman on reception only looks about twenty-five, and she welcomes me with a smile and a half-distracted air. She tells me they only have thirty beds, but they can easily fit me in. I take a single room, which reminds me of the first bedroom I had in London. It is crammed with cheap furniture, and hardly any carpet shows. I throw my bag on the bed, and I like the way it looks there.

Luckily for me, the woman just wants a bit of cash up front. I don't have to use my credit card yet. When I do, Mother and Papa will realise that I'm not in Madrid, and that I'm not on a Spanish course. It took me a year of pretending before they agreed to let me go. They drove me there and settled me into a spare room in the middle of a noisy Spanish family, and the next morning I went to the airport and flew to Gatwick. It was odd to be back in London, but all I was doing was changing planes, so I got a coach to Heathrow, and flew to Hong Kong. Then I caught a Cathay Pacific flight all the way here. Now I ought to be exhausted, but I'm too excited for that. I expect that Mother and Papa know I've gone, by now. I'm sure they must have called every day to check up on me.

I go back downstairs, because I can't wait any longer. I stand in front of the woman while she finishes a conversation on the phone, about the week's shopping bills.

She turns to me. 'Where in England are you from?' she asks. 'My husband's family are English. And I can tell you, this place is constantly full of you guys.'

'I'm actually from France,' I tell her, 'but I lived in London until recently. North London.' I am proud of my stay over there. Even though I got things slightly wrong, I wouldn't change a thing. I met Matt there, and fell in love with him. I think I love him more, now that I will never see him again. He is perfect, in my mind. All the same, he was much too cross with me when I vanished, and sent me a crazy email after Liz got back and told him all sorts of bad things I had supposedly done. I ignored him. I love Matt, but he is from my past, and I have proved to myself in the past year that there are many other men out there. Many other men who desire me, who are driven crazy by my sexiness and my allure.

I am an independent woman and my whole trip to London was an important part of the process, and now I am here.

'Can you help me out with some directions?' I ask politely. She says that of course she can, and she tells me that the street I am looking for is around the corner, ten minutes' walk away at the most.

'Wonderful,' I tell her. 'Thank you.'

I go straight there. I follow the woman's instructions, and find the house. On the way, I pass cafés and bars and restaurants, and I wonder whether I could get a job in one of them. I do have experience, after all, though probably not references.

I stand outside the house for a while, on the other side of the road, and look at it, and I am pleased. Unlike Liz, Beth lives in a whole house. It is lovely. It's pale green, and it's wooden, made of overlapping boards, and it has a pretty veranda, with wooden railings and wrought-iron decoration. The garden is green and there are trees all round the house. I think that I like New Zealand.

There is a red car parked outside. It's not a flash one, just something normal. I can see three of the house's windows, but I can't see inside any of them.

After a while, I take a deep breath, march up the drive, stand on the veranda, and ring the bell.

I know at once that I have the right person. Beth is my height. She has my blonde hair, Mother's blonde hair, but hers is short. She is slim enough, and pretty enough. She's wearing jeans and a nice, black top with a chunky necklace. She looks like a woman who is comfortable in her life. She doesn't look like someone who would bother to agonise about the mother who abandoned her, years and years ago.

She smiles at me, but she looks a bit fed up.

'Hello?' she says. I don't answer, because suddenly I'm too scared. 'Can I help you?' she asks. She sounds English, but she has a tiny bit of a New Zealand accent.

I smile my biggest smile. 'I hope so,' I tell her. 'I hope you don't mind my knocking, but I'm new in the area and I was wondering if you know anyone with a room to let? I'm looking for somewhere to live. I just love this area.'

She looks surprised. 'You're English?'

'Yes. Sorry, I didn't know where to start. I'm a bit lost, and your house looked nice, and your car was here, so I just . . .' I look at her expectantly.

She doesn't say anything for a while. I clench my fists and will a good reaction.

'Um.' She looks around. She doesn't know what to say, because this isn't something that normally happens. I smile at her, then look away, trying to look lost and harmless. 'Actually,' she says, 'I'm English too. Where are you from?'

I know the answer to this one.

'Brighton,' I say, innocently.

'No way! That's where I grew up. Look, I do actually have a friend who's going overseas next month. She was looking for a tenant for six months or so.'

'Oh, really? Could I contact her?'

She is still sizing me up. I stand there, doing my best to look like the right sort of person.

'I'm Isabelle,' I tell her.

She nods. 'I'm Beth,' she says. 'Why don't you come in?'